"Wicked" Women Whodunit

"Wicked" Women Whodunit

MaryJanice Davidson
Amy Garvey
Jennifer Apodaca
Nancy J. Cohen

KENSINGTON PUBLISHING CORP.
http://www.kensingtonbooks.com

BRAVA BOOKS are published by

Kensington Publishing Corp.
850 Third Avenue
New York, NY 10022

All Kensington titles, imprints and distributed lines are available at special quantity discounts for bulk purchases for sales promotion, premiums, fund-raising, educational or institutional use.

Special book excerpts or customized printings can also be created to fit specific needs. For details, write or phone the office of the Kensington Special Sales Manager: Kensington Publishing Corp., 850 Third Avenue, New York, NY 10022. Attn. Special Sales Department. Phone: 1-800-221-2647.

ISBN 0-7582-1026-4

First Kensington Trade Paperback Printing: March 2005
10 9 8 7 6 5 4 3

Printed in the United States of America

CONTENTS

Ten Little Idiots

(With apologies to Agatha Christie)

MaryJanice Davidson

For my husband, Anthony

Acknowledgments

Thanks to my husband, Anthony, for the tremendous amount of help he gave me on this story. Thanks also to the gang at Lori Foster's Yahoo group, RBL Romantica, my own Yahoo group, and Laurie Likes Books for their unwavering love of books and author support. It's so great to find people as passionate (in their likes and dislikes . . . TSTL, anyone?) about books as I am!

"Every murderer is probably somebody's old friend."
—Agatha Christie, *The Mysterious Affair at Styles*

"Murder is born of love, and love attains the greatest intensity in murder."
—Octave Mirbeau, *The Manuscript*

Prologue

Dana Gunn said, "I did it in the dining room with the candlestick."

She certainly didn't have to tell us, Caro Swenson thought. *And why do I feel like an extra on the set of CLUE instead of a vacationing nurse? "Professor Plum did it on the drawing room with . . ." Fer Christ's sake.*

The killer, a pleasant-looking blonde with curly Orphan Annie hair and big blue eyes, didn't have to make the announcement, because Caro could see for herself . . . the killer was standing in the hallway outside the bedrooms, calm as a cotton ball, the big candlestick in her fist actually dripping with the victim's blood.

Caro was a nurse, and long used to gore that would send a layman running for the toilet, but the cool way the killer held the weapon, the monotonous plink-plink of the blood hitting the carpet . . . it was startling, to say the least.

"Are you kidding?" Caro finally asked.

"I've already called the police," the killer declared, dropping the candlestick, which hit the carpet with a thick thud and rolled a few feet away. She rubbed her bloody palm on the skirt of her Anne Taylor knockoff, grimaced like Lady Macbeth, then continued. "I'm just going to wait here in my room until they get here." Then she stepped backward and shut the door in Caro's face.

After a long, thunderstruck moment, Caro turned to the other guests and said, "I don't know about you guys, but this wasn't in *my* brochure."

One

"This is all Jeannie Desjardin's fault," Caro declared to the people in the hallway.

Lynn Myers blinked at her. "Who-who's Jeannie Desjardin?"

"My friend. She's this awesomely horrible woman who generally revels in being bad. You know—she's one of those New York publishing types. But every once in a while she gets an attack of the guilts and tries to do something nice. Her husband and I try to talk her out of it, but . . . anyway, this was supposed to be *her* Maine getaway. But she gave me the tickets instead and stayed in New York to roast along with eight million other people." *And the yummy, luscious Steven McCord,* Caro thought rebelliously. *That lucky bitch.* "And now *look,*" she said, resisting the urge to kick the bloody candlestick. "Look at this mess. Wait until I tell her being nice backfired again."

"Well," Lynn said, blinking faster—Caro suspected it was a nervous tic—"we should—I mean—we should call the—the police. Right?"

Caro studied Lynn, a slender woman so tall she hunched to hide it, a woman whose darting gray eyes swam behind magnified lenses. She was the only one of the group dressed in full makeup, pantyhose, and heels. She had told Caro during the first "Get Acquainted" brunch that she was a realtor from California. If so, she was the most uptight Californian Caro had ever seen. Not to mention the most uptight realtor.

"Call the police?" she asked at last. "Sure. But I think a few things might have escaped your notice."

"Like the fact that the storm's cut us off from the mainland," Todd Opitz suggested, puffing away on his eighth cigarette in fifteen minutes.

"Secondhand smoke kills," Lynn's Goth teenage daughter, Jana, sniffed. She was a tiny brunette with wildly curly dark hair, large dark eyes edged in kohl (making her look not unlike an edgy raccoon), and a pierced nostril. "See, Mom? I told you this would be lame."

"Jana . . ."

"And secondhand smoke *kills,*" the teen added.

"I hope so," was Todd's cold reply. He was an Ichabod Crane of a man, towering over all of them and looking down his long nose, which was often obscured by cigarette smoke. He tossed a lank of dark blond hair out of his eyes, puffed, and added, "I really do. Go watch *Romper Room*, willya?"

"Chil*dren,*" Caro said. "Focus, please. Dana's in there holed up waiting for *les flic* to land. Meantime, who'd she kill?"

"What?" Lynn asked.

"Well, who's dead? Obviously it's not one of us. Who's missing?" Caro started counting on her fingers. "I think there's . . . what? Maybe a dozen of us, including staff? Well, four of us—five, if you count Dana—are accounted for. But there's a few of us missing."

The four of them looked around the narrow hallway, as if they expected the missing guests to pop out any second.

"Right. So, let's go see if we can find the dead person."

"Wh-why?" Lynn asked.

"Duh, Mom," Jana sniffed.

"Because they might not be dead," Caro explained patiently. "There's an old saying: 'A bloody candlestick does not a dead guy make,' or however it goes."

Jana was startled out of her sullen-teen routine. "Where the hell did *you* grow up?"

"Language, Jana. But—but the police?"

"Get it through your head," Todd said, not unkindly. "Nobody's riding to the rescue. You saw the Weather Channel . . . before the power went out, anyway. This is an island, a private island—"

"Enjoy the idyllic splendor of nature from your own solitary island off the Maine coast," Lynn quoted obediently from the brochure.

"Don't do that; it creeps me out when you do that."

"I have a photographic memory," she explained proudly.

"Congratufuckinglations. Anyway," Todd finished, lighting up yet another fresh cigarette, "the earliest the cops can get here is after the storm clears, probably sometime tomorrow morning."

"But they have helicopters—"

As if making Todd's point, a crack of lightning lit up the windows, followed by the hollow boom of thunder, so loud it seemed to shake the mansion walls. The group pressed closer to each other for a brief moment and then, as if embarrassed at their unwilling intimacy, pulled back.

"They won't fly in this weather. We're stuck. Killer in the bedroom, no cops, power's out. The perfect Maine getaway," Todd added mockingly.

"It's like one of those bad horror movies," Caro commented.

"Caro's right."

"About the horror movies?"

He shook his head. "Let's go see who's dead. I mean, what's the alternative? It beats huddling in our rooms waiting for the lights to come back on, don'cha think?"

"What he said," Caro said, and they started off.

Two

"Did you used to be a Boy Scout?" Caro asked Todd, who was briskly handing out large flashlights.

"No. When you're a smoker, you get to know the lay of the land pretty quickly."

"Secondhand smoke—" Jana cut herself off as the blond man glared down at her.

"*Anyway,*" he continued, "when you have to sneak around to take your cigarette breaks because the entire fucking world has gone crazy over cigarettes—don't start, you guys, I *know* it's bad for me; nothing that feels so good could ever be healthy—you get to know the place you're staying at pretty well. I found this little pantry the first hour I was here."

When they all had flashlights—with working batteries, for a change—Caro set off, and after a moment the others fell into step beside her. She had given up her vacation as ruined, but setting that aside, she had an urgent need to find Dana's victim. Sure, there had been blood, but the human body could lose a lot of it and still live to play poker the next day. She had seen it.

"First thing, we find who Dana clocked with the candlestick," Caro said, leading them down yet another long, carpeted hallway. She could hear rain beating against the windows and followed the signs to the main dining salon. "See if he—or she—is okay."

"You're a nurse, right?" Lynn asked.

"Uh-huh. Maybe I can do something."

"Raise the dead?" Jana muttered.

Caro ignored that, pushed through the double doors to the dining room, and immediately shivered. All the windows against the far wall were open, as were the French doors leading to the large balcony where they'd had a pleasant lunch—was it only eight hours ago?

"Then we try to figure out how come."

"How come what?" Lynn asked.

"Well, why did Dana kill whoever-it-is? She must have had a reason, unless she's a sociopath. And she didn't strike me that way at lunch. And—eesh, this is megacreepy."

White curtains billowed and plumed out from the windows, and another crack of lightning lit up the room. Caro hurried through the doors—

"Careful!" Todd said sharply. "Don't slip."

—and skidded to a halt right before the waist-high stone railing. She looked over . . . and nearly fell herself.

"There!" she said, pointing with her flashlight. "Down on the rocks! Oh, Jesus, what a fall . . ."

The others crowded around her, their flashlight beams poking like long white fingers. Far, far below, a body was washed up on the rocks. It was so far below, and so battered by the waves, it was impossible to tell if it was even a man or a woman. The head was so tiny, you couldn't tell the length of hair or even the color of the hair—the rain could have made a blonde brunette, could have made a brunette more of a brunette, could have made a redhead mud-colored.

The setting sun set a bloody, broody glow over everything through the clouds, the perfect horrible creepy touch—not that one was needed.

"Oh, my God," Lynn peeped.

About the only thing she could tell for sure was—

"Well, that poor bastard's deader than shit," Todd declared.

"*Very* helpful," Jana said acidly.

"Oh, why don't you go try to put this place on the market? That's what you do, right?"

"*I'm* the realtor," Lynn said. "Jana works in a CD store."

"Well, go listen to Trent Reznor's latest, then."

"Quit it, children," Caro said absently. "Why is he—or she?—naked?"

Jana shuddered. "I don't even want to think about it."

"Why would Dana undress the victim?" Caro said to herself.

"To keep us from knowing if it's a man or woman?" Lynn ventured.

"Maybe . . . but why?" Caro frowned and stepped back from the railing. "Why let us know she killed them, but not tell us who it was? I mean, pardon my French, but what the *fuck?*"

"She's a model. That's what she said at lunch earlier, right? Well. They're capable of anything." Todd shuddered. "*Anything.*"

Caro ignored the sarcasm. "Boy, there's just no way to get down there without breaking our necks, is there?"

"Get *down* there?" Jana's wild curls were plastered to her head in the driving rain, and she had to shout to be heard over the thunder. "Get *down* there? Have you lost your mind? We're not cops! I vote we all go back to our rooms and wait for the police to get here and take Dana back to the mainland."

"Yeah," Lynn added with a mighty sniff. She dashed rain out of her eyes and looked away from the body.

"Forget that," Todd said. "Just leave that poor schmuck down there on the rocks all night? For the birds and the fish and the—the whoever to do—you know. How'd you like it if it was you? Besides, he—she—they might be alive."

Caro didn't say anything. She certainly wasn't going to

argue with him, although his initial assessment had been correct: whomever-it-was was deader than shit. Not that she was going to take that road . . . she and Todd were on the same page—she wanted to get to the body. Skulking in her room waiting for rescue didn't exactly appeal. She wasn't happy to be in the middle of this, but by God, she was *in* it.

"Look at this," she said, pointing. There was blood on the stone railing, blood that trailed all the way back into the dining room. "That's Dana, carrying the candlestick. She clocked this poor guy, shoved him—or her—over, then walked back to her room."

"Naked," Lynn added. "Shoved them naked."

"Barf out," Jana said with a grimace.

"Then *told* us she did it," Todd added. "In the movies, the killer usually tries to, you know, cover up."

"She forgot to leave the candlestick behind—shock, probably," Caro continued, picturing it. "Didn't even remember holding it until she was talking to us. That's why there's a trail of blood."

"How handy for us," Todd said, trying unsuccessfully to light a new cigarette in the downpour. "Explains the blood in the hallway, too, huh, Sherlock?"

"Are you smoking those things, or eating them?"

"Hey, I'm stressed, all right?" he snapped back. "This isn't exactly my idea of a luxurious Maine getaway."

"What, it's *ours?* I could be in Minnesota right now, fishing on a lake."

"I could be in wine country," Lynn said mournfully.

"I could be indulging in minor property damage with my friends," Jana sighed.

"Aw, shaddup, you guys. Be nice or I won't tell you where the boathouse is."

"The boat—"

"I had a cigarette there earlier."

"Where haven't you had a cigarette?" Jana snapped. "Your lungs must look like a couple of pieces of beef jerky."

"Aw, shaddup. Look," he said, turning back to Caro, "we could take the little outboard, maybe try to rescue the—maybe try to get the body. Or whatever."

"Forget it," Jana said.

"Fine. Stay here. Alooooone," Todd said, wiggling his brows in a meaningfully scary way. "Hopefully Dana won't come out of her room and decide to decorate your head with another candlestick."

They stared at each other in the rain. Nobody consulted Lynn, but then, why start now?

Mother and daughter exchanged a look. Then, "So, where's this boathouse?" Jana asked, resigned.

Three

". . . just through here . . . a little bit farther . . ."

"That's what you said ten minutes ago," Caro pointed out.

"Well, we're getting close."

Under ordinary conditions—which was to say, when they weren't looking for a dead body in the steadily deepening dark, worried about the killer up at the mansion and being lashed by torrents of rain—this was probably a pleasant little path to the boathouse.

Not so much right now.

"It's just down there," Todd said, pointing. "See?"

They could see a small, squat building with a green roof just at the end of the path, and beyond that, a river gurgled alongside. Caro guessed the river must lead directly to the sea, and they could take the boat around to the back of the mansion, fish the body out, and then . . .

What?

She'd worry about that later.

"Is there a reason we aren't leaving this to the owner of the mansion?" Lynn ventured, stumbling in her pumps.

"He might be the dead guy," Caro replied. "And it's a big place. He could be anywhere. Heck, he could have gone back to the mainland after supper for all we know. I don't want to waste time looking for someone we don't even know is alive. I'd rather get to the victim."

"It's touching, yet a little on the creepy side," Todd said. "I'm sure it has nothing to do with your obsessive need to be in charge."

"Here we—ow! Son of a bitch!" Jana cursed and shoved the branches out of her face.

"*Jana!*" her mother gasped. "Watch your mouth."

"That probably stings like crazy," Todd commented, smothering a snicker.

"Does anyone know how to drive a boat?" Lynn asked timidly.

"I can do it," Caro said. "I used to go fishing with my old man on the Mississippi all the time."

"Aw, that's so cute," Todd said. "And when I say cute, I mean lame. Uh-oh."

Caro didn't ask what uh-oh meant. She and the others had reached the door to the boathouse . . . and the lock was smashed and hanging open.

"Dana's smarter than I thought," Todd said. "And that's really saying something—didn't she say she was a teacher?"

"What's so dumb about that?"

"She teaches modeling."

"Her evil knows no bounds," Caro said. "And she knows a few other things, too." Caro poked at the broken hasp. "Well, let's go see how bad it is."

She pushed the door open with tented fingers and walked in. Part of her couldn't believe this was happening to her, would-be author and pediatric nurse. Tramping around in the dark, in a spooky damp boathouse where she could barely see her hand in front of her face. Followed by the three musketeers: Larry, Moe, and Curly. Oh, Lord, what a day. *Next time,* she told herself grimly, *stay home or stay in bed. Possibly both.*

She took a deep breath and went in a little farther, feeling like every stupid horror movie heroine ever conceived. She could practically hear people yelling at the screen, "Don't go in there, dumb bitch!"

She kept her flashlight trained in front of her, which was why she didn't see the body at her feet and went sprawling.

"Ouch," Todd said, looking down at her. "That looked embarrassing."

Four

Caro scrambled back, away from the body. She could feel wet muck sliding down her shorts and didn't care. Wet snakes could be sliding down her shorts and she wouldn't care. The body on the floor . . . she cared about *that*.

"Oh, gross!" Jana cried.

"Another body," Lynn gasped.

"Dana's been a busy girl," Todd said. "Where's my lighter?"

"You dropped it on my back," the body said, rolling over and sitting up. The four of them screamed in unison. "Ow! Not so loud . . . my head . . ."

"You're alive!" Caro blurted. It was the first thing they taught in her nursing courses: determine if your patient is living or dead.

"Unfortunately, yes." The body rubbed the back of his head and squinted up at all of them. "Hey, thanks for coming to get me, you guys. I thought I was a goner when she nailed me."

He got to his feet with some care, then bent, winced, and helped Caro to her feet. She couldn't help staring at him. He was mussed and muddy and a little pale from the blow to his head, but for all that, yummy besides.

He was dressed in dark blue boat shoes and black swimming trunks, and nothing else. The mat of hair on his chest was dark and curly, the hair on his head a lighter color with streaks of gold, and his eyes were—she squinted in the gloom—dark green . . . almost exactly the color of the wet leaves all over the boathouse floor. She'd never seen eyes that color before.

"You're not a dead body!" Caro said again, because she honestly couldn't think of what else to say to him.

"I'm Turner."

"Last name Turner or first name Turner?"

"Just Turner."

"Like just Kramer on 'Seinfeld,' " Jana said helpfully.

"No, Kramer's first name was Cosmo," Todd said. To Turner, "I remember you. Breakfast, right?"

"Yup."

"Like Madonna, then," Jana was babbling.

"Or Cher," Lynn added.

"You guys, could we stay focused?" Caro demanded. "Turner's not the dead body. In fact, who *are* you? I didn't see you at lunch."

"Oh, I work here. Give tours, run the tourists down the river to some of those riverside restaurants . . . kind of an all around go-to guy."

"Oooh, ooh," Todd said, grinning. "Stop it."

The body quirked an eyebrow at him, then continued. "I came down here when the storm started kickin' up to make sure the boathouse was locked up, when—holy crap—you'll never guess—"

"Dana smashed the lock, damaged the boat, hit you over the head with something, came back told us what happened, and locked herself in."

Turner was gaping at them. "Well, shit. There goes my story. Figured it was good for a couple of beers at least. Not to mention, you guys know more of what happened than I do."

"I'll buy you a beer anyway," Lynn said.

"I got here in time to hear her rummaging in the boat and got my 'guests aren't supposed to use the boats unless I'm with them' lecture ready, when everything went dark and I went night-night. Didn't even see her coming." He rubbed the back of his head and winced. "Girl's got a swing like a Major Leaguer, I'll tell you that much."

"That's interesting," Todd said.

"Interesting as in psychotic? Interesting as in laughable? What are we talking about? Help me out."

"Well, you're a big guy, a *very* big guy, pardon me for noticing, and Dana's at least a foot shorter than you. She would have had to swing *up*. She must have really wanted you out of her way."

"Or didn't like you."

"At least she didn't kill me, and believe me, this isn't the first weekend I've had to say that. Well, let's check the boat anyway."

They did, and Turner announced, "Even if she hadn't punched that hole in the stern, I don't see any spark plugs, do you?"

"What does one look like?" Lynn whispered in Caro's ear.

"Search me," she shrugged. "So Dana knows about engines, too. Okay."

"But . . . how come?" Jana ventured. "I mean, grody enough that she killed whoever, but why come down here and fix it so we couldn't get the body?"

"Probably the same reason she won't tell us who she killed," Caro said. "Question is, now what?"

"Now we go back up to the mansion and wait for the cops," Lynn declared. "We're soaked, it's getting late, it's *dark*—"

"Aw, Mom," Jana whined, stealing another glance at Turner's legs.

"—and there's a body bobbing around the water somewhere . . ." Lynn shuddered.

Turner looked puzzled. "Well, who is it?"

"That's what we're trying to figure out," Caro explained. "Obviously, it's not you. And there's a few more of us missing. Four or five at least. We don't know who she killed . . . or even if she's done killing."

"Well, shit! Let's find out!"

"It's so nice to have a man in charge," Todd murmured, taking a deep drag.

Caro giggled. "Want me to look at that?" she asked, indicating the lump Turner kept rubbing.

"Naw. Got worse than this from my mama. Let's try to round up the others, make sure they're all okay."

"There aren't that many more of us," Caro reminded them. "Stop me if you've heard this, but . . . who the hell did she kill? And *why?*"

"I can get the list of guests from the register, and we can go from there."

"What a great idea!" Caro cried. "Shoot, we should have done something like that first."

"I thought you wanted to find the body first?" Todd asked.

"Well, now I've reprioritized. So, let's go get that list. You guys? Everybody game?"

"Okay," Jana and Lynn said at once. They both had identical expressions of hunger on their faces, which made them look more than ever like mother and daughter. Caro supposed they just needed the right incentive to be socially conscious. The right, six-foot, three-inch incentive.

Caro and Todd rolled their eyes. "All right, then," Caro said. "Let's go."

Five

"You know, you should go for it," Todd told her. They were trudging back up to the mansion/resort/hellhole, rain beating down on them like a live, malevolent thing. Todd and Caro were trailing behind the group. Jana and Lynn hovered so close to Turner, they were practically holding his hands. "I saw the way you looked at his butt."

"I was not," she said, jerking her gaze higher. "What are you talking about?"

"Oh, come on. You like him, I can tell."

"Todd," she said patiently, "I don't *know* him. Or you. Can we stay focused, please? Heck, a few minutes ago I thought he was a dead body."

"The only impediment to your budding romance, I might add. Make a pass. He'll be receptive, I bet. A little va-va-voom on your vacation, do you good."

"Todd! We're sort of in the middle of something, here. There's a time and a place, and this ain't it."

"Details," Todd grumbled.

"Why don't *you* make a pass, you think it's such a great idea?"

"Oh, believe me, I did. Right after breakfast. Hello, you see his pecs? Oofta. Alas, he politely turned me down." Todd sighed, then brightened. "But I bet he wouldn't turn you down." He squinted at her in the rain. "I bet your hair is past your waist when you get it out of that tacky braid. And it's probably not usually muddy and brownish."

"It's blond," she said, stung.

"Well, drowned rat is *not* a good look for you, darling. And you're almost as tall as he is. Actually . . ."

"That's enough."

". . . you've got sort of the forties starlet thing going, with your teeny waist and big boobs."

"That's the nicest thing anyone's ever said to me," she said sarcastically. "Now shut your face."

"Except for the glasses," he added heartlessly. "Big purple frames? In *this* decade? You should lose them and try contacts."

"I hate contacts. They itch my eyeballs. Can we please stop this?"

"But it's why you came here. It's why we all came here."

"That's not true!" she cried.

"Oh, sure it is," Todd went on cheerfully. "Not necessarily to hook up—like an island Love Boat, how lame would that be? And who does that make me? Doc? *Gopher?* But to be with people."

"I'm here only because my friend was too busy to go and she gave me her tickets."

"Okay," he said. "But why did you *come?*"

"It doesn't matter," she snapped.

"I'm just saying." Todd looked at the fresh cigarette and tucked it away without bothering to try to light it in the downpour. "You should ask him out. I bet he's into you. God knows he wasn't into *me.*"

"And who could resist you?"

"Exactly."

Caro grinned in spite of herself. "You're an asshole, Todd."

"Exactly."

Six

"Okay," Turner said as they all dripped across the lobby. The mansion had such a large foyer, it was used as a check-in area. He went behind the large mahogany desk, rummaged around, and produced a printout. "Here's the guest list for the weekend. Everybody on the island is on this. There's—"

"What do you think you're doing?"

"Aaiigghh!" they all cried, including Turner, who straightened so fast he clutched his head. Todd actually jumped behind Caro.

They all spun around to look. The manager of the resort was blinking at them from the doorway leading to the kitchen. He was dressed in a tan linen suit and looked like a sleepy Colonel Sanders with his closely trimmed beard and short white hair. His eyes were very blue as he stared at them. "Why are you yelling? And isn't it getting a little late for all this charging around? I was just about to retire for the night. And why are you all wet? Do you know what these carpets cost?"

"That's the owner guy," Jana said suddenly. "He checked us in this morning."

"I remember, miss. Richard Calque," he said. "What's going on?"

"Rich, you'll never believe this," Turner said. "One of the

guests is dead. I'm glad it's not you. Best boss I ever had," he added in a mutter to Lynn, who had sidled over to him.

"Dana killed him . . . remember from lunch? Short, red curly hair, wicked swing? And locked herself in and won't come out."

"What?"

"I know, I know," Caro said. "But it's true."

"But who is dead?" Richard asked, looking bewildered.

"That's just it. We don't know. I mean, we know it's not you," Caro said, "and we know it's not Turner. We came up here to get the names of the other guests. We figured we'd track them down and make sure they're okay."

"But the police—"

"Aren't coming. Not for a while, anyway. Stupid private island," Todd mumbled. "*Seemed* like a good idea at the time . . ."

"But there is a police officer among the guests," Rich said.

"Get out of town!" Caro hadn't expected some *good* news, not the way things had been going so far. "Really? Who is it?"

"Okay," Turner said as Caro, overcome with curiosity, went to him and read over his shoulder. "We got Dana . . . check. We got Jana."

"Check," Jana said, dimpling.

Caro glared at the teenager while Turner continued. "We got Lynn, we got Caro, we got Todd. We got me, we got the boss."

"Please," Rich said modestly, flicking an invisible speck off his spotless sleeve. "Call me Rich."

"That leaves the honeymooners—"

"Right, and the husband's a Brit," Todd added. "Great shoes."

"I remember," Lynn said excitedly. "Not the shoes, but I remember because they looked so odd together . . . he's this big strapping fellow, and she's this little tiny elfin thing; but he's a little starchy, and she's got this amazing foul mouth. They disappeared after lunch." Lynn colored. "You know, honeymoon business."

"The cook, Anna Barkmeier—"

"Room eight," Caro said, still shamelessly reading over Turner's (broad) shoulder.

"And that's it," Turner said, looking around at all of them. "Ten of us."

"What about the rest of the staff? There's, like, fifteen bedrooms in this place. There must be more than this."

"With only seven guests, I really only need two other people to help me run the mansion," Rich said mildly. "I haven't been the owner very long . . . it's a bit of an experiment."

"Keep owning it," Turner ordered.

"If dead people keep showing up, I'll likely sell as soon as possible and go see what my niece and nephew-by-marriage are up to," Rich retorted. "How do we know this person is dead, by the way?"

"They're dead," Todd and Caro said in unison.

"Well, I hope it's not one of the honeymooners," Turner said. "They seem like they're really in love and happy. I don't want to tell either one of them that the *other* one is dead."

"So let's go find them," Caro said.

Corinne Bullwinkle Daniels was on the brink of a truly profound . . . revelation . . . when someone started hammering at their door.

"Ignore it," her husband, Grant, panted beneath her.

"Way ahead of you," she gasped back, but the pounding, if anything, speeded up. Followed by the shrieking.

Her husband cursed as she climbed off him, then cursed more when she tossed a blanket over him, shrugged into her robe, and yanked the door open. "*What?*"

"You're alive!" the stunning blonde answered. She was wet, muddy, and completely bedraggled . . . and looked better that way than Corinne had looked on her wedding day. Not *too* annoying. "That's so great!"

"Thanks. We don't need any towels. Good-bye," she said, starting to swing the door shut, but the blonde stuck her foot out.

Corinne looked down at the foot, then looked up—up,

up!—at the tall woman. "Good way to get a fracture, bee-yatch," she warned.

"Is your husband all right?" she asked, trying to shove past Corinne.

"No, he's not all right, he's pissed off, and so am I." Corinne started leaning on the door. "We're on our honeymoon, fuck you very much, now *go away.*"

"Pissed off," the owner said, peeking over the blonde's shoulder, "as in, not dead?"

Corinne gave up, and the door swung open the rest of the way. Grant sat up and tucked the blanket demurely around himself. "What in the world is going on? Corinne, darling, let them in."

"Bad idea. Don't feed any of them," she said, stepping back, "or they'll never leave."

"We're dreadfully sorry to bother you, Mrs. Daniels—"

"Not as sorry as we are," Corinne grumped.

"But there's been . . . a murder."

Even though Rich said it with the appropriate dramatic pause, it was still hard to believe.

Corinne and Grant blinked at each other, then blinked at him. "There's been a *what?*" Corinne asked.

Quickly, the tall blonde—who would be breathtaking once she dried off and washed her hair, and her clothes—explained.

"Seriously?" Corinne asked when the blonde finished. "It's not a joke?"

"If it was, it would be in extremely poor taste. I understand you're a police officer," Rich said, "so if you could just—"

"Simmer down, Colonel Sanders," Corinne said, making the time-out motion with her hands. "One, I'm not a cop. I'm a private investigator—I quit the force when I got engaged."

"But—"

"Two, even if I *was* a cop, which, if you missed the memo, I'm not, this isn't my jurisdiction. In fact, we're about fifteen hundred miles from my jurisdiction."

"But—"

"Three, where's the killer?"

Their room was just *full* of people, Corinne saw to her annoyance, and they all stared at each other and then gaped at her. *Oh, SUPER helpful.*

"In her room," the blond woman finally said. "She locked herself in a couple hours ago when she told us what she did."

"And she's *still* there?"

"Uh . . . I think so."

"Did you—is anybody guarding the door so she doesn't get away?"

"Uh . . ."

Civilians. Lord help us. "Mmm." Corinne grabbed a pile of clothes out of her suitcase and marched to the bathroom. "Nobody go anywhere," she ordered. "I'll be right out."

A short silence fell, while everyone in the room tried to look everywhere but at the obviously mussed Grant Daniels. (Everyone except Todd.) Finally, the blonde said, "My name's Caro. This is Turner, Jana, Lynn, Todd, and Rich."

"Grant Daniels," he said, shaking her damp hand.

"So. Uh. How do you like Maine?"

"It's . . . exciting," Daniels said, eyeing the group with something close to wariness.

Seven

The tiny Mrs. Daniels, who really did look like an elf with those short limbs and tip-tilted dark eyes, hammered on Dana's door. "Hey in there!" she shouted. The amount of volume pumped out by that tiny frame was startling, to put it mildly. "Are you okay?"

"Go away!" Dana shouted back.

"Who'd you kill?"

"Mind your own business!"

"I'll tell the cops you cooperated!" Corinne yelled into the keyhole. "And they'll tell the D.A.!"

"History will exonerate me!"

"History will *what* her?" Lynn asked.

"I'm telling my whole story to the press!" Dana shouted. "But I'm not coming out there until you can guarantee my safety!"

"*She's* scared of *us?*" Turner asked. "Oh, that's rich."

"What?" Rich asked.

"Never mind, boss."

"Okay," Corinne said, turning back to the group. "So at least we know she's still in there. I guess the murder weapon's in there with her."

"No," Caro said. "It's—oh, shit!"

"Don't tell me, let me guess." Corinne paused dramatically, then rolled her eyes. "It's *gone*. Bum-bum-*bum!*"

"Completely gone," Rich said, eyeing the bloody patch of carpet with distaste.

"It was *right there,*" Todd said, pointing. "Right there!"

"So she either came out to get it, or somebody took it."

"Who would take it?"

Corinne shook her head. "Okay, so the crime scene is totally fucked."

"Totally fucked?" her husband teased. "As opposed to only partially fucked?"

She ignored him. "We'll worry about that when the locals land. There's no way to properly process the scene anyway, not without the right equipment. It's too bad, because the more time that gets wasted . . . anyway, it's better to just leave the whole place alone and try to find out who's dead. Is there a way to lock her in?"

"Yes," Turner and Rich said in unison.

"So, let's do it."

Caro was impressed. She so rarely met a woman as forceful as herself. And this one was half her size! Bet she gave her husband hell on a regular basis. "Good idea."

"Uh . . . darling . . ."

"I know, Grant," Corrine replied, holding up her hands. "I'm not a big fan of squashing constitutional rights, either. Well, usually. Sometimes. But she admitted to murder. I think for everyone's safety, we lock her up until the cops come."

"Come on," Turner said, and to Caro's complete surprise, he grabbed her hand and pulled her away from the group. "I know where the keys are."

"That's nice," she said, unnerved by the pressure of his big hand around hers. "Are they so heavy you need help carrying them?"

"No. But I'll feel better if I know you're with me."

The evening was getting more surreal by the minute. Dead

bodies she was used to—she worked in a Minneapolis emergency ward, for God's sake. Criminals she was used to—bad guys as well as good guys got sick. But scrumptious-looking handymen wanting to be with her? Being protective of her? That was just too damn weird.

"Uh . . . uh . . ."

"You know, I noticed you at breakfast."

"I didn't notice you," she confessed. "I was too busy listening to Mr. and Mrs. Daniels debate whether or not King George was a bad enough king to justify the Revolutionary War."

"Right."

"Apparently he wasn't such a bad guy."

"Right."

"I mean, to hear the British guy tell it."

"Right. Are you okay?"

"I'm a little nervous," she gasped.

"Oh, sure. Understandable. You know, with dead bodies and killers and ex-cops running around."

That's not why I'm nervous, buddy boy. "Uh-huh."

Turner was rummaging around behind the big desk, and then he emerged with an old-fashioned set of keys on a large metal ring. "Haven't seen something like this in a while, huh?" he asked her. "Amazing how fast we all got used to key cards. But this place is two hundred years old, and Rich refused to put modern locks on the doors."

"Uh-huh." *Oh, you're really impressing him with your wit and style! Good thing you don't LOOK LIKE HELL or you'd really be in trouble.* "That's . . . uh-huh."

"Listen, Caro," he said, fixing her with a look and then grabbing her hand again. "I want you to stay away from Dana."

That broke the spell. Thank goodness! "No shit. Thanks for the tip."

He had the grace to look abashed. "Well, it's probably tempting to talk to her, try to get some details, right? Tempting for you, I mean."

"Well . . . yeah . . ." *How does he know that?*

He grinned at her. "You seem like the curious type. But she's dangerous. Like, drooling crazy dangerous. Network-executive-run-amok dangerous. Steer clear. For my sake, okay?"

"Why in the world do you care?" She had to restrain herself from slapping her own forehead. *Oh, shit! That was out loud!*

"I just . . . do. I wouldn't want anything to happen to you." He rubbed the bump on his head. "She just knocked me cold, but that could have killed someone else. And I—I knew her. From before."

"Knew Dana?"

"Well, yeah. We sort of have a history. Not much of one," he added, seeing the alarmed look on Caro's face. "She was out here our opening weekend, and I—we—we sort of spent the night together. But she wouldn't have anything to do with me afterward." He shook his head. "My own fault. One-night stands never lead to anything good. Should have kept my pants on."

"I guess *so*." *Ya big pig,* she thought but didn't say.

"She was sort of—uh, she came on kind of strong. And I was kind of lonesome, and—look, I'm not proud of it, okay? I'm just saying, please stay away from her."

"Don't worry," Caro said. "But if I do get near her, I promise not to fall into bed with her."

He blushed. Blushed! Red to his eyebrows. "Look, I just wanted to tell you, okay?"

"How come? I mean, why me?"

He shrugged, looking uncomfortable. "I—I think you're kind of cool."

"You don't even know me," she said, flattered in spite of herself.

"No, but I'd like to. I noticed you earlier and tried to figure out how to talk to you, but you're so gorgeous and classy . . ." He trailed off.

"*I* am?" she practically gasped.

"I hate to say it, but as awful and scary as this whole thing is, it gave me a chance to, you know, talk to you."

Okay, this is getting weirder and weirder.

"Come on," he said. "Let's go lock her in."

Wordlessly, she let him lead her back to the others.

Eight

"Why would she kill the cook?" Caro mused aloud, after Dana had been locked in her room. Turner had jammed a chair against the doorknob for good effect, and everyone had breathed easier. Now they were all in the small dining room where breakfast had been served earlier. Lit candles gave an appropriately spooky glow to everyone's face. "That's the only one we haven't found, right? The cook? Anna what's-her-name?"

"Barkmeier," Rich confirmed. "She's been in my employ for about a month. And I don't know why."

"You never heard them—Dana and the cook?—arguing about anything?" Corinne pressed. "About money, men, whatever?"

"No. Nothing. I barely saw Dana before she . . . you know."

"This might be kind of a dumb question," Turner said, "and it's off the subject, but has anyone tried their cell phone?"

"Yes," Todd and Caro said gloomily. Todd added, "The storm must have taken out the tower, or whatever cell phones have. Nobody can get a signal."

"And land lines are out, needless to say," Corinne observed.

"Right."

"Well, getting back to the subject, as a former cop, I can tell you, people kill other people for the dumbest reasons in the world . . . or no reason at all. I once arrested a guy who shot his wife because she burned the pork loin. Honest to God."

"Well, maybe Dana didn't like Anna's cooking," Todd said, trying to smile.

"Maybe Anna had something she wanted. Or did something she didn't like. Or knew a secret Dana didn't want to get out. Seriously, you guys, it could be anything."

"I just wish we could get her body," Caro said.

Corinne shook her head. "It's better you leave it where it is. The first commandment of crime is, Thou shalt not fuck up thy crime scene."

Grant snickered, then sobered when everyone looked at him. "Sorry. That was amusing to me."

"So . . . what?" Todd asked. "We're just going to sit here in the dark and stare at each other? Blurgh."

A short silence, followed by, "Well, there's really nothing we can do, right? Dana confessed, and we locked her in. We can't get the body—and shouldn't, anyway. We know who's dead. Everyone else is accounted for. And it's now . . ." Corinne grabbed her husband's wrist and squinted at his watch. "Eleven-thirty-two P.M. And the storm . . ." Another crash of thunder. "Isn't letting up anytime soon. And . . . frankly, you guys . . . I'm on my honeymoon, here."

"Darling, you're insatiable."

"Shut up, Grant. Anyway. I vote we all go back to our rooms and hit the sheets."

"That sounds all right," Lynn said cautiously. "I mean, I was against tromping around in the woods from the start. If there's really nothing more we can do . . ."

"I'll post watch outside Dana's door," Rich volunteered.

"I'll do it," Turner said, shooting a glance at Caro. "Maybe I could have some company?"

Caro opened her mouth, but Rich interrupted with, "No, no. It's my mansion, I'll do it."

"Okay, but then I'll relieve you at . . . what? Three o'clock?"

"That sounds fine, my boy." Rich rose, adjusted his pleats, and bowed. "Until tomorrow morning, then."

"Turner, will you walk me to my room?" Jana asked. "It's so dark . . . and scary . . . and you're so . . . big . . ."

"I can't," he said. "I promised Caro I'd . . . look at her JAMA collection."

"What?" Caro asked.

"JAMA?"

"Journal of the American Medical Association," Caro said automatically. Then, "Oh. Oh! Right. I've been dying to show you my, uh, collection."

Later, as they scampered down the hall like kids freed early for recess, Caro asked, "How in the world do you know about JAMA?"

"My sister's a doc," he replied easily. "Thanks for going along with it. Badly, I might add."

"Well, give a girl some warning next time!"

"How about this?" he asked, and pulled her into his arms and, right below the painting of the elderly woman with the flashing eyes and wispy moustache, kissed her.

Nine

"Just so you know," Caro gasped, coming up for air, "I never do this."

"Me neither. Okay, I do it sometimes."

"You did it with Dana!"

"Believe me, that was *way* more her idea than mine. I thought she'd be there in the morning so I could buy her breakfast, maybe we could spend the weekend together, get to know each other, but . . ." He shook his head. "Gone."

"Oh, like that's the first time that's happened. You probably horndog after all the girl guests."

"No," he said soberly, pulling back and looking at her. "I don't."

They were in her room, and she couldn't help noticing it was just romantic as hell with the candles and the lit fireplace. How was a girl supposed to resist? Not to mention, Turner must have been a Boy Scout in his youth, because with the help of four matches and several pages from *US* magazine, he had a blaze going in no time.

They kissed again, hungrily, exploring each other's mouths, and she traced her fingers along his jawline and across his shoulders. He was as firm to the touch as he was candy to the eyes, and smelled delicious . . . if slightly damp.

His hands were busy beneath her BLO POP T-shirt, grazing the flesh just beneath her bra, big warm fingers sending shivers down her spine . . . the good kind of shivers, for a change.

"Seriously," she said again, breaking the kiss. "I mean, I *never* do stuff like this. When I'm not working, I'm writing. Doesn't leave a lot of time for a social life."

"You're a writer?"

"Would-be. I'm still trying to get published."

"Well, if you came out here for inspiration, you got it in spades."

"Are you talking about the murder?" she teased as he nibbled on her earlobe. "Or other things?"

"Mmmf," he replied, then pulled his lips away from her ear. "Uh, listen, Caro, I really like you . . ."

"Well, I didn't think that was a roll of Life Savers in your pocket."

"Life Savers?" he said, offended.

"Caro, I really like you . . . ," she prompted.

"That's about it. I mean, I wasn't really going anywhere with it."

"Very romantic," she grumbled. "As it happens, I like you, too, but don't ask me why. I mean, five hours ago, I didn't know you. This is *so* unlike me."

"You keep saying that," he murmured, kissing the base of her throat. "And then you keep doing things."

"The whole thing. Isn't like me, I mean. Oooh, that's nice, don't stop doing that."

"Don't worry."

"I don't even read mysteries, y'know? I'm strictly a cookbook girl. Well, and maybe a few Star Trek novels. I just love Commander Riker."

"Could you not reveal your major geekiness right now? It's sort of killing the mood."

"Give me a break. It's just so weird to be in the middle of all this. The last mystery I read was . . . I can't even remember. Miss Marple I'm not."

"Definitely not," he said, nuzzling her other ear. "I sort of liked the way you took charge."

"You weren't even there."

"Oh, Jana and Lynn were bitching about it."

"Figures," she snorted. "I doubt Jana's legal, by the way, so don't get any ideas."

He actually shuddered. "Don't worry. Neither of them is my type. She's too young, and her mom's too annoying."

"Nice way to talk about guests," she teased.

"And if this is all so unlike you, how come you're here?"

"Well . . . I'm just trying to be polite . . ." Her fingers brushed the front of his shorts. "And I did pack some condoms. It's been so long since I bought some," she added grumpily, "the pharmacist laughed his ass off."

He pulled away from her. "Oh. That's good . . . that's great. But I wasn't going to, y'know, push you or anything."

"You were quick enough to jump into bed with Dana!" she said, stung.

"*She* jumped in with me. I told you, the whole thing wasn't exactly my idea," he said patiently. "I don't want to wreck things with you. I mean, a one-night stand isn't exactly what I'm after. They don't work for me."

"Well, what are we doing here, then?"

His brow clouded. "Oh, I'm like your summer vacation boy toy? Bonk the help and then go back to the real world?"

"You're not the help," she said, shocked. Then she thought about it. "Well, I guess you are. But I didn't think about you that way. Honest."

"That's true," he said. "First you thought I was a dead body."

"But then you got better!"

He laughed. "Sorry. I guess I'm a little touchy. I felt really used by Dana, you know?"

"Sure, I can understand that."

"It's just, you're so classy and beautiful, I didn't think you'd even talk to me. And now that we're here . . . it's like it's too good to be true. I don't want anything to ruin it. You know, anything more than felony assault and homicide."

Classy and beautiful? Was he high? Was *she?* But he was right about the too good to be true part. The whole night had a definite surreal cast. Death and sex . . . whodathunkit?

She was right about one thing. This *wasn't* like her. But for once in her life, she was going to do something irresponsible and weird. And Turner was going to help!

"Anyway," she said, determined not to waste the opportunity, "about those condoms . . ."

There was a sudden rap at the door, and they both jumped. Then Caro laughed nervously. "Dum-dum-*dum!* I guess it's been that kind of night."

"I'll get it."

She pushed him back on the bed. "Stay put. And how about losing those shorts? It's my room, I'll get it." She crossed the room and called through the door, "It's not the killer, is it?"

"No," a confused-sounding female voice said from the other side. "I'm looking for Turner."

Caro opened the door and beheld a freckled, red-haired woman who was almost exactly her height. Her hair was sleek and damp, the color of strawberry pie, and she was barefoot and dressed in denim shorts and a red polo shirt. "Hi," she said, extending a large hand.

"Hi. Listen, you've found Turner, but you can't have him."

The redhead looked confused. "But I need him."

"Join the club, babe."

"No, I mean, he's supposed to help me with the garbage bins. I can't move them by myself, and I've got to prep for breakfast."

Caro stared. "Uh, why?"

The redhead stared back. "Because it's my job. I'm the cook? Anna Barkmeier?"

"Aigh!" Caro cried, and slammed the door shut.

Ten

"What? What?" Turner was at her side in a second. "What's the matter?"

"It's the body!" she cried, leaning against the door. "The body is here, looking for you!"

"You mean *Anna?* Move." He jerked the door open. "Holy shit!"

"You slammed the door on me," the body complained, aggrieved. "I hate that."

Caro goggled. "You're not dead!"

Turner gave her a curious look. "That seems to be a thing with you. You're always shocked to find out someone's alive."

"No, I'm *not.* I mean, I am tonight, sure. But it's not 'a thing' with me. Not normally. Jeez, Anna Barkmeier! I can't believe it!"

"Anyway," the body continued doggedly, "if I could just borrow Turner for a few minutes . . ."

Turner grabbed her by the elbow and pulled her into the room. "Where the hell have you been?"

Anna tripped on the rug and nearly went sprawling, then jerked her elbow away and glared at them both. "I was stuck in town, of course. Miserable storm. Why, were you looking for me?"

"Actually, no. We thought you were—uh—it's a long story," Caro finished sheepishly.

"Well. Now I'm way behind on breakfast prep, so I really need you to—"

"But who's dead?"

"Corinne! Open up!" Caro hammered on the door. "We found the body!" Silence from inside the room. Caro hammered more. "I'm sorry to bother you again, but the body's here!"

Suddenly, the door was jerked open, and a disheveled, hastily robed Corinne stood there, glaring. *"You're* going to be the body if you don't quit interrupting us," she growled.

"I know, I know, I'm sorry. But the body came looking for Turner."

"The body did *what?"*

"For heaven's sake," she heard Grant say from inside the room. "Let her in, Corinne, or she'll beat on our door all night."

"I didn't know you were into that stuff," she snapped, then stepped back.

Embarrassed, Caro scuttled into the room. "Hi again," she said breathlessly as the scrumptious Grant, looking resigned, once again rearranged the covers over himself. "Sorry. I'm really sorry. But this is important."

"Oh, you always say that. 'Come quick, there's been a murder.' 'Come quick, we found a dead body . . . again.' " Grant smiled at her to take the sting out of his words. "Can't you come up with anything good?"

"Funny," she said. "But we really need you guys. See, Anna being alive poses kind of a problem."

"You got *that* right," Corinne replied. "For starters . . ."

Eleven

"Who the hell is dead?"

"I—I don't understand," Anna said faintly. "What's going on? Why is everybody up? Have you filled out your breakfast orders?"

"Screw breakfast," Todd said. "We've sort of had a few other things on our mind tonight while you were slumming in town."

"I wasn't—"

"One of the guests killed somebody," Corinne explained. "We don't know who, because with you being alive, everyone's accounted for."

"But—but—who—?"

"Whom," Jana corrected loftily.

"Shut up, Punky Brewster," Todd ordered.

"Dana Gunn killed someone, then confessed and barricaded herself in her room," Caro said. "Before she did that, she conked Turner over the head and wrecked the boat so we couldn't get the body. Which is weird in itself . . . she confessed to murder but she won't tell us who she offed? What, like she's embarrassed? Don't you guys think that's weird?"

"This whole awful night is weird," Lynn said.

"Dana . . . Dana *killed* . . . ?" Anna rubbed her temples, as if a sudden, throbbing headache had appeared. Which, for all Caro knew, it had. "I don't understand . . . and you thought I was . . . ?"

"Well, you were the only one we couldn't find," Jana said peevishly. "Thanks tons for disappearing, by the way."

"I don't believe it," Anna muttered, still rubbing. "I just don't believe it."

"Believe it, sis," Todd said, exhaling a cloud of smoke and looking not unlike a sulky blond dragon. "But you turning up begs the question . . . and stop me if you've heard this before, but who'd she kill?"

"Whom did she kill," Jana corrected.

"And why?" Caro asked, ignoring the teen. "I still want to know why."

"If you knew *why* she killed, you'd probably know who," Corinne pointed out.

"This is decidedly freaky," Turner commented. "Now what do we do?"

"The storm must be letting up," Grant said. "If Anna was able to get back."

Corinne frowned. "Anybody try their cell phone lately?"

"Why do you think I was stranded?" Anna snapped. "My cell wasn't working, among other things."

"All right, all right, don't foam at the mouth. I suggest we all go back to what we were doing—"

"Insatiable," Grant murmured.

"Works for me," Caro said cheerfully.

"—and we'll get together again when the police are here."

"That sounds all right," Lynn said tentatively.

"Well, it's not like you've got a lot of choice. You'll all have to give statements, anyway."

"But I've got breakfast to get on with," Anna protested.

Corinne gave her a look, and the redhead subsided.

Twelve

"Well, if there's nothing else we can do . . ." Her shirt went flying, followed by her bra.

"I'm a handyman and you're a nurse. We're not the police." His shorts joined her shirt on the floor, and then they tumbled to her bed. "Now, if they needed something repaired . . . or if someone needed a vaccine . . ."

"Then we'd be there for them. But they don't. And . . ."

"And we've got to pass the time somehow."

"Right!" She pulled the covers up over both of them and gasped with delight as he suckled her breasts.

"Or the minutes will just drag by . . ."

"And we can't have that!"

"Damn, you've got the best rack I've ever seen."

"That's so romantic," she sighed. "Ooooh, don't stop. That's wonderful."

"And your ass isn't bad, either."

"Turner, maybe you shouldn't talk while we do this."

He laughed, then abruptly sobered, which was startling. "Do you think we should be enjoying this? I mean . . . someone's dead."

"Yeah, but what can we do? I think we just established that we're mere observers."

"Good point." His hand slipped between her legs, and she wriggled against him. "Oh, God, you feel so sweet . . ."

"Just wait," she promised him. "I'll—"

There was an abrupt knock at the door, and they both froze.

"Hey in there!" Corinne called. "Let us in!"

"Fuck," Turner swore.

"No, we'd better not," Caro said, then called, "Just a minute!"

"Where'd you put my shorts?"

"Where'd you put my bra?"

Twenty seconds later, she was pulling the door open. "What?"

"Ha!" Corinne crowed, instantly analyzing their flushed faces.

"Shut up and come in already. What is it?"

"Terribly sorry to interrupt," Grant said, looking embarrassed. "But Corinne had some thoughts . . ."

"So?" Caro asked rudely.

"Well, there's a couple of things," Corinne said, kicking Caro's bra out of her way, marching across the room, and sitting on the bed. "Anna said she was stuck in town, right? And she said her cell phone doesn't work?"

"Right. So . . . ?"

"But ours does. We just called the locals, like five minutes ago."

"Well, maybe she's got a different service than we do . . . ," Turner said doubtfully.

"Right, anything's possible, but that *did* get me thinking. If she lied about her cell, maybe she lied about being stuck in town. And if she hasn't been stuck in town, what's she been doing?"

Caro's mouth popped open. She had just flashed back to seeing Anna standing outside her door, with wet hair and bare feet. And . . . there was something else, wasn't there? Something . . .

"She's tall," Caro said slowly. "But Dana's short. I remember being surprised when I saw Anna, because I hardly ever meet women as tall as me. But Turner got hit in a bad place . . . low, almost on the back of the neck. Dana would have had to swing up . . . but *Anna's* a big girl. She wouldn't have had any trouble conking him a good one."

Comprehension dawned on Turner's face. "So *Anna* went down to the boathouse, to prevent us from getting the body. And she probably took the bloody candlestick, too. But that means Dana . . ."

"Dana's been in her room the whole time," Caro said, feeling a definite chill race down her back. Bad enough the killer was in the house with them, but knowing Anna was scuttling around, covering things up for the killer and lying herself black in the face . . . that was fucking creepy. "Anna never went to town. She's been here all along, covering up for her . . . protecting her . . ."

"Because she *didn't know Dana had confessed!*" Corinne finished triumphantly. "That's why she looked so totally poleaxed earlier. Not because she was shocked about the murder . . . she was shocked that Dana had told us *she* was the killer! It made all the crap she's been doing totally unnecessary. No wonder she looked sick!"

"But . . . why?" Grant asked.

"Well," Corinne said, "let's go ask her."

Thirteen

"I don't know what you're talking about," Anna said through tight lips, peeling potatoes so rapidly her hands were practically a blur. "Now that the power's back on, I'm way behind. Why don't you go back to your rooms?"

"Anna, you want to cut the shit? We *know,*" Corinne said impatiently. "Your story doesn't hold water with us, and it sure as shit won't with the local cops, who, by the way, should be here in about ten minutes."

Caro nodded, and glanced around the large, spotless kitchen. Something was missing, but she couldn't quite put her finger on it. What was wrong? There was a small shelf full of pictures, but that wasn't it. Distracted, Caro stepped closer to the pictures. Family stuff, mostly, Anna posing in front of various gorgeous scenes . . . and one was flipped down.

"Not to mention, where are the groceries?" Corinne gestured at the large kitchen. "No damp bags, no extra food . . . because you never went to town."

That's what was wrong, Caro decided, fingering the turned-down photo. No food. Anna hadn't had time to return from shopping, put everything away, *and* find Turner. Because, of course, she had never been shopping. Heck, where could she go? Was there even a grocery store on the island? She supposed they could check the garage, see if Anna's car engine was warm. Another nail in the coffin.

"You'd better cough up the truth," Corinne went on relentlessly, "because it'll just be that much worse for you if you lie to the locals."

Caro flipped the picture back up, positioned it where it belonged, started to turn back to the group . . . then took another look at the picture.

"So why don't you just talk?" Corinne finished.

"Jesus Christ," Caro whispered, staring at the photo. Everything made sense . . . a horrible, skin-crawling sense. Poor Turner. Poor Anna. And poor . . .

"I don't know what you're talking about," Anna repeated stubbornly, peeled potatoes flying into the pot. "I didn't go to town for food, I went for . . . for . . ."

"You're covering up for Dana. By my count, you've destroyed property, tampered with a crime scene, and committed felony assault, and that's just for starters. The cops are going to want to talk to you. We'll make sure of that. So all this crap you pulled was basically for nothing. Why not tell us?"

Anna glared at Corinne, and her grip tightened on the potato peeler. Grant stepped protectively in front of his wife and got a poke between the shoulder blades for his pain. "Don't do that," she snapped, elbowing him out of the way. "On my slowest day, I could take her."

"Let's stop provoking unbelievably dangerous people, what do you say, dear?"

"Anna, won't you tell them why?" Caro had flipped the picture back down. For her, there were no more questions. But the others . . . Corinne was definitely on the right track. Anna looked as though she was going to puke. Or faint. Or both. "Why in the world would you do all this stuff? Steal crime scene evidence and hurt Turner?" Especially hurt Turner, who was only guilty of being in the wrong place at the wrong time, *both* times, poor dope. "What was it all for?"

"Yeah, we work together, Annie," Turner added. "You and me and Rich, we were making this place into a real weekend getaway for people." He rubbed his head and looked at her reproachfully. "I kind of thought we were a team."

"A team!" Anna spat. "Ha! *You're* the cause of all this, Turner, you ass."

"Me?" Turner gasped.

"Him?" Corinne gasped. "What'd he do?"

"You led her on, that's what. That whole 'studly handyman looking for love' nonsense you give off like . . . like pheromones."

"I'll admit he's cute," Grant said, "but I fail to see . . ."

"She's my sister," Anna said in a small voice. She put the potato peeler on the counter and stared at the floor.

Caro could practically hear the air being sucked out of the room as everyone gasped. "Dana's your *sister?"* Corinne managed, while Caro nodded tiredly.

"I didn't lead her on!" Turner protested. *"She* was all over *me."*

"That's kind of a minor detail you could have mentioned," Corinne said. "The killer being, you know, *a blood relative* and all."

"Not just that," Caro added. "Isn't that right, Anna?"

"No, no. I mean, yes, she is, but she killed . . . our sister."

"The body's your sister, too?"

"I think I'm going to faint," Grant murmured.

Anna looked peeved. "Turner, you ass, don't you remember? I brought them both out here on opening weekend."

"Well, yeah, I remember Dana from before," he said slowly, "sure I did. But . . . nothing ever came of it, and I figured . . . I just figured she was here *this* weekend as a returning guest. Rich wants to build up repeat clientele, so I didn't think anything of it. I tried to be friendly, you know, talk to her, but she was totally cold to me. I guess she . . . I guess she didn't like me from before."

"That's not true," Caro said quietly.

Anna snorted. "Didn't think anything of it . . . that's you in a nutshell. And I suppose you don't remember Tina?"

He frowned. "Tina? No, I didn't meet her. I only met Dana."

"No, you met Tina *pretending* to be Dana."

"How could she pretend—"

"She had a crush on you. She would have done anything for you."

"Who are you talking about?" Grant asked.

"But I only talked to her for five minutes! I—"

"So your sister fixated on Turner," Corinne interrupted. "And it sounds like Dana did, too."

"But I didn't do anything!" Turner was looking more horrified by the second. "I was nice to her!"

"You slept with her!"

"No, I didn't! I didn't! I slept with Dana!"

"Somebody give me a notebook," Corinne muttered. "I'm gonna have to start writing this down to keep track. Who'd you sleep with, Turner?"

Anna ignored the interruption and went on in a tone that stung. "Tina wanted to see you again . . . and Dana did, too, only she didn't tell me." She looked at the floor again. "So I snuck Tina out here this weekend—"

"Which is why she's not on the registry," Grant observed.

"—but Dana didn't tell me she was coming, too, as a guest. And Tina . . . Tina was going to—well, I guess she was going to, what's the phrase, make a play for you? And Dana . . . she didn't like that."

"So Dana beaned her with a candlestick and threw her into the ocean?" Caro hoped she didn't look as horrified as she felt. She wanted Anna to keep talking.

"You know how sisters are," Caro continued dully.

"Sisters?"

"As far back as I can remember, they competed for everything . . . fought to win everything. Toys. And when they were older, boys. And I guess Dana wasn't going to let Tina win this time."

"You mean Dana had a wicked sister?" Turner looked flabbergasted. "Or, wait a minute, Dana *was* the wicked sister? Christ, how complicated is this going to get?"

"Turner, I don't think you've . . ." Put it all together, Caro was going to add, but then, she had the benefit of the photo. Anna, standing with her sister, Dana. And someone who looked a lot like Dana.

"But that means . . . when I slept with Dana, her sister made up her mind to sleep with me, too?" Turner looked horrified. "I wouldn't have hurt Dana. But she must have thought—"

"And you tried to protect the sister who was still alive, right, Anna?" Corinne prompted.

"I saw it happen . . . I'd come down to the dining room to see if they wanted to go into town for supper. I was there to hear them fighting, rounded the corner in time to see what happened, but I wasn't in time to stop it. I've—I've never been able to stop them."

"Tina was found naked," Caro said softly, "because she was going to try to seduce Turner wasn't she? And that did it. Dana had had enough."

Anna nodded. "So I told Dana to lock herself in her room and not come out, and I—"

"Made yourself useful, covering up the crime."

"I didn't know she'd confessed," Anna said bitterly. "I thought if I could prevent any of you from finding the body—"

"And not noticing the way Tina looked exactly like Dana," Caro added dryly.

"—that I could get Dana away before anything—anything happened. But then Turner came snooping around, and none of you would stay in your rooms. And one of you turned out to be a cop, for goodness sake."

"Ex-cop," Grant and Corinne said in unison.

Anna raised her head and glared at Turner. "This is all your fault."

"Uh . . ." Caro held up a finger. "Actually, I think it might be all Dana's fault."

"Dana just wanted something—someone nice for herself, is that such a crime? She doesn't even think it's a crime, and if you knew how Tina taunted her . . . tormented her . . . all their lives . . . it's not really a crime, right? Wanting to be able to hang on to something nice, for once? Wanting something your sister can't have?"

"No, of course not," Corinne said, "but murder *is.*"

"All this," Caro said, "for a crush? Because Tina pulled one over on Dana, and Dana wanted to get even? That doesn't make any sense!"

"No," Anna said. "All this because one of them had to be the winner. All the time."

Fourteen

"I still don't believe it," Turner said, shaking his head. "Those poor girls."

"And poor Anna," Caro added. "One sister's dead, and the other's headed for prison. I know it wasn't too cool that she, you know, practically killed you, but I can't help but feel sorry for her."

He nodded. "No wonder Dana wouldn't tell us who she killed. How could she confess to killing her own sister? And over something so dumb? I'm serious, Caro, I barely knew the girl. *Girls.*" He shivered. "And here I slept with the killer . . . and now her sister's dead. God . . ."

"More of their sick games," Caro commented. "Like Anna said, in the end, it wasn't about you, or even love. It was about winning. You know what's the worst? That picture I saw, the one Anna kept in the kitchen. Of the three of them? None of them are smiling. They're someplace warm, on sand that looks like sugar, they're wearing tropical flowers around their necks . . . and none of them are smiling."

"Those poor girls," Turner said again.

There was a short silence, and then Caro, the night catching up with her, yawned. "Listen, we've got some time before . . . I mean, we're done talking to the cops and stuff . . ."

Turner looked at the bed, then looked at her. "Let's just lie down together, all right?"

"Very much extremely all right."

She crawled into the bed, noticing the sun was starting to come up over the horizon. Turner climbed in beside her, and they curled up like spoons in a drawer, and slept.

"All checked out, then?" Rich asked.

"We're ready to rock," Corinne said. The group had, by necessity, been forced to become close in an obscenely short amount of time, and now they found separating difficult. "Listen, you guys, if you're ever in Minneapolis . . ."

"I live there," Caro said, smiling.

". . . or San Diego," Lynn added.

". . . or Boston," Todd said.

"Well, I'm not telling any of *you* weirdos where *I* live," Jana huffed, snatching her bag away from Rich.

"But you live with me, dear," Lynn began.

"This was, like, the lamest vacation *ever.*" She glared at the group. "The absolute worst." She tossed her curls out of her face and stomped off.

"I'll miss that bitch," Todd sighed.

"I wouldn't go that far," Grant commented.

"All I can say is, I hope to God I can score some smokes on the way to the airport." He bent and kissed Caro on the cheek. "It's been real, blondie. And what that means, I have no idea." He hefted his bag and waved at the others. "Hope to see you all again. Under less interesting circumstances."

"Heck, I don't mind so much. It made me lonesome for the force," Corinne said. "I gotta admit, it was one for the books."

"Not much of a honeymoon for you two, though," Turner said.

"Oh, we'll get it right next time," Corinne said airily. She slung her duffel bag over one shoulder and sketched a salute. "Later, gators."

"Good-bye," Grant said, shaking hands all around, then

followed his wife out the front door. "You know, darling, there's always the Mile High Club . . ."

"Well, 'bye," Lynn said, and hurried after them.

"You know, I don't think she said twenty words all weekend," Turner commented, watching her go.

"Yeah, but she's got a great story to tell when she gets home. And I've got a great story to write. Although," she added as Rich looked vaguely alarmed, "I will change the names to protect the innocent."

"Bad enough I'm short a cook," he grumbled. "That kind of publicity I do not need."

"You kidding?" Turner asked. "People will swarm to this place just to see where the candlestick got dropped . . . where poor Tina went over the rail. You could double your prices and they'd still come. People are weird."

"Ugh," Caro said. "The whole thing was a waste, if you ask me. Tina's dead . . . and for what? Dana's in jail, thinking she's the winner . . . for what? Over a guy they hardly knew, but decided to fight over. A guy who was a doll in their tug-of-war."

"Beats me," Turner said, looking honestly puzzled. "There's lots of guys out there."

Caro took another look at his tousled dark hair, his vivid green eyes, the long, tanned legs. Poor bastard. No clue how finger-lickin' good he really was.

"I hope we'll see you again, Caro," Rich said, shaking her hand.

"Next weekend?" Turner asked hopefully.

"Jeez, I really couldn't afford . . ."

"Oh, you'll stay as a guest of management, of course," Rich said. "It's the least I can do."

"Well," Caro said, stealing another peek at Turner, "maybe I will."

Epilogue

She arched her back to meet his thrusts and clutched his shoulders to bring him closer. He shuddered over her and bit her lightly on the ear, and her orgasm burst through her like a shooting star. Moments later he stiffened, went deeper than he had before, and then he collapsed over her.

"Oh, thank God," Turner groaned.

"Yeah, *finally,*" Caro sighed.

"I'm glad you came. Uh, to visit again."

She giggled. "Me, too." He kissed her again and rolled away, and she sat up. "Although, I have to say, it's been extremely weird to be here and not worry about, you know, dead bodies."

He laughed and patted her leg. "It's not usually like that. Last month was the exception, big-time."

She snorted. "Prove it."

"I plan to."

She glanced at her watch. "Let's see . . . I've been here for an hour. How do you want to fill the rest of the weekend?"

"I'll need another ten minutes . . ."

"Not *that*. Although it's tempting. But don't you have work to do?"

"Don't you?"

She stared at him. "Oh, come on. You don't mean Rich was serious."

"You kidding? I bugged him about it constantly until you came back."

"You guys don't need a live-in nurse on the grounds."

"After what happened last time?" He rubbed the back of his head.

"You guys are serious?"

"Caro, get it through your head: we want you to stay here. *I* want you to stay here."

She was flattered, thrilled, and scared. All at the same time. Kind of like last month. "But we barely know each other."

"Look, you're right, it's definitely crazy, okay? But so what? I'll tell you what I *do* know; I thought about you constantly while you were gone. That month felt like a damn year."

"I missed you, too," she admitted.

"I want you to stay. Rich has a job for you. Give it a try," he coaxed. "There's worse things than hanging out on a gorgeous secluded island off the coast of Maine and trying to hurt each other, you know, sexually."

"I guess." She grinned. "I guess we could give it a try. If I survived what happened last month, I could try anything." She sobered. "But if I'm going to stay here with you, I have to know one thing."

"Anything."

"What's your full name? I can't just go around calling you 'Turner' all the time."

He grimaced. "I'll tell you, but you should know, only my mom and my sisters know it. You'll have to take an oath of secrecy."

She held up her hand, palm out. "I swear."

"Seriously. You can't tell anybody."

"I won't tell anybody."

"It's Fred."

"Fred?" She bit her tongue so she wouldn't laugh. Fred! Oh, that was a riot. "Well, that's . . . it's very . . . classic. Yes, it's a very old-fashioned, nice, classic name."

"I hate it," he said gloomily. "A Fred does your taxes for you. A Fred wears a tie and drinks cheap scotch."

"A Fred is giving me a whole new life," she said, stroking the tip of his ear with her finger.

He brightened. "That's true."

"So, it's not so bad. Not, you know, *murder* bad."

"That's true, too. You know, I'm sort of falling for you, here. You didn't go into gales of humiliating laughter when I told you my name. My mom always said the one girl who didn't laugh at my name was the girl for me."

"Your mom's pretty bright, then. Fred."

"No."

"What's wrong, Freddy?"

"No."

She glanced at her watch again. "So, is that ten minutes up yet?"

He pounced on her. "Close enough."

"I'm with you on that one . . . Fred."

Dear Reader:

My editor asked me to do a Letter To My Readers, the slave driver, and I agreed to get right on it after I finished my other very important errand. It's 4:00 p.m. and the pan of brownies has been polished off (no need to make supper!), so now I'm writing to you, my readers. Here it is: Dear Readers, thank you for buying my book. Please buy three more copies. Collect the set! Sincerely, MaryJanice.

But seriously (I always say "but seriously", which is fairly lame as my rampant immaturity usually prevents me from being serious, accepting compliments gracefully, sitting through a movie without talking, or resisting the urge to give my mother-in-law a Wet Willy), thanks for giving this book a try. It's the first mystery I've ever done, and I can't tell you how much fun I had with it. Unlimited laughing gas fun. Free trip to the amusement park fun. Every mystery I've ever read centered around the concept of "who killed this guy?", and being contrary Mary, I thought, "What if they knew who did it, but didn't know who was dead?" Thus, *Ten Little Idiots* was born.

Meanwhile, if you liked *Ten Little Idiots* and want to check out some of the other stories I've churned out (churned = agonizing creative process), there's *Hello, Gorgeous!* (Legally Blonde meets The Bionic Woman) coming this month, *Undead and Unappreciated* (the latest in my vampire series, coming from Berkley in May), and *Really Unusual Bad Boys* coming in October. Again, the purchase of multiple copies will be looked upon by me with great favor, and it'll sure make my boat payments easier.

So, curl up (with a brownie!) and enjoy. And thanks for taking a look.

Later, gators,

MaryJanice
maryjanice@comcast.net

Single White Dead Guy

Amy Garvey

One

When this weekend was over, Lanie Burke told herself, she was going to seriously investigate the idea of karma. Not the concept itself, but specifically whom she had offended in some former life. There was no denying anymore that someone, somewhere, was spitting mad at her, and she was paying for it now, with interest.

Squinting through the snowflakes swirling furiously beyond the windshield, she blew out a frustrated breath and reached blindly for the volume dial on the rental car's stereo. Louder would be good. Deafening would probably be better, especially if Dave Matthews drowned out the "told you so" voice in her head that was making it really clear this impromptu weekend trip had been a bad idea.

The problem was, her life was beginning to seem like one unending bad idea, she thought as she tried to follow the narrow strip of country road in the rapidly fading light. It had been a bad idea to make the color scheme for *Elan*'s latest fashion section shocking pink. Sitting at her desk and staring out at the sooty gray bricks of the building across the alley last December, she'd imagined something quintessentially springy, pretty but cleverly hip, and instead the whole eight-page spread had looked like a Pepto Bismol-induced nightmare.

It had been a bad idea to give her sister advice about her marriage. Discussing something as simple as the weather with Bell could sometimes be treacherous, but offering an opinion on her brother-in-law's latest almost-midlife crisis had been a mistake of epic proportions. Especially since Bell was apparently now considering leaving him, at least temporarily, and moving in with Lanie.

Picturing her sister—and her sister's luggage, overweight cat, and armfuls of self-help books—crammed into her studio apartment on Second Avenue, Lanie shuddered. Small was a generous word for the place. Even "tiny" would be kind. Most days she was amazed that she managed to live there alone without tripping over something. Another adult-sized human would be asking for disaster, not to mention more stress than Lanie could handle at the moment.

Which was the reason her friend Jess had offered the use of her husband's cabin for the weekend. "Go away," she'd said. "Just get in the car and drive, go up there and sleep and read and forget about everything for a few days. You deserve it." Lanie hadn't been sure she wanted to make the trip; after all, what was there to do upstate by herself but sit around and think about the big fat mess her life had become? But when Jess had added, "Or you could come over and look at the pictures from the wedding," Lanie had sighed and asked when she could pick up the keys. She'd tripped over a stray purse and fallen into the buffet table at Jess's wedding two months ago, squashing three hundred dollars' worth of shrimp canapés and mini lobster ravioli, and photographic evidence of it wasn't exactly going to improve her state of mind.

So she'd packed her comfiest pajamas, two good books, a bottle of Shiraz, and a box of Clairol #37—Champagne on Ice—with a positive attitude and only a medium-nauseating quantity of chocolate for backup. Maybe a weekend away was exactly what she needed. Her batteries were fizzling, so she'd recharge them. She was running on empty, so she'd refill her tank. Her mental cupboards were bare, so she'd restock them.

And then she'd work on cutting all the annoying analogies

out of her vocabulary instead of cursing the weatherman for not predicting a freak spring storm, she thought, maneuvering the unfamiliar car around a curve and frowning in dismay at the snow. It was nearly dark, she wasn't sure how to get to the cabin, and the roads were becoming more slippery with every mile.

It figured. Of course it did. This was her life lately, a dictionary-ready example of Murphy's Law. The knowledge didn't make driving through the snow any easier, though. Huddling deeper inside her coat, she turned off the county route and onto the main street of Churchville, skidding to a stop along the curb a moment later as the Ford fishtailed with a terrifying *swish*.

"Not good," she muttered, catching her breath and waiting for her heart to stop hammering in her chest. "Very bad, in fact." A weekend away from her life was one thing, but not if it meant risking her life in the process. Shoving the gearshift into park, she scanned the quiet street and focused on the warm gold light spilling from the window of what looked like the local bar, just a block away. It was a picturesque little town, especially in the snow, like something out of a New England postcard. Another day, it would have been nice to sketch it.

Right now she had different choices. She could either trudge through the snow to the bar and ask for directions, if not a snowmobile, or freeze to death drinking the bottle of Shiraz, happily drunk but ultimately a human popsicle. Sighing, she buttoned her coat, turned off the engine, and grabbed her purse, opening the door into a sudden gust of wind and blinking fat, wet snowflakes from her eyelashes. Slogging through at least five inches of snow, she staggered into the Coach and Four wet, shivering, and wishing like hell she'd worn something other than the cute spring mules she'd bought on sale at Saks' the week before.

And realized she was standing in the doorway like an idiot, staring at the crowd gathered at the bar and huddled up to the tables off to the right, all of whom were staring right back with curiosity.

"It's snowing," she managed, sniffling and shaking snow from her hair.

With that, everyone turned back to their drinks, and a flush of embarrassment melted her frozen cheeks. There was nothing like an idiotic understatement as a way to introduce herself.

She edged her way up to the bar, murmuring apologies as she tapped on shoulders and tugged on coat sleeves. Directions could wait. She needed a hot drink, and she wouldn't say no to a half dozen warm towels, either.

The bartender was ignoring everyone to stare at a round little brunette in a fuzzy purple sweater at the opposite end of the bar. Lanie edged closer to lean on the solid oak surface, sniffling and trying not to bump up against the mountain of warm wool on her right.

"Um, you're dripping on me," the mountain said.

She was tempted to snap at him, just to burn off the irritation of being miles from home, freezing, and looking like five miles of wintry road, when she turned to face the man instead and blinked at the warm, deep blue eyes twinkling at her.

Wow. They didn't make guys like this in the city. She'd have to keep that in mind when her lease came up for renewal. She'd love to sketch him, too—all those masculine planes and angles of his face, the gentle curve of his mouth, those fascinating eyes.

She wrestled the damp edge of her coat away from his leg, smiling what she hoped resembled an apology while she stared back. Rough around the edges in a scruffy, completely masculine way, he looked like a guy who knew how to fix more than the virus in a computer. Like a guy who would rather spend his money on baseball tickets and hot dogs than off-season Armani. Like a guy who'd never heard of Armani, in fact.

In short, he looked good. Blond, and solid, and just a little bit mischievous, with those eyes twinkling at her. How did he do that in the smoky half-light of the bar?

Not that it mattered. Good was bad, definitely. At least in her case. With her luck lately, flirting alone would result in grievous bodily injury and/or a hazmat team bursting through the door.

"Tongue's frozen, huh?" *Twinkle.*

He was so big and burly and sweet, that ridiculous sparkle in his eyes should have reminded her of a young Santa Claus, but it didn't. The eyes in question were too blue, but not at all chilly. They were as deep as the Caribbean, where it was hot and lush and wet . . . Suddenly the jukebox that sometimes clicked on in her head cued up the theme from *A Summer Place.*

Oh, God. What the hell had he asked her?

"Tea's good for that," he said, reaching out to unwrap her scarf and drape it over the back of his chair. Then he slid off his stool and patted it. "Sit. You'll thaw faster. And I'll be out of dripping range."

"Thanks," she managed with a slight croak, cursing the heat in her cheeks. "I'm a little, uh . . ."

"Stunned?" When she nodded, he told her, "It happens. We're used to snow as late as May around here, but tourists aren't. They come for crocuses and go home with frostbite." More twinkling.

She was doomed.

Two

He called for the bartender, who left the brunette and her sweater with a grunt of frustration, and ordered hot tea while Lanie peeled off her sodden coat and rubbed feeling back into her hands.

"Will DeMaio," he said, offering his hand, which was huge and dry and very warm against hers.

"Lanie Burke." Damn it, was her nose running?

"Short for Elaine?"

"Long for Lane." She smiled up at him, trying to ignore the happy little thrill that rippled through her when he grinned back. "A family name. My sister's Bell, which is just for . . . well, Bell. My mother has a thing about genealogy."

"Good thing no one on her side was named Hockenschmidt, I guess." He slid the mug of tea toward her. "Sugar? Milk?"

Who was this guy? She'd stopped shivering, but it didn't make the urge to snuggle up to his broad, sweatered chest any less appealing. Her flirting instinct was coming to life despite her best intentions, and since the ceiling hadn't caved in and she was fairly sure she didn't have broccoli stuck in her front teeth, she figured it couldn't hurt. Much.

"Something artificial and probably very, very bad for me, if it's available," she said, wrapping her hands around the steaming mug. Will handed her two packets of Sweet 'N Low, and she stirred them in before tilting her head up to his. "Do you live here?"

"All my life. DeMaio Carpentry and Construction, that's me. What about you?"

"I don't live here." She sighed and wriggled her still-frozen toes inside the soaked mules. Delicious buttery black leather ruined for nothing. "I'm looking for a little house on Gallows Hill Road, which actually doesn't sound very appealing now that I think about it. Any idea where that is? And if I can get there without a snowmobile?"

He grinned, and she watched in amazement, wondering how his mouth had learned to curve into such a sensuous, cat-with-a-canary shape. Nothing that sexy could be a genetic accident. "I live there, if you can believe it. On Gallows Hill, I mean. And you won't need a Sno-Cat, but you might need a little help plowing through the storm if you're planning to stay here long enough to drink that tea."

She glanced past a group of old-timers arguing about the Yankees' latest trades, and out the front window, where only a thick white blur was visible beyond the dusty glass. A "gotcha" spring snow shower was one thing, but a blizzard was another. She'd be lucky if she made it back to the city on Monday night.

"And you'd be offering to help?" she asked, turning back to catch that irresistible twinkle in his eyes again.

Before he could reply, a rough hand settled on his shoulder, and a voice from behind him barked, "Who the hell do you think you are, DeMaio?"

Well, there was the beauty of a local bar, Lanie thought. Everyone knew everyone else, and no one had any respect for an out-of-towner's attempts at good old-fashioned flirting.

Will shrugged off the hand and turned halfway around, giving Lanie a view of a guy who might as well have had "crotchety" tattooed on his forehead. Right underneath "curmudgeon."

"I think I'm exactly who I was this morning, Vic." Will's tone was even, if slightly amused. "Who do you think you are at the moment?"

"Save the smart remarks, asshole," the other man growled, swiping what could only be called a paw under his nose. "I want to know where you got the balls to underbid me by fifteen thousand on the high school job. You printing money in the basement now?"

"Have they made that legal finally? Good to know." Will shrugged and turned back to Lanie, who gave him a weak smile. It was nice to discover that he was an optimist. If he thought Vic was just going to walk away, he obviously subscribed to the "glass half full" philosophy.

"I want an answer, DeMaio," Vic shouted, and Lanie winced. One lit match within six feet of his breath, and the bar would go up in flames.

"I don't have one for you, Vic." Will's voice was suddenly as no-nonsense as a piece of rebar, and about as friendly. There was no sign of that twinkle, either. "Not unless you're looking for something along the lines of honest bidding, fair pricing, and a crew that spends more time with their tools than down here drinking."

Oh, dear. Fighting words, definitely. And, strangely, kind of a turn-on. Had her brain frozen on the trudge over from the car? She'd never gone for the alpha type, not that she'd actually met a lot of them in the city. Not genuine ones, anyway. Not the kind who made a girl tingle by showing off his sexy twinkle as he took over, ordering tea and putting her into a chair. Well, put that way it didn't sound very alpha, but going Neanderthal on the local drunk qualified. Still, she bit her bottom lip, praying that a bar brawl wasn't imminent. She really didn't know Will, but he'd been so nice before the other man showed up. He'd unwrapped her wet scarf. And plus, she wasn't even close to finished admiring his face yet.

She was trying not to picture the angled strength of his jaw purpled with a bruise when a younger guy walked up behind Vic, who had just reached the rolling boil stage. "Not the time for business, Vic. Come on. We'll handle this Monday."

The stranger's dark eyes flicked over Lanie, and she fought the urge to shudder. Something about the way he'd said "business" sounded much too ominous for an everyday argument between rival contractors.

"Sounds like a plan," Will said smoothly, and turned back to Lanie as Vic was steered away. "Sorry about that."

"Not very neighborly of them." She watched as they disappeared into the crowd at the back of the bar. "Do contractors up here come to blows every day?"

"With Vic, only the ones that end in *Y*." Will flashed another grin and propped an elbow on the bar. "Speaking of neighborly, though, I think I know where you're headed. Dave and Jess Seaver's place, right? My house is just past theirs, and I look after their place when they can't come up for a while. So we'll be neighbors as long as you're here."

At least sipping her tea was one way to hide a ridiculous, pleased grin. He was honest to God coming on to her. Either her flirting muscles were in better shape than she'd thought after six months on vacation, or the dusky light of the bar was hiding her half-thawed red nose and what was sure to be *Bride of Frankenstein* hair by now. On a good day it was two parts *Felicity* to one part Carrie Bradshaw (from the first season of *Sex and the City*, of course), but get it wet and it looked like she'd borrowed Elsa Lanchester's wig.

She was about to reply when she heard a voice from across the bar and watched Will's jaw tighten in irritation.

"Hey there, Will DeMaio." A redhead in a thick black coat and a metallic gold scarf rubbed her shoulder against his, her lower lip caught between two very white, very large front teeth. "Who's your friend?"

"Jill, this is Lanie Burke." He'd edged closer to the bar to escape her friendly nudging, and his eyes had darkened to a furious navy blue, despite the courtesy in his tone.

Jill stopped rubbing and nudging, her overplucked red eyebrows drawn into a frown. "I don't think we've met. Lanie. That's a weird name, huh?"

The last few words were delivered with a falsely bright smile. Marking her territory, definitely, Lanie thought. She wondered when Jill would figure out Will wasn't interested.

"No weirder than Jill, I guess," she replied, and wanted to bite her tongue. Cattiness wasn't the most attractive trait to put on display in this situation, but she couldn't help it. Will had been flirting with *her,* damn it, and if Jill was her bad luck personified, she wasn't going to give in without a fight.

"She's here for the weekend," Will cut in, taking Lanie's hand. The contact was so unexpected, Lanie nearly jumped. "And we're busy catching up."

"Well, don't let me interrupt," Jill said, swallowing hard. Her injured sniffle puffed out her chest, which Lanie was pretty sure had been fortified with a padded WonderBra.

"That was flouncing," Lanie whispered as the other woman headed for the back of the bar, red hair swung violently over her shoulder. "There are some hurt feelings there, if you ask me."

Not that he had. Not that it was any of her business. She hadn't come up here to find a guy, and she didn't really know Will DeMaio at all. His romantic troubles were his problem—although it surprised her to realize how glad she was that dyed red hair and Spandex didn't seem to be his taste.

"Her feelings have been hurt since the seventh grade," Will said, shaking his head. "I've been giving her the 'not interested' signs since then, without much luck. She's the most single-minded woman I've ever met."

Hmmm. Lanie sipped her tea and glanced down at his left hand, which was wrapped around an icy bottle of beer, checking for the pale white stripe that would prove a wedding ring was nestled in his bureau at home. But he was clean—his hand was uniformly tan, with just the kind of long, capable-looking fingers she liked on a man.

"It's the truth," he said. *Twinkle. Sparkle.* "There's no secret tragic history there, believe me. That probably doesn't sound very convincing, but . . ."

"The way my life has been going lately, I'm actually inclined to believe you," she said, and looked down to find her hand resting on his wrist. This was flirting, all right. Two-way, official flirting.

"What's wrong with your life?" He slouched against the bar, and his body was suddenly much closer. His big, strong, beautifully built body. She could smell the crisp, spicy scent of him, and for one wild second she had to resist the urge to lick her lips.

But before she could answer, someone shouted at the other end of the bar, and a beer bottle shattered with an explosive crash.

"Oh, cry me a river, Nick! Do you think I give a shit about your shop or your new goddamn girlfriend? You can both starve to death for all I care!"

A skinny guy with a moustache that looked very much like a moldy caterpillar stood up, his cheeks flaming, his thin shoulders trembling inside an oversized leather jacket.

"No blood from a stone, Staci, you ever hear that? I don't have your fuckin' money!"

Staci, who was almost as tall as he was and much broader, squared off in front of him, jabbing a finger toward his chest. "So *your* kids'll just have to make do again, huh? Even though you got the money to be here with *her,* drinking your fill?"

The "her" in question, a bleached blonde who had narrowed her eyes and folded her arms across her chest, defiantly picked up her mug and took a thirsty swig.

"That does it, you fuckin'—"

The end of Staci's threat was cut off as a man shaped like a steamroller grabbed her from behind, one arm around her waist and the other hand clamped over her mouth. "Time to go, honey," he said, shaking his head. "You wanna fight, you take it somewhere else."

He carried her, kicking and grunting, out of the bar and into the snow, and Lanie watched as the other patrons shrugged and turned back to their drinks. The name Churchville was all wrong for this town.

"In case you were wondering," she said to Will, setting down her empty mug of tea, "I've reconsidered moving up here permanently."

His laugh was a deep rumble of relief. "Do you want to get out of here?"

"I think it's probably advisable at this point."

There was that grin again, complete with twinkle. Her insides did a slow, warm roll. "What were you planning to do for dinner?" he asked.

"There's a big bag of peanut M&Ms in my car."

He arched an eyebrow, and she shrugged. "Hey, it's . . . nutritious. Kind of. Half carbs, half protein."

He grabbed his coat and put it on, handing her her scarf. "I think we can do better than that, if you let me stop in the kitchen. I'll drive your car, and I can walk from there to my place."

She let him help her into her coat, savoring a pleasurable little thrill at the feel of his hands on her arms, lingering on her shoulders as he wound the scarf around her neck. Wondering if he'd stay at her place instead of going home was premature. Ill-advised. Just plain asking for trouble. The half hour she'd spent with him so far had been more fun than every date she'd been on in the last six months. Wishing for more—the touching, kissing, pulse-pounding, blissful kind of more—would lead to nothing but disaster. It was just her luck, or lack of it, lately. No use denying it.

But as she let him take her hand and lead her through the crowd toward the back of the bar, she couldn't help imagining what he would look like without the heavy sweater and the faded jeans. What his hands would feel like on her bare skin, instead of the still-damp fabric of her shirt. What his mouth would taste like on hers.

And when he rested his hand on the small of her back, letting his words shiver against her neck as he asked if she wanted her cheeseburger medium or well, she decided that maybe, just maybe, her karma was finally turning around.

Three

"Who knew Shiraz and cheeseburgers would be a perfect match? We should alert *Gourmet*."

Will snorted and reached over with one finger to catch a bead of ketchup on Lanie's lower lip. "I don't think you're allowed to use the word 'cheeseburger' in that magazine. But I'm glad you like it. Rick knows his way around a grill."

They'd waited in the back hall while his friend rushed through a takeout order, and then Will had given Lanie a piggyback ride to her car, the plastic bag of cheeseburgers and fries hanging from her wrist, and those ridiculous, entirely feminine shoes dangling from her feet.

It was still snowing, hard and fast, and the wind was wet with it, but they'd laughed all the way down the street. And he'd needed that more than he'd realized. Lanie Burke was nothing like the women he knew in Churchville, and that was a very good thing.

Staring at her across the coffee table, where they'd opened the Styrofoam takeout containers in front of the fire he'd built in her borrowed cottage, he wasn't exactly sure *what* she was, but at the moment he didn't care. There were a couple of options, among them hopelessly impulsive, in love with danger, and just plain flaky, but none of those descriptions fit right. He could have been a serial killer, for all she knew, or at the very least a not-so-nice guy who was just hoping to score.

Not that he wasn't hoping, of course, watching Lanie daintily dip a French fry into a puddle of ketchup before sliding it into her mouth. He hadn't consciously tasted any of his meal, because he kept wondering what her lips would taste like instead. Lanie Burke was smart and funny, and that head of riotous dark blond curls had made his fingers itch to touch them since she'd walked into the bar, looking a little bit lost and a whole lot interesting. He'd never wanted to take care of a woman as much as he wanted to sleep with one, but Lanie had managed to inspire both urges. Churchville wasn't crawling with cads or serial killers, as far as he knew, but still, when he looked into those funny hazel eyes—green and brown and gold all at once—he was much too glad he'd been the one she'd dripped on.

He stretched his legs out and propped himself up on one elbow, biting back a grin as she twirled another fry in the ketchup and then washed it down with her wine. After the week he'd had, Lanie Burke was a very promising answer to a question he hadn't even known he'd been asking. She wasn't local, she was flirting back, and he'd reached the end of his rope sometime between Vic Landry's drunken threats and Jill Manetti's clockwork come-on. His life wasn't action-movie material—which was the way he liked it—but lately it had begun to feel a little too much like a rerun. The same people, the same sights, the same old routine. He'd spent a few days in Boston this week with his college roommate, and even that had been a big yawn—he went up there every year at this time, and they always went to a Red Sox game, had fried clams and seafood chowder at No Name, and spent at least one afternoon in Harvard Square fantasizing about the Radcliffe undergrads. Boring.

Yeah, spending the evening with Lanie—and her wild curls and that funny little upturned nose and hopefully the rest of her—was exactly what he wanted. And the only way to find out if he would be spending it with her in the bedroom was to gently remove her wineglass from her hand and kiss her.

Lanie shivered as Will's hand slid to her nape, tugging her toward him. *Here we go,* she thought, hoping he didn't mind ketchup breath and immediately not caring if he did. She'd been staring at him for what seemed like days in the warm glow of the firelight, and somewhere in the last half hour, he'd begun to look like dessert. When his finger had slid over her lower lip earlier, she'd had to fight to keep herself from nibbling it.

This morning, while she was packing her bags and trying out a new hair color, digging into a new book had seemed like a reasonable way to de-stress. This morning, her hormones had apparently already been on vacation.

She leaned forward, wondering what Will would taste like, but she didn't have time to think about it for long. The pressure of his lips on hers was gentle, then firmer, then lingering, savoring, tasting her until she opened her mouth and met his tongue, letting him explore.

She sat back, breathless and disappointed, when he broke away, but he was only stripping off his heavy sweater and coming around the coffee table to lower her onto her back in front of the fire. She didn't argue. At the moment, every nerve ending and hormone in her body was in agreement: Will DeMaio knew how to kiss.

So far, there wasn't anything he didn't know how to do, she thought, stroking her open palms over the back of his T-shirt as he kneeled over her, his lips teasing her cheekbone, her jaw, the side of her neck. Will DeMaio and his fabulous mouth felt much too good to worry about potential consequences. It was against all her rules to fall into bed with a guy on the first date—and hot tea in a crowded bar, with subsequent takeout food, hardly seemed like an official "date," anyway—but her life lately, to be completely blunt, sucked. In a way that definitely called for a capital *S*.

She deserved this. She was a twenty-eight-year-old woman perfectly capable of making her own decisions, even if most of them lately had been just this side of disastrous. She was overdue for a night—hell, an *hour*—like this, and with Will doing such incredible things to her collarbone with his tongue, this was no time for standards. She shivered as he licked toward the base of her throat, one of his hands, warm and strong, cradling her head while the other delicately unbuttoned her shirt.

She had to fight the restless urge to slap it away and do it herself.

"Patience," he murmured, and she blushed. So much for her poker face.

Even his voice was delicious, low and slightly gruff, a gentle rumble against her skin. Which was wide open to him now, chest to belly, since he had reached behind her to unhook her bra, and was even now sliding the sheer pink material toward her throat so he could kiss her breasts, teasing her with each soft, introductory brush of his lips.

Oh, yes, this was much better than an evening with Miss Clairol.

And there was more, she realized with another shudder of anticipation. He hadn't even seemed to notice that she existed below the waist yet, and there was still his body, beneath his T-shirt and well-worn jeans, to explore.

Well, there was an idea whose time had come. She tugged the worn white cotton out of his waistband, eager to feel the broad expanse of his back, and suddenly heard a warning voice in her head.

Bad and Luck, it whispered. *Your new middle names. You've had too much of a good thing already tonight.* Will probably had a third nipple or a cult tattoo or—she swallowed hard—parts missing altogether. Important parts.

"Disappointing" was going to be a completely inadequate word if that was the scenario. Hands frozen on his lower back, she realized she had stiffened in dismay when Will raised his head and caught her gaze.

"Stop talking to yourself and kiss me," he whispered. "I don't bite."

Her shaky laugh was equal parts relief and embarrassment. "What if I want you to?" she whispered back, squirming in pleasure as he shifted over her, his thighs parting hers.

"In that case, I think we can work something out."

She arched her back as he took one nipple between his teeth, lightly, until it stood at attention. Will obviously wasn't going to give her one spare moment to second-guess this situation, because—oh, God, yes—he was far too busy reacquainting her with every sexual desire she'd ever had. If a hazmat team did end up crashing into the picture, she was pretty sure she'd be too limp and sated any time now to care.

But still . . . maybe they should know a little more about each other. Maybe she should throw a few details out there, just to be polite.

"I work for a magazine," she murmured to the top of Will's head, trying to concentrate on what she was saying over each zing of pleasure. "In the art department. As a designer."

He raised his head to look at her, a vague smile on his lips. "Uh huh."

"I just thought you should know. What I do, I mean." She lifted her naked shoulders in a kind of apology, suddenly very sure he was going to pat her on the head, grab his sweater, and head out into the snow. And now her mouth was opening again. Oh, God. To hell with bad karma—apparently she was going to sabotage this all on her own. "Since I know you're a . . . carpenter. Or a contractor. Or whatever it was you . . ."

He was staring now, without even a shadow of a twinkle. Perfect. She angled up on one elbow, biting her bottom lip, waiting for him to tell her she was crazy, or maybe just annoying. Or, possibly, both.

"I'm going back to kissing you now," he said, and she heard amused laughter behind his words. "If you want to tell me more about your job, you just keep going. But I'm hoping you'll tell me later instead." He kissed the valley between her breasts lightly, then ran his tongue up her breastbone to the hollow of her throat. "Actually," he murmured, "what I'm really hoping is that in a few minutes you won't even remember anything that isn't happening on this rug."

"That . . . sounds like a plan." She hitched in a ragged breath as his hand ran over her hip and down her thigh, then inside it to stroke up toward her crotch, which was already too hot to be humanly possible. "Pants . . . off."

God, now he was making her incoherent, with just one teasing pass below the waist. She didn't care, she wanted out of her still slightly damp pants, and she wanted him out of his. *Now.* And as she caught his gaze, a hot dark blue, like the heart of a flame, she realized that everything that had been playful just a moment ago had become something else—something much more serious, maybe even a little bit dangerous—and it took her breath away.

He wanted this, too, and her sudden demand had just kicked slow and languorous up to fast and hot and *right now.*

He pushed up and away from her, kneeling, and his hands were just rough enough to be exciting when he yanked at the zipper on her pants and tugged them away. She wiggled out of them, feeling a flush of purely female satisfaction when he got a look at her panties. Pink, sheer, and on clearance at Bloomie's, they were obviously not what he'd expected to find beneath her plain khakis, if the shuddering breath he drew was any indication.

But they were history a moment later, along with her shirt and the matching pink bra she'd forgotten was tangled up around her collarbone, and she was scrambling to her knees, too, sliding her hands under his T-shirt and pulling it off, then fumbling with the zipper on his jeans. Beside them the fire snapped as a log fell apart, and she shuddered at the sudden blast of heat on her naked skin.

Will shifted to kick off his jeans, and she reached for his briefs, her tongue darting out to wet her bottom lip when her hands found the hard curve of his ass. He grunted and grabbed her, rolling onto his back and pulling her on top of him, his erection nestled between her legs, thick and solid and deliciously hot. Nothing missing there, no sir.

"Condom . . . ," she managed, her elbows shaking as she raised herself off the rough expanse of his chest, but he only nodded, muttering, "Soon," before he fastened his mouth around one nipple. Wet and smooth, his tongue pushed at its bottom curve as he suckled hard, and she groaned out loud.

"Now . . . ?" It was barely a word—more like a primitive plea. Her body was rushing ahead, trembling, impatient, one great big demand, but he wasn't listening. Damn it, why wasn't he listening? Why was he rolling them over again?

"In a minute." His voice sounded as ragged as hers, but his hands were doing a much better job keeping it together as he slid her legs open, the carpet vaguely itchy beneath her thighs and her back. The heel of his hand pressed gently against her, and she wriggled, wanting more. Her breath caught in her throat as she watched him admiring her, the light from the fire throwing crazy shadows against the side of his face. His fingers splayed through her curls; then he opened her with his other hand, one long, firm finger stroking through the wet, circling, exploring the swollen knot of flesh there, and it was too hot, too much. She bit her bottom lip, torn between the hypnotic, delicious pleasure and the sharp jab of need that wanted more, now, to make that wonderful sliding sensation double and triple and break wide open as she slid over the edge.

"Will, please . . ." She thrust up with her hips, but he wasn't making her wait any longer—his finger had worked its way inside her, deep and deeper, pulling out only long enough for him to add another, and she shuddered when they hit the sweet spot on the far wall.

No more fooling around, she wanted to yell. Unless what she really meant was, *Much more fooling around, please, please, please!* She propped herself up on one shaky elbow and reached for his cock, learning the solid, heavy shape of it, reaching beneath it to stroke the taut sacs. He grunted when she traced the velvet tip with one finger, then fumbled on the rug for his jeans.

She took the foil-wrapped packet when he handed it to her—Extra Sensitive! some distant part of her brain noticed—and ripped it open, rolling the slippery latex over his erection. When she looked up at him, his eyes were glittering with need, and that was the last thing she knew before he nudged her onto her back, parting her thighs with his knee.

Then everything was heat and contact, the length of his body pressed to hers as he entered her with one sure thrust, making her gasp as she opened for him, her legs suddenly wrapped around his waist and her fingers digging into the solid knot of muscle that defined each of his shoulders.

Oh, so very, very much better than Miss Clairol . . .

She found the pulse in his neck with her lips and kissed it, and he groaned when she let her mouth wander higher, taking his earlobe between her teeth, teasing, licking, clinging to him at the same time. Then she let go and threw her head back, pushing up against him, thrust for thrust, unable to focus on anything but the dark, wet heat where they were connected.

She almost never came this way, but it didn't matter, it felt so damn good, Will felt so good, the whole heated, delicious length of him, this curiously sweet-sexy guy with his twinkle and his scrumptious ass . . . and his incredibly hard, perfectly shaped penis thrusting into her . . .

She gasped when his teeth grazed her jawbone, and opened her eyes. The twinkle was gone again—instead his gaze was an intense, hot blue, as deep as his cock inside her, and she shuddered when he whispered, "Look at me, Lanie."

Like she could look away now. He thrust harder, his thighs solid and rough between hers, and as her mouth fell open, he kissed her, his tongue as wet and hot as she was inside, and then she didn't know anything but the fact of them sliding together, pleasure rippling outward from that sweet, fiery spot where he was deepest, now and again and again and . . . oh, God, *now* . . .

She held on as she came, breathless with each shuddering

wave of it, quivering down her legs and curling her toes, and he answered with a deep, guttural groan as his thighs tightened and he rocked into her one last time. His forehead met hers as his orgasm shuddered through him, and she breathed in the spicy tang of sweat and heat slicked over them both.

"So you were saying something about your job," he murmured, rolling to his side and taking her with him. He was still buried inside her.

She nestled into his chest, licking away a bead of sweat and dropping a light kiss on his breastbone. "Oh. Oh, yeah," she whispered. "I, uh, have one."

"That's good. Me, too." He kissed the top of her head, then pushed her away to sit up. "I think I hear the bed calling. Wait . . . yup, there it is. Lanie, it says, come on in, and bring that guy with you."

She giggled, and let him take her hand and pull her to her feet, shaky in the best possible way, boneless and light-headed and just a little bit—damn it—in love. Will DeMaio was an unexpectedly dangerous temptation for her heart, but she trusted him, too.

She really did, she thought as she lay on the wide, comfortable bed a moment later, not even bothering with a polite protest of the "your turn" variety when he crawled between her spread legs and licked his way up the inside of her thigh. Who said there were no really nice guys left? And who said nice guys couldn't be a little bit bad where it counted?

Stupid people, she told herself, shivering as his tongue found the slippery heat of her clit and swirled against it. Anyway, Will was more than nice.

At the first deliciously shivery pulse of another orgasm inside her, she decided he was damn near perfect.

Four

In the morning, he was gone.

Lifting her head from the downy warmth of the pillow, Lanie blinked and stretched, pleasantly sore and wondering why—until she recognized the cozy bedroom of Jess's cottage, and remembered where she was.

All alone, apparently. Rubbing sleep from her eyes, she pushed away the tangled mess of the comforter and sat up, sighing.

It figured. She should have known better than to believe the gods of fate or karma, or whatever they were, would give her a night like the one she'd just spent and offer a morning-after bonus, too.

But it didn't mean she wasn't disappointed. Sometime late last night, when Will had made her laugh so hard she was weak with the combination of giddiness and sexual bliss, she'd let herself imagine this morning—a little preshower snuggling, then the two of them together under a hot, pounding spray, wet and soapy and starting all over again . . .

Tossing the covers to the foot of the bed, she swung her legs over the side and stood up, shivering. It was a lot colder in this cottage without Will's body wrapped around hers. Without the best parts of Will's body *inside* hers . . .

No more pity party, she told herself, flinging open her suitcase and pawing through it for a pair of jeans and a sweater. She was just lucky he hadn't been the proverbial axe murderer mothers everywhere warned against. Or a bondage junkie with the only key to an S&M dungeon. It had been stupid enough to invite a complete stranger into her bed for the night—it had been stupid of monumental proportions to even fantasize that a few hours of really good sex would lead to something more.

Even if the only "more" she'd really been counting on was the physical, "oh, yes, *more,* please" kind.

Pulling her hair into a loose ponytail and tugging the thickest socks she could find over her feet, she wandered into the kitchen, avoiding a look at last night's takeout containers and wineglasses on the coffee table. The aroma of wood smoke still lingered in the room, but she ignored it and dug into the small bag of essential groceries—coffee, filters, sweetener, and, of course, chocolate—that sat on the kitchen counter.

By the time she'd brushed her teeth, brewed a pot of coffee, and fished her sneakers out of her suitcase, she was restless. It was far too quiet, and none of the radio stations came in without static. It was still snowing hard, and the coffee was only making her jittery. She cleaned up, finally, noticing with surprise an empty bottle of Jack Daniels under the sink, and an overflowing ashtray on the windowsill overlooking the backyard. Jess didn't smoke, and neither did Dave, so that was weird, but even weirder was the fact that Jess obviously wasn't the neat freak Lanie had always believed she was. For a second, at least, the thought made her happy.

But with the remains of dinner taken care of, she was left once again with nothing to do. The appeal of hair coloring had long since worn off, and there was no way she was going to be able to concentrate on a book, not when she could still smell Will on her skin and in her hair, when she could close her eyes and taste his tongue on her lips, feel his big, slightly rough hands on her breasts . . .

Time for a distraction. A big one. Anything to take her mind off last night and the weekend-long repeat performances she'd imagined in graphic detail as she drifted off to sleep.

Not to mention that other fantasy, the know-it-all voice in her head whispered. *The one where Will chucks it all to move to the city with you, to dedicate his life there to your eternal, daily sexual pleasure and maybe learn to cook, so you can watch him making scrambled eggs in an apron and nothing else . . .*

"Stop that," she said out loud, setting down her coffee cup and standing up. This was ridiculous. Maybe she should have checked into a sanitarium. Her life had obviously taken a big toll on her sanity if one night with a nice guy—okay, a funny, sweet, deliciously sexy guy with the most talented tongue she'd probably ever know—had turned her into a sniveling, moping fool. Men left the morning after—happened all the time, to her and every other woman she knew. Men and commitment, even the simple next-day kind, didn't mix on a regular basis, unless the planets were aligned just right and all the portents were favorable.

And lately, her life was a favorable-portent-free zone.

Arms folded over her chest, she surveyed her options. She could poke around the cottage. She could rummage through the cupboards for something other than chocolate, which always seemed pointless in situations like this. She could take a shower. She could . . . take a walk! In the snow. Down the road.

Which was, conveniently, where Will lived.

Even to her, the idea seemed vaguely like something a stalker would do, but she could play it cool. "Oh, hey there," she imagined herself saying as she bumped into him, all innocence. "Will, right? Great body you've got there. If you're not doing anything later, bring it on over, and maybe we can reacquaint it with mine."

Maybe cool wasn't in her repertoire. Not that it mattered—she probably wouldn't even see him. He'd most likely holed up in his bachelor bedroom for a daylong nap, and nothing short of a lightning strike would wake him up after all that sex.

But it couldn't hurt to get a little exercise, she told herself, poking through the hall closet for a stray hat and a pair of mittens. She'd just burn off some calories with a trudge through the snow, and then she'd come back, curiosity satisfied and her quota of healthy behavior fulfilled for the day. Or maybe the weekend.

He'd mentioned that his house was farther down the road, so she went out the back door, wrapping her arms around her middle when the frigid, wet air hit her face, dismayed at the amount of snow piled on the back porch steps. But she could see a house through the trees, the bare branches frosted with thick white powder. It was like a storybook out here, white-laced and quiet, the snow still falling in fat, twirling flakes.

And Will's house fit right in, a neat gray cottage trimmed with gingerbread and an inviting porch, the dark blue shutters edged with snowy fringe.

To hell with it, she'd just plow through the accumulation on the steps and worry about the ruin of her sneakers later.

But two steps down, her right foot hit something solid, and she drew back, wincing.

And then gasping, as she realized the contact had dislodged the topmost layer of snow from what looked very much like the back of a man's head.

Inching down the other side of the steps, she stood in the snow and squinted at the shape, her heart thudding like a wild thing in her chest.

It was a man, all right. A very dead man. Faintly, her internal jukebox cued up the music from *Psycho*.

Shaking it off, she bit her lip and reached out with one mittened hand to brush the snow from his face—and realized she was staring at Will. Blond hair spiked with icicles, that gorgeous jaw blue with cold, his mouth a grim, frozen line . . .

"Oh my God oh my God oh my God," she whispered into the still air. Her bad luck had just reached previously unknown heights. The poor guy had slept with her once and wound up dead.

Dead. Dead! Dead? How the hell was he dead? He couldn't

be dead; he'd been perfectly healthy, if stamina was any marker, and very much alive just hours ago. Unless he'd left in the middle of the night . . . in which case maybe he hadn't enjoyed himself as much as she'd believed . . .

Oh, God, she was really losing it. Here she was staring at this beautiful man's snow-covered corpse and trying to massage her ego at the same time. It was panic, plain and simple.

But she couldn't panic. She had to . . . what? Call 911. That was the first step in any emergency. But did they have 911 up here? Would it matter? Trembling hard now and slightly nauseous, she glanced up at the sky. The storm wasn't even over, and the roads probably hadn't been plowed.

Then again, it wasn't like he needed an ambulance.

"Oh, my God," she whispered again, sitting down abruptly in the snow, fighting tears that were going to be truly hysterical if she let them come. Will DeMaio, her gorgeous one-night stand, was really, truly dead.

And it hadn't been kind—he looked awful. Stunned, and somehow older. Not that it mattered. Because he was dead.

But . . . how? She stiffened, picturing the angry contractor from the bar. What had his scary friend said? That they would "take care of business" later?

Good God. She'd had no idea that a streak of violence ran through the construction business.

But then there was Jill . . . It wasn't completely out of the realm of possibility that Stalker Girl had snapped, following them out of the bar, waiting, maybe *watching* . . .

She shivered, but this time the cause was revulsion, the creepy, skin-crawling kind, instead of the cold. If Jill had done this, waiting for her chance when Will left, she could still be waiting, to finish the job . . .

Oh, God. She sniffled, trying to get herself together and think, when a hand on her shoulder tore a startled scream from her throat. Scrambling to her feet, she looked up and felt a dizzy wave of confusion that seemed very likely the precursor to a faint.

It wasn't Jill. It was a man standing beside her, a brown bag of groceries in one arm and a concerned frown on his face. And the man was Will.

"Lanie? What's wrong?"

"Will?" She backed away from him, her face as white as the snow, her eyes huge and confused and . . . glistening? Was she crying? What the hell was going on? He'd just gone into town for bagels, for God's sake, and he'd left her a note.

"Lanie, it's me," he said, looking around for a place to set down the bag when he saw what had spooked her.

And found himself more than a little spooked in turn.

Stumbling, he swallowed hard and blindly shoved the bag at Lanie. What the fuck had happened here? Where had his father come from, and why the hell was he dead on the Seavers' back porch?

"Will?"

Lanie's voice was shaking, but he knew it was more than the unwelcome shock of a corpse. It was whom she'd thought the corpse was—*him.*

"Lanie, it's me," he said, turning to drag her close, running his hands over her trembling back, the brown bag a lumpy obstacle between them. "I mean, I'm me, and that's . . . that's my father, Mike DeMaio. Oh, Jesus."

"Your . . . father?"

"The same." He couldn't stop staring at the body, even though his hands continued their soothing circles through Lanie's wildly inappropriate spring coat. Somewhere in the back of his mind, he knew she was in shock, as well as nearly frozen, but his feet wouldn't work to move them into the house. In a minute, maybe he could manage it, but right now he needed to process the fact that his father—the lazy, bitter, selfish sonofabitch who had given Will little more than his name—was gone. The bloody, gaping wound in his neck was proof of that.

And then he needed to start thinking about the why and the how and the who.

"Will, I'm so . . ." Lanie shook her head, her eyes wide and grief-stricken when he faced her. "Well, sorry, obviously, but the word seems pretty inadequate for this situation."

"It's okay," he said vaguely, turning to look back at his father. When had he shown up in town, and why was he on the Seavers' back porch? The questions racing through his head all needed answers, but first, he wanted to get Lanie in the house and sit down himself. Preferably with a double shot of something alcoholic.

Willing his feet to move, he steered her toward the steps, careful to help her past the body, and realized only as they entered the kitchen that she'd been chattering nervously all the while.

". . . you'd left," she was saying, her mittened hands gesturing wildly, "so I thought I'd take a walk, see your house, you know? And *I* know that sounds a little desperate, but I was confused, because last night seemed so great—and I really do get that it doesn't matter right now, but I wanted to explain why I was out there and—"

He held up a hand to stem the rushing tide of words, guiding her into one of the chairs and setting her down in it. "I went to get bagels, and my car. I left you a note."

Her pretty pink mouth opened in surprise. "Oh."

If only he could spend the rest of the day focusing on that mouth, he thought, straddling a chair and resting his chin on his folded arms. That would be good. Even better would be focusing on the rest of her, too, head to foot and all the sweetly lickable parts in between.

"I guess you didn't find it," he said, raising his head to reach out and take her hand. Her wet mittens were still in place, and he pulled them off. "You looked so peaceful this morning, I didn't think you'd be up for a while."

"I tossed the covers." Now her cheeks were pink with embarrassment. "It's probably on the floor somewhere. And it really doesn't matter, not with . . . your dad."

Right. Actually, wrong. Mike DeMaio had fathered him, but he'd never, not for a minute, been his "dad." Heaving a frustrated sigh, Will got up and paced the length of the kitchen. He'd wanted a lot of things from the man over the years, like for him to wake up and remember he had a kid who needed a guy to play with, to come to back-to-school night, to give a thumbs-up to a Halloween costume. That had changed to simply wanting him to get a job and stop mooching off Will's mom whenever he needed beer money. For the last twenty years, he'd just wanted him gone. Still, he'd never wanted *this*.

"Should we call the police department? Or 911?" Lanie asked him. "I wasn't sure which, and I was still pretty much panicking when you showed up, and since I'm not from around here I didn't know . . ."

Something too close to hysteria edged Lanie's voice, and Will stopped beside her chair, absently noting the wet, striped knit cap squashed over her messy curls. He plucked it off her head before squatting to take her hands in his, and she bit her bottom lip as he searched her eyes.

"The roads aren't cleared yet—I couldn't even dig my car out," he told her. "And the girl at the store told me there was a big crash on Route 26—every cop in the county is probably over there now. Just let me think for a minute before we do anything—he's not going to be any less dead by then."

He swallowed hard when he'd said the word aloud. Dead. Christ, what the hell was going on? The last he'd heard, his dad was somewhere in the Carolinas, scraping together an existence with his most recent girlfriend. Will hadn't received one of his "Hey, old buddy, old pal, got any spare cash?" calls in almost four years. Neither had his mother, although now that she was in Maryland with her sister, he wouldn't know if she was telling him the truth. Her reserves of pity went far deeper than Will's, and she dipped into them a little too often for Will's taste.

And now Lanie had found him dead on the back steps of the Seavers' cabin. Lanie—Jesus. She'd come to Churchville for a quiet weekend away from the city, and stumbled into a murder.

A murder?

Holy fuck. Staring at Lanie, he realized his face must have registered his shock because hers went pale and scared as she looked at him, her bottom lip caught between her teeth.

"Will?"

He didn't answer, because his mind was racing. Who would want to kill his father? Thirty years ago, he might have said Grandpa Tom, but he was long dead, and the rest of his mother's family had pretty much washed their hands of the whole situation.

"Will?" Lanie sounded terrified now, and he dragged his gaze to her face.

"Did you . . . *see* anything out there?" he said. "Aside from the body, I mean?" Even in his own ears, his voice sounded gruff.

"See anything like what?" Then it struck her, and her mouth opened again, a tempting pink O that should have been reserved for nothing but satisfied sighs. "Oh, God, you mean like a . . . murder weapon?"

"Pretty much." He stood up, suddenly too restless to stay in one place. A *murder* weapon. This was not how he'd pictured spending this morning. Or any morning. In this or any other lifetime.

"But . . ." She shook her head, making her curls bounce, and twisted around to follow his progress as he paced. "Who would want to kill him? Does he have any, I don't know, enemies?"

"He hasn't lived here in more than ten years." He ran a hand through his hair, spiking it restlessly. It didn't make sense, any of it. Unless . . .

Lanie's voice broke into his thoughts. "But who would want him dead, then?"

"That's just it," he told her. "No one I can think of. Not here, a dozen yards from my house."

He watched as the idea struck her—he didn't think her face could get any paler. She looked ghostly in the wan light.

"So you're saying maybe he wasn't the real victim." Her voice was little more than a whisper. "Maybe someone . . ."

He finished the thought for her, gripping the edge of the counter so tight, his knuckles ached. "Maybe someone wanted to kill *me.*"

Five

It couldn't be, Lanie thought, trying to ignore the frightening way her heart had sped up again, like a train out of control. Why would anyone want to kill Will?

Maybe he is an axe murderer. Or a bondage master. What do you really know about him?

No way. It was ridiculous, it was maybe even naïve, but in her bones, she knew that Will DeMaio was a nice guy. A *good* guy.

And no one was killing a good guy on her watch.

Especially not if it was her bad luck that had set off this whole nightmare.

Will was pacing again, his jaw set in a grim, tight line, and he was talking more to himself than to her. "I just don't get it," he muttered. "I mean, why was he here? And why *here?* This house, I mean. It doesn't make sense."

This house . . . Lanie sat up straight, glancing at the end of the counter. "Will? Did he drink, your dad? And smoke?"

"You better believe it." He snorted. "He rarely did anything else."

She got up and nudged him aside to open the cabinet door below the sink. "I found this earlier," she said, pointing to the empty bottle of whiskey, "and those," she added, gesturing to the crowded ashtray. "Do you think he was staying . . . here?"

"Could be." His eyes narrowed as he crossed his arms over his chest. He was so tense, he looked as if he would snap if she brushed against him accidentally. "He knew the people who used to own this place before your friends—he might have known where a spare key was."

"That doesn't make sense, though," she said, sitting down again. "Wouldn't you have noticed him over here?"

"I was away until Wednesday, up in Boston."

She squashed the urge to ask him whom he'd been visiting—or, more specifically, whether his friend was the female variety. It wasn't important, not right now. Not with his dad murdered in very cold blood on the back porch, and Will most likely the bullet's intended recipient.

It didn't really make sense, because she certainly didn't have any experience with murder—and she took it for granted Will didn't either—but while her life was far from perfect lately, it was sort of like a dresser with a wobbly foot. It was irritating, a little troublesome, but ultimately fixable, even if in the short term all she could do was shim up the wobble with a matchbook.

This was like the whole dresser falling apart after someone had taken an axe to it. And then setting it on fire.

No way was she going shake Will's hand, thank him for the lovely orgasms, and leave him with a charred and smoking ruin.

She couldn't explain that to Will, of course. But she was going to have to inform him that she intended to help pretty much right now, because the look on his face screamed, "Thanks for everything, but we should probably say good-bye now."

And it was a decent motivation, as far as she was concerned. Not many guys would expect a woman he'd slept with once to stick around when messing around turned into murder. But she was damned if she was going to let her recent run of disasters trickle over onto him. Violent death was a whole other level of really bad karma. It wasn't her violent death, thank goodness, but it was on her back steps, and it was the father of her one-night stand.

Will was opening his mouth, and before he could get a word out, she scrambled for something that wouldn't make her sound like a lunatic.

"I want to help," she blurted, squaring her shoulders for the argument she desperately hoped wasn't coming. "This is . . . well, this is kind of a nightmare, actually, but for you, not for me, but I'm here, and I really like you, and I just . . . well, if you want the truth, it's all my fault anyway."

So much for not sounding like a lunatic.

But Will was even more adorable when he was stunned, in the I-have-no-idea-what-you-just-said way, of course, not the my-father's-been-murdered way. It took him a blinking, mouth-gaping minute to process what she'd said, and then all he could manage was, "Excuse me?"

"It's not really my fault, of course." She gave him a weak smile, wishing she sounded a little more confident. A little more stable, in fact. "It's just that my karma, or something, is in one of those off-again phases. It's bad luck, and it's screwing up just about everything I touch, and since I touched you, last night, I just figured . . ." Her shoulders slumped when she realized he was trying not to laugh. "I know it sounds weird, but just concentrate on the other part, okay? I want to help. What I mean is, I'm not going to shake hands and pack my bags and leave you holding the . . . well, the dead body."

"This isn't some long-cherished Nancy Drew fantasy, is it?" he asked, but he was teasing, and when he held out his hand, she took it, letting him draw her against the length of him.

This was going to be dangerous, she thought, her body softening all over as she breathed him in, snow and pine and, faintly, the yeasty warmth of the bagel shop. Not because of what they might find. Because of the way Will DeMaio made her feel.

* * *

Stepping onto the back porch, Lanie decided that she talked a good game for a girl whose biggest adventure, before last night, was mixing diet Coke with diet Pepsi. As they'd made their way down the icy steps, it was suddenly all too real that there was a very dead body on the steps, and they were going to look at it. Up close.

Will had called the police, who promised to send someone over as soon as they could, but in the meantime, he was determined to take another look at his father.

"Before they start in with the yellow tape and the latex gloves and all that," he'd told her. "I didn't love him—hell, I didn't even like him—but he's dead, you know? And if someone wanted *me* dead, in a weird way it's my fault."

She didn't know which was scarier—that someone would figure out he'd killed the wrong person and come after Will again, or that despite what a shit his father had been, Will felt guilty that the man was dead. The last being frightening for how much more evidence it stacked in the "Will DeMaio: Incredibly Nice Guy" category.

Squinting against the snow glare, Will pulled a pair of leather gloves out of his jacket pocket and put them on. Lanie stood behind him, craning her neck to see past his shoulder, and rubbing her arms briskly in the frigid air.

Taking a deep breath, Will reached toward the body, murmuring, "You ready?"

"As I'll ever be." She nodded, but as he turned back to his father's body, she fought the urge to squeeze her eyes shut. She wasn't going to be a delicate girly-girl about this. *Think of all the great female detectives,* she told herself. *Miss Marple, Harriet Vane, Stephanie Plum. Okay, they're fictional, but—*

"Oh, man," Will murmured, and Lanie risked a peek. If the storm hadn't lasted through the night and into the morning, the way the man had died would have been obvious. Brushing the wet snow from his gloves, Will stepped back, and Lanie got a good look at the front of his father's coat, where a rime of blood had made a huge, frozen stain. It was lacquered on his throat, too, surrounding an angry wound where a bullet had ripped into the flesh.

"There should be a trail of it," Will muttered. "Or maybe . . . a splatter? God, I don't know."

Shuddering, Lanie backed away from the body and turned to face the frozen field between the cabin and Will's place. She needed a deep breath, a good lungful of the clean white snow.

"I don't see a gun conveniently lying around." She peered down at the snow, but the surface was already brittle, sugary and bright even in the weak sunlight. "And I don't see any blood, but since it snowed all night . . ." She let the thought trail out in a white puff of breath. Oh my God, they'd been getting hot and sweaty while Will's father was out here the whole time . . .

Will passed a hand over his eyes, a bright, startled blue before they disappeared, then dug out the snow around the body. "Yeah, he's sitting on the bare step, not packed snow. Don't even think about it. And especially don't talk about it anymore. Let's just see what else we can find here."

She nodded, trying to wiggle her toes in her frozen sneakers as she set off in one direction, kicking gently at the snow to look for a blood trail beneath the surface. Will set off the other way, and every time she glanced back at him, the grim set of his shoulders in his heavy jacket made her heart squeeze. The sun was almost directly above them now, and it flashed warm gold on his hair. He reminded her of a very determined little boy, shouldering a burden much too big for him but resolved to carry it anyway.

"I'm not getting anything," he called from half a dozen yards away, "and if we mess with this much more, we're going to be trampling the evidence."

"I think that's a given already." Rubbing her mittened hands together, she surveyed the crisscrossed web of trails they'd made, an abstract in the snow.

He'd jammed his hands in his pockets when he walked back to her. "I just wish I knew what he was doing here."

"What about his pockets?" Lanie said quietly, turning her gaze up to him. He looked unsettled by the idea, but he nodded and walked back to the body, reaching toward the coat.

"There's a wallet," he said, lifting it out, "and that's it."

"Maybe there's a receipt for something?" This was so much harder than she'd thought—not that she'd believed it would be a piece of cake in the first place—and she couldn't begin to imagine what it was doing to Will.

At least the practical aspect of figuring it out was giving him something to do. He thumbed through the worn billfold and retrieved a scrap of white paper, which he waved at her. "The motel out on the highway," he said. "Makes sense."

He looked up suddenly and jerked his head toward the road. "Here comes the cavalry."

Gently sliding the wallet back into the jacket pocket where he'd found it, he pulled her against him, briskly rubbing her back as they watched a salt-spattered black SUV with the local police emblem emblazoned on the door pull up, crunching through the snow.

"Cavalry, huh?" she murmured.

"The not-so-esteemed Jackson Holby," Will murmured back. "Voted Most Likely to Be a Security Guard in high school. This is going to blow his mind."

"Hey there, Will," a stout, red-cheeked man called as he climbed out of the truck, zipping up a huge gray parka. He looked like a sooty version of the Michelin man. "Got a dead body here, huh?"

"And you'll never guess who it is," Will called back, murmuring to Lanie, "even though I already told the dispatch officer."

"Let's just take a look, shall we?" He was having a hard time wading through the packed accumulation, each massive booted foot pulled up with effort. He stopped at the bottom of the steps, chest heaving, and squinted down at the corpse. "Holy shit, Will—pardon my language, miss—but this looks just like you."

"That's because it's my father, Jackson." Lanie didn't dare look at Will for fear of giggling, but she could picture his eyes rolling.

"Your dad? Didn't he leave town, oh . . . ten years ago?"

She thought she could feel the frustration vibrating off Will in waves now, and she sighed. If this was the best the local police force had to offer, they'd be better off investigating on their own.

"He did, Jackson, but there's no law preventing the occasional visit, you know? I'm not sure why he was here, but he was, and now he's dead. About a hundred feet from my front door, as a matter of fact."

"Huh." As noncommittal grunts went, this guy had them perfected, Lanie thought, watching as he used his nightstick to nudge open the dead man's coat. If he understood Will's inference, he didn't show any signs of it.

She had halfway decided to introduce herself, offer her statement about finding the body, when two more police cars pulled up, and a team of four men, two in street clothes and two in police-issue parkas, got out.

Thankfully, the thumbnail on any one of them seemed more intelligent than Jackson Holby, and she and Will were separated and questioned immediately as the evidence techs started their work on the body and the surrounding area. By the time they were allowed inside, where Lanie gathered her things and stuffed them into her bag, she was truly frozen, and the idea of trudging across the snowy field to Will's house was mitigated only by the chance to crawl into what she hoped was his big, warm, snuggly bed, with him.

When the detectives had given them permission to leave, however, Will had other ideas.

"We should get out of here," he murmured. "Let them do their thing, take the body away, all that."

"And go where?" she whispered back. "And do what? Shouldn't they be protecting you? Didn't you tell them that you may have been the target here?"

"It's a small town, Lanie." He backed her up against the

bathroom sink, where she'd been collecting her toothbrush and deodorant. "They're going to go off and question everyone who might have it in for me, and I thought we could concentrate on figuring out what my father was doing."

"Won't they do that, too?"

"Yeah. But we've got a head start while they're here dusting for fingerprints and whatever else it is they do, and I don't feel like sitting over there at home watching them cart my father's dead body away."

She frowned, suddenly very sure that his bed was not in her immediate future. "Okay, but how are we going to get anywhere? The rental car barely made it here last night, and that was ten inches of snow ago."

She squinted up at him when he didn't answer immediately, and her stomach gave a nauseating little lurch of anxiety. "I have a feeling this isn't going to be good."

Even his tired grin wasn't reassuring. It was far too mischievous for the present circumstances.

"Remember when I mentioned the snowmobile?"

Six

Maybe she wasn't intrepid enough for sleuthing, Lanie thought, clutching Will's jacket with hands gone completely numb in the frigid afternoon air. Maybe she needed to update her image of discreetly poking around for clues in a saucy convertible, wearing a bag to match her shoes. No one dressed like that anymore but her grandmother, anyway, whose white leather pocketbook was stored in her closet with her white leather church shoes, right beside the black patent leather set.

As far as she knew, Nancy Drew had never ridden on the back of a snowmobile that resembled a New Age rocket, icicles dripping from her hair and her rear end smarting with each jolt of the contraption over the hard-packed snow. Which was traveling much, much too fast for her taste.

". . . there," Will shouted, only a fragment of his voice carrying over the icy wind as he jerked the snowmobile forward with a groan from the engine.

"What?" she yelled back, hanging on and digging her knees into his hipbones, just to make him uncomfortable.

"We're almost there!" He took one hand off the steering bar and pointed at the highway, now visible as they cleared a small rise, and Lanie blinked frost from her eyelashes to squint at the faded motel sign sitting dejectedly by the side of the road. The Come On Inn, dented metal letters spelled out. Maybe that was what passed for romance up here in the country.

A minute later, Will steered the snowmobile across the deserted road and slid to a stop in the parking lot, cutting the engine.

"You okay?" He held out a hand as he jumped off, shaking snow dust from his hair.

"My ass has been better," Lanie grumbled. Her foot shook as she stepped down, and she caught Will's eye in time to say, "Don't even think about it," when she noticed his mouth opening in a retort.

But she let him pull her against him as they made their way through the unplowed snow to the front office. Warmth was warmth, even if it was coming from a kamikaze snowmobile driver.

"What if no one's here?" she said. The window was grimed with salt from previous snows, and probably a decade's worth of road dust besides. There were no cars in the parking lot, which stretched the length of the squat white brick building, and no lights visible behind the heavy drapes in the guest rooms' windows.

"Clarice will be here," Will said, pushing open the door, and Lanie followed.

He was right. When the bell jingled, a head of wild raven hair jerked out of the doorway behind the counter, and an enormous pink bubble snapped and deflated. "Hey, Will. What's up?"

"Stayed here again last night, Clarice?" Will said, folding his arms on the counter and leaning over it, sniffing. "Any coffee brewed?"

"I end up staying here every night," Clarice said. "I told Henry we could get reservations on the Web if he put in a cable modem—I've only got dial-up at home. You need a room or what?"

"I need some information." *Bastard,* Lanie thought. He was

twinkling at the girl. "But even more than that, I really need some caffeine."

"It's almost four o'clock, Will. What does this look like, a diner?"

"Come on, Clarice. You mainline coffee and HTML all day." *Twinkle, sparkle.*

Lanie rolled her eyes and settled on a cracked black leather chair beside the window. She would just sit and contemplate the effects of frostbite while Romeo flirted them up something hot to drink. At this point, she didn't care if it was a twenty-year-old package of Swiss Miss.

A minute later, he thrust a steaming cardboard cup into her hand and settled into the chair beside her. Clarice perched on the counter, swinging a pair of electric purple high-tops and snapping her gum. "What do you want, Will? I'm coding stuff for the Web site, and I want it to go live later today."

"What's your Web site about?" Lanie asked politely, blowing on her coffee. All the good detectives—at least the ones who didn't rely on brute force as a rule—always made small talk.

"*Farscape* fan fiction," Clarice said, taking her gum out of her mouth and rolling it between two fingers. Her nails were painted bright green. "And the possibility of alien life on earth."

Lanie swallowed her coffee too fast and coughed. "Oh."

Will bit back a grin and leaned forward, elbows on his knees. "Was an older guy, looks just like me, staying here any time recently?"

"Your dad?" Clarice slid off the counter and walked around it, flipping open the guest register. She shrugged when Will frowned at her. "The name kind of gave it away. Here it is, Mike DeMaio, Tuesday the fifth, till this Thursday. Why?"

"Just wondering." Staring into his coffee cup, his tone was casual when he asked, "Anyone hanging around here with him? Any trouble?"

"This isn't a baby-sitting service either, Will," Clarice said with an exasperated huff, but when he turned his blue gaze up to her, she gave in. "I think Chick Statler stopped by once, and what's his name? Um . . . yeah, Petey Petrowski, too, a couple of times."

"Chick?" Lanie asked, setting her empty cup on the floor and wondering if she should have been taking notes.

"It's a nickname," Will explained. "For Jason Statler. If you saw him you'd know it's kind of like calling Michael Jordan 'Shorty', but he doesn't seem to mind."

"Is that it?" Clarice interrupted, popping a fresh piece of gum into her mouth. Her dark eyes were bored beneath the coat of thick black eyeliner. "I've got two more pages to design."

"What room was he in?" Will stood up, and Lanie followed, hoping they weren't headed back to the snowmobile so soon. "If it's free, can I have it for tonight?"

"If it's free . . ." Clarice snorted, and handed him the key to Room 10. "I think I can squeeze you in."

"Charming," Lanie said, fingering the faded blue spread. It felt like early-issue polyester, and there was a questionable stain on one corner. The walls were a grim beige—she suspected they'd once been white and were now just dirty. A nondescript nightstand had been set beside the bed, and a lamp was bolted to its scarred surface.

"No one comes here for the ambience," Will called from the bathroom. "Personally, I'm a little disappointed there are no Magic Fingers. Find anything?"

"Maybe Clarice cleans up better than you thought," she called back. "There's nothing here but a trusty King James and a phonebook."

"Nothing in here, either. Damn it." He came out of the bathroom and dropped onto the bed, frowning. "What do we do next, Nancy?"

"I'm not sure, Ned." She sat down beside him and shrugged off her coat. He'd cranked the thermostat when they came in, and warm, stale air gushed from the clattering unit by the window. "It's been a while since the whole thing with the old clock and figuring out the password to Larkspur Lane."

"I have no idea what you're talking about," he said, and

lay back, throwing an arm across his face. "And I have no idea what to do next."

"Well, we could interview his old buddies in town," Lanie said, toeing off her sneakers and scooting backward to cross her legs on the end of the bed. "Figure out who else he saw while he was here. But we could also try to trace his movements, check out your office, and . . . what?" She'd glanced back at him and stopped when he removed his arm and looked at her blankly before his eyes warmed with amusement.

"You watch a lot of cop shows, Lanie?"

"No," she said with an injured huff. "Just *CSI* once in a while. And *Law and Order*. Well, and the occasional rerun of *NYPD Blue*. You know, when it was still worth watching." She bit back a smile as Will snorted, and added, "Okay, I watch my share. What do you watch?"

"Baseball. Football. Basketball. Hockey." He grinned when she rolled her eyes, and added, "And this surprises you? Hello, guy here. I wasn't going to mention the adult movies on Cinemax After Dark, but if you really want to—"

"I don't, thank you." She sniffed, and then turned around to face him. "We could just stop, you know. The police are handling it, and they probably wouldn't like you poking around on your own anyway. The thing is, you could still be in danger, especially if someone really mistook your dad for—"

"Lanie."

She took in a breath at the sound of his voice, low and gentle, and felt a flutter of excitement when she realized his gaze had darkened to that smoky, heated blue she'd seen last night. The man could make her tingle all over with just a look, and if she stopped to remember what he had made her feel when touching was part of the equation, she'd melt into a messy puddle right here at the foot of the bed.

"Maybe you could just help me talk it out," he said, but it was really more of a murmur. A persuasive, you're-too-far-away murmur. "It would be easier if you were up here, though." He patted the bedspread in invitation.

"Within groping range?" She lifted an eyebrow, but she scooted up next to him, curling into the circle of his arm and against the heat of his body with a satisfied sigh. *Go ahead, grope me,* she wanted to say. *There's nothing I'd like more.*

"Something like that," he said, but he only reached up to twine his fingers in her hair. She wanted to push against his hand like a cat, urge him to stroke, but they had a murder to figure out, after all. Her body was embarrassingly oblivious to the business at hand.

"So, enemies," she said idly. "Apparently, you have some. When I found the body, and thought it was you, my first thought was the contractor who confronted you at the bar. What was his name?"

"Vic Landry." He angled up on his other elbow to look at her. "That doesn't work, though—from the looks of it, my father was probably dead before we even got back to the cottage, and Vic left the bar before we did. Even if he was somewhere waiting for me, the timing's all wrong—my dad was shot sometime early in the evening, before there was much snow."

"Okay, so he's out. Which is a shame, because he's got a motive." Tracing a figure eight on his sweater with one finger, she looked up at him and noticed his raised eyebrows. "Not a *good* one," she added, "but still."

They were silent for a few minutes, each thinking, with the low rumble of the heater in the background. In the comfortable nest of the bed, Will's body a great big warm temptation beside her, it was hard to believe they were trying to piece together the clues to a murder instead of how quickly they could get undressed.

"I guess that leaves out Jill, too, huh?" Lanie said finally. "I thought maybe she'd gone totally stalker-psycho and followed us back to the house, but if he was dead before we got there . . ."

"Yeah." Will sat up, running his fingers through his hair. "Besides, she may be a little single-minded, but I don't think she's homicidal. You know, yet."

"Maybe if we knew what your dad was doing here, it

would lead us to something," she suggested. "What about the people Clarice mentioned?"

"Well, I can't think of a reason Chick would want me dead," Will said doubtfully.

"What's Chick's deal? He sounds . . . interesting." Focusing was difficult when she was breathing in the clean, warm scent of him.

"He runs a Harley shop out near Finley, and it's not strictly aboveboard. He's not a bad guy, really, but he looks like one, and he uses that to intimidate people." Will sighed, and his arm tightened around her. "Chick has always been just scummy enough to encourage wanna-bes to fetch and carry for him, you know? Actually, Petey, the other guy Clarice mentioned, used to run errands for him sometimes back in high school. Go out for another case of beer, lock up the shop when Chick had a date, that kind of thing. He always thought it would make him one of the cool guys."

"How did your father even know Chick?" Lanie asked. "He had to be years older."

"Not as many as you'd think." Will's voice was rueful. "He and my mom were just eighteen when I was conceived in the proverbial backseat of someone's Chevy, and Chick's a few years older than me—left back twice, and the kind of guy who likes to be a big fish in a little pond, hanging out with kids just enough younger to look up to him."

"Sounds like a really upright member of society," Lanie murmured. "What about Petey . . . what was his name?"

"Petrowski. I fired him a month ago, actually—he's been working for me on and off for years, but I got fed up with his bullshit. He's lazy and about as intelligent as a bottle cap, and I just stopped feeling sorry for him."

"But what would your dad want with him?" Lanie asked.

"They were probably commiserating about what a rotten guy I am," Will said with a bitter laugh. "I wouldn't give either of them a handout as often as they liked."

"So that means we're back where we started," she added, sitting up in frustration. Outside the slightly parted drapes, the afternoon was completely still, a dark, threatening gray. "Nowhere."

With that, as if she'd uttered the words to a spell, it was suddenly even darker. With a wheezing gasp, the radiator went off, and then the lights went out.

Seven

"I didn't do it, I swear," Lanie said, shaking her head. "Not my fault this time."

"It's probably the power lines." Will laughed and climbed off the bed to grab his coat. "When the temperature drops like it did today, the lines get icy and heavy, and then they collapse. Let's go see what's what."

"Out there? In the snow? Again?" She sighed, but she got up and put her sneakers and her coat back on, and he threw an arm around her shoulders as they headed back to the office.

"Power's out," Clarice called from the back room when they walked in, the bell over the door jingling their arrival. She came out to the counter, and Will realized her green nail polish glowed in the dark. "No refunds, though."

"Not a problem," Will told her, even though Lanie had rolled her green-brown eyes in disgust. "Well, it's going to be *cold,"* she whispered.

"Wait here and let me walk down the road a bit," he said to Lanie, installing her in the leather chair near the window again. "If it's out all over, we're better off just staying put."

It was—he didn't go far, but no lights were visible in the twilight, not from the lane heading off the main road, or from farther down the highway, where a Mobil sign should have been a big blue beacon. He walked back into the office, stomping snow from his boots and blowing on his hands, and found Lanie examining a tattoo on Clarice's stomach.

"Anything to eat around here?" He took a casual step closer to get a better look, but Clarice pulled down her sweater with a smirk.

"Not much that doesn't require a zap in the microwave," she said, "but we could raid the cash drawer for change and hit the vending machine."

"It's that old," Will said when Lanie frowned, glancing at it. "Circa 1969, I bet. All mechanical."

"If it's got candy, I don't care if it's from the last world war," she retorted, following Clarice to the cash register, which was another conveniently retro model. Clarice opened the drawer with a loud *ding* and handed out quarters.

"I don't think there's enough chocolate in the world to balance out the events of this weekend," Lanie said as they trudged back to the room, nibbling delicately on a Hershey bar with almonds, and then attempting to spit mitten fuzz from her tongue.

Will set down the two candles Clarice had scrounged from the storeroom, and unloaded the M&Ms, chips, and peanuts he'd chosen from the vending machine. Soda was out since that machine was refrigerated, but Clarice had given them each a bottle of water from the tiny motel kitchen, and a bottle of cheap tequila some college kids had left behind two weeks ago, just in case they needed artificial warmth. The room was already chilly, and he grabbed the extra blanket from the luggage rack near the closet.

"Maybe not chocolate," he said, taking Lanie's extra candy and tossing it on the bureau. "But we could try something else."

She licked a creamy brown smudge from the side of her mouth and glanced at the bed. "Something like . . . ?"

"You know the old theory about sharing body heat, don't you?" He flipped down the covers and took off his coat. "I say we test it."

She crumpled her candy wrapper and threw it vaguely in the direction of the wastepaper basket, and shrugged off her jacket.

"It's not . . . you know, disrespectful?" she whispered as he sat her on the bed and removed her sneakers, then reached down to take his own off. "I mean, your father's dead, and we're supposed to be . . . I don't know, sleuthing. Mourning. Something."

"I'll mourn him," Will whispered, sitting down and pulling her onto his lap, sighing when she pressed her breasts against him. Nice, but it would be much better when they were naked. Time to work on that. "Right now I still can't really believe he's dead. And as for sleuthing, I think we've done our share for the day." His hands slid up her back, beneath her sweater, and then under her bra strap.

"If you say so . . ." She met him halfway when he angled his mouth toward her, and the taste of her tongue was sweet and dark and delicious. When she arched her back, he unhooked her bra and ran his palms over the bare, silky skin, lingering on the wings of her shoulder blades. She made a sound so close to a purr, he almost growled in response.

He'd been imagining this all day, and if it made him callous or cold or just plain weird, he didn't care. Lanie Burke was the best thing to happen to him in a while, and a small, admittedly petty part of him was pissed off at his father for nearly screwing it up. He'd made excuses for him when he was a kid, and when he'd given up on that, he'd tried his best to deny the hot flare of bitterness in his gut whenever his father's name was mentioned. Mike DeMaio had never given him anything of value but his life, and for that Will owed him at least some measure of justice for a murder that was most likely an accident.

Right after he took a little comfort in Lanie.

And that was all it was, or at least that's what he'd been trying to tell himself since last night. He slid Lanie's sweater over her head when she raised her arms and then took her bra with it, tossing the clothes to the floor. Fastening his mouth on

to one side and leaned in to take his pulsing, already aching cock in one hand and lick up the shaft with just the tip of her tongue. A whisper of wet, a bare hint of pressure, teasing, promising—Christ, he was going to black out himself if she didn't take him into her mouth real soon.

"Lanie," he managed, bracing himself on the mattress with his elbows, resisting the urge to take her head in his hands and guide her. The part of his brain that was still rational wanted her to do it her own way, in her own time.

It was just that he wanted her own time to be right now.

And it was—he groaned when she closed her lips over the swollen head, sucking gently, swirling against the cleft with her tongue, and he groaned louder when she bent her head to slide his cock farther into her mouth.

He was going to fucking explode if she didn't stop . . . and in a hazy red flash, he realized what he really wanted was to explode fucking. Fucking Lanie, with those luscious breasts soft and hot against his chest, and her amazingly strong legs wrapped around his hips, her little heels digging into his ass.

And her hands—her small, very feminine hands holding on tight, like she was having the ride of her life.

He grunted as her mouth tightened around his erection and her hand wandered between his legs to cup his taut balls and stroke the extra-sensitive skin behind them. Okay, time to stop. Time to get inside her, where he could hear that shuddering little sob when she came.

Gently, he pushed her head away, easing himself out of the slippery bliss of her mouth, and even in the almost nonexistent light he could see the question mark in her eyes.

"My turn," he said, and pulled her to her feet.

She wriggled away when he tried to steer her toward the bed, and backed up instead. "Ever do it standing up, Will DeMaio? I haven't." She swallowed hard, her chest still rising and falling fast, and then she said, "I bet you could teach me."

Oh, yeah. He grinned, and she grinned back, opening her arms to let him lift her, wrapping her legs around his waist and lowering her head to kiss him, deep and hard and so, so hot.

Her mouth was on fire, dark and wet and greedy, and he shuddered when the hot, slick center of her made contact with his abdomen.

Oh, *yeah*. His cock was wedged between the round cheeks of her ass, which was a good thing on its own, but right now he wanted *in*. Deep, then deeper. Then, if possible, deeper still.

The thought of it made his cock twitch with impatience, and he stalked forward as she hung on, nibbling at his earlobe and twining her fingers in his hair.

"Condom," he grunted between gritted teeth, trying to figure out where his jeans were and if there was any way he could find a condom, open it, and roll the damn thing on without letting go of her.

She slithered off him without warning and scrabbled over the carpet, coming up with a handful of denim. "Give," she panted when he pulled out the foil-wrapped packet. "I like this part."

He let her smooth the slick rubber over his erection, shuddering when she managed to work in a few sly squeezes around the rock-hard base, and then he grabbed her. She climbed up him, her skin flushed with heat everywhere, warm silk, and once he'd staggered back to the wall, resting her against it, she pushed herself up using his shoulders so he could aim.

He eased in with one thrust, and for a second everything went a fiery red, his nerve endings blazing at the relief of being inside her, where the heat was searing and she was so incredibly wet.

Then she wriggled, seating him deeper with a funny little sound that was half groan and half sigh, and he braced himself with one arm against the wall to rock into her.

It wasn't going to take long, damn it, and he wanted it to take forever. He wanted to thrust into her deliciously slick center until everything was obliterated and time had stopped, it felt so un-fucking-believably good.

She was levering herself up and down, using his shoulders, digging her fingers into the knotted muscle, and with every bounce she gasped, a steady "Oh, oh, oh" that became "oh-ohohohoh," a fierce, frantic hum.

Every syllable urged him deeper, harder, faster, the head of his cock burying itself against the far wall, stroking her, and suddenly he felt her tense up, her thighs tightening, and she came in a trembling wave, pulsing around him.

That was all it took. He groaned as he exploded with one last thrust, the aftershocks rippling through his belly and his legs until he was shaking.

With one unsteady step backward, they were on the bed, sweaty and panting, and he grabbed at the blankets when the reality of the chilly air hit him.

Lanie snuggled against him, a warm, comfortable weight. As his head fell back on the pillow, she whispered, "I don't know about you, but I think I definitely deserve an *A* for that," and as he drifted into a boneless, sated doze, he realized he was laughing.

Eight

"So he doesn't work?" Lanie whispered. "I mean, didn't?"

Will grunted and pulled her closer, still drowsy, but Lanie edged away, propping herself up on her elbows to look down at him. She couldn't see much—it had been too cold to sleep for long, at least under one blanket, and when she woke up shivering she'd lit one of the candles and shaken Will until he climbed under the covers, sheets, comforter, extra blanket, and all. The gentle, flickering light cast eerie shadows across his face, and she'd lain beside him, thinking, until the question she'd just asked—and several others—had occurred to her.

"Will, wake up." She nudged him again. "What was your father doing here, and for so long?"

He opened one eye and frowned. "I don't know. That's what's weird. He doesn't have family here anymore. I mean, except for me."

"Exactly." She tapped his chest with one finger. It was so beautifully firm. Chiseled, in fact. Construction was clearly a good way to keep in shape. She dragged herself back to the conversation and added, "But he didn't call you, right? Didn't leave any messages on your machine while you were away?"

He stared at her, uncomprehending. "No. That's why I was

so shocked when I saw him. Aside from the fact that it was his dead body, not him. What are you getting at?"

She sighed and sat up, wrapping herself in the extra blanket. "I'm not sure. But it just seems odd to me that he would come all the way up here from where, North Carolina? Then not even give you a call, and *then* wind up dead."

"Well, when you put it that way, yeah." One of his hands snaked under the blanket to fasten on her calf, his thumb tracing lazy circles on the skin. "I stopped caring what was going on in his head a long time ago, mostly because what was usually up there was the easiest way to score groceries and rent money from a new girlfriend, or mooch off me and my mom. The truth is, I don't know what he was doing up here, but I can practically guarantee it was something slimy."

"Hmmm." She nodded, but she was still thinking, trying hard to ignore the sensation of his fingers on her skin, climbing higher now, venturing into the ticklish spot behind her knee. The whole thing was too coincidental. They were missing some connection, and she was never going to figure it out if Will kept distracting her. Like that. Oh, God, and like *that* . . .

And with a phone ringing?

"What is that?" Will said, sitting up and squinting into the darkness beyond the circle of candlelight. "It's not the room phone."

"It sounds like a cell," Lanie said, twisting to move her ear closer to the headboard. "It's down there somewhere."

"Let me see."

She moved to the foot of the mattress, swathed in the blanket, while he dug between the headboard and the mattress. The phone was still ringing, but the voice mail service was bound to pick up soon.

"An old"—he made a face—"Oreo." Tossing the stale cookie to the floor, he dug deeper, cursing when the shrill electronic ring stopped. "A lighter. What did you say about Clarice cleaning in here? And, too late, the phone."

He held it up, a slim silver flip phone.

"Oh, it's so pretty. I wanted one like that," Lanie said, taking it from him to scroll through the call log. They'd never be able to figure out the voice mail password. "Where's the two-five-two area code?"

"Two-five-two?" Suddenly, he sounded very serious, and not at all happy.

"Yeah, why?"

"Because that's a North Carolina number."

She glanced up to find his eyes wide and dark. "You think it's your father's phone?"

"He stayed in this room last. And it's obviously still charged, so it was left here recently. And someone—someone who doesn't know he's dead—is calling him."

"Oh, God." There wasn't much to mourn about the man himself, according to Will, but for a moment she pictured some unknowing girlfriend, wondering when her man was coming home, and she felt a momentary stab of pity.

"Let me see if there are any local numbers in there." Will took the phone back and scrolled through the call log himself, his brow creasing.

"What's wrong?"

"Well, he called Petey . . . I don't know, two dozen times? What the hell?"

The frustration in his voice was sharp enough to cut glass. But there was something beneath it—anger, and what sounded like betrayal. She crawled back into the bed and pulled him with her, nestling under the covers beside him. The temperature in the room was rapidly moving from uncomfortably chilly to meat-locker worthy. And the chill running up the back of her neck as her thoughts raced was practically icy.

"Petey's the one you fired, right?"

"Yeah." He met her gaze, understanding her meaning. "And I think I know where I might be able to find out what he's been up to this week."

She grabbed her own clothes while Will pulled on his pants and socks. She was searching the floor for her shoes when Will turned around, tugging his sweater into place, and frowned at her. "What are you doing?"

She ignored this and asked him, "I assume we're getting on the snowmobile again. God, I wish I were an Eskimo."

"I don't think you'd look good in fur." He put a hand on her arm as she reached for her coat, which was draped across the bureau. "And I'm asking again, what are you doing?"

"Getting dressed." She folded her arms over her chest. If he pulled a he-man macho act now . . . "Why?"

"I think you should stay here, Lanie. Really," he said, his shoulders sagging in exasperation when she raised an eyebrow and shook her head. "Look, it's freezing out . . ."

"Oh, yeah, and it's really toasty in here. Think again, Will DeMaio. And don't think I won't use 'William' if you really piss me off."

"Lanie . . ."

"You're getting close now," she warned, wagging a finger at him. "What do you think is going to happen out there? I mean, worse than taking a chance on a one-night fling and waking up to find a dead body on the back steps? You can't seriously think you're protecting my delicate sensibilities here."

"Actually, I'm rethinking the issue of your sensibilities right now," he said, shaking his head as he zipped his jacket. "All right, but I don't like this. This is a *murder,* for Christ's sake, and I don't want you in any danger. You know, I never thought I'd actually say that to a woman. Not as a carpenter living in Churchville, at least."

She grinned as she put on her coat and wrapped her scarf around her neck. "Think how much more macho it would have sounded if you'd said 'I'm coming out firmly against this.' "

"Funny," he said, and lightly slapped her bottom on the way out the door.

The worst thing was, she thought as they climbed on the snowmobile and she wrapped her arms around him, she didn't mind it at all.

* * *

The Black Bear was past Churchville center in the other direction, set off a winding county route in a converted barn. In the dark, it hulked beneath the bare trees like something out of a horror movie, only three pickups parked haphazardly in front. Lanie took a deep breath as they climbed off the snowmobile, which wasn't easy—even her lungs seemed frozen.

"Why are we here?" she asked, trying to make out the vague path of footprints in the snow. The moon was only a thin sliver in the black sky. "There's no power out this way either, is there?"

"Nope." Will jerked the heavy door open, and she caught sight of five men gathered at the long bar, where lit candles and old-fashioned oil lamps threw warm light on the wood. "But blackout parties are kind of a tradition at the Black Bear."

"Hey there, Will," one of the men called, raising a mug. "Who's your friend?"

"This is Lanie Burke," he answered, winding a heavy, protective arm around her. She didn't protest. Everyone looked fairly tame, but it was frigidly cold in here, too. "She picked a hell of a weekend to visit, huh?"

"You can't count on spring up here till the end of May, honey," an older man said with a sympathetic smile. His hair was the color of polished steel, pulled off his neck with a leather band. "But the snow sure is pretty if you like this kind of thing. How about a beer?"

"I'd love one," she said, making her way to the bar and hoping she'd regain the feeling in her feet while they were inside. "Petey's not here, is he?" she asked Will under her breath.

"Not unless he's in the men's room." He pointed toward the back of the bar, where a rough wooden sign with a bear seared into it hung above a door. Over the door next to it, the bear on the sign was carrying a purse.

They settled into a booth near the bar, and the older man brought them an oil lamp and two very frosty mugs. "What are you doing dragging this pretty little thing out here on a night like this, Will?"

Pretty little thing. Against her better instincts, Lanie smiled at him—he was old enough to be her grandfather, and his old-fashioned charm seemed part and parcel of the little town with its antique shops, statuesque trees, and quaint clapboard farmhouses. If you discounted the murder, of course, she thought, taking a thirsty swallow of her beer. It was icy and bitter, like too many things this weekend.

"There's been a little . . . trouble," Will told him, examining a deep gouge in the tabletop with interest. "And I think Petey Petrowski might be part of it. Has he been around lately? Today, even?"

The older man scraped a chair away from the table with a sigh and sat down heavily. In the dusky light, Lanie noticed a silver scar on his cheek that looked suspiciously like something a knife had left. Okay, maybe a little less her grandfather and a little more aging Hell's Angel.

"Normally, what gets said in here stays in here," he began, his gaze shifting between her face and Will's, "but in this case . . ."

"Has he been around, Ray?" Will's tone had lost its warmth and taken on a distinctly let's-get-on-with-it edge.

"Does this have to do with your dad, Will?"

"Could be."

Lanie swallowed hard, her stomach twisting in dismay. Whatever Ray had to tell them, it wasn't going to be good, she knew it.

Ray shook his head with another rueful sigh. "They were here Thursday, and Petey was drunk. Well, they both were—they'd been ordering kamikazes all night. They were arguing for a while, and at one point Carter had to give them a warning because your dad got up and shoved Petey clear into the pool table. They then switched to straight J.D., no chasers, and I was getting ready to throw them both out . . ." He looked up and caught Will's impatient stare. "When your dad left, Petey started babbling, you know the way he does sometimes, about the 'plan.' How it was going to work, and he was the man to do it, and something about how he wouldn't get caught because it was all figured out, and it damn well sounded like . . ." He turned his faded blue eyes to Lanie momentarily. "It sounded like he was talking about killing someone."

It certainly did sound like a guy talking himself up, convincing himself he could commit murder. That much Lanie agreed with. But now she wasn't sure whom he'd intended to kill. She held her tongue as Will downed half his beer in a single gulp and stared out the black square of the window.

"So what was the trouble?" Ray asked, his voice as low as Will's. At the bar, the others were arguing the relative merits of cable and satellite dishes, noisily.

Will didn't answer, and the tension at the table suddenly seemed strung taut enough to snap. This weekend was feeling more like a noir movie every minute. She should have been wearing heels and a kicky little suit, with her hair piled up under a hat.

"You know it'll be all over town by tomorrow, once the land lines are up again," Ray reminded him, and Lanie squirmed. Will was missing his cue, and suddenly she was worried the scene was going to end in, if not violence, something equally unpleasant. The old guy wanted his gossip, and now.

When Will finally finished his beer and set it down, she could tell he was going to cave, and breathed a sigh of relief.

"My father's dead." The words were punctuated with a bark of laughter that didn't sound anything like the low, amused rumble she was used to. "How about that? All these years, I've wanted him gone, to leave my mom alone, and now he's dead."

Lanie's heart squeezed as the rigid line of his jaw trembled with rage or grief, or maybe both. But he wasn't finished. He gave Ray a mirthless smile as he added, "And the fucked-up thing is, I think I was the one who was supposed to die."

Nine

This whole thing was crazy, Will thought as he steered Lanie out to the snowmobile. Twenty-four hours ago he'd been anticipating his usual weekend—odd jobs left over from the work week, watching whatever game was in season on TV, knocking back a few beers with the guys, and possibly finding someone nice and soft and female to share his bed. It was all starting to seem like a far-off, really happy dream.

Well, he'd gotten the soft female part right, and more.

A *lot* more. Lanie was sexy as hell, and somehow made to fit against and around him like the last piece to a puzzle, but for the first time in a long time, the two parts of him that usually took a vacation when he had a woman in his bed were the two parts demanding his attention—his head and his heart. Lanie fascinated the first, and had, to be completely greeting card corny about it, stolen the second.

And instead of lying next to her in his bed at home, exploring every inch of skin and every funny, slightly off center thought in her head, he was dragging her around on the back of a snowmobile in the freezing cold. Rather than enjoying the lazy, fuzzy glow of good sex, he could feel the beginnings of a pure, icy rage that would put last night's storm to shame.

All because his father, apparently, had asked Petey Petrowski to kill him. And Petey, major fuck-up that he was, had screwed up and killed his father instead.

"Will, talk to me." Lanie's voice was muffled against his shoulder as he coaxed the starter to life. "What are you thinking?"

He'd hustled her out of the bar so fast, she'd barely had time to zip up her coat, and when he twisted around to look at her now, he could see that the upturned tip of her nose was red with cold, and her hands, when he reached to take one, felt brittle even beneath her mittens.

She didn't get it. Hadn't made the connection. Couldn't imagine that a man would want his own son dead. And that was just one of the reasons he wished like hell he could start this damn thing up, drive her away somewhere warm and safe, and love her until she was weak with it.

"It was my father, Lanie," he said, feeling his heart sink as she frowned in disagreement, her brow screwing up more adorably than was probably possible for a woman on the back of a snowmobile in the middle of the night. "Really. Think about it."

"I did," she said, shaking her head. "They were arguing, had been seen together a couple of times. There were all those calls to Petey's number on your father's cell phone. I think we were wrong—I think they cooked something up that went bad, and Petey decided to kill your dad."

"You don't know Petey." He pulled her close and kissed the top of her head. "He fucked up, Lanie. That's all. My dad wanted me dead, for whatever twisted reason went through his head that day, and Petey got drunk and killed him by accident."

She swallowed hard—he could see the muscles working in her throat as her eyes filled with tears, glistening in the weak moonlight. She didn't want to believe him.

"Think about it," he said. "Think about where we found him, the empty bottle and the ashtray at the Seavers'. He had a front-row seat. He expected to watch Petey find me and kill me, and Petey just . . . fucked up."

"Oh, God, Will." She twined her arms around him, and even through their coats he could feel her warmth, the strength of the comfort she was trying to offer. "But that means that Petey could have realized his mistake by now. He really could be looking for you. We should go to the police right now. Stay there. They'd give us a cell, right, just to sleep in? Do they have a cell, even? I don't know how big the station is—"

"Lanie." Then he shushed her with his mouth, pressing his lips to hers firmly. "You're going to the police station. I'm going to take you there right now, before we have to defrost you."

"What do you mean, you're taking *me?*" She wriggled away, careful not to stamp down too hard in the snow. The feeling in her toes was only a fond memory. "Are you going to start that macho woman-in-danger stuff again?"

"Lanie . . ."

She supposed his low, rumbling tone was meant as a warning, but it wasn't as if she'd paid much attention to those lately. And she wasn't going to start now, "danger" or no danger.

Will DeMaio made her feel a thousand things it would take her weeks to list individually, but among the important biggies were whole, sexy, and, above all, competent. Despite every horrible thing that had happened since she arrived—and the revelation that Will's father had been the one scheming to kill his own son was so far past horrible, she didn't even know how to categorize it—she didn't feel like a walking bad luck charm when she was with Will. She felt good. She felt . . . powerful. A woman who knew what she was doing and what she wanted.

It had been a long time since she'd felt that way.

"If you're going off in search of him, I'm coming, Will, so don't even try to argue," she said, scampering out of reach of his hands and climbing on the back of the snowmobile again. Besides, she couldn't bear the idea of letting him out of her sight even for a minute. The last time he'd disappeared, she'd tripped over a dead body, and she was afraid if she let him go, she'd be hearing about his corpse next.

Her rear end protested another ride on the snowmobile, but Will didn't argue, which made her momentarily suspicious. But she knew she had him when he climbed on, too, and twisted around to grab her head and pull her mouth to his for a long, lingering kiss.

That's right, she was powerful. Competent. *Confident.* God, it felt good. And they were going to figure this out together, because Will believed in her, too.

She adjusted herself on the seat when he pulled away, wrapping her arms around him in preparation. Then she tapped him on the shoulder.

"Now, where are we going again?"

Her face buried in the back of Will's coat, her teeth chattering hard enough to break, Lanie gave a sigh of relief when Will steered the snowmobile behind the white mound of what was probably a hedge and cut the engine.

Next time she decided on a weekend away, she was definitely going to Florida.

"The office is just down the street," Will murmured, climbing down and helping her off. They were on the edge of Churchville's tiny business district, and he nodded toward the silent block of converted houses, all boasting what looked like shingles on the lawns, most likely announcing salons, realtors, and law offices. "But I didn't want to pull up right in front. I'm thinking stealth is probably a good idea until we know where Petey is."

"So we're not looking for him?" Lanie asked, relieved.

He rolled his eyes and shook his head. "No, because I don't actually have a death wish. Even a drunk idiot with a gun is more trouble than I want tonight. We're looking for flashlights, extra batteries, and a can of gas for the snowmobile."

"I don't see why we don't call the police right now and tell them what we know," she grumbled. It was cold, she was tired, and more than that, she was hungry. For food, for a decent cup of tea, and ultimately, for a few minutes alone with

Will in a warm, well-lit room. Wait, not minutes—hours. Preferably the whole night.

They'd sleuthed. They'd figured it out. Okay, some of their finds had been lucky coincidences, but for beginners she thought they'd done pretty well overall. They deserved heat, sustenance, and the chance to celebrate with something other than yet another ride on the Snowmobile From Hell.

"We will call them. Inside, where it's probably a little bit less cold than it is out here," Will said as they trudged through the snow. "Although, you know, I wouldn't say no to a little face-to-face time with Petey before he's in protective custody, if you want the truth. Just enough for a word or two."

"A word?" She snorted. "I have to say, the alpha male thing is going to lose its appeal if you get arrested for battery. Especially if your face gets messed up."

"And they say men are the shallow sex." He fumbled for his key and finally slid it into the lock. "Next time, I just might have to tie you to the bed and do this investigating stuff on my own. But, you know, I could make that very much worth your while."

Damn him. The pleasurable little thrill that rippled through her belly and between her legs was a tangible reminder of exactly how well he could deliver that promise.

"The bed would have blankets on it, right?" She tilted her head up at him, wondering if he could feel the hot flush on her cheeks. "Lots of them?"

"Whatever you want." He kissed her before he opened the door, and then guided her into the office, muttering that he had a flashlight somewhere in the front desk.

She heard drawers opening and more muffled muttering as she squinted into the darkness, trying to get a feel for the place. This was where Will worked, and since she hadn't been to his house yet, it was the first place she'd seen that might provide a few more clues to who he was. Not that Will was secretive, but she was a medicine cabinet peeker from way back, and the things found on people's desks and bookshelves, even on their kitchen counters, were sometimes a surprising window into their personalities.

Oh, stop sleuthing, she told herself, but she edged forward anyway, hands out, wondering where the door on the wall to her right led.

"Is this your office?" she asked him, and just as she twisted the knob and pushed, she heard Will's fiercely whispered, "Lanie, no! The door is—"

And then the door fell into the next room with a resounding thud, onto something that definitely wasn't the floor.

"Broken," Will finished bleakly.

She backed away, mortified, but realized something—or, more accurately, some*one*—was groaning beneath the heavy plank.

"Jesus, get back," Will shouted, rushing toward her, the flashlight's thin yellow beam bobbing against the wall.

Well, this time she wasn't going to argue. She scrambled out of the way as he lunged at the fallen door, shoving it hard over the obstacle beneath it and revealing a man.

A scrawny, moaning, leather-jacketed man sprawled on the floor, clutching his forehead with one hand and a gun with the other. The pistol shook as he pointed it, and Lanie's heart nearly jumped out of her chest.

Will said his name even as it came to her: "Petey."

Ten

Spitting blood out of his mouth and grunting as something in his knee popped loud enough for Lanie to hear it, Petey scrambled to his feet. "Will! I've been looking for you, man!"

Oh, my God. To finish the job, Lanie thought, squeezing her hands into fists. What the hell were they going to do now? Her tongue seemed to be frozen, but in her head, she was screaming. *Will, move! Duck! Something!*

"I've, uh, been looking for you, too," Will said evenly, still crouched by the fallen door, "all day."

He was stalling, which was good, but Lanie wanted him stalling somewhere out of range of the gun. Like Mexico.

"You found him, huh?" Petey said, backing up into the desk, its metal front reverberating. If he'd been drunk last night, he'd obviously kept drinking. "Your dad, I mean. Bastard."

Bastard? What did he mean by that?

Will stood up slowly, moving directly between her and Petey. "My friend Lanie here found him," he said. "And I think you should let her leave. Right now. She's not going to say anything to—"

"Hey, I don't wanna hurt anybody," Petey argued, waving the gun as he gestured, slurring his words into one long, barely intelligible sound. "I'm sorry, miss, you had to see that and all."

Did he mean the body? Lanie wondered, her hands beginning to unclench. What on earth was he talking about?

Will seemed just as confused, but he was edging closer to Petey now, inch by inch. He didn't seem to notice and, in fact, put the gun down on the desk with a sudden clatter so he could dig in his pocket for a cigarette.

"He wanted me to do it, you know," he told Will, sliding onto the desk, his heavy boots banging against the metal. "Kill you. Can you believe that?"

I knew it! Lanie wanted to crow, but she kept quiet as Will took another step closer to the desk and grabbed the gun while Petey lit a Marlboro. He hadn't mistaken Mike for Will. Whether he'd ever intended to kill Will was another question, but somewhere along the line, he'd decided to shoot Mike DeMaio instead.

"Why?" Will backed up, handing the gun to Lanie, handle first. Her hand shook as she took it, wondering if it was still loaded. "Put it on the front desk," he whispered.

Petey was smoking, and leaning back on the desk swinging his feet; he looked as casual as an office drop-in, just come for a quick hello and a cup of coffee.

"Why'd he want you dead?" he asked from behind a thick blue cloud of smoke. When Will nodded, he went on. "Money, I guess. I said you were doing okay when he asked me, and he figured maybe he could get into your bank account on the Internet or something. Use your place for a while."

Lanie took a step toward Will as his face hardened in fury. Money—God. It probably would have been easier to hear that it was revenge or jealousy or some other gut-level emotion, but for whatever Will had in his savings account? Mike DeMaio had been either completely desperate or lacking even the simplest moral compass, or both.

"And he asked you to do it." It wasn't a question, and Petey frowned.

"Yeah, he asked me, and you should be glad, man!" He knocked the ash from his cigarette onto the floor before taking another long drag. " 'Cause I played along, you know? I told him I'd do it, that I knew you, I knew where you hung out, and I still talked to guys on your crew . . ." He nodded, thinking back, a small, unbelievably creepy smile quirking his lips, and Lanie shuddered.

"And why would that make me glad?" Will asked, crossing his arms over his chest.

" 'Cause I was never gonna do it, man!" Petey dropped the butt and ground it out with his boot, grinning like a lunatic. "I'd never do that to you, Will! Not after everything you've done for me all these years, you know?"

"Oh, right! Like . . . firing you. Telling you you're a fuck-up and an incompetent. That kind of thing, huh?"

"Don't make him mad," Lanie whispered, grabbing Will's elbow. "It's over."

"We have the gun," Will muttered back, "and you could probably take him in a fair fight. I want to hear this."

She swallowed, knowing what was coming, and Petey didn't disappoint her.

"I just thought . . ." He shrugged, all wounded innocence. "I just thought you'd be proud of me, you know? For putting it over on him, for going along with it so he didn't run off looking for somebody else to do the job."

"You thought I'd reward you." Will snorted, and for the first time Petey looked mad.

"I thought you might, you know, appreciate my loyalty," Petey said, obviously trying hard to enunciate each word with something like dignity. Unfortunately, "appreciate" came out like "preejate."

"You killed his father," Lanie said in a rush, unable to stop the words. "You *killed* his father. Dead. *Murdered.* That's not like running out for another six-pack or picking up the dry cleaning. It's—"

"Who the hell are you to say?" Petey shouted, climbing off

the desk and taking a step toward her. Will stopped him with one fist, swinging out of nowhere and landing below Petey's right eye with a sickening crunch.

"Don't touch her," he growled, stepping back as Petey staggered to his knees, holding his cheek. "And *don't* do me any more favors."

Eleven

"What was this for?" Will asked, holding up the box of Miss Clairol. He was sprawled naked on his bed, pawing through Lanie's suitcase. Her midnight blue panties with the floral embroidery had elicited a very impressed "mmmm."

Lanie snatched the box and stuffed it into her tote bag, fighting a blush. "I was thinking of going blonder. Somehow, I never got around to it."

He grinned and made a grab for her, which she did nothing to resist. Settling her on top of him, he ground his hips into hers purposefully, and she let his borrowed robe fall open to feel his solid thighs against hers.

It looked like she wasn't going to have time for hair coloring this afternoon, either.

They'd waited for the police to come last night, with Petey bound in electrical tape on the desk chair, and had made as many excuses for their impromptu investigation as possible. None of which Jackson Holby had bothered to argue. At least not with any real steam. He'd lazed at the station house while his detectives were out doing the hard work, albeit not too effectively, and Will had solved his father's murder. Even Lanie could tell Holby was secretly pleased more hadn't been required of him.

Then they'd gone back to Will's. Despite everything they'd been through together, Lanie had been convinced staying there for the rest of the weekend would be awkward. With Petey arrested and nothing to do but grieve, or rage, she was sure Will would finally break. Lose it, just a little bit. And no one wanted an audience for that.

But he hadn't. He'd been quiet after he got back from the Seavers', and she'd offered him the hot tea and toast she'd made. When they climbed into bed, he'd simply held her for a long time, fitting his long, firm body against hers, and stroking her hair like a talisman without speaking until she was nearly asleep.

And then he'd started talking, in a low, rambling murmur, about his childhood. The memories were a little disjointed, and without context Lanie had a hard time following some of it, but the point wasn't for her to understand what Will was relating about growing up with Mike as his absentee dad, and his mom doing the best she could on her own, but simply to listen.

So she did. And when his hand wandered away from her hair and down her body, caressing her breasts and smoothing over her belly, she'd turned over and opened herself up to him, heart, mouth, and sex.

She was fairly sure he cried at one point, the rusty, hard-earned tears that were the only kind most men seemed able to shed, and in the end he'd driven into her with such intensity that she knew she'd left half-moon marks on his shoulders where her fingernails had bitten into the skin. And when he came, he'd roared, thrusting over and over until he'd emptied himself of everything he had, collapsing into a deep sleep minutes later, with his arm still circled around her.

And that was it, Lanie thought, rubbing her cheek against his collarbone now. They'd slept until noon, but when they got up he'd been fine, teasing her with kisses and dragging her into a steaming shower while she was still half asleep.

He'd woken her up the rest of the way very effectively while they were in there.

And that was part of the mystery of Will DeMaio, she realized. Not that he wasn't grieving for his father, or letting loose any of his justified rage that the man had been willing to kill him for little more than a few bucks and a place to stay for a while, because he was. He was doing it in his own way, in his own time. What stuck in her throat was the idea that she might not be around at the end of the process. That she might never have the chance to put together all the pieces of the puzzle.

"Jackson said the highways are fine now," he said, setting her away from him. "If you have to leave tonight, that is."

Her heart sang, a cheery little pop tune. He didn't look happy about the idea at all.

"I was thinking I might take an extra day," she said slowly. *Don't screw this up now,* that hateful voice in her head whispered. *Don't push your luck.* "If, well . . . if you wouldn't mind me staying, that is."

"Your investigative skills go right down the toilet when you've had one too many orgasms, don't they?" His eyes were that warm Caribbean blue again. Screw Florida on her next vacation—*that* was where she wanted to go, the Island of Will.

"Well, I don't want to . . . you know, wear out my welcome. Push my luck." God, she sounded pathetic. What happened to powerful, confident Lanie Burke? Mentally, she kicked herself. Of course, *that* Lanie hadn't been faced with a good-bye in a few hours' time.

"It doesn't have anything to do with luck, Lanie," Will said, taking her hand in his. When she looked up at him, their eyes locked, and she felt her heart turn over, just once, a hopeful, joyful little hop.

"It's not about luck or karma or fate," he went on. He was serious now, and even so, she couldn't help admiring the beautiful line of his jaw as he spoke, the full, lovingly shaped mouth. "It's about what you do, what choices you make. There's no such thing as bad luck."

"So you're saying the wedding buffet disaster was my fault,

then?" She arched an eyebrow at him, but she had to bite her lip to keep from smiling.

He paused, looking at the ceiling as if he was going to find the answer conveniently written there. "I'm saying . . . that maybe all the choices you made led you here. To this particular weekend, to that particular bar."

"So you're saying . . . meeting you *was* fate." She crossed her arms over her chest, watching in delight as he realized she'd cornered him. "In fact, I think what you're saying is you *are* my fate. Is that right?"

"I think what I'm saying is you're *my* fate." He smirked, proud of himself, and then added, "And I'm your good luck charm. Or something."

"I don't think you have any idea what you're talking about anymore." She laughed, and leaned forward to whisper, "But I like the idea that it's *your* good luck I'm going to stay another day. And it's your good luck that I may invite you to stay with me in the city. I'm fairly certain we won't have to solve any murders, either. New York's crime rate has gone way down."

"You drive a hard bargain, Lanie Burke." He grinned and lunged at her, rolling on top of her with a long, hot kiss. "I have a feeling I'm going need a long, long time to figure you out."

"Years, I bet," she murmured, groaning when his fingers found her nipple and tweaked it playfully.

"Well, you're in luck," he answered, and she melted when she saw that adorable twinkle in his eye. "Because I'm pretty sure I'm free."

Dear Reader:

The one thing I love more than a delicious romance is a great mystery. Even my childhood copies of *Jane Eyre* and *Wuthering Heights* were shelved right alongside my Nancy Drews. So when I was given the chance to combine the two genres, I jumped at it (figuratively, of course). Mixing in some humor made the whole process even more fun, and after some brainstorming about hot sex, dead bodies (not together, naturally), and laugh-out-loud situations, "Single White Dead Guy" was born.

I hope you enjoyed reading it as much as I loved writing it. And look for my next Brava romance/mystery, *Murder in the Hamptons,* in May 2005!

Happy reading,

Amy Garvey

Fast Boys

Jennifer Apodaca

One

"Tess? Tess!"

"What?" Tess Collins turned from the TV. Then she flushed when all three of her long-time friends burst out laughing. Damn, she was caught lusting after Ark Underwood while watching his interview in the NASCAR winner's circle after winning the race. The four of them gathered every week during the NASCAR season to watch the race and root for their favorite drivers. Ark was Tess's favorite. To head off the onslaught of teasing, Tess said, "I was thinking about one of my patients." Yeah, right. She never thought about her patients in her marriage and family therapy practice the way she thought about Ark Underwood.

Josie ate the last brownie from the plate on the coffee table and said, "Ha! You were thinking about Ark. And not as a patient or you wouldn't get to see him naked."

Nikki laughed. "Who could blame her? Look at the cover of *People* magazine." She picked up the magazine where Ark was this month's featured "Fast Boy of NASCAR." Against the background of a race car track, Ark stood with his arms crossed over his well-formed chest while staring at the camera with his mysterious hazel eyes and wicked half smile.

Tess sighed. She was in for it now from her friends. But she had to admit, Ark looked hot on the cover. Nicknamed "Hollywood," Ark was a natural-born bad boy. The man was made for sex. But that wasn't why her friends were warming up to their topic. It was because they cared about her. And since the last of Tess's close family, her grandmother, had died a few months back, her friends had been on a crusade to get Tess into a relationship with a man.

They felt it was time Tess worked through her fears and took a leap into a relationship with a man so she didn't end up old and alone like her grandmother.

Tess tried to relieve their worries. She picked up the tabloid, *The Breaking Buzz*, and said, "I'm dating Fred Ranger. He's a journalist."

Gwen fixed her silver-blue eyes on Tess. "Bet you haven't slept with him. That you are holding him off while fantasizing about Ark."

She wasn't holding Fred off. Not exactly. "We're planning to go away for a weekend soon." Someday. She wasn't sure how she felt about Fred yet. He traveled, was ambitious to become an on-air entertainment journalist, and he had great stories about people he had met. He was different from her usual nine-to-five suit-type of dates. They had been safe. Okay, boring. Tess knew she had dated those men because she shied away from men who stirred real passion in her. Her parents had had real passion, and it led to a turbulent marriage, and finally to their deaths in a car accident when Tess was fifteen. That made Tess cautious in relationships with men.

But she was taking a chance on Fred. He was different; he wanted her opinions on his work. Asked her advice on how to approach different people he needed to interview. He seemed to value her. Tess hoped that when she slept with Fred she'd feel sexual passion, a great orgasm. But not the darker side of passion that drove people to crazy behavior.

Josie sat forward. "Oh, yeah? *When* are you going away with Fred?"

Figures Josie would nail her. "I haven't committed yet." He'd been pushing more and more lately. He wanted a weekend with her. He had said he liked to be prepared ahead of time. Tess assumed that meant he wanted to create a romantic scene.

Gwen, the mom figure of their group, said, "Why? What's holding you back? Is there something off about Fred?"

Nikki shook the *People* magazine. "Ark Underwood is holding her back."

"He is not!" Tess said, but it was true. Embarrassing, but true. She had a PhD in marriage and family therapy, and she had been a licensed therapist for a few years now. And yet, she shielded herself by holding on to a fantasy built around her one meeting with Ark when they were kids. Tess's father, a sports photographer, had been doing shots on the beach of Ark's dad, a famous stunt car driver. Tess had been nine, and Ark around twelve or thirteen. They had played in the waves to pass the time. Suddenly, Tess had gotten caught in a riptide. She could still feel the terror of the current dragging her under. But then Ark had grabbed her hair, gotten an arm around her, and dragged her to the shore.

It had been Ark's dad who scooped her up into his arms and soothed her, while at the same time pulling Ark into his side and telling him how proud he was of his son.

Her parents had yelled at her for getting in the way. Tess had always been in the way of her parents' jet-setting lifestyle.

"Hey! Tess!"

She blinked and saw the three of them staring at her—again—with Nikki waving the stupid *People* magazine. "All right." She grinned. "So maybe I'm a little hung up on Ark. Or my fantasy of Ark. Big deal."

Josie stood up. "Well, then, we will fix that. Stay right here." She headed to the foyer table by the front door and picked up Tess's laptop case.

Tess frowned at her. "What are you doing?"

Josie sat between Nikki and Tess on the floor, took out the laptop, and set it up on the coffee table. "We're going to heal you, Doctor."

Tess groaned. They had done this since their college days.

When they wanted to change a behavior or something along those lines, they wrote an e-mail and sent it to all four of them. It was a kind of therapy. That's what she got for hanging out with women who all had PhDs or MDs. They just weren't normal.

And Tess loved them all. They were her family.

"All right." Josie turned the laptop toward Tess. "Sign on to your Internet service."

She narrowed her eyes. "What are we doing exactly?"

Josie grinned. "Ark Underwood is ruining your sex life. We're going to fix that by pointing out all his flaws."

Nikki clapped her hands. "Now, this sounds like fun!"

Gwen jumped up. "Wait, let me get some wine. We need wine!" She raced off to the kitchen.

Once they were all settled with glasses of wine, and after a great deal of giggling, Tess came up with the e-mail:

ARK UNDERWOOD AND SEX THERAPY

Professional Assessment of Ark Underwood, the hot Fast Boy of NASCAR, known for being a bad boy. The very personality that drives him to succeed and win also has some serious drawbacks for personal relationships.

1. Self-centered and used to being the center of attention. A woman with a career would threaten his over-inflated manhood.
2. All flash but no substance. Called "Hollywood" for his brat antics, Ark is probably as shallow as his reputation. Can't hold a conversation unless the subject is about his penis or race car.
3. He has a competitive, risk-taking personality that drives him on to the next conquest. Could even suffer from erectile dysfunction if he doesn't have the adrenaline rush of a new babe or some other sexual device.
4. Serious commitment phobia since he never stays

with any woman very long. Probably harkens back to self-centeredness, competitive streak, and risk-taking traits.

5. In short, Ark Underwood needs a mother, not a girlfriend or life partner. Who wants to sleep with a man who needs a mother?

So, in conclusion, I declare myself free of my fantasy of Ark Underwood. The next time my sometime-date, Fred, asks me on a long weekend, I am there!

"Perfect!" Josie declared. "Send it!"

After two glasses of wine, Tess was mellow. She clicked onto all three of her friends' e-mail addresses and sent the e-mail.

Tess came home later than usual after a long day at the office and a ninety-minute workout at karate. She was beat. She locked her front door and started flipping on lights as she headed toward her bedroom and a shower.

She detoured when the phone rang and picked it up by her bed. "Hello?"

"Hi, Tess. Miss me?"

"Fred! I didn't know you were back in town." She hadn't seen him in over a week. She glanced at herself in the mirror over her dresser. Dressed in her karate gi with her long wavy brown hair pulled back in a ponytail, and what little makeup she wore sweated off, she wasn't up to a date tonight.

"Just got in. I have a surprise for you."

Tess relaxed and sat down on the bed. He'd be tired, too, if he just got home. "What's that?"

"Tickets for us to the NASCAR race on Sunday. And pit passes."

She perked up. "Really? That sounds like fun."

"There's more. I also booked us a room at the Speedway Hotel. We have the room from Thursday afternoon until Sunday. I'm hoping you'll stay with me, Tess. We'll be hot together."

His voice had an interesting promise. Fred was nice looking with his brown hair and blue eyes. He had the face of a guy who could make it on TV. Not extraordinary, but a firm profile and pleasant. She liked him, and yet . . .

Ark. God, she was just stupid. Fred was here and real; Ark was a fantasy.

"Yes, Fred. It sounds great. I can meet you at the hotel after I see my patients on Thursday." Tess only had a group session on Friday, and Josie could cover for her. They shared an office suite. Her group knew and trusted Josie since she often sat in on the sessions with her expertise as a sex therapist.

"I'm looking forward to it, Tess. I missed you." He took a breath she could hear on the phone, then added, "I'll be ready for you when you get there Thursday."

Tess hung up. It was time she got past her Ark fantasy and her fear of passion. She was determined to go and have a good time with Fred.

Ark Underwood spent Thursday at the California Speedway track in Fontana, California. His crew was going over the car before storing it away for the night. He'd done some practice runs, and things were looking good.

He could feel the promise of a win on Sunday. He was pumped. Ready. Ark hadn't won a race in California. His bad boy rep made him both loved and hated here, and he had something to prove. This was going to be his race, his win, and his chance to prove he was proud of his nickname.

Hollywood.

He'd earned that nickname because his dad had been a well-known stunt driver before he suddenly died when Ark was sixteen. The joke was that he thought himself from Hollywood royalty, one of the sex-drugs-and-rock-'n-roll brat pack, and he considered himself too good for the Southern Boys that dominated NASCAR. Every time Ark lost his temper on the track, everyone shrugged and asked one another what they could expect from a Hollywood brat.

Ironically, now Ark was sponsored by a major Hollywood movie studio.

In three days, on Sunday, Ark was going to show them all exactly what they could expect from Hollywood Ark Underwood.

His best friend, Giles, brought his car into pit road. Ark watched while Giles unhooked his restraints, took off his helmet, and climbed out of the race car. He looked hot and sweaty with his dark hair damp and matted from his helmet. But his brown eyes and easy smile indicated he was pleased with his car. Ark went up and slapped him on the back. "Not bad. Not as good as me, but not bad."

Giles took the hat his crew chief held out to him and put it on his head. "Today's just practice, Hollywood. Sunday, I'll leave you in my dust."

Ark laughed and asked, "We on for tonight?"

Giles nodded. "Meet you in the sports bar about six."

"Dinner and a movie. Hell, Giles, we're getting old."

"I'm only twenty-nine. You're the old man at thirty. Besides, you've been shying away from the ladies. I keep tellin' ya to try the blue pill."

"Fuck off," Ark responded, then slapped Giles on the back and headed off the track.

A young woman sidled up beside him. Ark glanced over at her. "Heidi, what are you doing here?" He'd known Heidi for a couple years. A Paris Hilton look-a-like, she hung around the track or the NASCAR hangouts and slept with whoever had a hard-on. Ark was all for sex; hell, he loved sex. But he'd grown up in the last few years and was getting more discriminating. Sex for the sake of sex bored him. Now he wanted to make love to a woman, not screw a girl. Hell, maybe he was getting old.

"Maureen got me in." She smiled. "I have a lot of connections. I always get in."

Damn, he was going to have to talk to his publicist. Again. Maureen Michaels had been his publicist for seven years. The studio hired her to parlay his bad boy image into the right kind of publicity. That was what they told Ark, but Ark knew that he had been used to give the niece of the studio head a career. Maureen had wanted to be a publicist, so her uncle had created an agency for her and given her Ark as a client. Ark had always been her biggest client. And for a few years, Maureen did a great job.

But ever since her divorce a year and a half ago, she was focusing in on Ark too much, pushing too hard to keep his name in the media. Ark didn't want to go to clubs with socialites and party girls. It bored him. Maureen, however, was pushing to do the social scene, especially right before a race.

Ark had told her last week to back off.

So now she sent a groupie—probably to entice him to a club. He realized Heidi was talking and forced himself to pay attention.

"I overheard you talking to Giles. Why don't you come see me at the club tonight? I'm way more interesting than dinner and a movie." She leaned in, her long, straight blond hair brushing his arms. "And you won't need Viagra with me."

More like penicillin, Ark thought. Even in his horniest days, he'd had standards. "Sorry, Heidi, but I already promised Giles. See ya around." He strode off.

"I'll be around!" she called after him.

Tess was a little overdressed for a sports bar. Her apple green halter dress stood out among the jeans-and-shorts crowd. There were four big screen TVs blaring NASCAR, BUSCH, and INDY races. Tess loved the races as much as anyone, but when she had arrived at the hotel and Fred had said he wanted to take her to dinner, this wasn't what she had in mind. The menu was mostly beer, hamburgers, and variations of Buffalo wings.

They took their seats across from each other at a polished round table with a big screen TV rising up like a cliff over her left shoulder.

Tess was about to suggest another restaurant when Fred's cell phone rang. He pulled it out and looked at the screen. "Sorry, Tess, I have to take this." He put the phone to his ear. "Yeah?"

The waitress arrived. Tess ordered iced tea.

So, okay, maybe she wasn't fully committed to the weekend, to sex with Fred, or she'd have ordered a beer or some wine. What would Josie say about that? Tess wondered.

Fred pulled the phone away from his face and ordered a beer. As the cocktail waitress moved off, Fred went back to his call. "He's coming out now?" He paused, then added, "Got it." He hung up and put his phone away. Then Fred reached across the table and took her hand. "You're the most beautiful woman in here, Tess. I'm so lucky to be with you."

She smiled, feeling her irritation at the phone call lessen. "Thank you."

"I have a little bit of a confession."

She squeezed his hand. "What confession?" She was in the mood for seduction.

He fixed his blue gaze on her face. "I knew you were the woman for me when I read your e-mail. We'll make a great team."

Tess blinked, trying to follow him. "What e-mail?" She hadn't e-mailed him this week.

He grinned at her. "I was pretty sure you sent it to me by accident, but that e-mail told me so much about you." He leaned forward and took hold of her hand. "About your fantasies."

Fantasies . . . oh, no! Horror slammed into Tess. She knew what had happened. The e-mail she had composed with her friends on Sunday—she had sent it to Josie, Gwen, and Nikki. Fred's e-mail address sat right between Gwen and Nikki in her address book.

What did she want to bet that she had accidentally clicked on Fred's e-mail address instead of Gwen's or Nikki's? Or in addition to Gwen's and Nikki's? Oh, God. This was awful, and unethical.

And exactly what the hell was Fred getting at? She pulled her hand from his hold. "What e-mail?" She repeated her question to make sure she had her facts straight.

Fred lifted his beer and took a drink while watching her. "The e-mail with your professional assessment of Ark Underwood."

A sinking feeling mixed with clear realization. She'd said the next time Fred asked her away for a weekend . . . Tess narrowed her gaze. She had misjudged Fred. He was after something more than a weekend of making love with her. This whole thing, the weekend at the Speedway Hotel, tickets to the NASCAR race . . . it wasn't a coincidence. One thing she knew for sure, she wasn't wrong about Fred's ambition. She controlled her rising anger. "What are you after?"

The waitress arrived and set down their drinks and a bill. The roar of car engines from the big screen TVs competed with the loud conversations around them. The waitress finished and moved off.

Fred assessed her with his blue eyes. "I'm after the same thing you are—to show the world who Ark Underwood really is. The beauty of it for you is that you get to screw Underwood, both literally and figuratively."

Tess stood up. She glanced at her iced tea but refrained from dumping it on him. She didn't know what his plan was, but she was not going to be a part of it.

Fred reached out and snagged her wrist.

Tess took a breath to stay in control. She hated losing control. She glanced down at his hand gripping her wrist, then up to his flat blue eyes. "I'm going to give you five seconds to let go."

He sneered at her. "You either sit down and listen to me, or I'm going to forward your e-mail to every newspaper in Southern California."

Tess considered breaking his hand that gripped her wrist. But then she'd never know exactly what he was trying to accomplish. She sat down. "Let go of my wrist."

Fred must have gotten a good look at her face because he released her. Then he said, "I'm going to fulfill your fantasy for you, Tess, so listen up. Ark Underwood will be down here any minute, according to my source that just called me. You are going to meet up with him and seduce him. He's got a rep for being a horn dog, so he'll go for you."

She said nothing, only lifted an eyebrow. Inside, she bubbled with anger.

"And while you have him naked and happy, you're going to find out some information for me."

Years of karate had taught her self-control, but Fred was testing her resistance to creating a public scene by smacking him. "Am I?"

"You are. Or after I send this e-mail to all the newspapers, I'll send it on to the licensing board for Marriage and Family Therapists, and they'll have some serious questions about your ethics in trying to destroy a public figure you've never even met."

He thought he could blackmail her. Right now, she was damned glad she'd never told Fred that she had indeed met Ark once. "Keep going."

Fred nodded, apparently convinced he had her where he wanted her. "Here's the deal. You know I did that series of articles on *Exclusive Sex Revives Dying Town*. I heard some rumors tying Ark Underwood to those places, but I haven't been able to get any hard evidence. Now my source that helped me with those articles has evidence."

Annoyed at her stab of disappointment in Ark, she shoved that away and focused. Fred was going to try and use her to destroy Ark Underwood. She needed to know how and then find a way to stop him. "And?"

"The evidence is some pictures of Ark naked as the day he was born and engaged in some wild sex with several women at once. This source is blackmailing Ark for money or the source will release the pictures to the mainstream media." Fred stopped talking and took a long drink of his beer.

Tess fought to hold her temper. Being a public figure sometimes had to suck big-time. Whatever Ark did sexually wasn't anyone else's business as long as he wasn't hurting anyone. She winced, though, when she remembered the things she'd put in that e-mail. Erectile dysfunction, needing variety to get it up, even sexual devices . . . and calling Ark shallow.

She couldn't believe this was happening to her. One stupid

e-mail she'd written as sort of a joke, as a way to help her let the fantasy of Ark go, and look at what her actions had done. Fred had set up this whole weekend to blackmail Tess into destroying Ark. His blue eyes shined with passionate ambition. How had she missed it? She was a trained therapist, but she had ignored her own instincts. In a flat voice, Tess said, "You think Ark Underwood is your ticket from tabloid reporter to an entertainment journalist spot on TV, don't you?"

Fred leaned forward. "You bet your ass. First the talk show circuit, then an offer . . . but first, you have to get Ark on tape talking about the pictures of him having sex with multiple women at once, and his need for orgies and sex toys. I have a little recording device in a hairpin that you can—"

She hit her limit. So much angry adrenaline poured into her bloodstream that her arms and legs trembled as she stood up. Even her voice shook as she glared at Fred and said, "No. Go ahead and do your best to destroy my career. But I'm going to do everything in my power to make sure the media knows that e-mail is a hoax."

"You'll ruin yourself if you do!"

She looked down at the worm and hated herself for having done the very thing she often saw her patients do—she'd convinced herself that Fred's ambition was healthy. But his interest in her opinions hadn't been personal; it had been professional. He'd used her from the first, and she had refused to see that. So he would think she'd put her career over her ethics. She set him straight. "I'd destroy myself if I didn't." In a blind rage, she turned to leave and slammed into another man. Tess looked up and damn near choked.

Ark Underwood. Could this get any worse?

He reached out, curling his large hands around her upper arms to steady her. "Hey, sugar, you okay?"

"Uhh . . ." Tess couldn't get her brain to work. It was his hazel eyes fixed on her with concern. And his hands on her bare skin. And—God he was a hunk. He even smelled hunky, all leather and spice. Ark Underwood in person looked like . . . sex. What was wrong with her? Tess forced herself to step back. "I'm fine. And very sorry for running into you." *Not.* Not a bit sorry. She kind of wished she'd plowed him down to the ground and landed on top of him.

It was her anger. She'd let her emotions get out of control, and now she was thinking of sexually assaulting Ark Underwood.

Tess reached out for her brimming iced tea and took a drink.

"No problem," Ark grinned down at her. "Run into me anytime you like."

Dear God, could he be flirting with her? Tess opened her mouth and prayed for a clever answer when Fred jumped up out of his chair and used his shoulder to get in front of her.

Tess's iced tea sloshed over her fingers as she reached out to the table with her other hand to steady herself.

"Ark Underwood!" Fred said in a booming voice. "What's your comment about the rumor that there are pictures of you engaged in orgies? Will you pay blackmail money to keep the pictures out of the mainstream media?"

"Fred!" Tess yelled at him. "Stop it!"

Then she saw over Fred's shoulder that he held up his cell phone camera to get a picture of Ark. She lifted her gaze to Ark's face.

Boredom was stamped over his hard-cut features. The shallow cleft in his chin went flat with disinterest. His hazel eyes shadowed. "Get lost."

"Fred, please!" Tess took her hand off the table to tug on his arm.

Fred shoved her back, then reached into his front pants pocket and pulled out a folded sheet of paper. "And this e-mail is from a therapist who claims you have a whole list of issues. Is that why you go to sex shops? You can't get it up without help? You have mommy issues?" He held up the paper with one hand and snapped a picture of Ark looking at it with the other.

Tess saw it all through a thickening haze of red fog. Everything slowed into underwater motion. There was a buzzing in her ears that fed her rage.

Fred was using her e-mail to destroy Ark. He couldn't get

legitimate facts on the NASCAR star, so he was twisting her e-mail to get the story. The story Fred thought would propel him into television journalism. She had to stop him. Now.

"No comment," Ark said as if Fred had asked him about the weather.

Fred didn't even flinch. "What about the sex orgies? I'm told the pictures show you . . ."

Tess looked down at the sweaty cold glass of tea in her hand. She lifted her arm high and centered it over Fred's head; then she poured out the entire glass. She hoped, prayed, the tea would destroy the e-mail and the cell phone.

Fred jumped. "Shit, what the . . ." He turned around, and his blue gaze slammed into Tess. His face flamed red beneath the dripping tea. "My cell phone! You goddamned bitch!" He lunged at her.

Two

Ark reached out to grab a handful of the prick-who-had-to-be-a-reporter's shirt before he could attack the woman.

But all he got was a handful of air. He saw it and still didn't believe it.

The woman had seen the attack coming and stepped to the side, then swung her foot to knock the man's feet out from under him and pinned him facedown on the table.

She had his arm wrenched up behind his back.

His cell phone plopped to the ground, but he still held the e-mail in his other hand. It appeared to be undamaged from the iced-tea bath.

The woman said in a very reasonable tone, "Fred, you are seriously pissing me off."

Ark couldn't take his eyes off of her. She had long, wavy brown hair, expressive brown eyes, and one hell of an attitude, all wrapped up in a kick-ass package. The dress she wore hugged her breasts and exposed her slender, muscular back. The dress covered her ass, but the way she leaned over the reporter offered him a mouthwatering view.

She looked up at him. "This would be a good time for you to leave, Mr. Underwood."

The impact of her gaze slammed into him. She had to be the

most unusual, and sexy, woman he'd come across in years. He closed the distance between them. "But things are just getting interesting." He barely glanced down at the reporter. It was the woman that appealed to him. "What's your name?"

"Tess." Then she added, "Take my advice, Fred here is a tabloid reporter trying to use you to get a headline. Leave now and I'll help him understand that he needs to rethink his plans." She jerked his arm slightly, twisting it farther up behind his back.

"Ouch! Goddammit, Tess! Get off of me!"

Ark dropped his gaze to Fred. His neck was arched up and streaked with swollen veins as he fought her hold, his face a sweaty red around blazing blue eyes. He held the e-mail clutched in his hand. Ark seized the e-mail and read through it. Then saw the signature line, *Dr. Tess Collins, Marriage and Family Therapy.*

His gut went stone cold. The warmth he felt, that flicker of interest in Tess, died. He looked up at her, at the *doctor*. And for a second, he thought he saw a shimmer of tears and regret. But she blinked, and all he saw was determination. Just another shrink who thought she knew it all. He held up the e-mail. "This is you?"

Fred answered, "That's her. She wrote that e-mail! Called you a mama's boy. Says you can't get it up! What's your comment?"

Ark turned to Fred. "Shut up."

Fred's blue eyes froze with fear. He shut up.

He looked back to see Tess watching him. She said, "Yes, it's me, and I'm very sorry. I sent that e-mail to Fred by accident, but the damage is done. I'll do whatever it takes to fix it."

Ark looked into Tess's eyes, into her brown eyes with amber flecks, and was surprised by the flash of hurt he felt. She had really intrigued him; something about the way she handled Fred made him think she was honest. Until he'd read the e-mail. Shit. Ark dropped the e-mail back on the table by Fred's nose. "Fix what, sugar? That's me, all flash and no substance."

Fred angled his head around to sneer at Tess. "Guess you won't be getting laid by your fantasy now."

Ark stared at Tess. Her face flushed, and white lines appeared around her mouth. But her pressure on Fred's arm she held behind his back never changed.

Ark had the urge to reach out and slam Fred's head into the table. Or ignore Fred altogether and sweep Tess away to talk about her fantasies. Turns out that he was still interested in the doc, in spite of her e-mail. But a hand on his shoulder checked the urge.

He turned to see Giles standing there with another man. Behind them were another dozen or more people watching the scene. Damn, he'd been so intent on Tess, he hadn't noticed the growing scene. He supposed he'd see himself in the papers tomorrow.

Giles grinned. "This all looks interesting. Are any of us going to jail? Getting on the six o'clock news? Need an ambulance? Or maybe the nice manager, Al here, can help?"

That was Giles, always the good guy. He swept in right on cue to solve everything with calm and reason. He was like that on the track, too, appearing like a gentleman who plays by the rules, right up until he decided to go for it, leaving all the drivers behind him stunned. Giles operated on pure charm and deceit. Ark shifted his gaze to the manager. He had his name stamped onto a white rectangle nametag pinned to his black shirt.

"What's the problem here, Mr. Underwood?" Al inquired.

Ark glanced at Fred. "This reporter tried to attack the lady."

Al puffed out his chest. Then he had to let the air out in order to bend down and see Fred's face. "Sir, you'll have to come with me."

"Get this bitch off of me!"

Tess let him go and stepped back, but she didn't say a word to defend herself. She just stood there quietly while Al convinced Fred to go with him. Fred had the presence of mind to remember to pick up his wet camera phone from the floor and the dry e-mail Ark had dropped back on the table. Then he glared at Tess and said, "You can get your suitcase out of the Dumpster, bitch."

Tess didn't say a word as she watched the manager steer Fred away. The crowd faded back to their drinks and Buffalo wings.

Ark looked down at Tess and was slapped with a huge case of lust. What the hell was wrong with him? She was just another woman who somehow wanted to capitalize off his fame and money.

But his gut told him something else. She'd tried to prevent Fred from getting a story from him. Ark wanted to know more about her.

She met his gaze. "I'm sorry. This is my fault. I'll do what I can to make this right."

Before he could react, she smoothly turned and left.

Ark watched her walk through the sports bar to the door that led to the lobby of the hotel. Oh, hell. She was going to get her suitcase before Fred got back to the room. As best as Ark could determine, Tess was staying with him, but had been somehow blindsided by Fred having the e-mail. He couldn't let her confront that idiot again alone.

Tess punched the elevator button six or seven times until her finger hurt.

Damn, damn, damn. And she had no one to blame but herself. She wrote the e-mail that triggered this whole nightmare.

Could she have been any more stupid? To actually have believed Fred cared enough about her to book a weekend around the races that she loved? Ha, he'd just wanted to use her to advance his own career, and destroy another career in the process.

She punched the elevator button again and told herself not to think about Ark. About the look on his face when he read that e-mail.

"You're going to break your finger."

She whirled around, and her mouth dropped open. "Ark!"

"That's a relief. I was afraid you'd forgotten me already." His mouth curved wickedly.

Tess narrowed her eyes. And tried not to notice how good the short-sleeved, black button-down shirt looked on him. Or the way his jeans sat on his hips. Or the fact that his sun-streaked light brown hair looked good against his tanned skin. And his eyes . . . deep mysterious hazel eyes that made her think of—

Sex.

She was a sick woman, and she should know. Sheesh. "Umm, is there something I can do for you?"

Ark leaned forward, bracing his hand over her head on the wall. "Funny that you should ask. Give Giles here your key-card to your room. He'll put your suitcase in my room while we're having dinner."

Huh? "We're not having dinner." She glanced away from Ark to see Giles. He looked amused.

Ark got her attention back. "Of course we are, sugar. We have to find out how accurate your diagnosis of me is. And I want to hear all about your fantasies of me."

Tess just bet he did. He probably got off on the idea of women fantasizing about him. "I don't think so." She tried not to inhale the clean scent of leather and spice.

Ark didn't move. "Let me put this another way. First, you're not going up to the room to get your suitcase alone."

Like she was going to take orders from him. "I can take care of myself." Since that didn't impress him, she added, "I'm a black belt."

"I'm guessing Fred-the-prick didn't know that. But about dinner, I believe we need to come up with a strategy to deal with the press—once your little e-mail gets out, that is."

Guilt slammed into her. What could she say? She had to go to dinner with him to help him. "That's a dirty trick," she pointed out while reaching into her purse for her keycard. She knew damn well he was manipulating her, but he was right; she owed him all the help she could give him. She pulled out her card.

"Just let me get my suitcase, then I'll meet—hey!" Ark snatched the card from her fingers.

He turned and handed the card to Giles, then looked back at her. "Room number?"

"Four-oh-two." She relented. So she'd get her suitcase after dinner. What difference did it make? *The difference,* her rational brain pointed out, *is that I'll have to go to Ark's room to get it.*

Ark put his hand on the small of her back. "There's a steakhouse a few blocks over. We'll take your car."

Fifteen minutes later, they sat in a booth at the restaurant. Tess ordered a glass of Cabernet and followed that with an order for steak cooked medium rare, baked potato, and a kill-me-now chocolate cake.

She tended to eat when she was nervous.

Ark ordered steak and ribs, rice, cole slaw, and a slab of corn bread.

Tess didn't think *he* was nervous, just hungry. She sipped her wine, pretended it was courage, and said, "Ark, this whole thing is a big mistake. I never meant for Fred to get a hold of that e-mail."

He studied her in the dim lighting across the Formica table. "How did he get it, then? Why did you write it in the first place?"

She had debated what she'd say for the last fifteen minutes. But he deserved the truth. "It was a cross between a game and self-therapy. My friends believe my . . . uh . . . infatuation with you is interfering with real relationships with men. Other men can't live up to you. So we wrote the e-mail as kind of a joke, giving you flaws to destroy the fantasy." Wow, Tess finally found something more humiliating than her yearly gynecological appointment. She took a quick but deep drink of her wine and finished her pathetic story. "So I wrote the e-mail and meant to send it only to my friends' e-mail accounts. But I must have clicked on Fred's e-mail by mistake."

He didn't say anything, just stared at her.

Tess knew the trick. Cops used it, and so did therapists. But still she fell for it, compelled to fill the uncomfortable silence.

"I never meant the e-mail to get out! It was just a tool of therapy."

Ark took a drink of his wine and said, "Let me see if I understand this. You have a case of lust for me, so you wrote an e-mail to cure yourself and accidentally sent it off to Fred, a tabloid reporter. Whom you were going to spend the weekend with?"

She had to laugh at herself. "I'm afraid that's about it."

He laughed, too, and then settled his gaze on her. "Why me, Tess?"

That surprised her. She hadn't thought he'd care why. Didn't he have thousands of women throwing themselves at him? She ran her thumb and forefinger up and down the stem of her wineglass. "I guess because I met you once when we were kids. I know it's stupid." She saw no reason to lie to him. Not now, not after the e-mail that was going to cause him problems.

He looked surprised.

She went on before she chickened out. "My father was Miles Collins, the sports photographer. Your dad brought you with him for a shoot on a beach in San Clemente. You and I played in the waves while my dad did the shoot with your dad." She didn't mention her mother hovering around her father in her role as his greatest fan.

Ark's gaze sharpened as he thought for a second, then softened. "That was you? That scrawny little girl who got caught in the riptide?"

He remembered. She rushed on to just get it over with. "Yes. Anyway, I've followed your career. My friends and I are huge NASCAR fans. And . . ." She shrugged. How did she explain being such an idiot? Sitting across from the man made her fantasy seemed even more stupid. "Anyway the e-mail was half a joke and half a way to put you out of my mind." Tess slowed down and met his gaze to deal with the real issue. "I don't know what Fred's going to do with that e-mail, or if it can be fixed."

"There's no fixing it. I just deal. And win." He picked up his wineglass and drained it dry.

Tess stared at him. At his large hand around the glass, then up at his hazel eyes. What she saw there reached deep inside of her. There were layers to this man. "Winning fixes it?"

"No. Winning makes it worth it. Winning proves that I didn't get where I am because of my dad, or pity after my dad died, or by breaking faces. It proves I earned my place."

Tess got that. It made sense. "I'm sorry about your dad, Ark. I heard when he died. He seemed like a very nice man. I'm sure he'd be very proud of you."

Ark shrugged. "Maybe."

Beneath the charm and humor of Ark, there was a man who had suffered and endured. It made Tess even sorrier about her e-mail. She had cut the man when she had only been thinking about a cardboard fantasy. "What happens when you don't win?"

His face relaxed. "I break faces."

Tess studied him. "Not anymore. You're losing your bad boy touch, Hollywood. I can't remember the last time you got in a fight on the track."

"I can." He flexed his right hand in some kind of automatic gesture. "Seven years ago when I was twenty-three. I broke my hand when I tried to punch a driver who spun Giles and damn near killed him. Went home to my mom's house to recover. I was there one day when the school called. Bobbie, my youngest brother, had been in a fight. Again. It didn't take long to figure out that Bobbie was emulating me, his big brother. That was the day I decided to clean up my act and get control of my temper."

She knew much of Ark's history from following his career. After his dad died, his mom continued to let him race. Probably, Tess guessed, he needed to race. It was his connection to his dad. But she also knew he'd lost his same-sex parent, which was essentially his guide to manhood. Without his dad, he'd had to figure out himself how to be a man. To a sixteen-year-old boy, that often meant being aggressive and fighting. But Ark had recognized his destructive path and skidded to a stop to turn his behavior around. For his brothers—to be the role model of manhood his brothers needed.

That's what family meant to Ark.

Her stomach hollowed. It left her feeling off balance. She was growing to admire Ark for more than his driving. "The newspapers still call you the bad boy of NASCAR."

"It sells papers and tickets. And I give them reason occasionally. My publicist likes it; it gives her something to do."

Tess laughed. He had a great sense of humor.

Ark leaned his forearms on the table. "You know, Doc, you're very good. You've kept the conversation on me. But I want to learn more about you."

"There's not much to learn." She reached for her wine. It was easy to talk about him. She didn't want to talk about herself.

"But there is. I want to know all about your fantasy of me. Why would a beautiful woman like you choose a fantasy over a real man? Any man would be damn lucky to have you."

She sipped more wine and struggled for a way to deflect his question. "Who knows? Maybe I'm just not the passionate type."

"That is bullshit," he said in a soft voice.

Startled, she set her glass down and looked at him. "How would you know?"

He reached out and took hold of her hand. "Because you're a doctor and a black belt, both those things take passion. I know about going after what we want, Tess. I didn't get where I am by being indifferent. I got here by wanting it bad enough to suffer broken bones, concussions, humiliating loses . . . whatever it takes. And you didn't get a black belt in karate unless you took a few bruising punches, kicks, or suffered the pain it took to master the technique. So maybe you haven't been with the right man, but it's not lack of passion on your part."

She blinked. He wasn't what she expected. He was more . . . sexy, thoughtful, and yet, she could feel the physical strength in his hand. He was also honest. And what he said about the passion it took to succeed was true. She just hadn't thought about herself as passionate. "I can't believe I'm talking to you about this." She also couldn't believe she just said that. But it felt good to talk about it.

He shrugged. "Why not? Isn't talking what you do?" He looked down at his hand holding hers, then back up to her eyes. "You got me to talk."

"I just asked you questions." People liked to talk about themselves if you asked the right questions.

He held her gaze. "You were interested in what I had to say. In who I am. And I'm interested, very interested, in talking to you about passion and sex. Tell me about your desires, Tess." His voice was rich and seductive.

She blushed, shook her head, and reached for her glass of wine with her free hand.

He didn't laugh at her, but said, "How about I tell you mine? I'm tired of sex with girls after me for my fame or money. I want to make love with a woman who isn't after something from me, except honest pleasure." He turned her hand to rub his thumb along her palm.

His touch on her palm was firm, yet light. Frissons of pleasure and desire mixed with the wine to warm her skin. A craving for more of Ark's touch formed deep in her belly. Before she could think of a response that didn't include crawling over the table and into his lap, their waitress came with their meals.

Ark let go of her hand. After the waitress got their plates situated and brought them more wine, she left.

Tess busied herself slathering sour cream on her potato, a little salt and pepper on her steak, then cutting into her meat. Finally, she couldn't stand it. "How do you know I'm that woman? The woman who wants honest pleasure?"

Ark bit into a rib and chewed. He watched her for a second, then grinned, deepening the cleft in his chin. "You told me the truth about the e-mail. About yourself. No one would admit to a story like that unless it was the truth."

He had a point there.

He kept his intense hazel-colored gaze on her. "And we

have chemistry. You can't fake that. I knew from the first moment you ran into me."

Tess realized she hadn't had chemistry with Fred—she had been trying to force herself into another safe relationship that wouldn't cause her pain. That troubled her. Her life's work was about facing problems, not hiding from them. She ate some of her potato and got her thoughts in order.

He added, "I want to make love to you. I want to have the entire night to concentrate on you. Just you. Every single part of you."

Her breath shot up into her throat, while a tingling spread from her thighs straight up to her breasts. Tess ate some more of the tender steak and tried to look normal, not like a slut in heat. She needed a dose of reality to cool her lust. "Supposedly you like more than one woman at a time." If he was going to probe her weakness, and talk about sex, then it worked both ways.

"Are you asking me if I'm into the orgies? If the accusations Fred tossed around are true?"

She looked him in the eyes. "Yes."

The waitress came and cleared their plates, then brought Tess's cake and two forks.

Ark stared at her the entire time.

Finally they were alone again. Ark picked up the forks and handed her one while holding her stare. "No, Doc, I'm not into orgies or multiple partners. I like to focus on one woman. I want to see her, smell her, touch her, and know everything there is to know about her." He nudged her hand to take the fork from him and added, "And then drive myself into her until she explodes beneath me."

When his fingers touched hers, the contact slammed into her, and heat curled inside of her stomach. He made her want to lean closer to him, get closer to him. Okay, face it, she wanted to get naked with him. God. "But you don't know me." She took the fork and dropped her gaze to cut a piece of cake.

He reached out and caught her hand. "I know you don't

sleep around, have a conscience and care about your work, are disciplined enough to get a black belt, and don't tolerate idiots like Fred. I know you trust your friends."

She raised her eyebrows at that one. Though she was shocked at how much he did know. How much he had heard and processed.

He grinned. "Or you wouldn't have sent them the e-mail about me."

"True."

"And I know I'm that man who stirs your passion. I can see it in your eyes, feel it in the tension in your hand." He brought her hand to his mouth.

Tess watched him move his mouth over her hand, felt his lips brush her sensitive skin and shivered. A once in a lifetime chance to see what the whole passion thing was all about—with the very man she'd fantasized about for years.

He had saved her life once, and though he had been just a boy, Tess didn't think the grown man would hurt her. She really did feel she could trust Ark.

And damn it, she wanted him.

Three

Ark poured two glasses of wine from the wet bar/kitchen combo in his hotel suite. Then he walked toward the leather couch.

Tess sat there looking at a list of movies he'd handed her. He remembered her. The rush of fear when he looked over and realized Tess had been swept away by a riptide was part of the reason she stayed in his memory. His dad's obvious pride in him for getting her out of the riptide was another. But what really cemented the memory was what his dad said to him on the way home. *"Ark, I love you more than driving stunt cars. You know that, don't you? You, your brothers and your mom, you guys are my life."* As an adult now, Ark understood that his father had been upset at the coldness of Tess's parents. That he didn't want his family to ever feel as if they were in the way of his career. But at thirteen, he'd been a little surprised and embarrassed.

But those words had lived with Ark after his father died, a reminder of his dad's love and his belief in him. That memory had helped him deal with his dad's sudden death. Tess had no idea of the gift she had left him with.

And now she was here. Grown up from a scrawny kid to a warm, vibrant, and sexy woman.

It'd been years since he'd wanted a woman this badly. She was beautiful with her long brown hair cascading down over her shoulders, left bare by the halter top of her dress. Her brown eyes were on the movie list, but he could practically see her mind working.

He doubted she'd read a word of the list. Instead, he guessed that she was going over her decision to be here with him. Typical shrink.

But it was more than her looks that got him. It had been her honesty. She'd been in an awkward, humiliating position with that e-mail, and she'd told him the truth. She believed in the truth. Ark lived in a strange world where the press and media and, to be honest, his sponsors, agents, publicist, etc., created their own truths. Being the bad boy of NASCAR generated controversy that attracted more fans.

And a few drivers out to slam him into walls. He got along fine with most drivers now. But a few resented the media coverage he got. It was war out there on the track.

So Tess's honesty touched him. Writing an e-mail was such a shrink way of attacking a problem. Sex problem. A woman who earned a black belt had passion. A woman who earned a PhD had passion. What she'd lacked was a man she could trust.

Until now.

This was why he was determined to watch a movie and give her time to relax. He held the glass of wine out to her. "See anything?"

She jerked her head up. "Not really."

Ark sat down next to her on the couch. He took the list and tossed it onto the coffee table. "Tell me more about yourself. When did you get your black belt? What discipline is it in?"

She eased back against the couch. "Five years ago. One of my friends, Josie, and I both took karate in college and got involved. It's American-style karate. Now I teach a class."

Her eyes lit up. He could see that she loved karate. But he wanted to know more about the core of her. He decided to ask about her family. "A PhD and black belt . . . your family must be very proud. I bet your sisters and brothers don't give you a hard time. You could either analyze them to death or beat the crap out of them." He could smell the orange blossom scent—he thought it was from her hair. He wanted to touch the long wavy strands, wrapping them around his hand.

Tess looked away. "My parents died in a car accident over a decade ago. No brothers or sisters." She took a sip of wine, then turned back to him and said, "You have two brothers, right?"

Christ. He hadn't expected that about her folks. Her parents hadn't seemed like June and Ward Clever but to lose them both had to be awful. He also noticed she changed the subject, but left it alone. "Yeah, Nick and Bobbie. Nick's doing some stunt driving around finishing up college. He's good at it, just like our dad was. Bobbie is into football and girls. Mostly girls." First year of college, the boy had hormones the size of Rhode Island. "My mom held us all together after my dad died." Who held Tess together? He leaned forward and set down his wine.

"You're close with your mom and brothers?"

Ark put his arm around her, resting his hand on her bare shoulder. "Yes. They'll be around this weekend, so you'll probably meet them. But I'm more interested in you. How old were you when your parents were in the accident?"

"Fifteen, it was a long time ago. Does your family come to all your races?"

He moved his hand to rub circles around the curve of her shoulder, enjoying the feel of her firm muscles beneath soft, smooth skin. "In California, they do. Our home is in Valencia. Otherwise, they fly in if they have the time or inclination. I usually take a suite so there's plenty of room."

She tensed up. "They will stay here? I should leave." She sat forward.

Ark dropped his hand to her waist and was surprised at the stab of panic. He didn't want her to leave. "Tess, relax, they won't come until Saturday. It's a two-room suite, and this couch pulls out to a bed. You don't have to go."

"Oh." She didn't move.

Ark wondered what the hell her reaction to his family staying with him was about. "Tess, come here," he lifted her and pulled her onto his lap. Setting her firm ass on his thighs, it was all she could do to hang on to her wine. Which kept her from fighting him. Once he got her settled, he touched his hand to her face. "You're not leaving, not tonight. You had two glasses of wine at the restaurant and one here. I don't want you driving." She roused a protectiveness in him.

She took a breath.

Probably to tell him to go to hell. He didn't give her the chance. "I have two rooms. If you change your mind about sleeping with me, you're welcome to sleep in there."

She met his gaze. "I haven't changed my mind. I just thought . . . if your family was here . . . I wouldn't belong here."

He raised his eyebrows. "Why the hell not?" Most women tried to ingratiate themselves into his family. This was new. And if he wanted a woman friend in his hotel suite; he was thirty years old. He didn't have to ask his mother's permission, for Christ's sake.

She shifted on his lap. "Because, they are your family."

She was serious. Ark couldn't help but wonder why. Probably something to do with losing her parents so young and not having brothers or sisters. "Forget my family. All I want to think about tonight is you." He slid his hand into her hair—so thick and soft it slid sensually over his skin—and pulled her mouth to his.

She leaned into his kiss. Her mouth soft, her lips tasting like the wine. He wanted more, needed more. With gentle pressure from him, she opened her mouth. Her hot breath drove him crazy. He wanted to taste all of her and slid his tongue inside. She responded until he groaned as his cock strained against his pants to get to her rounded butt.

He broke the kiss. Took her wineglass and set it on the side table. Then he reached up under her heavy hair for the tie that held the top of her dress in place. "I like this dress, Doc. But I want to see your breasts." He pulled the tie open and tugged down the two ends. Leaving her bare.

Damn, she was hot. Full mounds topped with very erect nipples. A slight flush spread over the tops of her breasts and up her chest. *Can't have the doc thinking too much.* Ark took one full breast in his palm and drew his thumb back and forth across the distended nipple.

She shivered, her hands clutching his shoulders.

He wanted more. He leaned forward and took the other nipple into his mouth, suckling and moving the tip of his tongue on the pebbled surface.

She arched her back, and he took her more deeply in his mouth. Every time she shivered or squirmed, it was torture on his dick. Lifting his head, he looked up into her face.

Flushed. Swollen lips, and dark swollen nipples. She looked like a woman ready for sex. The way she responded to him was every man's wet dream. He had no idea why she thought otherwise. "I want to make love to you on a bed, Tess." He reached his hand down to her knee, then slid up to her smooth muscular thigh. "I want to pull off your dress, then your panties." He moved his hand higher, up to the edge of her panties around her thigh.

She stared at him, her brown eyes getting heavy with need.

"I can feel your heat from here." He drew his finger along the edge of her panties.

She licked her lips.

He was going to lick her lips. Both her mouth and between her legs. All night long. "Tell me you want me, Tess." He slid his finger under the elastic and touched her. Her heat made him groan.

She arched slightly against him. "I want you. I want to see you naked."

He could feel her holding back. That arch had been instinctive, seeking; then she had pulled back. He slid his finger between her folds and along her seam. God, she was wet. So damned hot. He felt the nub, gently circled it. "Sweetheart, I'll give you anything you want if you'll just open your legs a little more." He shifted her, pulling her back in the cradle of his left arm, using his hand to spread her thighs.

She tensed up.

He'd put her in a vulnerable position, so he spoke to her, wanting her to relax and trust him. "Lean back, let me hold you. I want to hold you against me while I touch you."

She relaxed.

He looked at her face, using all his self-control. "Close your eyes. Just feel me touching you."

She slid her eyes closed. Her mouth parted.

He tried not to think about her mouth. Just pleasuring her, getting her to trust him. Her clit was swelling, getting so wet his mouth went dry with his longing to taste her. He pressed his finger to her opening. He slid it inside of her, watching her face. Pleasure darkened her skin with a flush. He felt her hips rise.

But again she stilled them.

She didn't want to let go.

Too bad. Ark had every intention of making her let go and come. Over and over. While he touched her, while he tongued her, and while he was thrusting deep inside of her. He needed to feel her coming apart under him. Wanted it as much as he wanted to bury himself in her and come.

What started out as pure lust had become something much more. Deeper. Women like Tess did not come along every day.

He took his hand out from under her dress and slid it under her knees. "Put your arms around my neck."

She opened her eyes. "I can walk."

"You can also trust me." He stood up, heading to his room on the right side of the suite. Where he had a big bed and plenty of condoms. At the closed door, he stopped. Looked down into her face. She was watching him, probably thinking again. Probably realizing they really didn't know each other that well. But they had a very real connection. "You are safe with me. You can trust me, Tess."

Typically, she met his gaze directly. Her brown gaze locked on him. Then she said, "I believe you."

It eased something tight in his chest to hear her say it. He smiled. "Then lean down and open the door, Tess."

She proved she trusted him by reaching down and opening the door. Then she pulled back. "Ugh, what's that smell?"

Ark's muscles coiled. He stepped back and set Tess down. "Stay here." He had a bad feeling. It wouldn't be the first time someone, a fan or reporter, had broken into his room. Carefully, he reached to the wall and hit the light switch by the door.

The first thing he saw was the dead man on the floor at the foot of the bed. He was sprawled on his back with his pants at his ankles. His dick still had a bright pink erection enhancer ring around the base with a clitoral stimulator attached. Scattered on the floor were a few blue pills that appeared to be Viagra and Ark's box of condoms. What the hell was going on?

"My God, it's Fred!" Tess tried to get past him.

Ark grabbed her by the waist and hauled her into his arms. "Tess, he's dead." He had a hole in his forehead. A small gun, no doubt one with a silencer or the entire floor would have heard the shot. Ark wrapped his arms around her, holding her to his chest.

Then he realized what she had said. *Fred*. The tabloid journalist he and Tess had had a very public argument with a few hours ago. Tess had been with him and was now with Ark. Then Fred turns up murdered in his hotel room.

He was so screwed.

Four

Tess sat on the couch in Ark's suite. The horror would not leave her. Fred was dead—murdered in Ark's hotel room. It just didn't make any sense. Tess answered all the detective's questions and let them search her suitcase. They took her box of condoms. Other than embarrassment, she didn't care. One of Ark's lawyers had arrived and arranged for some kind of gun powder residue test for both Ark and Tess. They were clean.

The police had determined that Fred had been dead for more than two hours. He'd apparently been killed when she and Ark were at the restaurant. Ark's credit card receipt showed the time they left, and the waitress from the restaurant had verified it. They were semicleared as suspects.

Giles was questioned, too. He'd brought Tess's suitcase up to the suite. Fortunately, he'd had a woman, Ark's publicist Maureen Michaels, with him, who vouched they'd only dropped off the suitcase. Maureen had come with Giles to deliver some head shots for Ark to sign. The suitcase and pictures were exactly where Giles and Maureen said they'd be.

"Doctor?"

Tess looked up. Maureen stood in front of her. She resembled a short, less attractive, Nicole Kidman in a camel-colored power suit. Her long red hair was swept up into a French twist. Maureen had been huddled with Ark, Giles, and the lawyer at the bar for the last hour or so, all of them using cell phones and looking very concerned and important. "Yes?"

"We're getting Ark settled into another room for the night. I checked with the detective, and you are free to go home now."

She turned and saw the hotel manager talking to Ark. She knew the only available room was the one she and Fred had been in. The police had already searched Fred's room and found nothing. They wanted Ark's suite sealed off at least until tomorrow. They still didn't know how the killer had gotten into the room, but they must have had a keycard, or master card.

Ark rubbed the back of his neck and lifted his gaze to her.

It was time for her to leave. She was getting in Ark's way, giving him one more thing to worry about.

She looked back at Maureen and stood up. "Thank you." She headed toward her suitcase and purse by the door.

Ark met her there. "Tess, you're not going home. You're exhausted, and it might not be safe."

She frowned and looked up at him. "Not safe?" Did he mean because she'd drunk wine earlier?

"We don't know why Fred was killed. You were with him, so whoever killed him might be after you, too."

The detective said from behind her, "He could be right, Dr. Collins. Why don't you call a friend to stay with? I can escort you to your car, if you like."

Maureen walked up to stand next to Ark and said to Tess, "I'll call a friend for you, Doctor, if you'll give me the number."

Ark ignored both the detective and Maureen. "Tess, stay with me. I just need to know you're safe. Please."

She could call Josie and go to her house. Or Gwen's or Nikki's house, but she was tired. And sick, disappointed, sad . . . she'd been going to have mind-blowing sex with Ark. And it had come to a screeching end at Fred's murder. Poor Fred. What was he doing in Ark's room? God, she couldn't get the picture of him out of her head.

Ark touched her shoulder. "Come on, the room is ready. Let's go get some sleep."

A half hour later, Tess was sitting on the bed, wearing her short red nightgown and surfing through the late night programs on TV. Her thoughts of sex had been replaced by murder. Over and over, she wondered the same thing—who killed Fred? Why?

Ark came out of the bathroom. She looked up. "Have you ever . . ." She stopped talking, totally forgetting what she had been going to ask him. He wore only a pair of black boxers. She couldn't help but stare at him. Muscular chest, flat rippling stomach . . . she wanted to touch him.

His gaze was locked on her. She'd thought the moment for sex was over. They were worn out, confused, and worried. But his hazel gaze was sizzling.

His boxers were growing in front.

He tossed the clothes in his hand in the direction of his suitcase and came toward her.

She slid off the bed, reached for the covers, and pulled them back. Her nerves were so tight she felt as though she might snap. The whole night was too much. She didn't know how to handle Ark in bed with her—and with him sporting a growing hard-on. She wasn't in control of herself.

Ark yanked back his side of the covers, his eyes still watching her. Then he got into the bed, slid down, and rested his head on the pillows.

She looked at him stretched out. And hard. Watching her. "Uhh, do you want to watch TV?"

His face was tight. "Turn it off and come here, Tess."

She picked up the remote, clicked off the TV, and set it back down. Then she sat down on the cool sheets and lay on her back.

Ark wasted no time. He rolled to his side, put his arms around her, and pulled her to him, nudging her face into his chest. He smelled like soap and steam. The contact of his skin pressed up against her, his arms around her, eased her a bit.

Into her hair, he said, "Are you okay?"

She could feel his hard-on pressing into her thighs, but he

acted more concerned about how she was. "Yes. But I don't understand how Fred ended up murdered. What was he doing in your room?"

Ark sighed. "Looking for dirt on me, most likely. Maybe planting something. Obviously he wasn't alone."

"What was that . . . thing . . . on Fred?" Tess was curious. Who would leave him like that? Kill him, then leave him exposed to the world? Her training challenged her to understand.

"It was an erection enhancer with a clitoral stimulator attached to it. The enhancer goes around the base of his cock to hold in the blood, to get bigger and stay hard longer. Judging by the Viagra pills, Fred must have had a problem. The clitoral stimulator on the cock ring is to help a woman come to an orgasm while he's thrusting into her."

Well, she had asked. But she wasn't really embarrassed. Not with Ark holding her and answering her without judgment. "I didn't know they made stuff like that."

"It's for lazy men, sugar," he said softly. Then he reached down and pulled her face up to look at her. "We don't have any condoms. The police collected all mine as evidence and took the ones from your suitcase with your permission."

She could still feel his erection pressing into her. "It's not important." Not now, not with all that had happened.

His gaze stayed on her. "What's important is that you know how much I want to be inside of you. I want it all, Tess. I want to wait until we have condoms, and we aren't both wrung out from the shock of finding a body."

She smiled. "Afraid I'm going to attack you, Hollywood?"

He blinked at the nickname, then recovered. After kissing her softly, he pulled her back against his body. "Sweetheart, you have no idea what you are doing to me. I can't believe it, it's not like I've been hiding my erection. I'd give you anything you wanted just to feel you touch me."

Was that what he wanted? Just to get off?

"But I want to wait, Tess. The first time I come with you, I want it to be while I'm deep inside of you." He brushed his hand over her hair. "I want it all," he repeated softly.

His words touched her. Something warm and scary took root and blossomed in her chest. She didn't want to think about it. She just wanted to sleep with Ark. Just lie here and be safe with him for a few hours.

Ark held a cup of coffee and watched the breaking news on a morning show. "Ark Underwood, NASCAR star, linked with the Sex Toy Murder of a tabloid reporter who was found in the racer's hotel room last night. Police aren't releasing any more information, but an unnamed source says there's a connection to sex shops that Ark Underwood allegedly frequents. We're going live to the Fontana Speedway to get a comment."

"It's going to get worse, Ark."

He turned to look at Maureen. She'd arrived with the newspapers right before Tess got into the shower, her face tight with worry. He knew Maureen was convinced his career hung by a fraying thread. She was coordinating contact with his sponsors, the media, and various others, doing her best to control the damage. "It'll play out, Maureen. After a few days, and once the police find the killer, we'll be okay."

"Did you see the newspaper headline?" She picked up the closest one and read, "Ark Underwood Connected to Sex Toy Murder." She looked up at him. "Who leaked that little tidbit to the press?"

Ark set his coffee down. "Tess was here with me."

She shook her head. "I'm not accusing her. Could have been any of the cops, the hotel manager, anyone who wanted their five seconds of fame." She tossed the paper down and went to pour herself some coffee. "My point is that Tess being here is making it worse for you. And she's going to get smeared with the same brush the press is going to paint over you."

Ark winced at that. It was true. The press loved to portray him as the bad boy—what would they do to Tess? He knew what he had to do. Get her away from him. But he wanted her close by. He wanted her, period. More than once, more than as just a one-night stand.

"Ark, she checked into the hotel with Fred. Then the three

of you had a very public fight. Then when she's with you, you find Fred murdered in your hotel room."

He grit his teeth. She was like a bulldog once she latched on to something. "I get it, Maureen."

She looked at him. "I'm just doing my job, Ark." Then she took her coffee and left.

Tess came out of the bathroom. She'd been in the shower for a long time. He turned and felt a lump in his chest. She wore a short white skirt that revealed her long tanned legs right down to her sandals, and a red sleeveless top that left her smooth arms bare. Her hair was wet and sleek with just a hint of the waves that would form as it dried. Her face appeared tired and worried.

He wanted her more than he had last night.

But he had to do the right thing. It wasn't only his career; it was all the people who counted on him for a job. And the sponsors who invested in him. Everyone.

He resisted the urge to go to her, to take her in his arms. Instead, he asked, "Do you want some coffee?"

Her gaze shifted to the TV, then back to him. "How bad is it?"

It was better to just get this over with. "Tess, it's bad. The press and media will drag you into this if I let them. I'm not going to let them." He refused to look away. She would understand. "It will be better for everyone if you go stay with a friend. And stay away from the media."

The shower-induced color faded from her face. She nodded and went to her suitcase. She dropped in her nightgown and panties, along with her bag of toiletries. She lifted her head and looked around the room. Then she shut and zipped her suitcase.

He watched her. She did understand, didn't she? She looked . . . upset. "Tess, where are you going? You're not going to stay at your house, right?"

She lifted her suitcase from the bed to the floor and faced him. "No. I'm going to my friend, Josie's. I'll be fine. Go on and good luck qualifying today."

God, she was so beautiful with honest brown eyes, a mouth he wanted to kiss forever, and a will of iron. The whole thing about her not experiencing passion was bullshit. But Tess controlled herself. He could see the effort in her taut slender neck and the clench of her jaw.

As if she was trying not to cry. Like she had cried all those years ago when his father had held her. And her father had yelled at her. Ark had not forgotten, had never forgotten. Tess's mother had flitted around worrying about Tess getting his dad's clothes wet and ruining the shoot. His father had been disgusted with both her parents.

But this wasn't about a little girl getting hurt. He just needed to make Tess understand that he was trying to protect her, too. "Doc." He softened his voice, trying to get his own frustration at the entire situation under control. He felt as though he'd been handed a gift with Tess, and now it was being snatched away. And he couldn't do a damn thing about it.

She looked directly at him. "Ark, I understand. I saw the paper; I heard the news. I checked into the hotel with Fred. The three of us had a fight in public. Then I was with you in your hotel room late at night when we found Fred dead. It's all in the police record now. I get it. With some luck, the media will never find out I stayed here last night. And I'll be perfectly safe where I'm going. You just concentrate when you are driving. You have to concentrate; you can't think about the murder when you are on the track."

The knot moved up to his throat. She was worried about him. Shit. "It's just until this mess calms down."

She smiled a sad smile. "You just worry about your driving." She picked up her suitcase and her purse.

Ark went to stop her, to make sure she knew he wanted to see her again, when a hard knock sounded on the door.

He changed direction, went to the door, and opened it.

Giles walked in. "Get a move on, Hollywood. Time to roll." He saw Tess. "Hi, Tess."

She walked past them. "Hi, Giles, good luck qualifying today."

Standing in the hallway, on the other side of Giles, she looked at Ark. "Be careful, Ark. Bye." Then she turned and left.

He couldn't let her go like that. He started after her.

Giles put a hand on his shoulder. "Hasn't she been through enough, Ark? Call down to the manager and get someone to make sure she gets to her car okay. The media is swarming."

It took every ounce of self-control not to shove Giles out of his way and go after her.

Five

After two days of being a virtual prisoner in Josie's house, Tess had had enough. The media had found her at work on Friday after she left Ark at the hotel, then followed her to Josie's house. But enough was enough. She insisted on going to the store while Josie waited for Nikki and Gwen to arrive; then they would all watch the NASCAR race.

Tess headed to the checkout stand with the some chips and dip, soda, wine, and a bag of chocolate kisses. A tabloid caught her attention with the headline: *Exclusive E-mail Reveals Ark Underwood's Sexual Dysfunctions*. Beneath it in smaller print read, *Written by the same doctor that Ark Underwood and Fred Ranger fought over just minutes before the Sex Toy Murder of Ranger.*

Tess grew hot and sick. The race was due to start in just under two hours. Ark had to know about this. How the hell was he going to concentrate when the media was destroying him?

By her e-mail.

Tess had to fight the dizzy terror sweeping over her. What if Ark was too upset to drive and had an accident? Like her parents had after she upset them?

"Ma'am?"

She looked up to see the checker staring at her. She realized she was holding up the line and pulled herself together. She paid for her stuff and left, hurrying to her car. Once on Josie's street, Tess saw that more media was gathering around the house. Her stomach cramped, and claustrophobia set in as they swarmed the car. She refused to look at them and used the clicker Josie had given her to open the garage. She slid her Honda in next to Josie's car in the two-car garage and shut the garage door.

She was safe from the reporters. But her e-mail was out. Still, her reasoning was returning. Ark was a professional driver. She didn't think he'd lose his focus on the track. She opened the car door and got out, then turned and leaned back in to get the bag of food.

"Dr. Collins, what is your comment on the e-mail regarding Ark Underwood?"

Startled, Tess banged her head on the roof of the car. Her heart pounded in her chest. She left the bag in the car and stood up. A big man with thinning blond hair and blue eyes held out a microphone that must be connected to a tape recorder. *A reporter.* "You're trespassing on private property." She sized up her situation. The reporter had about five inches on her and probably sixty pounds. They were between the two cars in a confined space. She decided her best bet was to get inside the house. She shut the car door to get by.

He clamped his hand around her left wrist, stopping her from leaving. "What's your comment on the e-mail that appeared in the paper today?"

Real fear was quickly edged out by adrenaline pouring into her veins. She looked down at his hand wrapped around her wrist, then back up to his face. She forced a deep breath to get control. This guy smelled like root beer and something else—something more bitter, like unchecked ambition. "Let go of my wrist."

He had a wide face that hardened. "Did you sell that e-mail to the paper? Did you kill Fred Ranger to keep him from selling the e-mail and getting the money? Why are you trying to destroy Ark Underwood?" He tightened his fingers around her wrist until it hurt.

Anger washed through Tess, allowing her to ignore the pain. "I'm going to give you one chance. Let go and step back." She knew to make her instructions clear, not panicked. She wasn't panicked; she was pissed.

He tightened his fingers into a painful vise.

Tess grabbed his thumb that was wrapped around her wrist and yanked hard. As soon as he grunted in pain and instinctively let go, she turned and slammed her elbow hard into his stomach. He grunted and fell back against Josie's car.

Tess turned to run into the house.

The reporter recovered and caught hold of her hair and yanked hard. Pain stung her scalp and made her eyes water. "Damn it." She was furious. "Let go!"

"Answer my questions."

"Let go of her. Now." Josie's voice boomed through the garage.

Tess hadn't even heard the door to the house open. Josie stormed down the steps, followed by Nikki and Gwen.

The reporter let go.

Gwen opened the garage door.

The reporter started backing up toward the opening.

Tess followed him. "Get out." She was so mad, she wanted to hurt him. She wanted to kick him in the balls. But she had to get control of herself since he was leaving, and therefore effectively neutralized. He backed to the edge of the garage.

Josie went around Tess's car until she was even with the reporter at the opening of the garage. "Hey, asshole."

The reporter turned to her.

Josie grabbed his shirt, yanking him toward her as she swung her knee up and into his balls.

"Oofff!" He sank to the ground, then rolled to his side.

Josie ignored him and walked up to Tess between the cars. "Are you okay?"

"Jo, he could file a complaint against you." After he got

done retching. Ugh. He was writhing and making icky gagging sounds.

Josie started pushing Tess toward the door to the house. "Nah, he accosted you in my garage, and besides, he's twice my size. He doesn't know I'm a black belt. He'd never admit to me taking him down."

Gwen closed the garage, Nikki got Tess's purse and the bag of groceries from the car, and they all went into the house.

"We already saw the tabloid," Nikki said when she set the bag of groceries down on the kitchen table. "I bought it this morning." She picked up her copy and handed it to Tess.

Tess reached for it. "I saw it at the store."

Nikki snatched the tabloid back and dropped it on the table. "Tess, let me see your wrist."

Tess looked down. Her wrist was red and puffy. "It's fine, Nik, probably just a bruise."

"Bastard. I should have kicked him again," Josie said. She stomped over to the freezer and filled a Ziploc bag with ice.

Gwen joined Nikki to examine Tess's wrist.

Tess swallowed down a stab of irritation. They cared about her. "It's fine," she said in a calm voice. "I've had worse in sparring."

"Not broken," Nikki decided.

"Needs ice," Gwen agreed, and took the ice from Josie. "Let's go in the living room to watch the prerace stuff. We can talk in there."

Tess let them lead her into the living room. She sat on the floor next to Nikki, holding the towel-covered bag of ice on her wrist. Josie brought her some coffee and a couple Advil.

She rolled her eyes and looked at her friends. They were really worried about her. "I'm not going to break, guys. And I'm not going to let the killer get away with this. Someone, and I think it's the killer, stole the e-mail from Fred and sold it to that tabloid." She looked at the paper that one of girls brought with them into the living room. "I'm going to find out who it is."

Her cell phone rang before her friends could react to her

statement. Gwen got up and retrieved the phone from Tess's purse and handed it to her. Tess thanked her and answered it. "Hello?"

"Tess, how are you?"

Her heart kicked up. "Ark?" She hadn't heard his voice on the phone before, but it was him. Why was he calling? He had to race in less than ninety minutes. But her gaze fell on the tabloid, and she knew. "I just saw the tabloid featuring my e-mail. I didn't give it to them." She said it quietly.

"I didn't think you did. I just want to make sure you're okay."

His voice stirred the memory of the night in bed when he'd pulled her into his arms and asked her if she was okay. But this was different. Everything had changed the next morning when Ark woke up and realized what was at stake. And saw that she was in the way. He'd been right, smart. "I'm fine. But shouldn't you be getting ready to drive? You need to concentrate out on the track." It was just over an hour to the start of the race.

Silence. Then, "I'm worried about you, Tess. I'm trying to protect you, Doc. And all the people whose paychecks are dependant on me. You understand that, right?"

His responsibilities weighed on him. It hit her how much Ark had to consider every action. How much she had misjudged him in her e-mail. And how much damage she was doing to him. "I understand, Ark. I told you I understood Friday morning."

"That's another reason I'm calling. I want to see you, Tess. I'm off for the week after the race today. Just hang in there."

She thought of the media outside, of all the ramifications. "No, Ark. You already pointed out that you need to protect all the people relying on you. We can't see each other. Go out there today and concentrate on your driving. Bye." She hung up.

Her friends stared at her.

"What?"

Josie said, "He wants to see you?"

Tess tilted her head to the tabloid. "Did you see this? Ark can't be seen with me; it'll make things worse. He told me to leave Friday morning as soon as he realized the damage I was doing to his career."

Gwen looked at her. "Tess, maybe he cares about you."

Tess shook her head. "He can't afford to. But I'm done letting the killer and the media trap me in Josie's house. It's time I started fighting back." She adjusted her position on the floor next to Nikki. "And I need you all to help me figure this out." Tess started telling them the entire story, from the first minute she met up with Fred at the hotel Thursday afternoon, until she left Ark Friday morning.

She hung up on him.

Ark stood outside his motor home where his family was staying. He'd talked them into staying there where the media couldn't get to them. He'd left the sponsors' tent early to get a minute to call Tess. He was worried about her.

She thought he'd called her because he believed she'd given the tabloid the e-mail. Ark didn't believe that. He knew it had only been a matter of time before it got out. It was on Fred's computer.

Or Fred's killer took it off his body.

Tess had too much to lose by selling that e-mail . . . like her entire career. And nothing about her suggested she was after money. Ark had seen enough of that to spot a gold digger. So why didn't she want to see him?

"Ark, you'd better get your ass to the drivers' meeting."

He looked up to see Heidi striding toward him. Wonder who sent her to find me? All drivers were required to be at the drivers' meeting held an hour before the race. "Right, what time is it?"

"Time to go. Now. Your crew chief and Giles have been looking for you." She reached out and wrapped her hand around his bicep.

Ark shrugged her off. He was in a rotten mood, and Heidi's clinging annoyed him. "I'm going."

"I'll walk with you." She fell into step beside him. "Missed you at the club the last couple nights."

"Been busy."

"Yeah, the whole murder thing. And now that e-mail in the tabloid. You should be more careful who you hang out with."

Ark stopped walking. Heidi wore a black tube top and white shorts cut up her ass. She was thin and tall, and stood with her chest thrust out and shoulders pushed back in a pose. But while Tess got his blood running hot, Heidi just made him tired. And if Heidi had seen the tabloid with the e-mail, then everyone had. He was worried what this was going to do to Tess. She had been so honest with him about her reasons for writing that e-mail; she didn't deserve this. He said to Heidi, "Do you have a point?"

She arched a thinly plucked brow. "I'm just saying that you don't know what strangers want from you. You're rich and famous, you should be more careful."

"Thanks for the tip." He turned and walked away from her and into the drivers' meeting.

Tess finished describing everything to Josie, Gwen, and Nikki while the NASCAR race played in the background.

"An erection enhancer in pink, interesting," Josie said, lifting her coffee cup, but then she seemed to forget about the drink. "Whoever murdered Fred wanted him found like that. With the pink cock ring, the Viagra, and Ark's condoms. There's a message in that scene."

Tess agreed. This was Josie's area of therapy, so she had valuable insight. "Plus they got close enough to kill him with the gun without a fight."

Josie nodded. "A woman."

Nikki agreed. "Had to be a woman. A pissed-off woman with a grudge, and axe to grind."

"The woman who killed Fred had to be angry at Ark, too. It can't be a coincidence that the murder happened in his suite—not just his suite but his bedroom." Tess tried not to think of what she and Ark had been doing while Fred lay dead in the bedroom. "I know Fred's source was at the hotel because Fred told me that was who called him to say Ark was on his way down while we were in the sports bar."

Josie took a sip of her coffee, then set her cup down on the table. "The one that he told you helped him with his sex shop articles and had the pictures of Ark to blackmail him with?"

Facts started clicking into place. "Yes. But Fred must have betrayed the source. Okay, let's back up for a second." It was hard to keep it all straight. "Fred had to have that room booked for a while. They fill up fast for the NASCAR races. So he had it before he got my accidental e-mail, right?"

Josie, Gwen, and Nikki all nodded. Gwen said, "Makes sense. So he and his source might have had a plan. To what, though? Blackmail Ark together?"

"I think so. Then once Ark paid, I bet Fred was going to write an exposé on it for *The Breaking Buzz* tabloid. But he got my e-mail about Ark and he had a better idea. He could use me to write an article now—getting what he wanted faster. A story that was so big, he could get into the TV entertainment journalist job that he wanted."

Josie caught on. "So Fred double-crossed his source. First he planned to use you to seduce Ark, but when you refused, he jumped on the chance of asking him those questions in the bar, trying to shock him into an admission of orgies and pictures."

Tess frowned at that. "But the source hadn't even blackmailed him yet . . . had they? So Fred jumped the gun by shouting those questions at Ark."

"You rattled him," Gwen said. "Fred thought he had you cornered and you'd do what he wanted to save your career."

"Okay." Tess nodded, thinking that fit with Fred's ambition trait. He'd do whatever it took, obviously, to save or advance his career, so he had believed she would, too. "So then he's screwed up, and he's got nothing to show for it. So he breaks into Ark's room. No wait, the room wasn't broken into."

Gwen said, "Had to be an inside person at the hotel, like . . . maids. Maids have a high turnover rate. With a big race, they'd hire on anybody in a pinch."

Tess agreed. "You're right, and people tend not to even notice the maids. They can find out all kinds of stuff. But what happened? The source got a job as a maid? Then after Fred betrayed her, she killed him?

Josie sat up. "Wait, it can work. We agree the killer is a woman and most likely Fred's source, correct?"

Tess nodded. She'd been working on this for days in her head, but it was really coming together with her friends' help.

Josie's blue eyes were almost violet as she thought. "She's furious. She's lost her ability to blackmail Ark since Fred already warned him about the pictures, and Ark didn't seem to care. You don't believe the pictures were real, right, Tess?"

She shook her head. "No, Ark said he never . . ." She blushed and realized she believed him totally. Did they think she was stupid? "He didn't seem to be worried. And we all know people can use computer programs to make up photos like that."

Josie said, "Tess, I believe your take on Ark. We all do. The question is—what did he care about?"

Tess felt sick. "The e-mail. But he left it, probably because he knew it was on Fred's computer."

"Now the source has a new weapon. Not to blackmail Ark with but to sell to the papers."

"So she killed Fred for it. And the picture in Fred's cell phone camera. Because those were real."

Josie nodded. "They probably knew you and Ark would be gone for a little bit. Fred's beside himself with rage. The manager of the hotel has kicked his ass to the curb. The source, maybe dressed as a maid, lures him to Ark's room for revenge. She tells him they'll use the pictures in his cell phone with some new ones they'll take in Ark's room."

Tess got it. "As a maid, she'd have the master key to the rooms. They have sex and she kills him. And then she steals the e-mail. I doubt the pictures in the cell phone survived the iced tea. But she sells the e-mail that showed up today in the tabloid."

Nikki said, "The police will have a tough time getting the tabloid to reveal their source."

Tess agreed. "We have to go after another angle. The connection is the sex shops in Fred's articles. The source has to be connected to those shops since she worked with Fred on the articles about the sex shops." She stared at the TV, automatically searching out Ark's car.

"We can split up and look," Josie suggested.

"No, this could get dangerous. You've already been a huge help." She stopped talking when she caught the close-up of Ark's car on TV. Her heart slammed into her throat. The race was down to the last ten laps. The Fontana Speedway was a D-shaped track, and turn three was known to be tricky. Giles was in first place, with Ark drafting behind him to gain momentum from the air currents that Giles's car created. Behind them was a rookie looking for his chance to slingshot around them and win.

Tess clenched her jaw so tight her head throbbed. The rookie had it in for Ark. The feud had started last season when the rookie tapped Ark and sent him into the wall and caused him to have a DNF or *did not finish*. When reporters had shoved a mike and camera in his face afterward, Ark had shrugged his shoulders and said, "Rookies. Some of them don't learn very fast." Two races later, Ark caught the rookie and spun him.

The rookie had been waiting for his chance to pay Ark back.

Giles came off turn three, and Ark followed close behind him. Tess couldn't sit still. She stood up and walked closer to Josie's TV. She knew Ark wanted to win this race. But Tess just prayed he kept his concentration and focus, and stayed alive.

They came off another turn when the rookie made his move, using the draft to slingshot around Ark.

Ark's car suddenly got loose. Tess strained to see—did the rookie tap his bumper? Or had he suddenly lost the draft and got loose? She dropped to her knees in front of the TV, watching as Ark fought the car. Struggled to control thousands of pounds of steal going 180 miles per hour. The tires lost traction for a few seconds, starting to angle into a slide.

Several things rushed through Tess's head. Ark wore the

Hans device, a safety system to protect his head and brain in a crash. The announcer mentioned that Ark had gotten four new tires the last pit stop. Ark was a good driver.

One of the best in the world.

If he was concentrating.

Tess stopped breathing. Her world stopped, zeroed in on Ark.

Then she saw Ark's car straighten out. He'd dropped back to fifth position.

Eight laps to go. It all happened in just a few seconds.

The rookie was in second place and on Giles's bumper.

Ark was safe. She let out a breath, so dizzy she didn't dare stand up.

"Oh, God, that was close," Josie said from her spot on the chair.

Tess blinked, then felt fresh terror at what she saw on the screen. "Don't!" she said to the TV.

But Ark wasn't listening. He got the draft he needed from the fourth place car in front of him and did a slingshot around the two cars ahead of him, putting him in third.

Behind the rookie.

Six laps to go.

Tess couldn't stand the tension. It felt as if a dozen knives were buried in her shoulder blades and neck. Her world shrunk to the TV, to the scream of the race cars on the track. She could almost smell the hot rubber and her own fear.

"What's he going to do?" Nikki said.

"Kill the rookie," Gwen answered in a tight voice.

"Hush," Josie said.

Tess knew Ark's ability as a driver. She believed in him. So she answered in a faraway voice while focusing on his car, "Protect Giles. Ark's going to get between Giles and the rookie." She hoped that his intention was to help Giles, not spin the rookie for nearly causing him to crash a few laps earlier.

Two more laps down, leaving four more to the checkered flag. The crowd was on its feet—all one hundred thousand NASCAR fans roaring their approval or disapproval.

Ark alternately blocked the fourth place car from passing him, and then got back on the rookie's bumper.

Down to the third lap.

The fans stayed on their feet, but went silent. No one breathed.

They all came off turn three. The rookie was going to make his move. His car had been driving like pure gold all day long.

But Ark moved first, barely off the turn, and he shot out and got side by side with the rookie. All the way into the next turn. He held his place.

One nudge, one wrong draft, one tiny slip, and Ark would slam into the wall. Tess's teeth ached with worry and tension.

The second to last lap.

Ark pulled ahead and forced his way in front of the rookie.

Tess breathed. Her oxygen-starved lungs forced her to suck in air.

The crowd responded with cheers and boos.

The next lap, Ark protected Giles's ass until Giles passed the checkered flag and won the Fontana Speedway race.

Ark came in second.

Alive.

A few minutes later, Giles gave his interviews in the winner's circle. Tess saw Ark come into camera range to congratulate Giles.

All the cameras and mikes turned to Ark. Not to ask about his spectacular driving, but to find out about the Sex Toy Murder. They wanted to know more about the e-mail that had made the papers, the suggestions that Ark had sexual dysfunctions, and they especially wanted to know if he and the tabloid reporter had really fought over the doctor who wrote the e-mail.

Ark issued a terse "No comment" and forced his way through the media.

Tess stood up and looked at her friends. "I'm going to start with the last shop that Fred wrote about and work backward. I have to find Fred's source."

Josie met Tess's gaze. "Look for a woman on the fringe of

Ark's life. Someone who hasn't been able to get as close to him as she wants to."

Tess felt the hair on the back of her neck stand up. "A crazy woman?"

"With a wicked streak."

Six

"Josie? This is Ark Underwood. I'm looking for Tess. She won't answer her cell phone." He paced his hotel room. What was Tess's friend like? Loyal enough to tell him to go to hell? Should he lie to her? Tell her he had something of Tess's to return?

"What do you want with her, Ark?"

"I want to see her."

Silence.

Ark let her think. What could he do? He knew that Tess had gone to college with Josie and took karate with her. They appeared to be good enough friends that Tess went to her house to hide from the reporters. It was his impression that Tess trusted Josie. Now, would Josie trust him?

"She's not here, Ark."

Hell. "What do you mean, not there?" He reined in his temper. "I'm sorry, Josie, I'm worried about her. She didn't go home alone, did she?"

"No. But she's doing something she has to do."

A sweat broke out on his forehead, even though he'd just showered. As soon as he had done his interviews and sucked up to his sponsors after the race, he'd gotten the hell out of there. Now he had the next week off. He had to find Tess.

Touch her. Make this up to her. Into the phone, he asked, "Where? Where did she go?"

"Do you care about her at all?"

He closed his eyes for a second. When he opened them, he stared at the bed where he'd held her all night. "She's not like any woman I've ever known. I need to find her. First I need to make sure she's safe. Then I need to make her understand I only had her leave to protect her." He shut up, surprised he'd told her that much.

"The night her parents died, they were fighting about sending her away. Tess heard the fight. She was only fifteen years old. But her mom was starting to take an interest in Tess when her dad was traveling. She clung to Tess when he was gone on a photo shoot, turned her into her lunch and shopping partner, then forgot her once her dad came home. Her dad wanted to send her away to a boarding school for the gifted so he could come home and screw his wife without interruption. Tess's mom wanted a closer boarding school where she could bring her home at will. They both considered her to be in the way of their time together."

He sank down on the bed. "What happened?"

"Tess went downstairs and yelled at her parents. Told them she was tired of them treating her like a problem. She was gifted, Ark. An excellent student. Loved by her friends and teachers, but she was an outsider in her own home. But that night, she lost her temper. Cried, screamed at her parents—like a fifteen-year-old girl. They both screamed back. Then left for their party, still screaming at each other."

He knew the rest. "And died in a car accident, leaving her an orphan."

"She went to live with her mother's mother, who blamed Tess's father for taking her daughter. She was a woman destroyed by her daughter's death. Tess's grandmother told her over and over to never let a man destroy her."

"Christ." He had sent her away. It sure as hell explained her having trouble with trust and letting go. It also explained why she left when he told her to. And Ark hadn't forgotten how cold her parents had been to her after he'd pulled her out of the waves all those years ago. "Josie, I have to find her."

"She's researching the sex shops that Fred wrote about, trying to figure out who his source was."

He sat there speechless for long seconds. His brain kicked in. "Where?"

She told him.

Fred's last article had been on an exclusive sex shop located in the once-dying town of Prosper, California, not far from Fontana. Prosper had originally been a military town, and once the base closed, the life drained out of the town. But a few investors opened the Prosper Card Club and Resort, then began quietly adding upscale shops of a sexual nature to cater to upscale clientele.

Fred found out and wrote his *Exclusive Sex Revives Dying Town* articles.

On one of the main shopping strips that had sprung up around the Prosper Card Club and Resort was a sex toy shop called Sensual Delights. The shop didn't advertise or even have a large sign. The store front was tasteful with silhouettes of couples and "Sensual Delights" in scrolled gold letters across the silhouettes.

According to Fred, this shop catered to upscale clients. You had to be buzzed in the front door. If the owner didn't like your look, you didn't get in.

Tess wondered if the owner would like her look.

And if he or she killed Fred.

She pressed the doorbell discreetly inlaid on the door and was almost immediately let in. The shop was brightly lit and clean, with clear glass shelves and lots of scrollwork on the pale peach walls. When she inhaled, she smelled scented candles and exotic lotions—like a mix between the perfume counter at a department store and a candle store. Nervous, she looked around. She stood right next to shelves filled with scented candles, lotions, and games.

"Can I help you find something?"

She turned. The woman looked like a suburban soccer mom. Tess judged her to be in her late thirties or early forties with blond hair in a soft cut around her face, blue eyes, and an easy smile. She wore a pair of jeans and a sweater set.

Could she be Fred's source? And a murderer?

Tess said, "This is my first time in a sex shop." Her mouth was dry. "Could you . . . uhh . . . tell me a little about it?"

"Sure, do you have any particular interests?"

She had no idea. But she thought about Fred. "Performance enhancers. For men."

The woman nodded. "This way," she said, leading Tess through the store. "This is our video and DVD section. That's the viewing booth," she said, pointing to a small curtained booth. "You can see clips of movies in there."

"Oh."

"These are our vibrators and dildos." She gestured to the left.

Tess blinked at the section. All shapes and . . . wow.

"Here's a good selection of enhancers."

She stopped at a section of wall with fake male members sticking out. They were fitted with different erection enhancers. The simplest ones were a gellike ring that fitted snugly at the base of the penis. From there, they got more creative, adding clitoral stimulators, or a second ring that looped around the testicles . . . it was overwhelming. Tess tried to concentrate.

It was a little distracting to have a wall of penises staring at her.

"I'll let you look. My name is Linda, just give me a call if you have any questions."

Tess nodded. "Thanks." She watched the woman walk away and turned back. Could she remember what that thing Fred had on looked like? Did it come from this store? She stared at each one, trying to see if it jogged her memory.

"What are you doing?"

"Huh?" She turned around. "Ark!" What was he doing here? He wore a pair of jeans, a T-shirt, and a determined look in his hazel eyes. How did he—"Josie."

"She cares about you very much."

There was something different about him. His gaze held something different, something more, when he looked at her. "Yes, she does. And she means well, but she shouldn't have told you where I am. It's not a good idea for you to be seen with me or—"

He reached out, took hold of her shoulders, and pulled her into his body, and his kiss.

Tess opened her mouth in surprise.

Ark put his hand on the back of her head, kissing her with heat. His tongue touched hers and then sank deep inside her mouth. She would have protested, but she was too busy kissing him back. His other hand settled on the curve of her back.

Ark broke the kiss and looked down at her. "I've missed you."

She tried to think.

But he just kept looking at her.

"What?"

"I thought you'd be okay. I didn't think the media would track you down to your friend's house." He reached down and lifted her left hand. His face tightened in anger as he gently touched the bruise around her wrist left by the reporter.

Obviously, Josie had told him about their encounters with the media.

He looked up from her wrist. His face hardened into a cold look she hadn't seen before. "What's the name of the reporter that did this to you?"

She shrugged. "I didn't ask his name."

"You should have told me he did this to you."

Tess sucked in a breath. He looked furious. "It's not your fault. I'm the one who wrote that e-mail, and that's what interested the reporter in me. But I'm going to find out who was Fred's source. It's one thing to accept responsibility for what I did, but I'm not going to let a killer murder Fred, destroy my life, threaten your career, and then just walk away." She tried to step back.

He let her go. "So you are going to solve this yourself?"

"I'm going to take back my life." Tess didn't tell him that she needed to fix what she had done to his life. Or that she felt responsible in a distant way for Fred's death. Her e-mail seemed to have set off a chain of events that hurt a lot of people. But the thing that ate at her the most was hurting Ark. She had to fix that. To live with herself.

Ark stood silently, watching her. Finally, he lifted his hand and gestured toward the penis wall. "See anything matching the device Fred had on?"

Tess turned back around. "I can't remember it much. Except that it was pink. I distinctly remember his face, and that his pants were down, but . . ." Tess sighed. "Shock has a way of making a couple details vivid and blurring the rest."

He put his hand on her shoulder. "I remember it. It was similar to that one." He used his other hand to point past her to one that was a blue ring with a soft, gellike protrusion in the front. He slid his hand down her arm, his mouth going to her ear. "It had the clit kisser."

The urge to lean back into him settled on Tess. The man had a pull on her. She had to stop this. Turning back around, she faced him. "What are you doing, Ark? You should be celebrating. You and Giles. Why are you here?" She knew he'd wanted first place today, but second place kept him in the top five of the season points, which kept him in the running to win the NASCAR Championship at the end of the season.

He looked down at her. "Because you're here."

Ark was honest. All she had to do was ask the right question. "What do you want from me?"

He reached out, putting both hands on her shoulders and tugging her forward. "I told you, Doc, I want it all. Right now, I'll help you with your sex sleuthing." He grinned.

She could feel her resolve softening, her body and mind listening to him. But she knew it was just some kind of weird guilt or worry driving him. She lifted her chin. "You are that desperate for sex?"

He lifted one hand off her shoulder to touch her face. "I'm that desperate to see you."

"Oh."

Ark let go of her, then looped an arm around her shoulder and pulled her into his side. "I don't see the exact model of the cock ring. Let's browse around."

They ended up at the checkout stand. Ark didn't just look; he bought a box of condoms and charmed even more information from Linda. She and her husband had owned the shop together until he died two years ago. Now she ran it alone, though her stepdaughter occasionally helped.

Tess ignored the condoms and said to Linda, "I heard about the shop from Fred Ranger's article in *The Breaking Buzz.*"

Linda's smile faded. "I didn't know he was a reporter. He kept asking questions about our high-end customers. He pretended to be a wealthy client. Asked questions about how men in high-stress and high-risk jobs relieve stress. I thought he was embarrassed and described some submissive techniques that a few of our men in high-stress jobs like." She shook her head at the memory. "It's their way of taking a break from having to be in control. Here I thought I was helping him, but Fred just wanted to expose the wealthy clients." She looked at Ark. "He asked about you specifically. Said you told him about our shop, but by then, I was suspicious and asked him to leave."

Ark said, "I have been here. What made you so sure he didn't know me?"

Tess looked up at him in surprise. And disappointment? She wasn't sure. Why did it matter? Sex toys weren't a crime.

Linda shrugged. "He said he wanted the same toys you buy."

Ark nodded.

Tess stared at him. What did that mean?

He turned and caught her curious stare. "She means hardcore toys and fetish stuff, and I'm not into that. I'm pretty much a condom, bottle of oil, or lingerie customer. So Linda knew that I hadn't told Fred about the store."

Did she want to know what hardcore toys were? Probably not. She did like knowing Ark didn't go in for strange sex toys.

Linda added, "I never reveal our clients. It's no one's business."

Tess thought about what she knew. "Linda, how did Fred find out about this shop? You have to know it's here to find it. Did you just buzz him in like you buzzed me in?"

"I buzzed you in because I liked your look. I buzzed in Fred because he was carrying one of our bags." She held up a white bag trimmed in gold scrolling. "So I assumed he was a customer."

So where did Fred get the bag? It had to be from his source. Tess believed Linda—she wasn't Fred's source. Her business depended on her discretion.

Ark pulled out his wallet to pay for the condoms. "Can you think of anyone who would have helped Fred? Given him the bag so you'd buzz him in?"

Linda dropped her gaze to count back change. "No."

Tess knew she was lying. Her face went tight and stiff; white anger lines formed around her mouth. She didn't think the anger was at her and Ark, but rather whoever she might know that would sic Fred on her. But why wouldn't she tell them?

Ark accepted his change, then took out a business card and wrote a number on the back. "Here's my cell number. Call if you think of anything that could help us."

Outside the store, Tess looked at Ark. "She's lying. I think she suspects who Fred's source is."

He nodded. "I got that, too. I don't think it's her. And I don't think she has any reason to be out to destroy me. I've bought condoms or a gift basket from her occasionally. She was always professional—there's just no reason to think she'd be after me."

"But you think someone is?"

Seven

Ark looked around Tess's kitchen. The walls were painted a soft yellow. The wood floors and pecan-colored tile on the counters added to the warmth. It felt like a place to sit and have coffee with friends or lovers. It felt like a home.

He knew enough about Tess now to know that creating a home was very important to her. She understood her needs and found a way to fulfill them. She was an incredibly strong woman.

He liked that about her. A lot.

But she had a vulnerable side that touched him deeply. The side that had been hurt by her parents, and that she now guarded so carefully.

The side that brought out his protective instincts.

God, he wanted her. Needed her.

They had come to her house to do some research. The next place on her list to investigate was a dance club that had a secret sex club within it, *The Fantasy.* The dance club didn't even open until nine P.M. It was just after six now.

Plenty of time to talk and make love.

He looked over at Tess bent over her laptop at the kitchen table with Fred's articles spread around her.

She must have felt his stare. She looked up and asked, "How did Fred get into the exclusive shops in Prosper?" Her gaze was troubled, tired. "I never even knew these places existed. The Fantasy Club? It's in one of the rooms at the Prosper Card Club and Resort?"

They'd talked about this, and Tess knew Ark had been to the Fantasy Club. She had told him her theories on who killed Fred. He was impressed with her reasoning and thought she may be right. He nodded at her question.

She looked back to her screen. "I think the source stole the e-mail from Fred to sell to the highest bidder—another tabloid. Since you think the source is out to destroy you—it's probably reasonable to assume that it could be the same person who leaked the sex toy detail of Fred's death."

"Someone is getting around," Ark said, "but who?" He went to stand behind Tess. "Who would you protect if you were Linda, Tess? She was angry; we could both see that." He put his hands on her tight shoulders and kneaded.

She leaned back into his hands. "But she didn't want to tell us who it might be. A child? Sister?"

Ark tensed at a thought. "Stepdaughter. She said her stepdaughter sometimes worked at the store." Who the hell was her stepdaughter?

"Have you seen the stepdaughter when you have been in there?"

He strained to remember. "I don't think so. No. Sometimes I send Maureen. I could ask her." He pulled out his cell phone and dialed.

Tess looked up at him with her wide brown eyes. "You send your publicist to the sex shop for you?"

He put one hand back on her shoulder. "For gifts. They deliver baskets of bath stuff, massage oils, lingerie. I haven't done that in a long time, Tess. But I'm not a monk either. The one thing you need to know is that I am always careful—I choose nice women and use condoms." He wanted her to believe him. Before he could be sure she did, Maureen answered in his ear.

"Ark, where are you? We need to go over our strategy for dealing with this disaster."

He ignored her dramatics. He'd already told her he planned to spend time with Tess. "I'm busy, Maureen. I need to know if you've ever seen the stepdaughter of Linda at Sensual Delights. Do you know who she is?"

Seconds of silence ticked by; then she answered, "No, why do you ask? We need to be working on your image. I think we should get the press out to watch you play basketball with those boys."

Those boys. Ark hardened his jaw. "*Those boys* are off limits, Maureen." He felt Tess tense beneath his hand because his voice was ice cold.

"Ark, I'm trying to do my job here."

"Leave *those boys* alone." He hung up and stuffed the phone back in his pocket. To Tess, he said, "She doesn't remember the stepdaughter either."

She said softly, "Everything okay?"

He smiled to reassure her. "Yes, just an old fight. My brothers and I do work with the Big Brother program. It's something we enjoy, but Maureen wants to invite the press in."

"And you don't?"

"No. I want the boys to know that we care about the men they become. I don't want them to ever think they were just some kind of photo op." He knew how hard it was to grow into a man without a father. Ark had been lucky—he'd had a damn good father until he died. Many of these boys had virtually no role model.

Tess accepted that and turned back to the computer. She had hooked up to the Internet. "I'm on the Sensual Delights' Web site to look for Linda's last name. Or maybe the list of employees, something like that." She scrolled through and finally found an e-mail. *LRiley@Sensualdelights.com.* "Riley. I bet her last name is Riley." She looked up at him. "Ark, Josie thinks that it's a woman on the fringe of your life. Do you know a woman with the last name of Riley?"

"Not off hand. But I think Josie is right. And I'm worried about you. Whoever this is might be very jealous."

She looked startled. "Jealous? Of me?"

"Sugar, anyone in that sports bar would have felt the sexual tension between us. And I don't usually send a woman's suitcase up to my suite. I don't like to have women spend the night." He should have told her all this sooner. He should have let her know from the first moment that she was special to him.

She stood up and went to the freezer, absently pulling the door open. "Are you hungry? I could make something while we work on figuring this out."

She was nervous. Scared. Ark crossed the square kitchen and shut the door. He turned her to face him, looked into her wide brown eyes. "I want you, Tess. Don't close up on me now."

Heat rose in her face. She leaned her head back and closed her eyes. "We have to find Fred's source, the killer."

He touched her face, running both his thumbs alongside her temples and cheeks. "Later."

She opened her eyes. "We're going to end up in bed, aren't we?"

He smiled, amazed at her honesty. He curved his hands around her cheeks, cupping her face with his palms. "We both feel the chemistry, so yeah, I'm going to be inside you before the night is over. I won't let you walk away again."

"I didn't—" She stopped herself.

"I told you to go. I did it to protect you." He used slight pressure to tilt her face up. "And I regretted it every single moment you were away from me."

She raised her eyebrows. "So you tracked me down in a sex shop?"

He nodded. "That had a certain allure, but I'd have found you anywhere."

Her gaze stayed on him. "You've been in there a lot?"

She had a right to know. He'd touched on this a few minutes ago, but he wanted to make this very clear. "Upscale sex stores have the better condoms, and I'm very careful about details like that."

"You must think I'm incredibly naïve."

He didn't. He thought she respected herself too much to do what she wasn't comfortable with. A huge difference. "I think you are a woman who knows what she wants. Whoever you had sex with wasn't doing it for you. So you waited until you were ready to try it again. Or waited for the right man to come along."

"It wasn't Fred."

"Which I suspect you knew," he pointed out. "But what was the catalyst, Tess? What pushed you over the edge to open yourself up to a relationship that involved sex again?" From the first, it was clear that Tess didn't jump into bed with men.

Her eyes slid away from him. She had the faraway look of someone focusing on a memory. "My grandmother died. She was all I had left. I didn't want to end up alone like her. I had to take a chance."

He dropped his hands to her shoulders, tugged her to his chest, and wrapped his arms around her. He was going to hunt down Dr. Josie Montgomery and thank her. She took a huge chance on him. She never told him this part, but he'd bet she knew. The woman he'd talked to on the phone appeared to care very much about Tess, and she took the risk that Ark would be the man to . . . care about her, too. Admiration for Tess welled up inside of him. She, the woman who measured risks so carefully, took the biggest one to find someone to care about. To open herself up to the intimacy of sex when the idea of losing control scared her. She was brave as hell.

She pulled back and looked up at him. "So? Do you still want to make love?"

He brushed his lips over hers. "I ache for you."

Heat swept over Tess when Ark firmed up the pressure of his mouth, sliding his tongue deep inside. Desire curled a tight knot in her belly. She lifted her hands, running them up his arms, under the sleeves of his shirt, and up over the cut of his hard muscles.

Ark broke the kiss, looking up. His hazel eyes had a lust-induced haze to them. He glanced around the kitchen, then back to her. He reached to the hem of her shirt, pulling it up.

"We can go into my bedroom." She had the blind pulled in her kitchen, but—

He pulled the shirt off. "We will. But now I have to see you. I'm not going to let anything get between us again." He reached down to unsnap her jeans.

Tess caught hold of his shirt. She wanted to see him, to see all of him. Ark helped her get the shirt over his head. Then he reached back to push her jeans down. "Take them off, Doc."

She shimmied the jeans down and took a moment to step out of her sandals and kick her pants off. Then she looked up.

Ark was naked. Her mouth went dry. Her hands itched to touch him. He obviously worked out. No wonder *People* magazine had been so anxious to feature him, he looked hot both in clothes and out. At just over six feet, he had full, wide shoulders, a flat stomach, and slim hips that framed a big erection.

He was big. Everywhere.

She put her hand on his chest, just to touch him. Then she looked up into his face.

He had his gaze locked on her. She stood in only her bra and panties. She could feel the heat from his skin beneath her hand. She trailed her hand down and felt his stomach contract. She went lower to his penis. She wrapped her fingers around him. Hot and thick, it moved and danced in her hand.

Ark closed his eyes, his face darkening in pleasure. When he opened his eyes, he said in a thick voice, "Turn around."

She let go of him to turn and face the fridge. She felt him move her hair and unclasp her bra. She let it slide down her arms. Ark leaned down to her ear. "Put your hands on the refrigerator, Tess."

She blinked, staring at her side-by-side. But she trusted Ark and put both her palms flat on the fridge. The surface was cool compared to the heat of Ark's body behind her.

He caught hold of her panties, sliding them down.

Tess concentrated on keeping her hands on the refrigerator. She stepped out of the panties.

He ran his hands up her legs as he rose behind her. Then over her butt and up her back. She shivered, feeling vulnerable with her back to him.

Ark put his arms around her. She felt his dick pressing into the curve of her lower back. "You are so damn beautiful."

His voice was rich and whispery. He gently caressed her belly with one hand and stroked her breasts with another. His touch and words heated her up. She didn't feel vulnerable anymore.

He slid his hand down, tangling his fingers in her pubic hair. "I want you, Tess. But first, I want to feel you come. Just let me touch you, stroke you, until all you can do is feel white-hot pleasure. And I'm going to be right here, holding you up while you let go." With his other hand, he grasped her nipple and gently rolled it. The sensations shot from her throat to her core.

And he moved his hand deeper between her legs. "Spread your legs for me."

She shifted her weight and spread her feet to give him better access.

He moved his hand deeper between her legs, using his fingers to separate her. Then he found her swollen clit. "You're wet. Sexy." His voice was thicker and tighter. She could feel his heart slamming against her back, while her heart picked up speed. He began circling her clit.

"Ark." She arched back while pressing her hips into his hand.

"Keep your hands on the fridge." He increased the pressure between her legs and dropped his mouth to kiss her ear, down her neck, and the curve of her shoulder.

She pressed her hands flat into the fridge. The sensations slammed into her, rolled through her, until she couldn't breathe.

He slid one finger, then two inside her. His palm rubbed against her clit. "Move, sugar. Move your hips against my hand."

She did, because it was torture. Blissful. She leaned back against him and pumped her hips against his hand.

"God, yes. Perfect." He panted the words into her ear.

His words sent her over the edge into an orgasm. Shudders of pleasure rocked through her. Her legs buckled.

Ark dropped his hand from her breasts to loop his arm around her waist. "I got you. I'm right here," he whispered.

Ark had pulled her back, flush to his hard body, with his arm tight under her ribs. His cock pressed into her lower back; his breath feathered over her shoulder. Tess got her breath back, and she wanted more. She took her hands from the refrigerator and put them on his arm. "I want more."

He lifted his arm from around her waist and moved back from her.

Tess turned. He stood with his back to her at the kitchen table. He looked magnificent. When he turned around, he was rolling on a condom he'd pulled out from the Sensual Delights bag. He met her gaze. "Come here."

She walked to him.

Ark pulled her into his arms. Wrapped her tightly against him. "I'm desperate to be inside you, Tess."

She looked up. "My bed?"

"Oh, yeah. Later." He slid his hands down her waist and lifted her high against him. "Your bed, maybe the shower . . . but right now—" He walked while carrying her to the kitchen wall. "Put your legs around me and take me inside you."

His words were hoarse. He leaned her against the wall. She curled her legs around his hips, then reached down between them to guide his cock inside. Once she positioned him, Ark took over.

"Hold on to me, Doc. Now. Hold on." He drove into her and groaned a deep sound of satisfaction.

Tess put her hands on his shoulders, felt him tremble with desire and need. She leaned forward and kissed him.

Ark made another noise deep in his throat. He shifted his hands to her hips, then pulled out and thrust back into her.

Again and again.

Tess held on, kissing him and accepting him as he thrust deeper, reaching sensitive, tender places far inside of her. She was panting again, wanting again. And he gave it to her. She broke the kiss and buried her head in the curve of his shoulder as a second orgasm rushed over her.

"Tess," he groaned her name in a thick, shuddering voice and drove into her one last time with his orgasm.

Ark sat back at the kitchen table. They had another hour before they should leave for the Fantasy Club. They were back to doing research. He lifted his beer.

It was almost too heavy.

"Sugar, I think you killed me." Two more times. He'd gotten the chance to make long, slow love to her again on her bed. He used his mouth to make her beg. Then she paid him back in the shower.

She grinned across the table where she was back at her laptop. "You're the one who had something to prove, Underwood."

God, she was beautiful. She had her hair piled up on her head from the shower, and her skin did that glowing female thing. She had pulled on a tank top and her jeans. No bra. Her lean, toned arms flexed as she worked on the computer. "So what do you think, Doc, do I have erectile dysfunction? Need the rush of a new babe to get it up?"

She flushed red. "I'm so sorry I ever—"

Ark got up and went around the table. "Tess, I'm just teasing you." He dropped to a crouch next to her chair. "We've all done stuff like your e-mail. I'm not pissed about it. It was a private thing that got out into the public by accident. I'm pissed that someone sold it. I hate it when people use me that way." He wanted to make her understand. "I fought my way to the top, Tess. People who pull shit like this e-mail? They are cheating."

She met his gaze directly. "Honesty means a lot to you, doesn't it?"

Ark looked into her brown eyes and knew she understood. "Yeah. My dad was in a crazy business, too. But he always kept it real, Tess. I guess I learned from him. He put my mom and us kids first." He thought of a memory from so long ago. "Sometimes he had a late night and when he came home we'd all be in bed. But he'd wake one of us boys up to have ice cream with him. All by ourselves. It was pretty cool to a little kid."

Her gaze softened. "So he came home to his family when he could have been out partying with famous people."

Like her parents probably had done. He regretted that he'd said anything. It was like throwing up what he had into her face. "I'm just saying that he was honest. He said his family came first, and we did. I respect honesty. And you are honest. More honest than any other woman I've met."

She smiled. "Thanks. But I'm also more trouble than any woman you've ever met. I need to fix this. I've found something here—" She turned back to the computer. Then she asked, "Would any man go to a sex store and buy a pink-colored erection enhancer?"

Ark looked at the computer screen. She was back on Sensual Delights' Web site. "Not any man I know."

"So Fred's killer brought that with her. She had to get it somewhere. And if it's Linda Riley's stepdaughter—"

"But we didn't see any pink ones there," he pointed out.

She started scrolling through some screens. "But they may sell them on the Internet, meaning they have stock in the store to ship to customers. Here." She pointed to the screen where she found the erection enhancer like the one Ark saw at the shop.

Ark stood up and set his hand on her shoulder. "It's blue."

"Let's see what other colors they have." She clicked on the word *colors*, and a drop-down screen opened up. It listed black, blue, green, pink . . . "There!" Tess pointed.

"So the stepdaughter could have gotten the pink cock ring from Sensual Delights. And she could easily have given Fred a bag from there to get into the store to do his articles. Fred probably had the Viagra, and my condoms—I don't know what my condoms was about."

Tess turned around. "I do. She couldn't get you to use your condoms with her. So she used them with another man. Trust me, it's a female thing. You rejected her."

Ark rubbed his hand over his face. "Who?" He dropped his hand. "We have to get the first name of Linda's step-daughter."

"Yes, but let's think for a minute. Josie's take was that this woman is on the fringe of your life. To accomplish everything we think she has, she would have to have access to Sensual Delights. She would have had to have access to your suite somehow since there was no forced entry. She would have known that you and I were at the restaurant long enough to lure Fred into your room and kill him. Plus, it's likely the killer leaked the sex toy part to the media so they now refer to it as the Sex Toy Murder."

Ark was impressed as hell. "That's good. So who knows me that well? There's Giles, but he didn't do it, obviously. And who can get in my room?"

"Someone who works at the hotel. It'd be easy enough to get a job there right before the big race. Did you see anyone you recognized as a maid or something?"

He shook his head. "Don't think so." Something bothered him about getting into his room. "The police are checking all the hotel staff." But that wasn't it. What bothered him?

Tess said, "Ark, think—"

She stopped talking when his cell phone rang. Ark pulled it from his pocket and looked at the screen. It was Maureen. He felt a twinge of guilt. She'd been working day and night since the murder to try and contain the fallout and figure out a way to keep Ark's reputation, such as it was, from suffering too much damage. He answered, "What's up?"

"Couple things, Ark. First I got the name of Linda's step-daughter."

Ark started pacing the kitchen. Now they were getting somewhere. "What's her name?" He could feel Tess's gaze on him, but he concentrated on Maureen's voice in his ear.

"It's Heidi."

He stopped pacing. "Heidi? Groupie Heidi? She is Linda's stepdaughter?" Ark had trained himself to process information very fast. His life depended on it when he was driving upwards of 180 miles per hour. Heidi was on the fringe of his life, and he had rejected her sexual advances countless times. She had been there when Ark made his original plans with Giles. She could probably have gotten a job with the hotel . . .

"Yes, that Heidi. But, Ark, I have more information, and it's not good. You're not going to like it."

A twinge of uneasiness rolled through him. "What? Just tell me." He glanced at Tess to see her watching him.

Maureen said, "I found the reporter who published the e-mail. After using a little persuasion, I got him to tell me who sold him the e-mail."

The twinge took root inside of him. Ark knew how she persuaded the reporter—her uncle ran a large Hollywood movie production studio. All Maureen probably had to do was promise the reporter a chance to pitch his story. They always had a story. "Who?"

"Dr. Collins."

He looked at Tess. "No."

"I'm afraid so. She sold it to him Friday after she left the hotel sometime. They paid her five thousand. He said she put the check with the stub attached in her laptop case."

She looked so damned honest. He'd believed her—that the e-mail had been an honest mistake. But why? Did she need the money?

"Ark?"

"Yes, I'm here." He heard the coldness in his voice.

So did Tess. She frowned at him.

"We need to have a press conference, and you need to distance yourself from Dr. Collins. We'll say that you dated her once and realized she wasn't the kind of woman you admire . . . I'll have it all written up. Then we'll talk about how we are co-operating with the police, etc. In an hour, Ark. Be back at the hotel in an hour. I've already secured a conference room to use."

"Press conference at the Speedway Hotel in an hour. I'll be there." He hung up.

Tess started firing questions at him. "Who is it? Did she give you a name? Ark?"

Tess didn't kill Fred. Ark knew that, she'd been with him. But she'd lied to him, used him. She wasn't real. Hurt and a feeling of betrayal ripped through his gut. If she'd needed money, he'd have given it to her.

Obviously she'd been there at the hotel to sell Fred the e-mail. She'd been staying with Fred, too—so was there more? It didn't matter.

Her face tightened with anxiety. "Ark? What's the matter? Do you recognize the name Linda gave you?"

He walked toward her. Then looked down at the floor between Tess's chair and the wall where she'd put her laptop case. He'd seen her get it from its place by the front door in the living room and bring it in here, then pull out her laptop and boot it up. Ark went behind Tess's chair, bent over, and grabbed the case.

"Ark? What are you doing?" She twisted around to see him.

The part of the case that had held the computer was unzipped. He stuck his hand into the smaller pockets. He touched a piece of paper. His breath locked in his chest. He didn't want to look. He wanted, desperately, to believe in Tess.

But Ark dealt with life head on.

He pulled out the paper. It was folded in half. He dropped the case and unfolded the paper.

A check stub. The vendor was Dr. Tess Collins. The amount was five thousand. No check was attached. Most likely because it had been deposited.

He dropped the check stub on Tess's lap. He went to the other side of the table where he'd left his shirt and shoes while having sex with Tess.

Just sex as it turned out. Sex he paid for in a manner of speaking since she sold the e-mail about him for five grand.

Tess grabbed the check stub. Her face was blank and pale.

Ark said, "I have no room for liars like you in my life." He left.

Eight

Tess was stunned for about three minutes. Then devastated. She read the check stub over and over, trying to understand. She never sold her e-mail. She never went to a tabloid. She hadn't lied to Ark.

But he believed she had. She wasn't worth fighting for. She wasn't worth taking the time to ask for an explanation.

She didn't have an explanation.

A painful lump filled her throat. God, it hurt. Now she knew why she didn't take chances with passion, with caring so damn much. The pain was unbearable. Tears ran down her face, but she didn't care, didn't wipe them away. She couldn't even see her computer screen.

Wait.

Her computer had been at her house while she'd been staying at Josie's. She had found it in its usual place next to the foyer table by the front door.

How had the check stub gotten in there?

Someone had broken into her house. She had been gone for days. Someone set her up.

Tess shook off her heavy self-pity. Someone was trying to separate her from Ark Underwood. Someone who knew him well enough to do it. Tess got up and grabbed her cordless phone.

Heidi? Tess fought to clear her head and think. That was the name Ark said—*Groupie Heidi.* So Heidi was a groupie and Linda's stepdaughter? Had Ark rejected her advances and she decided to pay him back? Get revenge? Make money? Did she get a job at the hotel as a maid or something like that to get into Ark's room?

Who told Ark's publicist that Tess sold him the e-mail? Obviously that's what Maureen told Ark on the phone. That was the reason Ark knew to look in her laptop case for the check stub.

Tess dialed the phone and, when it was answered, said, "Jo?"

"Tess, what's wrong?"

She swallowed and took a deep breath to get control of herself. "Ark's meeting someone at the Speedway Hotel in an hour for a press conference. We have to get there. Something's wrong." Tess took the cordless phone with her to get shoes and her purse while explaining what happened.

Ark didn't want her. That was fine. She could live with that. Tess had a good life; she loved her life.

She might have loved Ark, but that didn't matter now.

What mattered was that someone was screwing with both Tess's and Ark's lives. With their decisions. That she was not going to allow.

Josie broke into her thoughts. "Tess, if it's Heidi, Ark will have the police on her before the press conference. So what are we going for? To tell Ark he's an ass? 'Cause if that's it, I'm there."

Tess walked back into her kitchen and was slapped with the memory of making love with Ark. And the pain. She closed her eyes. *Think,* damn it. "No. Jo—I'm not convinced this Heidi is the killer. That check stub has to be a fake, and someone had to plant it in my laptop." She pushed aside the creepy notion of someone breaking into her house to stay focused. "What would Heidi gain by convincing Ark I sold the e-mail?" She was trying to solidify her thoughts. Zero in on what was wrong, what didn't make sense.

Someone knocked at her front door.

Tess ignored the knock.

"Tess," Josie's voice was gentle. "I'm in my car. I'm on my way, honey. Just stay there."

Tess damn near cried just from Josie's caring. Ark might not want her, but her friends—they had chosen Tess just like she chose them. They loved her. And now, Jo heard the pain in her voice and was desperate to get to her.

She had a good life. And a damn good reason to fight to clear her name.

And yes, to protect Ark.

"No. Jo, I'm okay. I promise. I'm just trying to think this out. To get clear. It has to be someone close to Ark. Could a groupie get that close? Close enough to plant a check stub at my house?"

Jo added, "How would she know where you live, Tess? And that you weren't home? How would a groupie know that?"

"Exactly." Tess looked around the kitchen as the pieces in her mind came together. "That's it. Oh, God, Jo. Ark's publicist—how would she know about the check stub if Heidi planted it? Why would she tell Ark that? Jo"—she had that flash of everything suddenly making sense—"it had to be Maureen who planted the check stub." Was Maureen the killer?

"Tess! Get out of the house!" Jo's voice had an edge of panic.

"Meet me at the Speedway Hotel." Tess hung up and headed for the door to the garage, her thoughts whirling. Maureen had enough connections and experience to figure out where Tess lived. And she probably knew from Ark that Tess had been staying at Josie's house. Ark said he'd sent Maureen to Sensual Delights—she could have been Fred's source. And, God, how had she missed it? Maureen had been with Giles when he went in Ark's room the night Fred was murdered. She could have left the door unlatched or something. Tess pushed open the door to the garage and hit the button to open the garage door. She hurried to her car.

"Going someplace?"

Tess looked up just as the cell phone in her purse rang. She ignored the phone and looked up at the voice.

Oh, God.

Maureen. She had a gun. All the karate in the world wasn't going to help her against a killer with a gun.

Ark was fifteen minutes from the Speedway Hotel when he doubled back to Tess's house. He grabbed his cell phone, clicked on Tess's name, and hit send, praying that she would answer.

He was an ass. Christ. Tess hadn't sold that e-mail. It didn't make any sense. Why would she fight with a reporter earlier that day in Josie's garage if she had sold the e-mail? She would have just given a statement. He saw the bruise. And she had stayed with him Thursday night; he was reasonably certain she hadn't had the e-mail with her.

He was positive that she hadn't had her laptop with her. He had gone into her house with her and seen her get the case by the front door. The house had smelled closed up and musty. Not bad, just normal for a few days away. So Tess had clearly left her laptop at home while staying at Josie's house. Ark smelled a setup, and God knew he'd seen a few of them by reporters desperate for a story.

Tess had told him the truth from the very first moment. And he had called her a liar. Told her there was no room in his life for her.

Jesus, he knew he'd hurt her. Badly.

She wasn't answering her cell phone. He hung up on her voice mail and dialed again, hoping she'd answer.

So how had that check stub gotten in her laptop case? Someone had to plant it. A shiver of cold fear ran down his spine. It was one thing if someone was after him—Ark could handle that.

But not Tess.

Did someone break into her house and plant a fake check stub? How had they gotten into her house?

The thing that had been nagging at him suddenly popped up in his head.

How had the killer gotten into his hotel room? They knew of two people that had been in his room. Giles and Maureen.

Giles wasn't a killer. But he'd probably let one in. Then all Maureen had to do was tape the door latch, or not close the door, whatever . . .

Fear slammed into Ark. Deep, blood-freezing, mind-numbing fear. He dropped the cell phone and grabbed the steering wheel with both hands. And floored it.

Tess sat in the same kitchen chair she had occupied while talking to Ark earlier. Maureen stood with her back to the sink and the gun trained on Tess and said, "Ark Underwood is all I have left, so you'd better consider this deal I'm going to offer you."

A deal? The woman had forced her back into her own house at gunpoint and closed the automatic garage door. Now she wanted to offer Tess a deal? Something Ark had said at dinner Thursday night came back to her. Tess had joked that the newspapers still called him the bad boy of NASCAR. And Ark had answered, *It sells papers and tickets. And I give them reason occasionally. My publicist likes it; it gives her something to do.*

Maureen wanted to keep Ark as the bad boy? Tess had the sick feeling they'd been wrong all along. This whole thing from the blackmail scheme to Fred's murder hadn't been about money or revenge. It had been an attempt to force Ark back into his place as the bad boy of NASCAR.

Tess tried to take control of the conversation by picking up the check stub and saying, "This was clever. You did it on a computer?"

"That was easy. Harder was getting into your house but I have contacts with skills."

She'd hired someone to break into Tess's house to put a

fake check stub in her laptop case. This woman was determined or deranged. And scary.

Maureen didn't miss a beat. She reached into her black designer handbag and pulled out a paper. "A cashier's check for fifty thousand dollars. Here's the deal: shut up and stay away from Ark."

She glanced at the check, then back up to Maureen's face. Her freckles stood out under the glare of the overhead lights. "Why?"

Her jaw hardened. "You wouldn't understand. You just wouldn't. You have a PhD, a fancy career, friends. Ark is all I have. Uncle Spence created my publicity agency to give me a career. It went well for a while. I married a client. I was so damn good at putting out fires. I had all the connections, but my problems started when Ark stopped creating trouble. Suddenly there were no fires left to put out. He rarely dates these days, he doesn't drink much, and he doesn't lose his temper. My clients started drifting away to publicists who were getting famous for spinning bad behavior of other famous people." Maureen looked down at the check in her hand. "Then my husband left me."

Oh, Lord. Maureen believed she needed Ark to get her life back. The breakup of her marriage had probably been the final stressor that sent her over the edge. It was easier for her to blame Ark than to accept responsibility for her own life imploding. And to focus on fixing Ark, rather than herself. It was common to see people doing this in therapy.

Just not to this extent.

Maureen lifted her gaze back to Tess. "So I have to recreate the magic. Ark needs some controversy. Once I'm done spinning it, he'll have twice the fans. More endorsements. Commercials. I'll be the most sought after publicist."

Tess didn't have time to do the years' worth of therapy to help Maureen fix her life. But she needed to get her redirected. "Maureen, have you talked to Ark about this?" Maybe she could establish a connection while she figured out what to do.

The woman may have convinced herself she was going to pay Tess off, but Tess was sure Maureen was going to have to kill her. Tess simply knew too much now.

Maureen waved the check. "I've tried to talk to him. I've sent him girls that could attract publicity. But lately, Ark's complaining to Uncle Spence about me. He doesn't understand how much he needs me."

"So you killed Fred to prove to him how much he needs you?"

"The original plan was blackmail for orgy photos that would get into the media. Just enough to make Ark look a little bad again. Just enough to need me. I was going to prove those were doctored photos." Her face paled in anger. "But Fred . . . I should have known he'd double-cross me. He was a sleazy tabloid reporter."

Whom she was more than willing to use. And kill, Tess thought.

The anger cleared from Maureen's face. "But killing him was even better. Having Fred found murdered wearing the sex toy and in Ark's hotel suite bedroom, now that was a disaster for Ark. A publicity nightmare I could really sink my teeth into."

Tess fought down fear and assessed her situation. The entryway to the living room was behind her left shoulder. She could turn and run, hang a fast right, and get out the front door. "So you'd like me to take the check and pretend that I sold my e-mail to the tabloid?"

Her green eyes narrowed. "It's a fair trade-off. You get to live and have some extra money." She jerked the gun in a threat.

Tess's house phone rang.

Maureen jumped.

Tess leaped up from the chair, turned, and arced around the wall to race for the front door.

"Stop!" Maureen screamed.

Tess heard the gun fire. She tensed for a bullet to tear through her, but she kept running. No pain, no shock of a bullet ripped through her back. The door was only a few feet in front of her. She reached out for the door handle with two hands, one to grasp the knob, the other to turn the lock. Then she pulled it open.

"I'll shoot!" Maureen screamed, her voice getting closer behind Tess.

She would have run out the door, but Ark stood there in the entrance. Oh, God. "Run!" She screamed at him.

He was looking behind her. Then he leaped at Tess. He was fast. He bowled her over like a football player. Knocked her flat to the ground and covered her body with his.

They both heard the gunshot.

"Shit. Damn, that hurts," Ark said in a low voice.

Tess could hardly breathe. Her bruised left wrist screamed in pain. But all that went away when she realized Ark had been shot. She wiggled, desperate to get out from under him.

"Hold still!"

She entwined her legs around his, then levered herself and flipped him off her. He grunted in real pain, but she ignored that and rolled up to her feet.

Maureen held the gun in both hands, but her face had paled. She looked down at Ark.

Tess glanced down. Blood. Right calf. Tore through his pants. He was trying to get up. "Stay down," she ordered him, and then looked back at Maureen.

"You made me shoot him," she said in a thin voice. She lifted her gaze from Ark to Tess. "You made me shoot him!" Shock was giving way to anger. She moved the gun toward Tess.

"Maureen!" Ark bellowed.

Damn it, he was getting up! Tess didn't look away from Maureen, but in her peripheral vision, she saw Ark grab on to the foyer table to pull himself up to his feet. She sized up her options.

"Maureen." Ark's voice cracked, but he was up to his full height. He held out his hand. "Give me the gun. It's over. I called the pol—"

Tess knew telling her that was a mistake. "Shut up!"

"You needed me." Maureen shifted the gun to point it at Ark. "How could you call the police? You need me!"

Tess had only one chance. She took two fast steps and launched into a flying kick. She caught Maureen right in her upper abdomen and rib cage with both feet.

Maureen flew back, hit the couch, and crumpled to the floor.

Tess slammed into the carpet. She tried to roll, but she hit the coffee table with her bad wrist. "Hell." She rolled the other way and got up. She had to get the gun!

Ark was already there, leaving a trail of blood. He had the gun in his hand and looked up at Tess. "She's out cold."

Tess nodded. "We need an ambulance for you." She was still thinking, assessing, trying to manage the situation. Ark was hurt, shot.

Shot trying to protect her. He had saved her life. Again. Why?

He sank down onto the arm of her couch. "I already called 911 on the way over. Hear the sirens?"

"Thank you." What else did she say? It was over. Tess could face him now. He knew she hadn't lied. He didn't want her; she could accept that. "I don't know why you came back, but thank you." Her hair was falling down in her eyes from where she had it pinned up. Her wrist throbbed.

His face was becoming drawn from pain, with white lines forming around his tight mouth. "I don't want your thanks, Tess."

Well. Okay. She took a breath. Didn't help, she still felt as if she'd been slapped. It hurt a hell of a lot worse than her wrist. The sirens were closer. "I'll just get a towel and put pressure on your leg." She took a quick look to make sure Maureen was still out, then headed toward the bathroom.

Ark caught her right hand.

She looked down at him. "I know you're in pain. They can give—"

"Tess." He tried to pull her toward him but was interrupted when the police poured into the house.

* * *

The emergency room overflowed with people. Ark's family, his lawyers, Giles, some other drivers, and reporters. Reporters that had been at the Speedway Hotel waiting for Ark Underwood to show up. Apparently, Maureen had thought she could deal with Tess, then get back in time to conduct the press conference.

Tess sat in the waiting room with Gwen, Josie, and Nikki. Josie had showed up at her house the same time as the police did. Because Tess hadn't answered her phone, Josie knew she was in trouble. Nikki and Gwen had met them at emergency and insisted Tess get her wrist x-rayed. It was only a bad sprain. Tess had resisted saying, "I told you so."

Gwen leaned over. "Keep the ice on it, Tess."

She nodded and moved the ice back to her wrist. She knew she should leave before the reporters figured out who she was. The news of Ark Underwood being shot was so big, and then add in the fact that his own publicist shot him, Tess had become fairly inconsequential. But eventually they'd sort out that Ark had been shot at her house and remember her. She didn't want to make things any worse for Ark. She just wanted to know he would be okay. His family and Giles handled the reporters.

"Do you want some Tylenol? You should let me give you a shot for pain," Nikki said.

Tess looked at all of them. She loved them, but right now . . . "Do me a favor. Go get some coffee and bring me back some when you are done."

Nikki looked horrified.

Josie got up. "Come on, girls. She just wants a few minutes to herself." The three of them headed off to find the cafeteria.

"Dr. Collins."

She looked up. Damn, it was the reporter who had accosted her in Josie's garage this morning. He had slid by the Ark-family-and-friends barricade. His blue eyes were icy. "Do you feel your e-mail is responsible for Ark Underwood getting shot?"

Her stomach cramped. *Yes*. And she felt guilty because Ark had been shot while trying to protect her.

"No comment," she said tiredly. People didn't die from leg wounds. Ark would be fine. She should have gone home. But what if his leg was badly damaged? What if it ruined his career?

The reporter leaned over her, putting his hands on the chair arms to trap her. "No comment? You might have ruined Underwood's career. Was that your plan all along?"

Tess let the ice pack slide off her wrist to the chair seat and said quietly, "Step back or I swear to God, I'll kick your balls up into your tonsils."

His face went red. "You touch me again, and I'll—"

"You'll get away from her."

The reporter let go of the chair and snapped up at the hard male voice right behind him.

Tess jumped out of the chair so that she stood next to the startled reporter. "Ark!" He stood there, leaning on a pair of crutches. His family and friends were moving up behind him. He looked okay. "Ark, what did the doctor say about your leg?"

He ignored her questions and asked one of his own instead. "Tess, is this the reporter that hurt your wrist?"

She nodded, searching him over. His pant leg was cut and his calf bandaged.

"Ark Underwood." The reporter tried to get past her.

Tess shoved her elbow into his stomach.

"Ooff." He doubled over, then wheezed, "You bitch, that's assault!"

Tess ignored him, but she couldn't ignore all the people fanning out behind Ark and staring at her. More reporters were trying to shove through. Camera flashes started going off. It was a nightmare. She was making things worse.

Ark looked at her. "Tess, come here."

She glanced at the reporter to see that he was still doubled over. Sheesh, she hadn't hit him that hard. She walked a few feet up to Ark. "What did the doctor say?"

"I'm fine, sugar. You need to get behind me."

She looked at his family. His mom stood at his shoulder with two men who had to be his brothers. Friends had moved in tight, and reporters were behind them. There was no room behind him. And she didn't belong there with all his people. "It's time for me to go home. I just wanted to make sure—" Tears sprang up in her eyes, and she looked away, embarrassed. It had just been a long night. A long few days.

Ark reached out, took hold of her right arm, and pulled her up to his body. "Sweetheart, I'm not letting you go. We have something special, and I'm not going to screw this up any more than I already have. I will spend the next ten years making up for the fact that I doubted you or your honesty." He brought his hand up and wiped the single tear that slid down her face.

Then he looked behind him. "Mom, this is Tess. Take care of her for a minute." He gently nudged her to his mom's side. One of his brothers moved over, creating an opening. His mom took Tess's hand in hers; then they closed around her.

Ark's mom said, "I'm Stella, Tess. Ark's told us all about you."

She looked up at Stella's brown eyes. "He has?"

She nodded. "Of course, you're very important to him."

"Now," Ark said to the reporter, "you were saying?"

The reporter straightened up. "Do you hold Dr. Collins responsible for starting all of this with her e-mail?"

"No. I have only one statement to make about that e-mail. I will be grateful for that e-mail every single day because it brought Dr. Collins into my life."

"Ark?" Tess tried to step forward, but his mom had a death grip on her hand. "What are you doing?"

"Giving a statement, sugar. Be with you in a sec," Ark said over his shoulder, then used his crutches to take a step closer to the reporter. He added, "And, if you ever touch her again. Or threaten her. Or get in her space. Or just annoy her. I will find you."

The reporter's eyes widened while flashbulbs behind Tess went off at a dizzying speed from other reporters.

The reporter said, "She attacked me!"

Ark chuckled. "No doubt about it, Dr. Collins can take care of herself."

Swear to God, Tess heard pride in his voice.

"But, and here's the part where you really need to pay attention, Tess doesn't get all riled up about reporters abusing her. I do. That's the deal, reporters stay away from my family. And that includes Dr. Collins. Got that?"

The reporter turned and fled.

Tess just stood there. Ark's mom still had a hold of her right hand.

Ark turned and used his crutches to move up to her. "Let's go home, sugar. I'm going to make damn sure you fall in love with me. I need to get to work on that right now."

"Love? But it's so fast . . ." It was all too fast. Too much. She had loved him for years anyway. What was she thinking? This was crazy.

Ark smiled at her, the smile that deepened the cleft in his chin and shot straight through to her heart. "What did you expect, Doc? I'm one of the Fast Boys of NASCAR. I always work fast."

Dear Readers:

I hope you enjoyed meeting Ark and Tess as much as I enjoyed writing their story. Both these characters have been wandering around separately in some story ideas that weren't working. Then I tried pairing Ark and Tess up and they came to life. All I had to do was get out of their way and let their story unfold. But now Tess's three friends, Josie, Gwen and Nikki are starting to grumble that they want to meet a hot guy under mysterious and sexy circumstances too. We shall see . . .

In the meantime, I hope you will look for my latest Samantha Shaw Mystery, *Batteries Required*, coming out in May 2005. Sam and her girlfriend, Angel, quickly discover that a box of sex toys should come with the warning, *Too Hot to Handle*. What starts out as a lark turns into high voltage danger that has Sam on the run. Throw in Sam's sizzling PI boyfriend making sexy demands, a crazy stalker, a handsome but cranky police detective and the mix adds up to another one of Sam's blazing adventures. I hope you'll pick up a copy of *Batteries Required* and let me know how you like it!

Happy reading,

Jennifer Apodaca
www.jenniferapodaca.com

Three Men and a Body

Nancy J. Cohen

One

Reality show contestant Heather Payne couldn't believe her good luck. She had the chance to win not only her dream house, but also the business she could never afford on her own. The game plan sounded easy: get a bed-and-breakfast in Winter Park, Florida, up and running within seven days. With her experience as a real estate agent, that shouldn't be too tough, right?

Wheeling her Samsonite suitcase along the brick walkway from the parking lot, she scanned the house ahead with a critical eye. Two stories high, painted white with green shutters, the concrete block construction looked solid enough to withstand hurricanes. Ditto for the white tile roof. She surveyed the windows with their energy-efficient design, then swept her gaze to the double front doors finished in a cherry veneer. Fiberglass, most likely, as it made them more resistant to rot than wood, an important consideration in humid central Florida. Brilliant pink bougainvillea, red pentas, and white gardenias provided splashes of color against greenery poised to soak up water during June's rainy season.

Heather blinked rapidly to dispel the moisture brimming in her eyes. This house was everything she'd dreamed about, and more. Ideas flew through her head as she climbed a short flight of steps to a shaded front porch. If she added some wicker furniture, she could serve afternoon tea out here. Hanging plants would be a nice touch, too. Think what a blast she could have decorating for the holidays, and. . . . Swallowing, she rang the doorbell. The inn didn't belong to her yet.

"Heather, come in," said Logan Samuels with a wide grin. One of the co-producers, he'd interviewed her over the past month along with his female partner. As their host, he looked like the typical TV personality: short, wavy brown hair, perfect teeth, a straight nose between two deep-set gray eyes, and a chiseled jaw. Overall, he reminded her of molded plastic. Even his suit was freshly pressed as though he'd just come from the cleaners.

She entered a paneled foyer. Beyond an oak staircase, she saw a family room where several contestants lounged. They peered at her curiously. "Hi," she called in what she hoped was a confident tone. Over the next week, they'd come to know each other intimately.

"Put your stuff upstairs, then come on down," one of the girls replied. She had a mass of blond hair and a challenge in her eyes.

"I'll show you to your room," Logan said. "Since we have eight guest bedrooms, you'll each have your own accommodation. Michelle can show you around the house later." A woman with thick black locks gave a welcoming wave. "Once we're all here, we'll review the rules."

She noticed cameramen setting up their equipment while lighting and sound technicians took measurements. "Where will we be filmed?" she asked when they reached the upstairs corridor.

"You'll see. Here you go."

Logan opened the door to number four, a spacious, airy room with two double beds, an armoire, two chairs beside a writing desk, and a private bathroom. No telephone, television, or computer. Heather rolled her suitcase to a halt just as the doorbell rang below. After Logan excused himself, she took time to freshen her lipstick and unpack. Viewing the sparse furnishings, she pictured the coordinated linen ensembles and accent pieces she'd add to give the room a cozier ambience.

She jumped when a knock sounded on her open door frame. "You must be the new arrival," said a man's rich, deep voice. "Rex Gerard. Guess we're here for the same reason."

Her gaze latched on to a pair of the bluest eyes she'd ever seen. Their aqua hue reminded her of the Caribbean Sea. Leaning lazily against the door post, the man watched while she hastily shoved her last bra into a drawer.

"I'm Heather Payne. Nice to meet you."

"I hope you still feel that way by the end of the week." In no hurry to leave, he crossed his arms over his chest.

Her glance slid from his jet black hair to his broad shoulders encased in a ratty T-shirt. They had to wear their own clothing on the show, which didn't seem to faze him. Shorts and sandals completed his casual attire. In contrast, she'd spiffed up in an emerald dress that matched her eyes. Tendrils of dark walnut hair blew about her face from the air-conditioning. Aware that lines of fatigue etched her forehead, she hoped the makeup artist they'd been promised would give them tips for camera work. Not that Rex needed any help. Even with his worn outfit, he looked like a guy who knew how to take charge.

His blatant return perusal made her blush. "This should be exciting for all of us," she said, letting enthusiasm lift her tone. "I can't wait to get started."

"Me, too."

"Let's go see what Logan has to say."

He didn't move aside to let her pass. Instead, the corners of his mouth tilted upward while she wedged her way out the door, giving him a look down her cleavage. Was he hoping to score while he was here? If so, she intended to disappoint him. She had one goal, and one goal only: to win.

So did the rest of the contenders. After the last person arrived, Logan and his co-producer, Tanya, gave them the scoop. Seated in the family room that faced a screened pool deck beyond a set of sliding glass doors, the contestants draped over sofas, chairs, and sat on the carpet while Logan introduced them and told them the rules for the show.

"Today is Friday. We've filled the rooms beginning a week from tomorrow. That means you'll have seven more days to get this place ready for its first guests. It will be up to you to acquire all the provisions you'll need, design a marketing plan, prepare for registration, meet legal and insurance requirements, locate suppliers, and so on. We've told you how much money you're budgeted. Go over that amount, and you all get axed."

"Can we make calls from the house?" asked Kim, the blonde who'd given Heather the challenging look earlier. Chewing a wad of gum, she kicked off her shoes to display her scarlet toenails. Heather wondered what her dream business could be; the girl looked as though she'd rather spend the week sunbathing.

"Using cell phones is forbidden for the duration of the show," Logan replied. "That means you'll want to establish local phone service as soon as possible. Nor are you allowed to use any instructional manuals while you're here. That includes books on how to set up a bed-and-breakfast, menu planners, fix-it guides. You're to rely on each other's resources. Violating the rules is immediate grounds for disqualification.

"Each night at eight, we'll gather here to discuss your accomplishments. Beginning tomorrow evening, TV viewers will vote on your business abilities, and whoever drops the ball gets booted out. At the end, the best professional wins this house. You may sell it to set up your dream enterprise or keep it to run as your own. With its prime location, it's valued at over five million dollars. Questions?"

Heather raised her hand. "Where are the cameras located?"

"You're fair game to be filmed anywhere, except in the bathroom," Tanya answered with a grin. Their co-producer wore her swirled golden hair in the classic style of a television anchorwoman. "At this point, we'll be going behind the scenes. Our production van is parked next door on the neighbor's property we're renting. Logan, we're outta here. Good luck."

Heather exchanged glances with Rex. His teasing glimmer

indicated he didn't think he'd be the one to get the shaft. *You just wait and see,* she told him silently.

They'd started early, and by noon, everyone was hungry. The crew members had filed away to silent positions, until the eight of them faced each other.

"Cripes, there's no food in the refrigerator," exclaimed Sarah Jane Craig. A short blonde with a pixie cut, she'd traipsed into the kitchen ahead of everyone else.

"Yo, babe, we gotta remedy that fast," said Dave Molina with a grin. His heavy-lidded eyes gave him a perpetual hungover look. That might not be so far from the mark, Heather mused, regarding his black shirt open nearly to his waist. His jeans were slung so low over his hips that his briefs showed.

"Somebody has to go shopping," Gary Friedman remarked. "We need a lot of things, not just food." His serious demeanor went along with his collared blue shirt and black trousers.

"I'll do it," Jonathan Walker offered. "Give me a list." His ruddy complexion contrasted with his spiked pale blond hair that showed darker roots.

"Oh, I love lists," squealed Michelle, whose dark eyes sparkled with excitement.

"Wait, we need a plan," Rex said in an authoritative voice. "We should figure out who's going to do what."

This dissolved into a round of bickering. Brushing a strand of hair from her eyes, Heather stepped forward. "Wait a minute, guys. Why don't we start by dividing up each category? For example, supplies should include not only food, but also things like soaps and shampoos for our guest baths, linens, even dishes. Did you notice that the kitchen cupboards are bare?"

"You're right," Gary cut in. "Michelle, take this down. We need someone on marketing and advertising to keep the rooms filled. Then there's guest registration. Do we want to use a sign-in book or find a computer program that can do this?"

"First we have to get a computer," Rex pointed out. "Don't forget, we have to work these things into the budget. Who's good with numbers?"

Jon waved a hand. "I'll do procurement and keep the books."

Dave ran out to get pizza and drinks while they continued their debate.

"What about cooking and cleaning? I hope we aren't expected to do it ourselves," Kim said with a sexy pout.

"I'd love to be in charge of meals," Sarah offered. "I want to be the winner so I can open my own restaurant."

"Good, then you can clean up after lunch," Gary told her with a sneer.

An hour later, they sat around the dining room table, littered with empty pizza cartons and soda cans. The room held four other smaller square tables, none of which looked inviting with their plain wooden tops. They begged for tablecloths and decorative accessories, Heather thought to herself.

"Never mind the guests. Our most immediate need is to provide for ourselves in the upcoming week," she said. "Our beds have no sheets on them. Someone has to go to Target to buy some cheap stuff just for us. Meanwhile, do we want to design a theme with a logo? We could coordinate table linens, sheets and towels, guest toiletries. I'd be happy to take charge of the marketing angle along with advertising."

They finished assigning duties. While Sarah and Jon went shopping, the others got to work on their individual jobs.

Heather decided to write a blurb about the house before placing any ads. First she had to get a better idea of its amenities. Furniture had been provided, but not much else.

Upstairs, she'd just entered one of the larger bedrooms when she found Rex stalking her heels.

"What is it?" she asked, whirling to face him.

"I need to make sure things are working properly," he said with a disarming grin. "If I'm in charge of maintenance, we don't want the lights going out at inappropriate moments."

His suggestive glance told her what he might do under such circumstances. Heat swamped her senses. Resisting his appeal could prove to be difficult.

"Logan said this place is less than two years old," she replied, moistening her lips.

His gaze followed her movements. "Looks pretty good, doesn't it? But then, things aren't always what they seem."

"Like some of us? Gary dresses as though he works in an office, but if he bosses people around the way he does our team, he wouldn't last long in a management position."

"His fingers are grease-stained. I don't think he has an office job. Besides, if he had the money to set up his own business, he wouldn't be here. What do you do?" Rex asked.

"I'm a real estate agent. I've always loved houses. This one is wonderful." She couldn't keep the wistful note from her voice. "I've always dreamed of owning a bed-and-breakfast."

"Yeah? My goal is to captain a charter fishing boat. I want to live on one of those yachts."

"So you'd sell the house?"

"Definitely."

"But this place is so beautiful. If it were mine, I'd, well, cherish it."

"People should be cherished, not buildings." He stepped farther inside the room, closing the distance between them. She wondered if the microphones were picking up their conversation. "What do you do for a living now?" she asked.

"I'm in furniture repair and restoration. It's my father's business."

She heard the hard edge in his tone. "I gather that's not what you expect to do for your whole life."

"No, but I can't deny the skills it's given me. They'll come in handy when I'm fixing my boat."

What other skills do you possess? her naughty mind wanted to ask.

She stood by a wall. Reaching around her, Rex inspected the molding, caressing the wood with his strong hands. Heather imagined what it would be like to feel those hands on her body. Her knees weakened, especially when he turned his attention to her and laid his palm on her shoulder.

"You know, you seem more sincere than the other women," he said, his voice husky. "I see fire in your eyes when you talk about running this place."

You should see the fire racing through my veins. Her pulse thrummed in her ears as she sniffed his sandalwood cologne. "If you're trying to distract me, it won't work," she said, hoping he wouldn't notice how weak her protest sounded.

"No?" He reached a hand to trace the outline of her mouth. "All's fair in love and war, isn't it?"

"Only if you consider this a battleground."

"I do, and if you're smart, you will also. Stay on guard. I wouldn't put it past Logan to throw a few wrenches into the works."

Two

"What do you mean?" Heather asked.

"Did you ever watch 'The Bachelor?' One of the girls was a spy who told the bachelor everything they said about him behind his back."

"Are you suggesting someone among us might be a plant?"

"You never know." Cupping her chin, Rex tilted her face upward. "Tell me, Heather, do you have a boyfriend?"

Her skin flushed. "No, I don't, but that's irrelevant. My personal status has nothing to do with the job that's required."

"The rules don't say anything about our remaining celibate. I'm single, too."

Lost in Logan's mesmerizing stare, Heather gradually became aware of a splashing noise. "Do you hear that?"

His head jerked up, his nostrils flaring. "Sounds like water spilling." Spinning around, he lunged out the door.

Heather followed him two doors down to number six, where she couldn't help admiring the cherry king-size bedroom suite.

Rex cursed from the bathroom. "The toilet's overflowing. The floor is flooded. Get a mop."

Heather raised her hands. "We don't have a mop. Did you tell Jon to get cleaning supplies?" She watched his butt tighten as he crouched to shut off the water faucet. Nice view, by golly.

His sinewy arm muscles contracted while he wrestled off the porcelain tank cover and fiddled with the plumbing.

"No, but I have to visit a hardware store to get what I need anyway. Is there a Home Depot nearby?"

"I'm not familiar with this area. I'll tell you what, let's go into town together. I'd like to ask the merchants if there's a community newsletter and what they do for local advertising. We should get on the national B&B listings and into travel guidebooks, too, but that may take some time."

"I think Jon planned to pick up a computer at Best Buy. You can check out hotel reservation links on the Internet."

"We'll need a Web page, also. I can design one real quick using Netscape Composer. It's a free download. But Dave has to set up his registration program on the computer. I hope he told Jon to buy Microsoft Office. All this is going to take time to install."

Rex straightened his spine, shaking out his wet hands after looking futilely for a towel. "Speak of the devil."

"Hey, what are you guys doing in my room?" Dave demanded, hooking his thumbs into his jeans waistband.

"Take a look," Heather said.

She backed away from the bathroom door to give him a glance inside, but he stepped behind her and encircled her with his arms. "Maybe you wanted to get me alone, and *he* butted in, huh babe?"

She shook him off. "Not quite."

"So what gives?" His lecherous grin turned her stomach.

"Your toilet got stuffed. There's water all over your floor, and we've nothing to dry it with."

He jabbed a stubby finger at Rex. "That's his problem. He's maintenance. Where's your plunger, man?"

Rex looked as though he'd like to plunge his fingers down Dave's throat. "I'm going into town to get supplies. I have a feeling this won't be the last of our troubles."

She remembered his warning about Logan but thought it more likely that another contestant had tampered with the plumbing, hoping to disqualify Rex if he fumbled. Her glance met Dave's. "Aren't you supposed to be working with Michelle on listing our priorities?"

"She's down by the lake, looking at the possibility for a dock."

"Oh, yeah?" Rex said. "Maybe I should help her. I know about boats."

"No way. We're going into town." Heather grabbed his arm and pulled him close. Too close. She felt his body heat radiate toward her.

Dave gave them a speculative glance. "You'd better have this, like, fixed by tonight," he said to Rex. "We don't want no stains on the floor when our guests get here."

"Don't worry, buddy. I'll have it as good as new."

On their way downstairs, Heather prodded him. "I'll bet you already have in mind the kind of sport fishing boat you want."

"I can show you a picture." He drew a brochure from his back pocket. Its print had faded, and its creases were worn as though it had been unfolded many times.

"Wow, this is beautiful," Heather said, studying the sleek craft while alternately watching her footing on the stairs.

"It's a forty-five-foot Hatteras. Has two cabins, a salon, and a fully equipped galley. Here's the flybridge, and this is the cockpit. See this? It's a live-bait well."

She thought of squiggly creatures and shuddered. "Boating isn't my thing. I've always been afraid of drowning at sea."

"You're just a green landlubber. You'd love her if you saw her in person," he added with a grin.

He spoke of his dream vessel as though it were a woman. "Have you ever been married?" she blurted, wondering if his boat held more importance to him than a wife.

"Nope. You?" At the foot of the stairs, he slanted an amused glance her way.

"No, I've been too busy to give time to a relationship. Besides, I haven't met anyone who—"

"What?"

Could give me the security I need. "I'm still waiting to meet the right person," she said, shrugging.

"You must have kissed a lot of frogs already. Don't tell me an attractive woman like you doesn't have guys asking her out."

"I never said I don't date." Her chin thrust defensively.

"Then maybe you're picky."

"Oh, and you're not?"

His brows drew together. "I don't want the woman I marry to struggle like my mom. My dad's business pays the bills, but it doesn't give him the good things in life."

And you think fishing for a living will improve your prospects? "My parents live in West Virginia. Mom hasn't been well lately, and the doctor says a warmer climate would help her. I want to bring them down to live with me. This place would be ideal."

"So you feel obligated to them, just like I feel obligated to my dad."

She peered at him closely. "Is that why you haven't shared your dream with him?"

"I can't hurt the old man."

"Then let's hope he doesn't watch television."

"Oh, God, I forgot. We've probably been on camera all day."

After handing Rex back his brochure, she withdrew her car keys from the purse she'd obtained from her room. "Want me to drive? I'll tell the others we're leaving, in case they want us to pick up anything else."

Feminine giggles wafted from the family room facing the rear patio. Walking briskly in that direction, Heather spotted Kim folded around Gary, who'd been measuring the room's dimensions. Noting her arrival, Gary's face turned beet red while Kim untangled herself.

"I see you've been hard at work," Heather said in a sarcastic tone. "Rex and I are going into town. He needs some hardware supplies, and I want to talk to the merchants about advertising. Do you guys want us to get anything for you?"

"Telephones," Gary replied. "Jon is supposed to call the

phone company to set up service, but we need phones in each of the guest rooms in addition to the kitchen and entrance hall. Michelle has some lists from the others as well."

"Fine." She took his requisition sheet, afraid she'd get stuck shopping when she had to advertise their new business venture. Was this a ploy to sabotage her role?

Tanya waylaid her and Rex when they emerged outside. "You have to take a cameraman with you," the co-producer said. "Everything you do this week is fair game for our viewers."

Heather exchanged guilty glances with Rex. Just how much of their interaction upstairs had been videotaped?

That evening after dinner, they had a chance to see the first takes. Watching a monitor set up in the living room, Heather's jaw dropped when she saw the angle at which she and Rex were caught on film while in the bedroom. It looked as though he were about to kiss her. Her cheeks flushed as the others ribbed them.

"Whoa, looks like you two couldn't wait to have fun," Kim said with a snide undertone. Wearing a leopard tank top with black biker shorts, she lounged on the sofa with a languorous air.

"You and Gary got pretty close together in the family room," she couldn't help snipping back. "We're in confined quarters here. We're bound to interact with each other more quickly than under normal circumstances. It's our teamwork that counts, not what we do on our personal time."

As the camera continued to follow them on their trip into town, it focused on their excursion to Lake Osceola where a tour boat ran every morning. Rex had insisted on the detour after they'd completed their tasks. The small body of water wasn't the ocean that he longed to sail, but she'd seen the yearning on his face. Unfortunately, the way the camera captured the scene, his head angled toward her.

"Let's go over what we each accomplished today," Rex said, and Heather threw him a grateful glance. "Sarah?"

The short blonde, sitting in an armchair, grinned happily. "I've planned our meals for the entire week and created menus for breakfasts when the guests arrive. I've made another shopping list for whoever goes into town next. We'll need a griddle and an electric skillet. Otherwise, I think we're okay with all those things we bought today."

"Did you do what I asked?" Gary said. "Draw up an assignment sheet for each of us to rotate doing dishes? And what about the table linens, did you figure out how frequently they'd have to be washed, and if there's a commercial linen service that can handle our needs?"

Sarah's petite face creased into a frown. "I can't find out about the linen service until our phones are operational."

"Well, then you should be helping Jon tomorrow. He's our supply man."

"I'll be busy in the kitchen all day. I won't have time to do anything else."

Gary half rose from his seat, but Rex waved him back. "She's right," Rex said. "Sarah should focus her abilities where she can be the most use. Michelle has been prioritizing our needs. Now we've got our basic supplies in stock, what should we do first thing tomorrow morning?" he asked the dark-haired girl.

Heather liked Michelle. They'd talked earlier, and Michelle had confided how she wasn't happy in her current job as an assistant in an accountant's office. If she won the house, she'd sell it and use the money to set up her own stationery store. She did calligraphy and already made money on the side doing party invitations.

"Jon said apparently the TV studio had arranged for our phones to be activated on Monday," Michelle said. "Our cable service will be connected tomorrow. That makes things easier. Heather, keep working on your logo design, and then we'll see about ordering custom-made products for the guest rooms. Sarah, I understand every Saturday morning there is a farmer's market by the train station. I think you should meet the vendors."

"And what will you be doing, besides making lists for the rest of us?" Kim said in a syrupy tone.

"Speak for yourself," Michelle shot back. "You've been so

busy coming on to all the guys that I don't see what you've accomplished."

"Gary and I measured the rooms. He said we need to get some area rugs and lamps for better lighting."

"Gary's good at telling everybody else what to do but not at getting much done himself," Dave kicked in, grinning from his position on the floor.

"Oh, hell, I don't see how we'll pull it together the way you people act." Running a hand under his collar as though the room were too hot, Gary shot to his feet and stalked off.

"Now see what you've done," Kim snapped to no one in particular.

"Look, people, let's all be nice," Heather inserted. "We have to get along, and we should appreciate what each of us brings to the table."

They continued their discussion, during which Sarah excused herself to make a pot of coffee. She took an unusually long time to return with a plate of cookies. Kim went upstairs to use the bathroom, while Dave left with a mumbled excuse about looking in the garage for chemicals to clean the pool. The water would turn green otherwise, he insisted. Since his ambition was to open his own pool service, he volunteered for this duty.

"I've just thought of something else," Rex said. "We don't have any locks on our doors. Each guest will require a room key. We'll have to call a locksmith."

"I'll go count all the doors, including the ones outside," Michelle offered. "Is this place wired for a security system? While I'm at it, I'd better check the rooms for smoke alarms." She hastened away, refusing Sarah's offer of a coffee mug.

"Heck, you know what we forgot?" Rex said to the remaining three of them. His rangy body leaned against the fireplace mantel. "We'll need a business license."

"City offices won't reopen until Monday," Heather pointed out. Another problem popped into her mind. She turned to Logan, who'd just strode through the front door, his usually plastered hair in wild disarray. "Do we have insurance for the house, liability coverage, that sort of thing?"

"That's your group's responsibility to arrange," he said, smoothing his head and tugging his sport coat into place. "Isn't Tanya here yet? She's supposed to interview each one of you."

A chilling scream pierced the night before any of them could answer.

Three

"The lights were off back here," Michelle blubbered when they reached her on the patio. "When I turned them on, I saw it . . . him." She pointed a shaky finger.

Heather uttered a cry when she spied the body floating in the pool. "Oh, my Lord. It's Gary." Facedown, his undulating form told its own story.

"Call 911," Rex ordered. Jon peeled off to comply. "Dave, don't just stand there. Get me that pole so I can drag him in. And stop the cameras, dammit."

"No, keep filming," Tanya countered, showing up with a cameraman in tow. He panned for a wide-angle shot.

Heather considered what she could do while Rex and Logan hauled Gary's limp body over the pool's edge. Water splashed everywhere. She heard Sarah descend into sobs from behind while Kim cursed up a storm. As Rex and Logan began CPR, Tanya yelled directions to the camera crew. Heather stood frozen, watching the surreal scene unravel.

Help Rex, you twit. "I'll send the paramedics back here," she called to him. Jon hadn't reappeared. Maybe he was waiting out front. Turning, she fled past the open sliding glass doors.

Sirens wailed from down the street. Soon police and rescue personnel flooded the grounds. Following orders from the officer in charge, Heather and the other contestants gathered in the living room. Swirling red lights strobed through the picture window from rescue vehicles parked in the driveway.

She slid onto the sofa next to Sarah, who sat rigidly, her face as pale as bleached flour. Kim wrapped herself around Dave on a chair by the fireplace, while Michelle sank to the floor, the luster gone from her flamenco dancer's eyes. Jon's complexion, normally a ruddy contrast to his spiked blond hair, had deepened to resemble a cooked lobster.

No one spoke. She felt a grateful glow when Rex flanked her other side. His solid warmth gave her strength. Their hips touched, making her aware of his proximity and her inappropriate response. Parts of her that should be numb flamed into life. This wasn't the right time or place to react to his scent of soap and sandalwood. To distract herself from wayward thoughts, she focused on his admirable fortitude. A muscle twitched in his jaw, his only outward sign of emotion. Otherwise, the sharp angles of his face presented a rock-hardness as firm as Gibraltar. His forearm, sprinkled with dark hairs, rested just a few centimeters from hers. An uncontrollable urge to grasp his hand made her curl her fingers.

Logan, given permission to continue filming, withdrew into a corner for a huddled conference with Tanya and their crew.

Another official arrived, an ominous portent judging from Logan's audible curse and sudden pallor.

"Who's that?" she whispered to Rex.

"The medical examiner. That's not good."

Heather soon understood why. Shortly thereafter, a body retrieval unit carried away the covered corpse on a stretcher.

"Oh, no. I can't believe Gary's gone," she croaked, her throat dry.

"Believe it, babe," Dave said. "What I don't understand is what the hell he was doing by the pool."

"I'd like to know the same thing," said a dour-faced man in a rumpled suit, who stalked in from the rear. "I'm Detective Jackson. I'll have to take statements from each one of you. We can use that spare front room as an office. If you wouldn't mind giving me your names, we'll get started. In the meantime, there will be no discussion among you until I've interviewed everyone. Understand?"

Tanya stepped forward. Heather noted that she seemed less rattled than Logan. Her makeup and hair appeared perfectly in place. "This won't affect our show, will it, officer? I mean, we have an obligation to the network. We can't let this horrible accident stop our progress. Dealing with setbacks is part of the business. You can watch our videotapes if that would help your investigation."

Heather nearly choked. Gary's death was more than a setback. How could Tanya be so callous?

The detective furrowed his brow. "Thanks, that's what I intended. But you're under a mistaken impression here. This wasn't an accident. The victim was hit with a blunt instrument on the side of his head."

Heather's glance flitted to the male contestants. Now they were down to three men. How horrible. No one was supposed to leave the show in this manner.

She sat in stunned disbelief as Jackson called each individual to be questioned. She didn't even notice when Rex entwined his fingers with hers. When her turn came, he squeezed her hand and gave her a nod of encouragement. Maybe furniture repair wasn't such a bad job. He seemed to possess the same sturdiness as the wooden items he restored.

The detective's choice of milieu wasn't wood but stone, judging from the granitelike coldness of his eyes. "Please have a seat, Miss Payne." Instead of sitting behind the desk, he chose an armchair adjacent to hers. He tilted his head, peppery hair spilling across his forehead. "I'd appreciate it if you could tell me the sequence of events that you remember."

She bent her neck, folding her hands in her lap. "We were talking about what we should do tomorrow," she said in a subdued tone. "I don't know what you've been told, but we have to get this place ready for guests to arrive within the week. Will we . . . will the show be cancelled?"

"I don't think so. I'll review the tapes before they're edited, but I'm hoping we can wrap this up pretty quickly. So you were sitting in the—?"

"Living room. We viewed the video from today. Gary got angry and left."

"Angry at whom?"

"Dave accused him of not accomplishing much."

"I see." He consulted his notes. "Did Dave Molina remain in the room?"

"Yes. Michelle had been making lists, but we really hadn't organized ourselves. Rex aimed us in the right direction."

Jackson must have detected a note of admiration in her tone because he gave her a sharp glance. "Jon Walker said Gary took charge, telling everyone what to do."

She clasped her hands. "Gary tends to order people around, but he means well. That's his work style, you know? Rex, on the other hand, motivates you to do your job."

"So you think Rex Gerard set everyone on the right track?"

"Yes. He said Jon's good with numbers, so he should be in charge of finances and insurance. We hadn't even thought about establishing accounts with the credit card companies, banking, taxes, or billing procedures."

"Your producers said they'd given you a budget. Walker is the one handling the money now, isn't he? So it wouldn't be much of a stretch to put him in charge of financial aspects."

"Rex also suggested that Kim and Sarah take on guest services. Sarah will handle meals, and Kim will supervise housekeeping." Kim would make sure things were kept up properly. She liked her clean towels and perfumed soaps.

"So you respect Mr. Gerard's ability to tap into people's talents?"

She cocked her head. "Yes, I do." It was more than that. Rex didn't act competitively. He behaved as though he'd like them all to succeed.

"Did Gerard leave the room while the deceased was gone?"

Her hands clenched tighter. "No, and neither did I."

Jackson scribbled in his notebook. "Can you tell me about anyone else's movements?"

"Well, after Sarah went into the kitchen to make coffee, Kim left to use the bathroom, and Dave decided to check for pool cleaning supplies in the garage."

"At night? Were the exterior lights on at this time?"

"I didn't notice."

"Michelle said they were turned off when she went outside." He waited expectantly.

"We'd decided to bring in a locksmith," Heather explained, "and Michelle offered to count the bedrooms for the number of guest keys we'd need. She meant to check on smoke alarms, too."

"Then what do you think led her to the patio in the dark?"

"I don't know. Maybe she was looking to see if the patio doors were hooked up to a security system. That's one of the things we have to install, unless the house is already wired."

"Did the others return during this interval?"

"Sarah brought us coffee and cookies." After she'd been gone for at least fifteen minutes, Heather recalled. That was before Kim and Dave left. Could Sarah have gone outside, whacked Gary on the head, then run back in to fix them a snack? They hadn't heard a thing with the television blaring.

"You want to add something?"

Heather fixed a bleak smile on her face. For all Sarah's desire to win the prize, the girl seemed too timid to commit murder. "I don't think so."

"Who do you think is guilty, Miss Payne?"

"I haven't a clue. Is it possible that an intruder got Gary?"

"We'll investigate all the angles." He paused, his brows lowering. "Until this is solved, I suggest you trust no one. Is that clear?"

When Jackson left to scour the grounds outside, along with his crime scene technicians, the contestants grouped in the kitchen to rehash events. Unable to reach any conclusions, they shuffled off to their rooms after the clock struck midnight.

Too tired to think straight, Heather prepared for bed. She was about to step into her shower when a loud crash sounded from down the hallway. A woman's shrieks made her grab an oversized bath towel and rush out the door. She bumped into Rex, emerging from his bedroom. His glance skittered across her barely concealed body. Half-naked himself, he wore only a pair of khaki shorts. His hand reached out to steady her.

"What's happening?" she gasped, ignoring the heated trail from his touch.

He gestured toward Kim's room. "Come on, let's go see."

Following in his wake, she trotted into Kim's room where the others had congregated. Kim crouched on her bed, her plum negligee leaving little to the imagination. Blond hair streamed about her creamy shoulders as she pointed a shaking finger at the open closet.

"It's in there," she squealed.

"What?" Dave said in a fearful tone. Shirtless, he hovered in the doorway along with Sarah, who clutched at her robe. Jon stood just inside the room, looking uncertain.

"A giant cockroach. I've never seen one that big. It's enormous!" So were her eyes, round as the sapphire ring she flaunted.

Rex brushed past them all. "I'll take care of it, but we'll need to hire an exterminator on a regular basis. We don't want guests finding palmetto bugs in their bedrooms."

For God's sake, you scared us for a bug? Heather threw Kim a contemptuous look. Pressing a hand to her chest where her heart pounded, she felt an unsettling reaction rise from her toes to her crown. Oh, no. Her numbness from the evening's trauma dissipated, and she began to shake. Her knees buckled. Dave caught her as she stumbled.

"Hey, babe, are you okay?" His bedroom eyes regarded her with mock concern.

"No, I'm not. All Logan and Tanya care about is the stupid show, and their attitude is infecting us. Gary's dead. I can't go on pretending as though he never existed."

Whack. Rex killed the miscreant insect in the closet with one of Kim's fashion magazines. Its life was extinguished, just like Gary Friedman had been squashed in his prime.

Sarah began weeping. Spotting an opportunity, Dave shifted his attention to her. "Don't cry, babe. We'll be all right. The dude would've wanted us to continue."

"This gig is turning into a nightmare," Kim whined. "If I didn't want the money to open a day spa, I'd bolt, but I don't want to work forever as a nail tech."

"We'll get through this," Heather said, summoning reserves of strength. "We just have to work together."

Jon strode forward to give Kim an awkward pat. "Tomorrow will be better. You'll see." Despite his geekish appearance with his spiky hair, he displayed an impressive physique in a set of workout clothes. He must have been on his way to the exercise room they'd set up downstairs, Heather thought.

Kim smiled at him, sheets of blond hair screening her face. "Stay with me for a while. I'm scared."

So am I, Heather thought, feeling alone and cold when the air-conditioning kicked in. Cool air blasted her skin.

"You're getting goose bumps," Dave called to her, winking. "Nice outfit, by the way."

Finished with his job as champion bug catcher, Rex approached. "You can try, Dave, but she's not interested." Putting a proprietary hand at the base of her spine, Rex propelled her out the door.

Hoots followed them down the hall. Heather heard Dave announce he was going downstairs for a beer. Sarah and Michelle chimed in to join him. After they left, Kim's door quietly closed from within.

Outside her room, Heather turned to face Rex. "Today has been terrible. I'll miss Gary."

"We'll all miss him. Will you be okay?"

"Yes, thanks." Her body shivered.

He stepped closer. His hooded glance raked over her, then came to rest where her towel barely covered her breasts. She stood rooted to the spot, unable to budge when he looked at her that way. With his desire to go to sea for a living, he seemed the antithesis of what she wanted in a man, and yet, she felt drawn to him by some kind of magnetism. Her lips parted involuntarily.

His gaze ignited, and before she knew what was happening, his mouth descended in a kiss hot with passion and promise.

Four

Heather felt divine being held by a man who seemed able to fix any problem. Desire flared inside her, and she wondered if he'd be able to assuage the heat shimmering through her body. Letting her tongue explore the crevice of his mouth that he so tantalizingly offered, she pressed herself against him and wrapped her arms around his neck. The towel threatened to slip. Feeling his solid chest against her shoulders, she heard her own quick intake of breath and his guttural moan.

Applying pressure to her thighs, he forced her inside her room, kicking the door shut behind them. One hand gripped her head while the other supported her back. His mouth slanted again, giving her a taste of mint and merlot from dinner. *You're some dessert,* she exulted, realizing that she hadn't felt this aroused in ages. Beneath the terry cloth fabric, her nipples ached for his touch. Heather's remaining reserve kept her from shedding the towel completely. This was absurd. They barely knew each other, and yet the man captivated her senses. It must be a belated release from tension, she decided.

"Mmm, you taste so good," he murmured, coming up for air. His glittering gaze swept her face. "I don't know why you're doing this to me. I didn't intend for anything to happen, but I can't help myself. Maybe it's the stress from today," he said, confirming her notion. "Or maybe," he said, sliding his fingers along the inner rim of her coverup, "you're just a witch in disguise. Is this how you plan to disarm me?"

She leaned against him, her limbs languorous. "You're the one who is too distracting. I can't think straight around you." When he brought his other hand into play to cup her breast, she swayed. Between her legs, warmth pooled into a cauldron of sensation. He sealed her response with more kisses. Matching his ardor, she met his hot tongue with her own explorations. She knew they shouldn't be doing this, that both of them were reacting to Gary's death. But the wild abandon seemed so right for the moment. They could have fun tonight, forget about everything, and face reality tomorrow.

Rex squeezed her nipples, teasing them into tautness, while her eyelids fluttered closed. Not minding when her towel loosened, she splayed her fingers on the broad planes of his back, enjoying the ripple of muscles beneath his flesh. Wanting to explore all of him, she pushed down on his shorts.

"Cut the lights," he muttered.

"Huh?" Realizing what he meant, she sprang back from his embrace. "Dear heavens, I forgot about the cameras. They'll nail us."

"Wait, it's after twelve, isn't it? Logan said the video would be turned off in our rooms after midnight."

"They can still hear our conversation. The microphones are active."

"So? No one can see what we're doing."

His sexy grin threatened her resolve. So did the way his ebony hair tumbled across his forehead. Tightening her mouth, Heather met his steady gaze.

"Look, moral character is an important trait for a B&B owner, and I don't want to screw my chances just because I'm attracted to you," she said. "Don't you care that you might lose the opportunity to win your precious boat? Or was it your intent to show me in a bad light? There's usually a double standard where gender is concerned."

A shadow crossed his expression. "That's unfair. What I feel toward you is genuine."

"Oh, and what is that?"

"Respect. And something more. You can't deny that you feel it, too."

"We barely know each other. You want exactly the opposite of what I do."

"That's not true; we share more than you think. We both need to forge our own destinies, just in a different manner."

"You're aiming to live on a boat and sail off fishing every day. You said it yourself; I'm a landlubber. My place is here. Besides, I'm already in real estate. What have you done to work toward your goal?"

"My uncle used to take me fishing; that's how I got interested. I've been reading up on the boating industry ever since. Used to hang out at the docks and clean the big yachts when I had more free time. Now Dad keeps me busy in the shop."

"And you've never told him about your ambition?"

A painful look entered his expression. "He relies on me to carry on the business. Dad is one of the few skilled craftsmen left. He taught me all I know about woodworking. When I get my boat, I plan to fix her up real nice."

She tucked her towel in more securely. "How much will your vessel cost?"

"The owner is asking two hundred and fifty thousand dollars, but I'm sure I can get him down. That's why I need to win." He glared at her. "If I sell this house, I'll have enough money to buy the boat plus pay my expenses. You've got fees for dock space, fuel, electric. Then I can still help Dad when I don't have charters."

"So you're planning to spring this on him all of a sudden? I feel sorry for your father."

His gaze hardened. "I've been answering to him my whole life. I don't have to answer to you now, too."

"No, you don't," she said, gritting her teeth. "I'm glad you're so clear on your goals. That makes two of us." She opened her door for his departure. "Good night."

Wouldn't you know it, she thought to herself, *here I meet a hunk who seems to like me, and he's set on sailing off into the sunset. You just can't rely on anyone these days.*

They had to rely on each other the next day. Fortunately, their teamwork got a boost when high-speed Internet and telephone service were activated before noon. Guessing that the studio's influence might have speeded things up, everyone was thankful nonetheless.

Much of Saturday morning was wasted in answering more questions from the detective and stopping for personal interviews on camera with Logan. Applying her listening skills, Heather learned that the gardening implement used to crack Gary on the head had been found in the backyard. The shovel was clean of prints, making it likely the perpetrator had worn gloves, which had not yet been recovered. And Kim had a verifiable alibi for her time away from the group, but Jackson wouldn't say what it was.

Rex, in charge of lawn care as well as home maintenance, shrugged off the police investigation when the remaining contestants met in the dining room for lunch.

"Let the cops do their work. If one of us is guilty, they'll find out. In the meantime, we have a job to do."

"How can you overlook the fact that someone here might be a killer?" Heather retorted, dismayed by his harsh tone. Not that she believed her fellow contestants would stoop to such vile methods. It had to be an intruder who thought Gary was the homeowner, and that it would be an easy robbery.

"If you stop running your business every time something bad happens," Rex said, "you'll be out on the street before you take your next breath. You can't operate things that way."

"He's right," said Jon. "We have to focus on the tasks at hand. Hey, Sarah, these spinach crepes are really great."

"Thanks," their colleague yelled from the kitchen.

"Yo, dudes, we gotta eat and run, ya know?" Dave cut in. "I've set up basic programs for registration and billing, and contacted the credit card companies. We have to wait until Monday to do the legal stuff. So I'm gonna spend some time out back.

It's my job to balance the pool chemicals and skim the surface. Kim, babe, wanna take a dip when I'm done?"

Kim's face lit up, as though donning a bikini held more appeal than doing inventory and making more requisition lists for mundane things such as hangers. "Good idea," she purred, casting a smug glance at the rest of them.

"Who's signed up for computer time after me?" Dave said.

"I am." Heather raised her hand.

Taking her turn at the console set up inside the ground floor room they'd designated as an office, she set about finding supply houses that could customize orders for her tropical theme. After downloading Netscape, she created a rudimentary web page and uploaded it to her personal server. This would give them a presence on the Web for now.

Deciding she needed a break after designing a promotional flyer, linking to various reservation sites, and sending out a flurry of queries, she rose and stretched. Her mouth felt dry, so she meandered into the kitchen for a cold drink.

Opening the refrigerator door, Heather helped herself to a glass of iced tea, then leaned against the counter. "Lunch was delicious," she told Sarah. "You're a terrific cook." The shorter woman with the pixie haircut was just taking a batch of mouth-watering chocolate chip cookies from the oven.

"Thank you," Sarah said in her somewhat shy tone. "This kitchen is wonderful, but cooking for eight people isn't what I'm meant to do. If I win, I'll sell the inn and use the money to set up an old-fashioned diner. You know, mom's home-cooked meals served to order? I couldn't afford to go to a fancy culinary school, but I could make a diner work. What about you?"

"I love this house. It's what I've always wanted. I can't wait to accessorize the rooms and give them my personal signature, so it hurts that anyone might sell the place."

"Aren't you in real estate? Couldn't you get a good deal somewhere else?"

"I don't have the money. My parents live up north, and I want to bring them down to live with me. They'll have moving expenses. My mother is ill, so I can't wait too long."

In a way, Heather wanted them all to succeed. They had to work as a team to pull everything together in time. But after the show ended, only one of them would remain as proprietor.

Her glance slid over the granite countertops and stainless steel appliances before fixing on the window view to the pool and the lake beyond. If only this house were hers. Longing swelled within her and produced a lump in her throat so large that for a moment, she almost couldn't swallow.

She watched Dave cavorting in the pool with Kim. Loud splashes and laughter reached her ears while she snatched one of the cookies Sarah offered. The soft texture melted in her mouth. Baked cookie dough was one of the most tempting aromas. She couldn't resist taking another.

"Did you see anything outside last night?" she asked Sarah. "You had a perfect view."

Sarah's short blond hair fell across her face as she turned aside to wash the cookie sheet. "The shades were closed."

"Could you hear Gary at all? Or maybe you saw Dave on his way to the garage."

"No, I was busy, uh, doing the dinner dishes. I didn't notice a thing."

Why did Heather get the impression Sarah was lying?

"Oh, man, what's that good smell?" Rex stomped into the kitchen, tracking cut grass with his running shoes. Sweating, he wiped a hand across his brow. A band of cloth kept his hair from his eyes but not the grime from his face. "Whew, it's hot out there. That lawn hadn't been cut in weeks. I'm glad Jackson finished his inspection of the grounds so I could get it done. What are you girls up to? Hey, are those cookies? Gimme one." He grinned, a flash of white teeth against his tanned skin.

Heather's glance flickered over his powerful body, quite dashingly displayed in his gray T-shirt and shorts. She gulped at the view of his bulging biceps. Of all the people she hoped would remain on the show with her, he was the one, and yet his aspirations were in total conflict with hers. He wanted to get away from his father; she needed to bring her parents closer. He wanted to live on a boat; she set her roots on land. Yet the more she wanted to pull back, the more she felt attracted to him. He worked hard, and he didn't display any animosity toward anyone. His attitude could be ruthless, but he had their best interests at heart. They needed that right now. Just like she needed him, in a different way.

Rex caught her looking at him, and his grin broadened. His aquamarine eyes sparkled playfully. "I'd better get cleaned up before Kim comes back inside, or she'll howl at me for messing the floor. Did you get your brochure done?" he asked her. "There's a neat feature in my shower you might want to describe for potential guests. Come upstairs, and I'll show you."

Her blood surged at the notion of seeing him naked under the shower spray. "That's okay," she deferred, giving him a blatant once-over. "Remember, Logan said we need to dress up for tonight. It's an important session."

The doorbell rang, and she went into the hallway to see who was there. A delivery truck idled in the driveway. Jon beat her to the door, while Rex bounded up the staircase.

"Who the hell ordered these?" Jon hollered when he saw the invoice. "Gerard!"

The answer came to light when they all sat gathered in the formal living room at eight o'clock. Logan and Tanya were present, as well as various technicians who'd set up for different camera angles. Cables, normally absent from the hidden cameras during the day, trailed across the carpet.

"So which one of you ordered ten hand-painted toilet seats with gold-plated hinges at one hundred dollars each?" their host asked, beaming his capped teeth at them. "That'll take quite a cut from your budget."

When no one responded, Heather glanced at Rex, who had repeated his theory that the producers had planted someone to create havoc. She shared this with Jon beside her.

He snorted. "I wouldn't put it past them," he whispered. "Tanya especially needs this show to succeed. Logan mentioned that her last project took four months longer to complete at the added cost of two million dollars. The studio execs aren't happy with her. Then again, it could be one of you trying to bust my ass because I'm in charge of finances."

"Tonight, it's your vote that counts," Logan told the viewing audience. "Somebody here has to go. Who will it be?"

Five

Logan pointed to each one of them in turn, and they saw their close-ups on the monitor. "Kim Allen, who currently works as a manicurist and wants to open her own glamorous day spa. Let's see what Kim's colleagues at home think about her goal."

Kim's mouth dropped open as the monitor segued to a taped segment featuring interviews at the salon where she worked. "Omigod, when did you do this?" she cried.

Tanya smirked. "If you leave your current job, it's going to affect the people you work with. It's only fair to get their reaction."

Heather glanced over her shoulder at Rex, wishing they'd been seated closer together. His tight-lipped face had gone pale. Dear heavens, what if they'd spoken to his father? Now the older man would be aware his son planned to leave him.

"Jonathan Walker," Logan continued. "Jon works as a clerk in an attorney's office. He hopes to finish his college degree and open a collections agency. Jon, your boss wishes you the best."

None of them had been allowed to tell their coworkers where they were going, just that they needed a leave of absence for personal reasons. Heather had realized they'd be exposed on national television, but not everyone watched reality shows.

"Did you vote for him?" Logan said into the camera. "Is Jon

still in the competition? Stay with us, and we'll have the results coming up shortly."

Commercial break. Michelle, clearly rattled, rushed out to the bathroom. Heather got up to approach Rex.

"This must feel like a stab in the back. Perhaps your dad was too busy to be interviewed," she offered, touching his arm.

Rex's eyes glimmered. "He'll think I'm abandoning him. Damn, and we're not supposed to call home for the entire week."

"Rex seems to think he has something to hide." Tanya took over when they went live again. With instant replay, his dialogue was repeated over the air. Heather heard his muttered curse. "Rex Andrew Gerard works in his father's furniture repair and restoration shop. They are expert wood craftsmen, and his dad has owned the business for thirty years. Let's see what Gerard Senior has to say about his son's desire to captain a charter fishing boat."

Her gaze glued to the monitor, Heather soaked in the sawdust-strewn linoleum floors, worn worktables, upended chairs, and implements scattered throughout the studio. She could almost smell the lemon oil polish, paint varnish, and turpentine. A man with a sun-freckled complexion and gray hair shuffled into view, wearing a leather apron over a short-sleeved shirt and trousers. His eyes, shaded with a curtain of pain, exuded the same aquamarine clarity as Rex's.

"When I opened in the early seventies, this place was surrounded by cow pastures and horse ranches," Mr. Gerard said to Logan on-screen. "I worked hard to establish a reputation in town. Then an influx of New Yorkers swelled our ranks, and Davie, Florida, became more like a Fort Lauderdale suburb.

"The people who moved here brought a lot of their stuff from up north. My business thrived, and I was proud to be part of the community. Nowadays, you'll find very few men with these skills. We used to take Shop when I went to school. Now kids learn computers. I made sure Rex knew how to use the tools, though."

He cleared his throat. "He seemed to appreciate the craft. You could see it in his eyes when he'd sand down a piece. Wood likes to be caressed, you see, like a lady. Each cut has its own unique grain. Guess I was wrong about my boy."

Logan held the microphone closer. "How do you feel about his fishing enterprise?"

The older man shrugged. "Takes after my brother, I suppose. Jules got him started with the fishing bug. Took him out to sea every time he visited. I can't figure why the boy didn't say anything to me," he said, his tone gruff.

"If Rex wins the prize and gets his own boat, how do you feel about him leaving you here alone?"

Heather's heart sank. This couldn't be more painful for Rex than if they'd pried off his toenails. She didn't dare look back at him but imagined him staring stoically ahead.

"I reckon I'd manage, but it isn't easy these days. Arthritis, you know. I was kinda hoping to retire in another year if he'd take over. The boy never said nothing to me about giving it up." His voice cracked, and the camera focused on his bewildered expression. Then the monitor faded, and the live broadcast resumed.

"Well, Rex, doesn't that make you feel like a heel?" Logan said, grinning broadly. "So, American viewers, what have you decided? Will he remain on the show? Coming up next, advice for the person who leaves the competition."

Heather kept her place, hands clenched in her lap. Sweat dripped between her breasts. She yearned to comfort him, but not while the entire nation watched. Her own segment should be better. She'd already shared her dream. Thus, shock riddled her features when she saw an exterior shot of her parents' hovel in West Virginia. No, they weren't going there. What happened to her real estate office?

"We thought this next clip would have more impact if we spoke to Heather's parents," Tanya crooned when the session resumed. Perfectly coiffed, she spoke with sugary sweetness from her glossed lips. "Her real estate friends already knew she searched for the perfect bed-and-breakfast, but her parents had no inkling of her intention to bring them south. Let's see what they say on the subject."

Heather winced as the cameras followed Tanya inside the small two-bedroom house her parents called home. They had fought to better her life, and her success had been an elixir for them. But they hadn't known about her deep-down feelings that she hid even from herself.

"Did you know your daughter's ambition is to own a bed-and-breakfast and have you move in with her?" Tanya said.

Heather's mother, silver-streaked hair shaggy and unshorn, stared with world-weary eyes at the interviewer whose stylish suit put her outdated shirtwaist dress to shame. "I wouldn't know about that, ma'am. I'm happy for Heather, really I am. I hope she wins her dream."

"When's the last time you saw your daughter, Mrs. Payne?"

"Why, I don't right know. Do you, Al?" she deferred to her husband. Her wheezing breath descended into a cough. "Sorry, that's from all those years at the glass factory."

"We don't hear from our baby much," said her dad, shaking his coal-dust-blackened hair. "Just about once a month, she calls to see if we're okay. We understand her job keeps her busy."

Heather recognized the same look in his eyes that Rex's father had exhibited. *Forgive me,* she pleaded silently. *I'll check on you more often. I didn't mean to be neglectful.*

"How come you don't visit your folks?" Tanya asked her on live feed. "Are you ashamed of your origins, Heather? Is that why you want to get your parents away from there?"

Grasping her hands together, she dug her fingernails into her palms. "I'm concerned about their health," she said in a neutral tone. "The cold winters have taken their toll. They both need the warm, moist air in Florida to survive."

"That still doesn't explain why you ignore them. You've never even brought a boyfriend home. Is it because you don't have any suitors, or because you're too embarrassed to show a man where you've lived?"

She shot to her feet. "This has nothing to do with my ability to run a business. Why are you doing this to us?"

Tanya's smile stretched her mouth but didn't extend to her

eyes. "Your viewers want to see how you react to personal pressures. When you own a business, you don't work in a vacuum. You still have strings to the people at home. If someone who depends on you gets sick, what then? What if someone you love gets hurt or needs your help? Emotional issues affect people's efficiency every day. Sometimes, they can lead to failure."

Tanya paused, moistening her lips before zeroing in on her next target. "Isn't that right, David Molina? We interviewed your ex-wife to see what she thought about your arrest for hacking into your employer's personal computer files."

And so the heart-wrenching stories continued. Heather's stomach churned until she thought she'd throw up if they were on the air much longer. Then Tanya brought up the murder.

"As if these people don't have enough to hide, one of them may be a killer. The other night . . ." She showed the contestants talking in the living room, their discussion interrupted by Michelle's screams, and what ensued. "Just think, Heather, if you win this bed-and-breakfast, you can advertise that it comes with a ghost."

Heather closed her ears to the woman's laughter. When Logan took over, she breathed a sigh of relief.

"And now for the moment you've all been waiting for," their host said after the last commercial break. "The person with the least number of votes in their favor, who will leave us tonight is . . ." Heather froze. ". . . Kim Allen."

Heather's tense muscles relaxed.

"Kim, you would have been disqualified today anyway. When you went upstairs last night ostensibly to use the bathroom, you really went to make a forbidden call on your cell phone. We captured you on film. Watch this," Logan said.

A segment rolled that showed Kim grabbing something from her purse and dashing into the bathroom. She opened the door before emerging again, and her voice rang out. "I'll call you later," Heather heard Kim say in a clear tone.

"Oh, rats." Kim stood to accept hugs from the rest of them. According to the rules, she had ten minutes to pack her bags and meet the waiting taxi outside. Meanwhile, Logan and Tanya asked each of the remaining six contestants, "How do you feel about the decision tonight?"

"I feel horrible," Heather said to Rex when things quieted down. They trooped into the kitchen together after the others had gone upstairs. "I knew the show would be tough, but I never dreamed they'd shoot us with poisoned arrows."

He stopped her halfway to the refrigerator and turned her around to face him. His hands rested on her shoulders. "You shouldn't be ashamed of your parents," he said, his steadfast gaze making her knees weaken. "Their strength resides in you. It's given you a steel-hard core to go after your dream and make it into a reality. You *will* succeed."

Moisture tipped her lashes. "I've treated them so badly. Truthfully, it pains me to visit them. I can still remember the taunts of the other kids at school. Did you see my mom's dress compared to Tanya's outfit? We could only afford stuff from the thrift shop. I've been sending them money, but they use it for maintenance on the house."

"Well, I'm not the best one to offer advice. I don't know how I'll face my dad after this." His voice choked, and his grip tightened, as though he clung to her for solace.

"Explain to him that you didn't intend to leave him completely in the lurch. I think he'll understand that you didn't want to hurt him." She hesitated. "It's always painful for a parent when their child leaves the nest. Maybe he's been holding on to you for his own security."

"Yeah, I suppose that's part of it." He kissed her lightly. "I'm beginning to scare myself."

"How so?" She felt so protected, with him towering over her, his broad shoulders stretching his white dress shirt.

"I almost want you to win."

"No, you don't. Then you'd have to give up your boat."

He glanced away. "That would be tough. You'd understand if you went out with me." His gaze slid back to snag hers. "The bow slicing through the water, the white foam funneling below, the rocking motion . . . you feel as though you're one with the ocean. You should see how the sun divides the water into shards of light."

"It sounds incredible."

"Nothing could be better, except sex." He grinned, the transformation of his face making her breath catch. "Sometimes dolphins follow you. They like the bubbles that trail the boat. They speed along for miles, leaping and playing, then suddenly they'll peel off. It's amazing." His handsome features flushed as though the admission weren't manly.

She grasped one of his hands, callused from years of labor. Her forefinger traced a line from his thumb to his palm. "This may sound weird to you, but I'm just as entranced by houses. They're like people to me. They hide old secrets, reflect the personalities of their owners, and stand sturdy through years of change. I suppose you could say the same about the furniture you restore."

He tilted his head. "That's a unique way of looking at it. You know, Heather, at times you seem to understand me better than I do myself. It's uncanny."

Her pulse accelerated. He'd begun twirling his thumb inside *her* palm, and the effect made a muddle of her thoughts.

"I almost wish we'd met elsewhere, and we weren't competing with each other," she said. When he pulled her close, she didn't resist.

"I know. I could really dig someone like you."

This time when his mouth descended, his hot breath sifted into her mouth like an offering of his soul. His strong arms folded around her, crushing her against him as he pressed his lips to hers with searing intensity. Heather returned his passion, admiring his loyalty to his father and his closeness to the land . . . er, sea. Whatever. He seemed to provide something she lacked, and her intuition sensed it. She molded herself to him, oblivious to anything except the joy of his attention.

On the edges of her mind, she heard the microwave oven humming, as though it had just turned on. Crackling noises focused her awareness. The motor shouldn't sound like that.

Her head lifted just as an explosion blasted the kitchen.

Six

Heather ducked as a missile flew through the air. A loud crash resounded, followed by silence. She glanced over to where the microwave oven door had blown off, thanks to a shiny metal object someone had put inside the now smoking appliance. From its melted shape, the item's identity was no longer discernible. No matter. What concerned her more was the likelihood that this incident represented another case of sabotage.

"Someone waited until we were in the kitchen," Rex said, narrowing his eyes. "One of us could've been killed. Maybe it's the producers. They could be watching us on camera and activated the thing by remote control."

"Or Sarah set the timer. She was the last one in here."

"Why? To knock one of us from the competition?"

"Presumably. Or to scare us off the show. Or maybe she's working for the producers to stall our progress. You mentioned the possibility of a plant, remember?"

"This was no incident meant to frighten us or hinder our work. It could've caused bodily harm. Don't forget what happened to Gary."

Voices clamored as the others rushed to see what had caused the noise. Sarah's dismay seemed genuine when she saw the sooty residue on the kitchen counter.

"Cripes," she said, "I just cleaned up in here. Who could be so stupid to put metal in the microwave?"

"Maybe you did it, honey bunny," said Dave, crossing his arms. "It's an odd way to call attention to yourself, but the kitchen *is* your domain."

"You should talk, pool boy," Sarah retorted. "If you spent as much time on the computer as you did showing off your buff bod, our phone would be ringing with reservations."

Dave's bedroom eyes livened. "Oh, I get it. You're jealous of the time I spent out there with Kim. Well, don't worry, babe, she's gone, so now I'm all yours."

"Dave worked hard today," Heather said to smooth over their differences. "We all did well under the circumstances. Tomorrow we'll have plenty of time to get the place in shape, and Monday we can take care of business details. We should be proud of our accomplishments."

"I've made more lists of what has to get done," Michelle offered, her curly black locks spilling down her back.

"That's great," Rex answered. "What about newspaper delivery? Did you order it to start in the morning? I'm curious to see what the entertainment reporter says about our TV show."

"Tanya said no news until next weekend." Michelle grimaced. "She doesn't want us to be influenced by outside opinions."

Heather couldn't suppress her curiosity, however, so she corralled the lady producer on Sunday afternoon. Tanya had just finished interviews with the guys and had signaled for Sarah, Michelle, and Heather to come over. They'd set up cameras outside for a view of the lake in the background.

"Our ratings are great," Tanya responded to Heather's query. In the bright sunlight, her pancake makeup highlighted every crease in her face. "We have viewers calling in asking about the murder investigation. I knew that would score a hit. So tell me," she said when the sound tech signaled he'd begun taping, "how do you feel you're doing? Do you think you could handle running this place alone?"

Heather launched into her prepared spiel about her advertising plans and the themed home design accessories she'd add if the house were her own. "I'll make it succeed," she finished. "But getting things ready, I have everyone else to thank. The others are pulling their weight, too."

Voters seemed to like her answers when the contestants gathered that evening at eight for their next live segment. This time, Heather secured a place next to Rex. His solid presence offered reassurance, and when she shifted nervously, he patted her hand. She noticed he wasn't completely free from anxiety, though. He tapped his black dress shoe on the carpet while the show's credits rolled. What challenge would Logan have in store for them tonight?

"I'd like to introduce a surprise guest," Logan said, giving viewers his Colgate smile. "Let's welcome business expert, Mr. Steve Marcus."

With a dramatic flourish, Tanya flung open the front door. A tall, suited fellow strode inside wearing a tight grin and a comb-over to hide his shiny pate.

"Steve is author of the books, *Starting Your Own Business*, and *How To Succeed Without Crying*," Logan boomed. "He runs a multi-million-dollar trucking company and other enterprises in the transportation industry. We've asked for his critique on our contestants."

"Oh, no," Michelle groaned in the back row.

Marcus stripped each of them of their illusions concerning their capability.

"Heather, you're too nice to your teammates," he said, fixing his steely gaze on her while she shriveled in her seat. "You try to get along with everyone and end up making excuses for their inadequate behavior. You have to do what's best for the business. If you're always concerned about your colleagues liking you, or if you gloss over their deficiencies, you'll never exhibit true leadership. It takes guts to fire an incompetent employee. Similarly, you can't operate a machine with a defective part. You have to replace the weak link instead of repeatedly trying to fix it.

"Take Rex for your model." Marcus nodded at him, sitting stiffly at Heather's side. "He knows how to get the job done.

He's able to pinpoint each person's best potential, and he'll tell you if you're not up to speed. His problem, as I see it, may be that he's too goal-oriented and discounts the value of personal relationships to company morale."

Marcus continued in this vein for the rest of them until the moment they had all been waiting for arrived.

Logan took his usual stance. "So, America, what have you decided tonight? Who's going to stay, and who will go?" He took a printed sheet from Tanya's outstretched hand. "Aw, heck, Michelle. Looks like it's your turn. Our voters say you spend too much time planning and making lists, while others bear the burden of the work. Take my advice: learn to narrow your focus and follow your own tasks through to the end. So sorry."

With a muffled sob, Michelle embraced the others. Heather gave her a tearful hug.

"I'll miss you," she said. "In my opinion, you've worked as hard as anyone else."

While Michelle ran upstairs to pack, Logan solicited their reactions. "Okay, people, what do you think about this decision?"

"It stinks," Jon pitched in, forking a hand through his spiked blond hair. "Dave should be the one to go. He wastes time hanging out at the pool."

"Hey, I get my assignments done," Dave retorted. "And I don't cheat, unlike somebody else here. That person should get the boot."

"Oh, do tell us," Tanya called. "Who is it?"

"Sorry, my lips are sealed." Dave smirked. "For now."

After the interminable talks ended, the remaining five crashed in the kitchen, sharing beers and life stories. Time stretched past midnight. Jon, Dave, and Sarah eventually went upstairs, leaving Heather and Rex behind. Heather couldn't face the isolation of her room just yet.

"I hate the live sessions," she told Rex, seated across the kitchen table. "Bringing that businessman in tonight to judge us was unfair. You can't compare running a B&B to a large company."

"I agree. It's tough on all of us. But you know what? Even if I lose, I'm glad I had the opportunity to meet you."

Although he'd been clean-shaven earlier, dark stubble now shadowed his chin and gave him a rakish look. Combined with his tousled hair and disarming grin, he presented an irresistible package. Desire flared inside her. She wanted to get closer to him, but awareness of the hidden cameras inhibited her.

"I suppose we should retire," she said somewhat reluctantly.

His eyes twinkled playfully. "Yeah, we should go to bed."

Heather gathered from his tone that going to sleep wasn't what he had in mind, and her pulse rate soared. They had only a few days together. Why not make the best of them? Rising, she considered how they could be discreet.

Passing through the hallway, she glanced at the empty bookshelf standing against the side of the staircase. From her real estate agent's viewpoint, it seemed to be bizarrely out of place.

"That looks terrible there," she said. "We should move it into the family room, at least until we fill the shelves."

"Now?" he replied when she started over.

"Why not?" She shoved the bookcase away from the wall. "Hey, get this. There's a door back here. Would you believe it?" Its oiled hinges opened easily, making her wonder if the producers intended for them to find this closet under the stairwell. Her fingers fumbled along the inside wall for a light switch. A single bulb flashed on, illuminating the interior where stacks of cartons met her eyes. When she read the labels, her mouth dropped open.

"Oh, my gosh, these are cases of wine."

"No way." Rex investigated by tearing open a box and peering inside. "Unbelievable. We should tell the others."

"Later. Let's get some glasses and a corkscrew. We should at least see if the stuff is okay. You know, unspoiled."

"You're right." He left briefly and returned carrying the requested items. Rex made short work of removing one cork and filling a couple of inexpensive goblets from a bar set Sarah had bought.

The astringent taste of dry red wine slid down her throat. Closing her eyes, Heather took another gulp and savored the fruity flavor. She probably shouldn't drink any more after downing a couple of beers, but this evening's session had unnerved her, and stress relief suddenly became an urgent goal. Following several swallows that emptied her glass, she sank to the floor, feeling light-headed.

Rex sat beside her. He refilled their glasses, then put the bottle down. Glancing at the partially open door, he kicked it shut. "Now we've got this cozy little place all to ourselves."

And I have you all to myself. Twisting sideways, Heather reached out, brought his head down, and clamped her mouth to his. No time like the present, she thought giddily. His body stiffened in surprise; then he drew her into his arms so that they stitched together. She deepened the kiss, and his firm lips responded with fervor. Recognizing that his need matched her own, Heather pressed herself against his length until she thought her bones would melt. She wanted to obliterate Logan's questions and the business expert's opinions, to escape from momentary pain and experience pleasure so elemental so she could forget everything else. Rex was someone she could rely on, even though they both aimed toward the same prize that only one of them could take home. She let her gratitude expand and encompass him, showing how she felt by abandoning all reason.

Not all of her senses fled, however.

"We should go upstairs," she murmured, when they pulled back for air. "Logan might have put a camera in here, knowing one of us would find this makeshift wine cellar."

"That's true." His eyes glimmered as he regarded her. "Here, take our glasses and the opener. I'll bring another bottle."

"Your room or mine?" she whispered after they'd repositioned the bookshelf.

"Doesn't matter. Are you sure?"

"Absolutely," she answered, glad he cared enough to ask.

She'd just shut the door to her bedroom when he moved in like a vulture sniffing prey. Putting the wine goblets and corkscrew on her nightstand, she turned and sought his embrace. Her lips parted, and she snuggled against him. His gaze fired before his mouth descended on hers. She responded readily as he grazed her lips with hungry abandon. Her nostrils picked up his cologne, its scent sending tendrils of desire along her nerves. Warmth coiled through her groin, fueling her passion.

Eager for more, she let her tongue dart out, starting a duel that brought them to a new level of intimacy. She explored the far reaches of his mouth, probing his teeth, tasting the remnants of red wine and pretzels. Feeling naughty, she closed her lips to suck on his tongue. He groaned and squeezed his arms around her so tight she could barely breathe. His hips ground against her, inducing in her belly an upward spiral of need.

She could easily lose herself in his virility. It didn't matter what tomorrow would bring. Even if one of them got kicked off the show, they'd have memories of tonight to savor. She hadn't met a man who could be so giving while pursuing his single-minded goal. The heady mixture inspired her so she could do anything, have anything . . . or anyone. Instinct melded the two of them together, as though he were the only one for her.

She wrapped her arms around him, clutching his strong back. If only she could feel his bare skin, she'd run her hands over his powerful muscles. But his clothing was in the way.

Detaching her mouth from his suctionlike grip, she stepped back. "Take your shirt off, Rex." Her husky tone didn't sound like her own.

"Yes, ma'am." His breathing quickened, but his movements were deliberately slow. Watching her reaction, he unfastened his shirt button by button, while her eyes feasted on his exposed chest. He tossed the shirt to the floor, followed by his belt. When his hands poised on his pants zipper, she sucked in a sharp breath. Then he stood before her naked, grinning as she gaped at the evidence of his arousal.

"Your turn," he said with a devilish glint in his eyes. With a quick movement, he slipped her dress over her head. It joined his clothing on the carpet. Underneath, she'd worn her favorite black lace bra and panties, but he wasn't in any hurry to remove them. Her face flushed under his lazy perusal.

"Beautiful," he murmured in a thick voice, while impatience strained her limits.

Her blood surged, her body needing his touch. She closed the distance between them, thrusting her bosom against his bared flesh. But he wouldn't give her satisfaction yet. Bending his head, he brushed her mouth, tracing her contours with his tongue.

Still he didn't touch her.

Heather moaned in agony. Her breasts ached, her nipples swollen with need. Desire pooled in her core like bubbling lava seeking eruption through a sealed path.

When she was so weak-kneed she could barely stand, his hands found the upward slopes of her breasts. "Kill the lights," she said, reduced to monosyllables. Although video in their bedrooms was supposed to be turned off by now, she felt self-conscious being exposed in the bright room.

"More wine?" he asked, handing her a filled glass without waiting for her reply. He twisted his arm around hers, offering her his goblet. Feeling immersed in his power, she sipped the fruity ambrosia until her legs felt rubbery and she craved more than wine on her lips.

He took her glass and put it on the nightstand next to his own; then he flicked off the light switch. The room fell into darkness except for faint moonlight filtering through the blinds. Feeling bold, she unsnapped her bra, tossed it away, and wriggled out of her panties. Rex gave her a long glance south before he accepted her offering. He covered her breasts, massaging gently. His kneading reduced her to putty, especially when he stroked his thumbs across her tips until they peaked. Sensations sizzled directly to the female apparatus below her belly.

"Down," he commanded, pushing her gently onto the bed. Her eyes widened as he knelt at her feet. "By God, you're lovely." Slowly, he pushed apart her thighs to stare at her.

She felt streaks of lightning wherever he caressed her. When he tickled her inner leg, every nerve in her body quivered with excitement. He was determined to drive her to a frenzy. His fingers skirted her triangle, making her arch in response. When his hand returned, probing her folds and sticking a finger inside to assess her readiness, she thought she'd fly over the edge right then.

He wasn't about to allow her that luxury. Not yet. He straightened his body over hers, hard muscled flesh against her softness as his weight settled atop her. His lips descended on her mouth. While a maelstrom of desire swept her into a seething vortex, his tongue thrust hotly into her deep recesses.

Suddenly, she felt air cool her skin. He'd leaped from the bed and leaned over to retrieve something from the floor. "I don't want to forget this," he said, joining her again. He held up a foil-wrapped object. "Would you like to do the honors?"

Although Heather was on the pill, she was grateful for his intervention. She rolled it on him while he gazed at her with lust-ridden eyes. Then they resumed their previous pose.

As he slanted his mouth over hers to plunder her swollen lips, his strong muscles forced her legs wider apart. Through a haze of lust, she felt him prod her most intimate place. When he ground his hips from side to side, she tottered on the brink of ecstasy. The pressure became unbearable.

When she thought she couldn't hold on a single moment longer, he grunted, "Guide me inside you, sweetheart."

Breathing short, shallow breaths, she complied. He plunged into her welcoming heat.

Slowly at first, then with an increasing tempo, he timed his thrusts to an ancient rhythm. Heather wrapped her legs around his torso and gyrated with him. Sweat formed on her brow as the sweet ache in her pelvis expanded until she raced toward a climax. When she reached her upheaval, shudders of pleasure wracked her body.

While she was lost in the throes of her last spasms, Rex responded with his own spurt of hot desire as they joined together in a dance of the ages.

A dance that was interrupted by a sudden howl of terror from the hallway.

Seven

Tossing on their clothing, Heather and Rex slammed out of her bedroom and into the hall. Lights flicked on and doors crashed open. Sarah and Jon joined them in racing to the stairwell from where they heard a series of groans. At the bottom, Dave stretched on the floor, his left leg twisted at an odd angle.

"Someone pushed me," he gritted between clenched teeth. "My leg . . . I think it's broken."

"I'll call for help," Rex said while Heather knelt beside the stricken man.

"Shit," Jon cursed. "We don't have liability insurance yet."

"Is that all you can think of?" Heather retorted. "It wouldn't matter anyway. Dave is a contestant, not a guest."

"Yeah? Well, the studio should be doing more to guarantee our safety. Who's responsible for these incidents? You'd think the tapes would show someone we might recognize."

"Oh, dear," Sarah cried. "I-I'll get Dave a glass of water."

"The ambulance is on its way," Rex told them, replacing the phone receiver on its cradle. "I called the detective, too. I thought he should know about this."

"Who pushed you?" Heather asked Dave.

"I couldn't see. The person had something over their head."

He gasped as a spasm of pain caught him. "Maybe . . . check outside. Whoever it was ran out the front door."

Heather wondered if she could find any clues by looking outdoors. Not in the dark. That kind of investigating was best left to the police. Too bad the alarm system wouldn't be activated until Friday, or it would have alerted them to an intruder. She didn't see how someone from inside the house could have pushed Dave down the stairs, charged out the front door, returned through another entrance, and come upstairs. . . .

Wait a minute. She'd only gotten a quick look at the owner's suite on the ground floor level, with its private entrance on the other side of the living and dining rooms. Could there be a back staircase that she didn't know about? Her mind's eye pictured the door at the far end of the upstairs corridor. She had opened it briefly but assumed the dark space held a closet. Torn between wanting to investigate and providing support, she patted Dave's clammy hand, contemplating what his injury would mean to their team.

"You'll get fixed up and come back," she told him. His pallor alarmed her. Was he going into shock? "Rex," she said, her pitch rising.

"It's okay. I'm here." Rex knelt beside their colleague. "Hang in there, buddy. The medics are coming. Hear the siren? We'll save your place at the table for you."

"I don't think so." Dave's voice broke. "Looks like I'll have to work toward the pool service on my own. Maybe I can find myself a rich mama who digs hanging with a tough guy like me."

Heather's lower lip trembled as she fought tears. For all his masculine posturing, Dave was a whiz with computers. He'd carried his weight and deserved winning the prize same as the rest of them.

Just how valuable Dave's job had been became evident after daybreak when Jon sat at the computer to work on his spreadsheet. Heather heard his cry from outside, where she'd been inspecting the front lawn and shrubbery for clues to last night's visitor. She ran indoors to find Jon jumping up and down. "Everything is gone," he yelled, flapping his arms. With his ruddy complexion and spiked hair, he reminded her of a rooster.

She glanced at the blank monitor screen. "What do you mean?"

"The hard drive. It's wiped clean. I can't even bring up Windows."

"Oh, golly. All our files, the work Dave did. Lost?" She glanced around for Rex before remembering he'd gone into town to buy more supplies. Since when had she become so reliant on him? Sarah wouldn't be any help. Her skills centered in the kitchen. "Maybe the data can still be retrieved," she said. "Give me the phone book. I'll call a technician."

"It's a good thing I wrote our figures in the book," Jon said, giving her a dark glance. "Backups are essential. Did you copy your stuff to a disk?"

"Dave said he would do that for me." She bit her lip. Had last night's accident been an attempt to derail his efforts?

She called a computer expert who said he'd be out later that afternoon. Then she returned a few reservation inquiries left on their telephone answering machine. Already some of her advertising initiatives were showing results.

Her stomach growling, she entered the kitchen for a midmorning snack. Sarah, wearing an apron, was cutting vegetables in preparation for lunch. She had dark circles under her eyes, and her lids looked puffy. Heather had noticed earlier but hadn't taken the opportunity to speak to her privately.

"Be careful with that knife. The way you're chopping those carrots, your finger might slip. We don't need any more accidents," Heather warned.

Sarah paused, giving a furtive glance at one of the recessed camera lenses. "Can I talk to you outside?"

"Sure." They might get a quick minute in the backyard before a cameraman and sound tech bustled over.

The shorter woman walked with Heather toward the lake.

A clump of banana plants hung over the water, one of them sporting a deep purple blossom. Heather sniffed moisture in the air, a sign of impending rain. Cumulus clouds powdered the sky, a deep celestial blue. She glanced at the lake, where sunbeams showered the surface with sparkles of light.

"What's on your mind?" she prompted Sarah.

Sarah's brow knitted. "It's about Dave. I never told anyone, but I saw somebody on the patio the night Gary got clobbered."

"I thought you said the blinds were closed."

"They were lowered, but the slats weren't shut. I didn't get a clear look, though."

"This could be important to the police."

She lowered her pixie-cut blond head. "I didn't want to say anything in case it was Dave. He knew about my . . . he saw me . . ."

"What?" Heather swallowed her impatience.

"It would disqualify me. You have to promise not to tell."

"All right." She'd deal with the ramifications later. Right now, all Heather wanted to do was to prevent further incidents that caused bodily harm.

Glancing away, Sarah cleared her throat. "He caught me researching recipes in a cookbook. Remember Logan said we weren't allowed any instructional manuals? I'd brought it from home in my suitcase. Otherwise, there's no way I could have come up with all these menus on my own." Her pleading look engaged Heather's sympathies.

"So you kept quiet about what you saw because you thought it might be Dave outside, and if you told the police about him, he'd tell Logan about you?" She wrestled with her own anger. Sarah's selfishness could have been responsible for Dave's broken leg. He might have even cracked his collarbone tumbling down those stairs. Maybe he'd be unharmed if Sarah had spoken sooner and given the police some clues to follow.

"Did you see anything else? Was Gary struck from behind, or did he face the person who hit him?" Aware that a camera crew was heading their way, she spoke rapidly.

"I-I don't know. Dave passed through the kitchen on his way to the garage, if that's even where he went. I was upset when he caught me reading the cookbook, although he didn't say anything. He left after giving me this smirk, you know? I made sure to keep away from the cameras. After I'd stashed the book in its hiding place, I glanced up to see the barest flash of movement on the patio. I was afraid someone might be spying on me, so I shut the blinds."

Perhaps Dave had seen something significant on his way outside. That could be why he'd been targeted last night. But if that was true, why hadn't he spoken up?

Because he had something to hide, too. Maybe he'd been on his way to an assignation. With whom? Kim had been upstairs. Michelle, though, had been prowling the territory.

The camera crew reached them as they were heading back to the house. "What did we miss, ladies?" Tanya cooed, her face coated with the appropriate application of pasty makeup. Heather gave her a critical glance. *She must rise awfully early to primp herself in case the chance to be filmed popped up.*

"We were talking about Gary," she told the co-producer. "Tell me, did the police find anything on the tapes from that night?"

Tanya offered a chilly smile. "I'm afraid not. It was too dark. The lights were out."

"Oh, yes." Someone who'd been waiting on the patio might have switched them off when Gary appeared alone. It's possible he'd recognized, or even greeted, his assailant beforehand. Sarah had noticed movement in the shadows by the pool but nobody she could identify, and by the time Michelle had stepped outside, the deed was done. Michelle wouldn't have had time after leaving the rest of them in the living room to fetch a shovel, bonk Gary on the head, and ditch the evidence.

Something didn't play right about this scenario, but Heather couldn't determine the source. For now, she'd hold her tongue about Sarah's indiscretion. Ratting on her teammates wasn't in her nature. It was more important that they make this venture a success, regardless of who would win.

As they entered through the patio screen door, a pang of yearning stabbed her. How she wanted to claim this house for her own. *You can't kid yourself. You're dying to be the winner.*

Scanning the sparse outdoor furnishings, an oblong glass table with four chairs and two chaise lounges, she thought about how she'd add another dinette set, citronella candles, hanging plants, and chimes. Kim had contributed that pitiful potted green plant that acted as a centerpiece. If the house were hers, Heather would find something more suitable to her tropical theme.

Straightening things came second nature to her as a real estate agent. Her practiced glance noted the clumps of dirt marring the glass tabletop. Halting, she scooped the soil into her hand and dumped it into the pot. After righting the lopsided stalk, she followed Sarah inside.

Rex had returned with a report on Dave's condition. "His leg is in a cast," Rex said, unloading a bag of weed killer from the trunk of his Corolla. His arm muscles bulged. Heather watched the byplay of his powerful shoulders while he lifted the heavy purchases and stashed them in the garage. "But he'll be in the hospital a while longer, so I guess he's out of action as far as we're concerned."

"Someone wiped our hard drive clean," she told him. "Jon discovered it this morning. I arranged for a technician to come later to try to retrieve the data and reinstall Windows."

"Great." His eyes smoldered as he regarded her. "How are you holding up? Are you okay?"

She smiled. "I'm fine, but I'm glad you're home."

Home. How she wished those words were true. This house sang to her, as though it shared her longing. Its façade spoke to her of steamy summers and dry, balmy winters, of guests who enjoyed their stay so much that they made a return reservation for the following year. In her fantasy, Rex stood by her side, helping run the place, proudly skimming his hand over the polished wood during the day and stroking her skin, feverish with desire, in the evenings.

"You love this place, don't you?" he said, cocking his head.

"I do," she said, suppressing the urge to blurt out her feelings toward him. What *did* she feel? Had their lovemaking been merely an attempt to escape the tension building toward Friday evening, when one of them would be declared winner? Or did it mean more? Would she like Rex as much if she'd met him working in his father's store? Did she care for him enough to help him reach *his* dream?

"It's the house I've always wanted," she told him. "When I was young, I entertained myself by picturing the various rooms in my dream house and how I'd decorate them. I can't imagine anyone selling this place." Nor could she imagine how she and Rex would continue seeing each other after the show ended. Their lifestyles differed dramatically; never mind the geographical distance that separated them.

"Not everyone wants the same things you do," he spoke softly, regarding her with sad eyes.

"I know. Look at you. You'd like to live on the water instead of putting down roots on land."

"You bet. I can't wait to steer my vessel out to sea. Already I see myself holding the wheel, rocking with the motion as we hit each wave, being one with her as we slice through the water," he said with a dreamy, faraway look.

"Same as lovemaking." She smiled, but without cheer.

He reached out to stroke her cheek. "Not quite the same. I feel that we have something special, Heather. Regardless of who wins, I'd like to see you afterward."

"What for? You don't seem to understand that I have to provide for my parents. Their good health depends on me. So I need this house or another one just like it. I couldn't ever live on a boat."

"Couldn't we see where our relationship goes without worrying about living arrangements, or are you not interested?"

"Yes, I am, I mean . . . let's just wait and see what happens, okay? Neither one of us may win. Sarah or Jon could take home the final prize."

"Sarah doesn't deserve it," Rex said. "There's more to running an inn than cooking meals. Jon does his share, but I'm not sure he has the people skills."

"They'd both sell the place anyway, so what does it matter?"

His mouth tightened. "They wouldn't be the right people at the helm even if they wanted the B&B. Both of them are doing only what they're supposed to do and nothing more. You have to go above and beyond to be successful in any business venture. I don't think either one of them is capable."

Apparently, the viewers agreed, because on Tuesday night, Sarah got voted off the show. Logan had canceled the voting Monday because of Dave's departure.

Wednesday found three of them contending for the same goal. Excited that she was still in the race, Heather wondered why winning didn't seem like such a big deal anymore.

Eight

Wednesday evening found Heather, Jon, and Rex dressed in their best business clothes in the living room. As Logan ran through his opening sequence, Heather perched tensely on the edge of her chair. Twisting her hands, she felt adrift without their former companions.

"You three really accomplished a lot today," their host announced. "You've all become like a well-oiled machine, but now one of you has to go. Who will it be? It's a tough decision for viewers."

He waved to Tanya, who fed in taped sequences showing each of them at work. "Jon, who's handled financial, legal, and insurance matters, and taken over the computer programs from our accident-prone Dave Molina. Heather, whose advertising efforts already have reservations pouring in. She's assumed kitchen and housekeeping duties and enhanced the inn with her decorating touches. Her expenses have stayed well within budgetary restraints. And Rex: general handyman, lawn care specialist, pool maintenance and security. So, America, what's your choice?"

Tanya scurried over with the tally. Heather sat rigid, afraid to breathe. She'd come so far, it would kill her to lose now. She loved this house and had given her heart to it.

"The person with the least votes who will be leaving us tonight is . . . Jonathan Walker," Logan announced. "Sorry, Jon. Viewers feel you did a bang-up job with the business angles, but more is required when guests arrive. Our audience feels you may not have the requisite skills for being a proper host."

Heather jumped up to embrace him even while her heart fluttered in joyful relief.

"Congratulations," Logan told her and Rex after their colleague departed. "The next couple of days will be critical. We're not going to take a vote tomorrow night. Instead, we'll be giving you an assignment to test your merit. Now"—he winked at the camera—"we know you two have been fooling around, but only one of you can win this house. Is what you have going strong enough to last beyond the show, or will the competition tear you apart?"

The host bared his teeth. "Stay tuned, people," he told the TV viewers. "The remaining vote will make or break this couple. Come back tomorrow evening to see their new challenge."

"What do you think Logan will make us do?" Heather asked Rex after the production crew had departed. She headed for the kitchen, where Sarah had left a stash of cookies. Rex went for the leftover pizza.

"I haven't a clue. You?" He gave her an unreadable glance.

"No idea. I'm sure we'll manage okay, whatever it is."

She lit a vanilla candle, wanting to broach the subject of their relationship but leery of bringing it up. Maybe she was afraid Rex's ruthless business attitude would affect the outcome of their affair. Yet why should it, when he said he'd like to continue seeing her after the show, regardless of who won?

Her gaze swept his broad shoulders, strong features, and midnight black hair. He looked great in a dress shirt and tie, but from the way he kept shrugging, she guessed the formal outfit didn't suit him. Her imagination wandered, and she pictured him bare-chested at the wheel of his yacht, the wind tossing his hair and the sun blazing in his eyes. She had to admit the image stirred her female regions.

"What are you thinking?" he asked her, after polishing off a slice of cold pizza.

She smiled. "I'm imagining you on your boat."

"Do you believe that positive imagery can make things happen?" He licked a crumb off his mouth.

"People make their own destiny. If you view yourself as being successful, it'll happen. Persistence pays."

"And I suppose you view yourself as owning this house?"

She lifted her chin. "That's right."

"You should," he said softly. "Your heart is in it. Anyone can see it in your eyes, hear it in your voice when you talk about the things you'd like to do. You act as though you've come home."

"I have." She'd never wanted something so much in her life. But did this house mean more to her than what she felt for Rex?

"You're lucky that you can put your hands on your dream."

"So can you. Even if I win, you should still go after your boat. Don't hesitate because you're afraid of what your father will think. It's your life, and if he loves you, he'll want you to be happy. Write a business plan, apply for a loan. There are ways to make it work. You've already taken the first step by being on the show."

"That's true." He advanced until he was just inches away. Stroking her hair, he leaned close. "I've waited too long already. Sometimes sacrifices have to be made for the end to justify the means."

"Huh?" Puzzled by his statement, her hope for clarification ended when his mouth captured hers. Her wits fled, and before she knew it, they were stumbling up the stairs, divesting themselves of various articles of clothing.

Inside her room, Rex switched off the light. Their remaining garments ended up on the floor. They came together in a frenzied embrace, skin against skin, his hot breath fanning her cheek as he sought her mouth. He tasted her hungrily, greedily. Heather responded by clashing with his tongue, imbibing his remnants of pizza and beer as though they were blessed ambrosia. Closing her eyes, she drifted into nirvana. Nothing else mattered except the heavenly feel of his arms around her and the movement of his mouth on hers.

Need spiraled within her. Taking the initiative, she edged toward the bed until the frame hit her calves. Sinking down on the soft mattress, she stretched out, pulling him down with her. His weight settled atop her while he groaned her name. She parted her legs, thrusting her pelvis to welcome him inside. Reaching around, she splayed her hands on his butt, crying out when he entered her. Panting, she matched his rhythm until spasms of pleasure rocked them both on a sea of bliss.

"Damn, I forgot," he grunted, rolling his sweaty body off her. "To put on protection, I mean."

"I'm on the pill," she said, feeling delightfully satiated. "Not that I do this very often. Hardly ever, actually." She rubbed his arm, feeling his hard biceps beneath her fingers.

"Yeah? Hard to believe with that bod of yours. But don't worry, I'm very particular. I don't chase down every girl I meet. Just special ones, like you. So where do we go from here?" Leaning on his elbow, he traced her breast. His aqua eyes, deep as the ocean, bored into hers as she lazed beside him.

"I know where I'm going . . . into the shower." Twisting sideways, she bounded off the bed. She didn't want to answer his question yet. Getting serious with him didn't mesh with her visions of running a bed-and-breakfast, not when he planned to live on a boat and take people fishing for a livelihood. He'd said nothing about settling ashore on a permanent basis. Then again, he hadn't mentioned permanence in terms of their relationship. How much was he willing to give up to be with her, or her with him?

Feeling they still had issues between them to explore, she turned on the bathroom vanity lights, not minding that she was parading around naked. The cameras had gone dark for the evening. Needing to dispel the gloomy direction of her thoughts, she switched on the recessed light over the shower and then screamed, leaping backward, when the overhead bulb shattered.

"What the hell? Are you okay?" Rex stood at her side in an instant, covering her with his shirt. He couldn't use the towel; glass shards stuck to its terry cloth surface.

"The light burst. Oh, golly, if I'd been under it . . ." She blinked to make sure no pieces had gotten in her eyes.

Putting his arm around her, Rex guided her back into the bedroom and pushed her onto the mattress. "Stay here. I'll clean up the broken glass. Thank God you weren't injured."

Could this have been a true accident, she wondered when he left to get a broom, or was someone trying to scare her into quitting the show? As maintenance man, Rex would know how to short-circuit a light. Then again, Jon might have sabotaged it earlier, assuring his triumph in case Rex got voted off. No, that didn't make sense. She could've been the one axed by the voters. Or was her theory about a mysterious intruder correct?

She'd checked the closet at the end of the hall, and it had indeed led to a staircase descending to the master suite. Anyone could enter through the patio doors to come upstairs. But who would be so bold? A neighbor, who didn't want a bed-and-breakfast in the neighborhood? An investor, who hoped to buy the property when it turned out to be jinxed?

Her lips tightened. No one, and nothing, could stop her from winning this house.

On Thursday night, Logan revealed their assignment for Friday. "We've invited a group of town dignitaries for a grand opening breakfast tomorrow," their host said, wearing his plastic smile and moussed hair. "You can expect a full house: sixteen people. This will be a real test of how you can handle a crowd. Then that evening, our audience will make their final decision."

Tanya sauntered forward, looking slick in a form-fitting red suit. "Remember, you're not allowed to consult any manuals, like that cookbook Sarah had been hiding. But here's the catch: you're also not allowed to help each other. Separately, you will prepare breakfast for eight guests apiece. Whoever wins this place, after all, will be the house's sole proprietor."

"That's unfair," Heather complained to Rex later. "If I'm in charge here, I could use whatever resources were available."

Looking ruggedly handsome in a T-shirt and jeans, he gave her a disarming smile. "They don't want to make it easy. I'm beginning to think some of these so-called accidents have been staged. Tanya brags about how their ratings soar after every incident."

"Your idea about them planting a saboteur doesn't wash anymore with just the two of us left."

"You watch my back, and I'll watch yours."

She grinned. "I wish, but then I wouldn't get anything done." Standing on her toes, she kissed him. Her senses reeled from one sniff of his favorite cologne, but she tamped her reaction. No time for that now. She had to make a late-night trip to the grocery store, plan a menu, and get started in the kitchen.

Nine

By Friday evening, Heather's nerves were so taut, she thought she'd burst. She and Rex sat side-by-side on the sofa while Logan rattled through his introductions for their live broadcast. After tonight, she would never have to look again at the host's toothy smile or gelled hair. That was, if she lost. The producers planned to stick around over the weekend to film the first real guests arriving.

"Our contestants outdid themselves this morning when they each entertained eight of the town's top dignitaries for breakfast," Logan intoned. "This was a practice test for when they have to prepare meals every morning for the inn's residents. How did they measure up? Let's see."

Tanya took over, showing edited clips of their frenzied morning activity. Heather thought she and Rex had both done remarkably well, although Rex seemed unusually nervous during breakfast preparation, ducking outside periodically as though fresh air would energize him.

"Notice how Rex has trouble cracking an egg," Tanya said, chuckling. She wore a cloying perfume that irritated Heather's nose. "He burnt his first attempt at French toast, but then he got the hang of it. Let's backtrack a minute. See how he's taking the grapefruit pieces out of a jar? Compare his starter to

Heather's parfait of strawberry yogurt, granola, and fresh blueberries. Her main dish, broccoli and cheese quiche, served with melon slices shaped in a fan, came out perfectly."

The tape showed Rex stumbling as he poured coffee, nearly spilling it on the mayor. Heather risked a glance in his direction as the video continued. His flushed skin and clenched jaw were the only outward signs of tension. An urge to pat his arm took hold, but she kept her hands clasped in her lap, aware of the cameras trained on their faces.

Which one of them would win? She prayed it would be her. She had more at stake, needing to live here so she could care for her parents. But that was saying Rex's dream wasn't as important as hers, and that his boat was a luxury he could live without. Who was she to judge what he wanted from life? And what did she want, really? To live here alone, caring for her elderly folks, or to share her life with a man like Rex? How much would she be willing to sacrifice for that?

"And now, folks, we'll show you a scene from one of our hidden cameras that will blow your mind." Tanya crooned. "At this crucial moment, when a final decision is about to be reached, one of these people takes an incredible risk. Caught on video, this person's action means immediate dismissal. Remember the rule that disallows any instructional text? Watch this."

The tape showed Rex rounding a corner outside the rear of the house. At the big plastic garbage can, he lifted the lid and reached inside, pulling out a sheaf of papers. He studied them for several minutes before tucking them back into the can.

Beside her, Rex cursed and covered his face with his hands.

Tanya produced a stack of computer printouts, waving them as the live camera focused on her.

"Recipes, ladies and gentlemen. Rex Gerard downloaded them from the Internet because the man *never learned how to cook!* He's a complete novice in the kitchen, hence his bumbling efforts. Rex, you're out. Congratulations, Heather Payne. You've won your dream house."

Stunned, Heather stared at Rex, who rallied to give her a

hug. "You deserve it, sweetheart. I'm thrilled for you." Rising, he lifted her to her feet. "Until later." He kissed her, a brief peck on the cheek, nothing like the smoldering kisses he'd showered on her before.

Logan and Tanya bustled over to shake her hand and offer a ceremonial key. Too overwhelmed to react, Heather moved like a robot. Rex turned toward the stairway. The ten-minute limit to pack and leave still applied.

"Wait," Heather called out. She couldn't believe he'd tripped up like that. Rex must have deliberately screwed himself so she would win. But why? Now he'd have to confront his dad and figure out a way to get a boat on his own. Her heart sank. It wasn't right for her to feel that her goals were more important than his. He had to do what made him happy. Instead, he'd assured her happiness.

A lump rose in her throat. She had to tell him how she felt about his selfless act. But when she stepped forward, Tanya grabbed her arm and thrust her in front of the camera.

"How does it feel to be the winner?" Tanya demanded, while the sound tech positioned his equipment for her reply.

"I-I can't believe it. But I have to go—"

"Are you ready to greet your first real guests in the morning?"

"Well, sure, we've been preparing all week." Desperate to break away, she eyed Logan, who consulted with a lighting technician by the front door. Their host waited to get Rex's departure on camera. "Look, you'll have to excuse me . . ."

Her voice faded as Rex thundered down the stairs, a duffel bag slung over his shoulder. He must have packed his stuff the night before, Heather thought in dismay. Sparing her a wink and a wave, he exited through the open door before her limbs could react. After showing Rex's departure, Logan signaled to Tanya to resume her interview.

"Why do you feel Rex cheated at this critical juncture, when everything hinged on how the two of you managed under pressure?" Tanya persisted, her eyes gleaming. "Do you think he would have won the viewers' vote?"

"Who did get the most votes?" Heather said, confronting

the co-producer. Her knees felt weak, and her heart hammered. She still couldn't conceive that she'd won, so why did it feel as though she'd lost?

"That's a moot point now," Tanya said, grinning broadly. "The house is yours."

Something took hold inside of her, mustering reserves of iron strength. Rex said sometimes you had to show all your guns to get things done. She hadn't agreed, believing you won more battles with flowers. Now she understood what he meant. You had to be hard-edged on occasion for people to listen.

"It's not fair," she retorted, hands on her hips. "Your rules said we weren't allowed instructional manuals. Rex wasn't looking at a cookbook. So what if he printed out a few recipes? Now that this place is mine, I can use any resources I need."

"Nonetheless," Tanya replied in a syrupy tone, "he violated our guidelines."

Undaunted, Heather shook her head, her body trembling with the force of her emotions. "There has to be an appeal process. Rex deserves a chance along with me. The winning score should go to the best professional. You're disallowing the opinions of our viewers by ignoring their vote, and that was the whole point of this show."

"Aren't you just trying to appease your lover? We know you two have spent a few nights together. Does this mark the end of your affair?"

Mortified when tears brimmed her eyes, Heather turned and ran up the stairs to her room.

Desolate, she sobbed on her bed until her ducts went dry. Here she'd won her dream house, and she couldn't enjoy it. Without Rex at her side, earning the prize meant nothing.

Surprised by the intensity of her feelings, she resolved to make things right. Maybe those recipes in the garbage can were a plant. Rex may have received a tip to look in there, and he hadn't admitted he'd been duped because he wanted her to win. If she could prove they'd been put there by someone else, that would put him back in the running. She didn't think about what would transpire if she lost the house.

More importantly, she didn't want to lose Rex. He'd come to mean too much to her.

Gritting her teeth, she changed into jeans, a pullover top, socks, and running shoes. A few minutes in the bathroom freshened her face. Then she grabbed a flashlight and rushed downstairs, slipping outdoors through the family room patio doors.

Sniffing the warm night air laden with moisture, she prowled across the soft grass to the side of the house. There stood the incriminating garbage can, its lid awry. Peering inside with the flashlight, she felt a wave of disappointment. The can was empty. No clues in there. Now what?

An eerie stillness descended as she padded back to the screened patio. Aside from the steady hum of an air-conditioning unit and a chorus of crickets, she distinguished no other sounds. She was alone for the first time since she'd arrived at the house, and her nape prickled.

Gary had been assaulted out here. Detective Jackson, who'd shown up several more times to conduct detailed interviews as well as to search the premises, hadn't shared his findings with any of the contestants. He almost seemed to adopt a wait-and-see attitude. That didn't sit comfortably with Heather.

That stupid plant was lopsided again. Her hand automatically reached to straighten the tilting branches. She'd dump it outside tomorrow and find something more suitable.

Her fingers pushed on the stem. When it wouldn't right itself, she grabbed the entire thing in her hand. It lifted easily with a clump of dirt at the roots, but something impeded its repositioning. Shining her flashlight inside, she gasped. At the bottom of the pot nestled a pair of woman's gardening gloves.

Realizing what they represented, Heather stuffed the plant back into its container and brushed the soil from her hands. Then she stopped, standing frozen in the gloom. It shouldn't be so dark on the pool deck. What had happened to the outdoor lights she'd put on?

Her pulse accelerated, and she jerked forward toward the lit family room. *Get inside, and lock the doors.*

After securing the entrances, she'd call the police. Zipping around to the other doors, Heather made certain they were shut and locked. She remembered to check the private owner's suite at the opposite end of the ground floor. *My suite*, she thought with a sense of awe, standing in the center of the master bedroom with its king-size bed.

Her mind wandered to the home accessories she planned to add, picturing the bedspread and matching draperies, before she noticed the lingering perfume scent. *Oh, no.*

This room being unoccupied, they hadn't installed a telephone in here yet. She flew toward the front hallway. *Arm the security alarm while you're there.* The technician had connected the system earlier that day.

But just as she passed the kitchen entrance, the power cut off, and everything went dark.

That meant no camera feed to the production crew next door, no portable phones working, and no alarm system, because they hadn't chosen to pay extra for wireless backup.

She heard a scraping sound in the kitchen, and her breath caught. "Who's there?" At the same time, she realized locking the doors had been futile. Who else had a key? None other than the one person she hoped to avoid.

Still holding the flashlight, Heather flicked it on and leaped backward when Tanya's grinning face loomed in its beam. The producer edged toward her, a serrated knife glinting in her hand. Her eyes gleamed with a murderous light.

Icy fingers of fear clutched Heather's heart. "Tanya, what are you doing here?" she choked. "The game is over."

Tanya inched closer. "No, it isn't. Too bad the intruder responsible for those accidents will strike again tonight. I'll suggest it could be a neighbor, who opposes having a commercial property in the area. We'll get the highest ratings ever for any reality show, and then I can go on to produce movies."

"Is that why you killed Gary, just for the ratings? You used those gloves and then hid them inside the flower pot."

"I couldn't risk throwing them out. The police went through the trash. I would've gotten rid of them later when the heat died down. You might have lived, if you hadn't gone snooping tonight. I've been monitoring the video channels, and the cameras caught you going outside. The police will think the intruder followed you into the house."

Heather thought of her cell phone upstairs in her purse. If she could call for help. . . . Backed up against the staircase wall, she felt behind her for the empty bookshelf she and Rex had moved the night they found the wine. The door was just behind it.

"What about Dave?" she said hastily, shifting her position so she could slide the bookshelf sideways.

"I'd hoped to break his neck. Did you notice how the first people voted off the show were women? There wasn't any gender equality, so I had to even the score."

Heather stumbled, which pushed the bookshelf to the left. "Were you responsible for the pranks, too? The stuffed toilet? The bulb over my shower? Putting metal in the microwave?"

"Oh, that one was rich, wasn't it?" Tanya laughed. "I should've done more. But I'll make up for that now."

Tanya launched her body, knocking the flashlight from Heather's grip with an outstretched elbow. Crashing to the floor, the torch's light flickered and went dark, but not before Heather saw the sharp blade of the knife descending in an arc.

She screamed, dodging to her left. Her shoulder bumped the bookshelf further awry. She shot out her hand, grappling for the doorknob to the under stairs closet.

"Come here, you bitch," Tanya growled. Enough moonlight filtered in for Heather to see the knife aimed at her ribs.

Before she could regain her breath, Tanya lunged. Heather closed her hand on the closet handle and wrenched the door open. Tanya howled as the wood slammed her nose.

The knife clattered to the floor, and Heather kicked it away. A pounding sound reached her awareness, accompanied by shouts. "Heather! Are you in there? Open the door, dammit. Heather!"

Rex.

She turned toward the front door, a big mistake. Tanya flung herself onto Heather's back, shoving her to the ground.

The woman's heavier weight pressed her face into the carpet. She felt her arms twisted backward, held with an iron grip. Tanya grabbed her hair, pulling on her roots and forcing her neck back at a painful angle. Tears sprang into her eyes, but she couldn't cry out.

"Heather," Rex hollered, banging on the front door.

She felt her head being forced down, her face meshing into the carpet. Her teeth dug into her lip, and she tasted blood. Tanya pulled her neck back again, then shoved her head forward as though she were a rag doll. She squeezed her eyes shut, the bridge of her nose flaring with pain.

Wrestling to free her arms, she clenched her teeth when Tanya jerked her wrists higher, straining her sockets. What else could she do?

Rex's frantic efforts to gain entry gave her inspiration. Folding her knees, she whipped her legs behind, satisfied when she heard a grunt upon impact to her assailant's lower back. Tanya's grip loosened enough for her to twist her arms free. Rolling sideways, she smashed her fist into Tanya's face.

As though she had a glass jaw, Tanya registered surprise just before her eyes rolled up and she toppled over.

Ten

"Rex, thank God you're here." Breathless, Heather swung the door open after several failed attempts to slide the dead bolt between her shaking fingers.

"Are you all right?" Tall and powerful, he regarded her with a mixture of fear and relief before sweeping her into his arms. "I was afraid something like this might happen, so I came back. Stupid me, I should have kept the key. I've called Jackson. He's on the way."

She sagged against him, relishing the fold of his embrace. "It was Tanya. She's responsible for everything bad that's happened." Heather gestured inside. "The power is out. I gather Tanya flipped the circuits."

He took a few paces into the foyer. "Where is she?"

Heather drew a shuddering breath, pressing a hand to her chest. Her heart still raced. "Just over there. She's passed out, but—" Her jaw dropped as she strode farther into the house. "That's impossible. Where did she go?"

From down the street, sirens sounded. The clamor mixed with urgent voices as men from the production crew rushed through the front door.

"Did you see Tanya?" someone yelled. "She was heading

for the lake. She can't take that old rowboat out in the dark. It leaks, and she isn't a strong swimmer."

Rex directed the police to chase the producer toward the lake while a crewman headed for the circuit breaker. Remaining behind, Rex rubbed Heather's neck.

"I couldn't leave you," he said, while her heart leaped. "At least until I knew you were safe. Will you be all right?"

"Y-yes." What was he saying?

"I guess this is good-bye, then."

The lights snapped on. She looked into his eyes, hoping for any sign of doubt or regret, but couldn't read his feelings.

"You can't go. It's late," she said, trying not to beg. Was she misconstruing his words? Did he return only to insure her safety, not caring enough to stay?

"Tomorrow is your big day," he said, his mouth tightening into a firm line. "It's what you've always wanted, isn't it?"

She detected a note of wistful inquiry in his tone. "That's right. But you don't have to—"

"You need to establish your foothold here. I'd only get in the way. Besides, I have my own agenda, remember?" His lips twisted in self-mockery.

"Of course, and I wish you the best." So he would pursue his dream after all and sail into the sunset.

Meanwhile, this house was hers. She could set down roots here and have everything she'd always wanted. Almost.

"Thanks for coming back," she said stiffly. "Good luck when you discuss things with your dad. He'll rally around, you'll see."

"Yeah, right." His eyes glowed a deep aqua blue as he gave her a last scrutinizing glance. He looked maddeningly handsome in his V-necked sweater and jeans. "Well, enjoy the house."

"I will." She gave a tight smile. "Enjoy your boat. I know you'll get the one you showed me."

He left, and he took her heart with him.

It was the hardest decision she'd ever made, but there had been no other choice if she meant to fill the emptiness Rex had left behind. September rolled around before she approached the town Rex called home. Davie's rural origins were evident in the western-style architecture of its shops, his father's furniture repair store among them.

Pulling her blue pearl Honda Accord into a metered parking space, Heather got out and plunked quarters into the slot. The afternoon sun beat waves of heat onto the pavement. Thunder rumbled in the distance, while a spicy scent tickled her nostrils. Storm clouds funneled from the Everglades in the west, roiling like the emotions inside her. If she'd made a mistake, she'd be sorry for the rest of her life, but she had to try.

Swinging her leather handbag over one shoulder, she smoothed her white capri pants and turquoise top. Turquoise and silver earrings dangled from her ears, a gift from one of her friends to celebrate the inn's grand opening. Bitter dregs of regret filled her mouth. *Don't think about it. Go see if your sacrifice means anything.*

Mustering her courage, she pushed open the shop's door and entered. Chests of drawers, side tables, headboards, and dining room chairs stood in disarray, while from the far back, she heard a steady grinding noise. The smell of sawdust and lemon oil permeated the place.

An older man looked up from the counter where he'd been punching keys on a calculator. She recognized his face from the TV interview. In real life, he appeared more imposing, his large body and massive shoulders suitable to a life of labor. Crinkles around his eyes showed that he smiled often. His gray hair still held traces of coal black, the color his son had inherited.

She swallowed a lump in her throat. "Hello, Mr. Gerard. Is Rex here?" She heard her tremulous tone and hoped he couldn't detect her anxiety.

"He's in the back, ma'am. Who should I tell him is calling?" He squinted. "Sorry, don't I know you?"

"I'm Heather Payne."

"Oh, you're that gal from the reality show. Rex has been busy with Dorothy since he's come home."

His matter-of-fact tone took her aback. Was this the old gent's way of telling her that Rex's attentions had strayed?

"Maybe I shouldn't bother him, then."

"He'll be glad to tell you about her. The boy is obsessed. If you're hoping to hook him, you'll be competing with that lady of his."

Heather's cheeks warmed. *Oh, golly, I've made a dreadful mistake.* Rex hadn't taken long to get over her if he already had another girlfriend. Despite his assurances otherwise, their time together must have meant nothing to him except for a brief, passionate fling.

Mortified, she backed toward the entrance. "Perhaps I'll just—"

"He owes you a big debt." Giving a conspiratorial wink, Mr. Gerard lowered his voice. "If it wasn't for you, he'd never have been able to go after what he wanted. The boy was afraid he'd hurt my feelings, but I know a man's gotta follow his heart. He's been yearning for Dorothy all his life."

Heather suppressed a sob. Rex had never mentioned a former flame, but there were probably a lot of things she didn't know about him. Dorothy might have seen him on TV and returned to stake her claim.

"Suggesting he get a loan was the best thing you could have done for him," Mr. Gerard said. "It's good when a young 'un takes responsibility and strikes out on his own."

"He got a loan?" Heather stared at him.

"That's right," Rex said, sauntering into view. She inhaled sharply. He leaned against the door jamb, his jeans riding low on his hips, a tattered T-shirt covered with sawdust. Corded muscles ribboned his arms. Even grimy, he looked smashing.

"Hi," she said, her heart beating a rapid march.

"I didn't expect to see you here." His aqua eyes, warm and welcoming, eased her nervousness.

"Excuse me, folks," his dad said, giving them a bemused glance, "I need to finish that sanding job in the back."

As the elder man scuttled away, Rex raised his eyebrows.

"So, what gives, Heather?" Hooking his thumbs into his belt, he waited.

She felt the heat radiating from him. "Your father said you got a loan."

"I put a down payment on Dorothy." He must have seen her befuddled expression, because he added, "My boat. I named her after Dorothy in the *Wizard of Oz*, because it took me a while to realize my heart's desire."

"That's great." She felt as though she'd been broadsided. Was this good or bad, that *Dorothy* was his boat rather than another woman? Either way, she'd lost him to his dream. Speech evaded her, and she sought words to continue.

"How's the B&B?" he asked. "Have you had a busy season so far?"

She bit her lip. "I, uh, decided I didn't like the location. Too closed in for Florida, you know? I mean, Winter Park is a terrific town, but it's not near the ocean."

Fortifying herself with a deep breath, she plunged on. "So I sold it and bought a smaller B&B near a marina."

"You did what?" His jaw dropped.

She never thought she'd feel so nervous talking to someone. Being live on camera for the reality show hadn't been this bad. Her heart raced, and her fingertips felt icy. But she had to take the chance.

"Rex, tell me if I'm wrong, but I thought we had something between us. This way, you can have a slip for your boat, and I can have my house, and we can be together. I even have money left over. It's yours if you need it."

He looked as though he'd been hit by a truck. "I thought you wanted the place. It was the only reason I left. I didn't want to spoil your dream."

She stepped closer. "You taught me that sometimes sacrifices are necessary to get what you want. I realized that my house was empty without you. I've fallen in love with you, Rex."

His expression ignited as he clasped her shoulders. "I love you, too. You've given me a start on a goal I never thought I'd reach. Heck, I wasn't going to live on my boat. I'd decided to leave it at the nearest dock and come back to you, maybe offer your guests fishing charters on the lake. Whatever it took for you to have me."

"I'll have you just the way you are, Rex Gerard." She smiled. "I've reserved a private room for you at my new inn. When would you like to come?" She fluttered her lashes, letting him know the wicked direction of her thoughts.

"How about yesterday?"

His fierce kiss obliterated her rational mind, and she sank into an ocean of pleasure. Later, in her motel room, he showed her just how far they could sail together. Their dreams blended, strengthened by their union. And when they reached the horizon, she cried out in ecstasy, riding waves of delight.

Oh, yes, rocking on the sea with Rex could be fun, she thought, her fingers sifting through his soft strands of hair while he nibbled at a tender spot on her neck. And so would playing house on land. They'd have the best of both worlds.

In that respect, they had both won the prize.

Dear Reader:

Three Men and a Body was inspired by a stay at The Inn at Oakmont during the Annual Festival of Mystery sponsored by Mystery Lovers Bookshop in Pennsylvania. We had such a delightful time at this beautiful bed & breakfast that it inspired me to write this story. While my fictional reality show got a little too real, I hope you enjoyed the trials Heather and Rex experienced as they grew closer together.

For more reading pleasure, I hope you'll look for current and upcoming titles in my *Bad Hair Day* mystery series featuring sassy hairstylist Marla Shore. Elements of romance and humor blend with fast-paced action to keep you turning pages. Now available are *Died Blonde* and *Highlights to Heaven*. Next in the series is *Dead Roots*, where Marla's family reunion at a haunted Florida resort dredges up ghosts from the past along with dead bodies in the present. She and her fiancé, Detective Dalton Vail, launch another murder investigation in the midst of Thanksgiving dinner.

I love to hear from readers. Write to me at: P.O. Box 17756, Plantation, FL 33318. Please enclose a self-addressed stamped #10 business-size envelope for a personal reply. Email: nancy.j.cohen@comcast.net. Web site: www.nancyjcohen.com.

Please turn the page for a sizzling excerpt from
OUT OF CONTROL
by Shannon McKenna.

Available next month from Brava.

A poke in the eye, that's how it felt.

Mag Callahan curled white-knuckled hands around the mug of lukewarm coffee that she kept forgetting to drink. She stared, blank-eyed, at the Ziploc bag lying on her kitchen table. It contained the evidence that she had extracted from her own unmade bed a half an hour before, with the help of a pair of tweezers.

Item #1—Black lace thong panties. She, Mag, favored pastels that weren't such a harsh contrast to her fair skin. Item #2—Three strands of long, straight dark hair. She, Mag, had short, curly red hair.

Her mind reeled and fought the unwanted information. Craig, her boyfriend, had been uncommunicative and paranoid lately, but she'd chalked it up to that pesky Y chromosone of his, plus his job stress, and his struggle to start up his own new consulting business. It never occurred to her that he would ever . . . dear God.

Her own house. Her own *bed*. That pig.

The blank shock began to tingle and go red around the edges as it transformed inevitably into fury. She'd been so nice to him. Letting him stay in her house rent-free while he bug-swept and remodeled his own place. Lending him money, quite a bit of it. Cosigning his business loans. She'd bent over backwards to be supportive, accommodating, womanly. Trying to lighten up on her standard ballbreaker routine, which consisted of scaring boyfriend after boyfriend into hiding with her strong opinions. She'd wanted so badly to make it work this time. She'd tried so hard, and this was what she got for her pains. Shafted. Again.

She bumped the edge of the table as she got up, knocking over her coffee. She leaped back just in time to keep it from splattering over the cream linen outfit she'd changed into for her lunch date with Craig.

She'd come home early from her weekend conference on purpose to pretty herself up for their date, having fooled herself into thinking that Craig was only twitchy because he was about to broach the subject of—drum roll, please—the Future of Their Relationship. She'd even gone so far as to fantasize a sappy Kodak moment: Craig, bashfully passing her a ring box over dessert. Herself, opening it. A gasp of happy awe. Violins swelling as she melted into tears. How stupid.

Fury roared up like gasoline dumped on a fire. She had to do something active, right now. Like blow up his car, maybe. Craig's favorite coffee mug was the first object to present itself, sitting smugly in the sink beside another dirty mug, from which the mystery tart had no doubt sipped her own coffee this morning. Why, would you look at that. A trace of coral lipstick was smeared along the mug's edge.

Mag flung them across the room. Crash, tinkle. The noise relieved her feelings, but now she had a coffee splatter on her kitchen wall to remind her of this glorious moment forevermore. Smooth move, Mag.

She rummaged under the sink for a garbage bag, muttering. She was going to delete that lying bastard from her house.

She started with the spare room, which Craig had commandeered as his office. In went his laptop, modem, and mouse, his ergonomic keyboard. Mail, trade magazines, floppy disks, data storage CDs clattered in after it. A sealed box that she found in the back of one of the desk drawers hit the bottom of the bag with a rattling thud.

Onward. She dragged the bag into the hall. It had been stupid to start with the heaviest stuff first, but it was too late now. Next stop, hall closet. Costly suits, dress shirts, belts, ties, shoes, and loafers. On to the bedroom, to the drawers she'd cleared out for his casual wear. His hypoallergenic silicon pillow. His alarm clock. His special dental floss. Every item she tossed made her anger burn hotter. Scum.

That was it. Nothing left to dump. She knotted the top of the bag.

It was now too heavy to lift. She had to drag it, bumpity-thud out the door, over the deck, down the stairs, across the narrow, pebbly beach of Parson's Lake. The wooden passageway that led to her floating dock wobbled perilously as she jerked the stone-heavy thing along.

She heaved it over the edge of the dock with a grunt. Glug, glug, some pitiful bubbles, and down it sank, out of sight. Craig could take a bracing November dip and do a salvage job if he so chose.

She could breathe a bit better now, but she knew from experience that the health benefits of childish, vindictive behavior were very short-term. She'd crash and burn again soon if she didn't stay in constant motion. Work was the only thing that could save her now. She grabbed her purse, jumped into the car, and headed downtown to her office.

Dougie, her receptionist, looked up with startled eyes when she charged through the glass double doors of Callahan Web Weaving. "Wait. Hold on a second. She just walked in the door," he said into the phone. He pushed a button. "Mag? What are you doing here? I thought you were coming in this afternoon, after you had lunch with—"

"Change of plans," she said crisply. "I have better things to do."

Dougie looked bewildered. "But Craig's on line two. He wants to know why you're late for your lunch date. Says he has to talk to you. Urgently. As soon as possible. A matter of life and death, he says."

Mag rolled her eyes as she marched into her office. "So what else is new, Dougie? Isn't everything that has to do with Craig's precious convenience a matter of life and death?"

Dougie followed her. "He, uh, sounds really flipped out, Mag."

Come to think of it, it would be more classy, dignified, and above all, final if she looked him in the eye while she dumped him. Plus, she could throw the panties bag right into his face if he had the gall to deny it. That would be satisfying. Closure, and all that good stuff.

She smiled reassuringly into Dougie's anxious eyes. "Tell Craig I'm on my way. And after this, don't accept any more calls from him. Don't even bother to take messages. For Craig Caruso, I am in a meeting, for the rest of eternity. Is that clear?"

Dougie blinked through his glasses, owllike. "You OK, Mag?"

The smile on her face was a warlike mask. "Fine. I'm great, actually. This won't take long. I'm certainly not going to eat with him."

"Want me to order in lunch for you, then? Your usual?"

She hesitated, doubting she'd have much appetite, but poor Dougie was so anxious to help. "Sure, that would be nice." She patted him on the shoulder. "You're a sweetie-pie. I don't deserve you."

"I'll order carrot cake and a double skim latte, too. You're gonna need it," Dougie said, scurrying back to his beeping phone.

Mag checked the mirror inside her coat closet, freshened her lipstick, and made sure her coppery red 'do was artfully mussed, not wisping dorkily, as it tended to do if she didn't gel the living bejesus out of it. One should try to look elegant when telling a parasitical user to go to hell and fry. She thought about mascara and decided against it. She cried easily; when she was hurt, when she was pissed, and today she was both. Putting on mascara was like spitting in the face of the gods.

She grabbed her purse, uncomfortably aware, as always, of the 9mm Beretta that shared space with wallet, keys, and lipstick inside. A gift from Craig, after she'd gotten mugged months ago. A pointless gift, since she'd never been able to bring herself to load the thing, and had no license to carry concealed. Craig had insisted that she keep it in her purse, along with an extra clip of ammunition. And she'd gone along with it, in her efforts to be sweet and grateful and accommodating. Hah.

If she were a different woman, she'd make him regret that gift. She'd wave it around at him, scare him out of his wits. But that kind of tantrum just wasn't her style. Neither were guns. She'd give it back to him today. It was illegal, it was scary, it made her purse too heavy, and besides, today was all about streamlining, dumping excess baggage.

Emotional feng shui. Sploosh, straight into the lake.

By the time she got to her car, the unseasonable late autumn heat made sweat trickle between her shoulder blades. She felt rumpled, flushed and emotional. Frazzled Working Girl was not the look she wanted for this encounter. Indifferent Ice Queen was more like it. She cranked the air conditioning to chill down to Ice Queen temperatures and pulled out into traffic, the density of which gave her way too much time to think about what a painful pattern this was in her love life.

Used and shafted by charming jerks. Over and over. She was almost thirty years old, for God's sake. She should have outgrown this tedious, self-destructive crap by now. She should be hitting her stride.

Maybe she should get her head shrunk. What a joy. Pick out the most icky element of her personality, and pay someone scads of money to help her dwell on it. Bleah. Introspection had never been her thing.

She parked her car outside the newly renovated brick warehouse that housed Craig's new studio, and braced herself to see Craig's tech assistant bouncing up to chirp a greeting.

Mandi was her name. Probably dotted the *i* with a heart. Nothing behind those big brown eyes but bubbles and foam. She had long dark hair, too. Fancy that.

There was no one to be seen in the studio. Odd. Maybe Craig and Mandi had been overcome with passion in the back office. She set her teeth and marched through the place. Her heels clicked loudly on the tile. The silence made the sharp sounds echo and swell.

The door to Craig's office was ajar. She clicked her heels louder. *Go for it. Burn your bridges, Mag, it's what you're best at.* She slapped the door open, sucked in air and opened her mouth to—

She rocked back with a choked gasp.

And here's a preview of a romantic mystery,
MURDER IN THE HAMPTONS,
by Amy Garvey.
A Brava trade paperback available in May, 2005.

A door slammed, and the elegantly framed Picasso on the wall beside Maggie quivered. She reached up absently to steady it, wondering who had ended up on the other side of that door and who would be bunking on one of the sofas tonight. Not that it would be a hardship—if she wasn't mistaken, the drawing room sofas were upholstered in imported raw silk. The Axminster carpets didn't look too uncomfortable, either.

Beside her, Tyler held a finger to his lips, and she froze, listening as, around the corner, Ethan said, "Nell, open the door. *Nell.* I'm not going to ask you again."

Silence. The stillness practically hummed with the force of Nell's rage, even from down the hall.

Without warning, Ty grabbed her arm and the doorknob to her room at the same time, and she found herself shoved over the threshold into the darkness, where she banged her ankle on the secretary just inside the door.

"Ouch," she whispered, pulling her head back when she realized she was talking into his shirt. It smelled like salt water and sea pines, but beneath it was the unmistakable scent of hard, hot Ty muscle. She allowed herself one deep, irresistible lungful before she said, "Turn on the light."

"Shhh." His hand snaked out and clapped over her mouth,

but before she could wriggle away—or bite him in protest—she heard Ethan's muffled footfalls on the antique runner in the hallway as he headed for the stairs.

When Ty removed his hand, she ducked under his arm and reached for the lamp on the secretary. He closed the door and leaned against it.

"Sorry about that," he said when she turned around, blinking in the bright glare of the light. "Stealth is usually the way to go when you're eavesdropping."

"Which we shouldn't have been doing," she said, tucking her hair behind one ear. One day, she had to figure out how to say something like that without sounding like a prim maiden aunt.

"Why not?" He strode past her and sprawled on the bed like he had every right to be there. Of course, after last night, there was no good reason for him to think otherwise. Her brilliant plan to resist his charms wasn't going very well so far.

Especially when he was so out of place against the busily feminine and floral comforter. He was too big, too dark, too male. He was crushing the sprigged lilacs into dust, not reclining on them.

And rather than ordering him off the bed, what she wanted was to strip away the fussy linens, and then strip his clothes off him. Not necessarily in that order.

Stop staring, she told herself. As a distraction, she went to the window, peering down at the lawn and out at the dark, quiet bulk of the guest house. Amazing to think that just twelve hours ago, they'd all been gathered on the grass, staring at a dead body.

"Because this really isn't any of our business," she said finally. Well, there was a lame answer. It really wasn't fair. They'd spent the night in what some people would have called sexual gymnastics only to wake up to murder this morning, and he was as calm and collected as ever. Then again, she couldn't blame a little surprise homicide for her own case of nerves—Ty was the one who'd thrown her off balance the minute she saw him across that hangar-sized drawing room yesterday afternoon.

"We're not talking about tax returns, Maggie, we're talking about murder," he argued, and she turned around to find him toeing off one shoe and then the other.

She swallowed hard. She hadn't said the part about stripping his clothes off out loud, had she? *Keep going, big boy,* a lusty little voice in her head whispered, while her good sense rapped a metaphorical ruler across her knuckles and demanded, *Get him out of here while you can still remember your own name.*

"Exactly," she said quickly, nodding. "Murder. We're in the middle of a murder investigation. And that's no time to . . . to eavesdrop," she finished helplessly.

Obviously, she'd lost every shred of her intelligence somewhere in the sheets last night. The plan had to been to get him out of her system, hadn't it? One night, full stop, no more temptation. No more impulse kissing. No more accidentally-on-purpose touching. No more wondering if he still tasted as good as she remembered.

What a dumb plan.

"If you ask me," he said, shrugging out of his shirt and staring at her, "it's the perfect time to eavesdrop. Aren't you curious what the hell happened last night?"

"Of course I am," she said, realizing that her voice sounded far away in her ears. She was having a hard time taking her eyes off his chest. The ruler came down again, hard. *Stop it.* "But we don't—I mean, *I* don't know these people. Eavesdropping doesn't get you too far if you don't know what anyone's talking about in the first place."

"Not if you listen hard enough." He grinned, and she could see the devil in his eyes. "I'm not stooping to a drinking glass against the wall, though—it's strictly serendipitous eavesdropping for me. And I think I'm done for the night." He squinted at her thoughtfully. "You don't talk in your sleep, do you?"

God, I hope not. "Of course I don't." She scrambled for

something else to say when he climbed off the bed and walked toward her, cupping his hands on either side of her waist and leaning down to kiss the line of her jaw. "But I . . . I don't think . . . I mean, maybe it would be better if you stayed in your room tonight."

"Why?" His voice was muffled in her hair now, and she shivered when he blew it aside to trace a hot path down the side of her neck with his tongue.

Why. *Yes, why?* "Because we're . . . we're in the middle of a murder investigation. It seems . . . I don't know . . . rude."

"We're not in the middle," he argued, sliding his hands beneath her shirt and up her back. Oh, that was good. Too good. "We're on the sidelines. Actually, we're way up in the nosebleed section, in the bleachers. At least for now."

He was right, of course. After the chaos of the crime scene officers and the detectives' questions—not to mention Bobby's mini-breakdown and Nell and Ethan's argument—the house was finally quiet. There was nothing for them to do now. Nothing related to the murder, anyway.

Maybe if she gave in and spent one more night with him, she'd get him out of her system for good. In a permanent, definitely-not-going-off-the-deep-end way. Since he was tugging her shirt over her head, it seemed like the sensible thing to do, at least at the moment.

She groaned as a thrill of anticipation skittered up her spine—he was unfastening her bra now, his hands huge and warm and so very strong. There was no arguing with those hands, not when the two of them were stuck in this house for the duration, with nothing more pressing to do than exactly what they were doing. *And will be doing more of soon, and probably most of the night,* the bad girl's voice in her head reminded her.

She curled her fingers into the belt loops of his shorts, pulling him closer, and tilted her head up to look at him. His eyes were dark blue now, just like they'd been last night before he'd kissed her into blissful incoherence. There was no arguing with his mouth, either, she thought as it came down on hers, hot and hard.

Suddenly, he broke off the kiss, and when she opened her eyes, he was fumbling in one of his pockets, frowning.

She sighed and held out the foil-wrapped condom she'd found in his back pocket. Arguing was definitely over. She was way ahead of him.